Prai

LADY TAN'S CIRCLE OF WOMEN

New York Times Top 10 Bestseller

USA Today Bestseller

LibraryReads Hall of Fame Selection

"See shows how with the right people we can surpass our own expectations and that the hardships of life are often easier to endure if we don't have to survive them alone."

— *The New York Times Book Review*

"*Lady Tan's Circle of Women* has everything you could want in a dramatic tale of female friendship. A solemn vow. An arranged marriage. Conventions and traditions mixed with desire and independence. This novel will hold women's friendships up to the light paired with ambition, loyalty, and long-ago life."

— Katie Couric Media

"See envelops her story in the accepted practices of the time: arranged marriages, the buying and selling of concubines, the pressure to provide male heirs, and the crippling and sometimes deadly practice of female footbinding. Despite the inordinate limits placed on women, See allows their strengths to dominate their stories."

— *The Washington Post*

"If you loved *Snow Flower and the Secret Fan*, you'll love Lisa See's latest novel."

— *Good Morning America*

LADY TAN'S CIRCLE OF WOMEN

A Novel

LISA SEE

SCRIBNER

New York   London   Toronto   Sydney   New Delhi

Scribner

An Imprint of Simon & Schuster, LLC

1230 Avenue of the Americas

New York, NY 10020

First Scribner trade paperback edition June 2024

SCRIBNER and design are trademarks of Simon & Schuster, LLC

Simon & Schuster: Celebrating 100 Years of Publishing in 2024

For information about special discounts for bulk purchases, please contact Simon & Schuster Special Sales at 1-866-506-1949 or business@simonandschuster.com.

The Simon & Schuster Speakers Bureau can bring authors to your live event. For more information or to book an event, contact the Simon & Schuster Speakers Bureau at 1-866-248-3049 or visit our website at www.simonspeakers.com.

Interior design by Kathryn A. Kenney-Peterson

Manufactured in the United States of America

1   3   5   7   9   10   8   6   4   2

Library of Congress Cataloging-in-Publication Data is available.

ISBN 978-1-9821-1708-5
ISBN 978-1-9821-1709-2 (pbk)
ISBN 978-1-9821-1710-8 (ebook)

*In memory of Marina Bokelman,
second mother, healer, folklorist, embroiderer*

AUTHOR'S NOTE

This story begins in 1469, in the fifth year of the Chenghua emperor's reign, when Tan Yunxian was eight years old. The title of her book has been translated different ways: *The Sayings of a Woman Doctor*, *Miscellaneous Records of a Female Doctor*, and *The Comments of a Female Physician*.

I've adhered to the English-language tradition of capitalizing certain words related to Chinese medicine that have a different semantic meaning than their lowercase equivalents, such as Blood and blood. The first system to transcribe Chinese into the Roman alphabet was created by Matteo Ricci and Michele Ruggieri between 1583 and 1588, long after the events in this novel. That being the case, I've used the Pinyin system of transliteration for Chinese words, which was adopted by the People's Republic of China in 1979 and adopted internationally in 1982.

Last, you may be unfamiliar with the traditions of Chinese medicine—and I'm not here to advocate for or against them—but I hope you'll bear in mind the larger picture of the world when the story takes place. Columbus didn't lay sight on the Americas until thirty-one years after Tan Yunxian's birth, while the English settlement of Jamestown wasn't founded until fifty-one years after her death. The western tradition of medicine at the time of Tan Yunxian's practice explained sickness as either an imbalance or a corruption of the four humors—blood, phlegm, yellow bile, and black bile, which were thought to be the principal liquids of the body—or retribution for sins committed by the patient. Most western medicines were created out of alcohol and herbs, and bloodletting with leeches was the norm.

PREFACE TO *MISCELLANEOUS RECORDS OF A FEMALE DOCTOR*

Our ancient land has birthed many famous doctors, some of whom were female. It is the honor of our family lineage that my cousin Lady Tan Yunxian has produced a book of heart-mind lifesaving cases. The great physician Sun Simiao wrote, "Women are ten times more difficult to treat than a man." This is not just a matter of yin and yang or of the outside world of men and the inner chambers where women reside. It is because women become pregnant, give birth, and endure monthly loss of blood. They also suffer from having different temperaments and emotions than men. My cousin has excelled at treating women because she has shared in the losses and joys of what it means to be a female on this earth.

Ru Luan
*Metropolitan Graduate with
  Honors by Imperial Order
Grand Master for Court
  Precedence
Manager of the Royal Lancers*

PART I

MILK DAYS

The Fifth Year of the
Chenghua Emperor's Reign
(1469)

To Live Is . . .

"A thousand years in the past, a thousand years in the future—no matter where you live or how rich or poor you are—the four phases of a woman's life are the same," Respectful Lady says. "You are a little girl, so you are still in milk days. When you turn fifteen, you will enter hair-pinning days. The way we style your hair will announce to the world that you are ready for marriage." She smiles at me. "Tell me, Daughter, what comes next?"

"Rice-and-salt days," I answer dutifully, but my mind wanders. My mother and I sit together on porcelain stools under a covered colonnade in our home's courtyard. It's monsoon season, so the sliver of sky I can see is heavy with clouds, making the air feel humid, suffocating. Two miniature orange trees grow side by side in matching pots. Other containers hold cymbidiums, their stalks drooping under the weight of the blossoms. Rain is coming, but until then, birds titter in the gingko tree that provides a touch of coolness on the summer day, and I can smell the sea—something I've only seen in paintings. The fragrance doesn't, however, cover the unpleasant odor coming from Respectful Lady's bound feet.

"Your thoughts are elsewhere." Her voice sounds as frail as her body looks. "You must pay attention." She reaches over and takes one of my hands. "Are you having pain today?" When I nod, she says, "The memories of the agony you felt during your footbinding will never leave completely. There will be days from now until you die when the anguish will visit—if you've stood too long or walked too far, if the weather is about to change, if you don't take proper care of your feet." She squeezes my hand sympathetically. "When they throb or smart, remind yourself that one day your suffering will be proof to your husband of your love. Focusing on something else will distract you from the pain."

My mother is wise, which is why everyone in the household, including my brother, Yifeng, and I, calls her Respectful Lady, the honorary title she carries as the wife of someone with my father's high rank. But if she can tell I'm distracted, then I can see she is too. The sound of a woman singing reaches us. Miss Zhao, my father's concubine, must be entertaining my father and his guests.

"You know how to concentrate . . . when you want to," my mother goes on at last. "This ability—to be fully absorbed—is what saves us." She pauses for a moment as male laughter—my father's voice distinct in the appreciative choir—swirls around us like a fog. Then she asks, "Shall we continue?"

I take a breath. "Rice-and-salt days are the most important years in a woman's life. They are when I will be busy with wife and mother duties—"

"As I am now." Respectful Lady gracefully tips her head, setting the gold and jade ornaments that hang from her bun to tinkle softly. How pale she is, how elegant. "Each day should begin early. I rise before dawn, cleanse my face, rinse my mouth with fragrant tea, attend to my feet, and fix my hair and makeup. Then I go to the kitchen to make sure the servants have lit the fire and begun the morning meal."

She releases my hand and sighs, as though exhausted by the effort of getting so many words to leave her mouth. She takes a deep breath before continuing. "Memorizing these responsibilities is central to your education, but you can also learn by observing as I supervise the chores that must be done each day: bringing in fuel and water, sending a big-footed servant girl to the market, making sure clothes—including those of Miss Zhao—are washed, and so many other things that are essential to managing a household. Now, what else?"

She's been teaching me like this for four years already, and I know the answer she likes me to give. "Learning to embroider, play the zither, and memorize sayings from *Analects for Women*—"

"And other texts too, so that by the time you go to your husband's home, you will have an understanding of all you must do and all you must avoid." She shifts on her stool. "Eventually, you will reach the time of sitting quietly. Do you know what this means?"

Maybe it's because I'm feeling physical pain, but the thought of the sadness and loneliness of sitting quietly causes tears to well in my eyes. "This will come when I can no longer bring children into the world—"

"And extends into widowhood. You will be the one who has not died, waiting for death to reunite you with your husband. This is—"

A maid arrives with a tray of snacks, so my mother and I can continue our studies through lunch without a break. Two hours later, Respectful Lady asks me to repeat the rules we've covered.

"When walking, don't turn my head," I recite without protest. "When talking, don't open my mouth wide. When standing, don't rustle my skirts. When happy, don't rejoice with loud laughter. When angry, never raise my voice. I will bury all desire to venture beyond the inner chambers. Those rooms are for women alone."

"Very good," Respectful Lady praises me. "Always remember your place in the world. If you follow these rules, you will establish yourself as a true and proper human being." She closes her eyes. She's hurting too. Only she's too much of a lady to speak of it.

A squeal from my little brother interrupts our shared moment. Yifeng runs across the courtyard. His mother, Miss Zhao—free of her performing duties—glides behind him. Her feet are also bound, and her steps are so small they give the impression she's floating like . . .

"Like a ghost," my mother whispers as though she's read my thoughts.

Yifeng flings himself at my mother, buries his face in her lap, and giggles. Miss Zhao may be his mother by birth, but Respectful Lady not only is his ritual mother but has formally adopted him as her son. This means Yifeng will make offerings and perform all the rites and ceremonies after my mother and our father become ancestors in the Afterworld.

My mother pulls Yifeng onto her lap, brushing the bottoms of his shoes so the soles leave no dirt or dust on her silk gown.

"That is all, Miss Zhao."

"Respectful Lady." The concubine gives a polite nod and then quietly slips out of the courtyard.

My mother turns to the afternoon's teaching session, which Yifeng and I share. We will spend each day learning together until he reaches his seventh year, when the *Book of Rites* orders that boys and girls should not sit on the same mat or eat at the same table. At that time, Yifeng will leave our company and move to the library to spend his hours with private tutors in preparation to take the imperial exams.

"Harmony should be maintained in a household, but everyone knows how hard this is," Respectful Lady begins. "Consider the written characters that incorporate the radical that means *woman*. *Slave*, *demon*, *envy*, *greedy*, *traitor*. Put *woman* and *horse* together and you get . . ."

"*Mother*."

"Because her work never ends."

"But the character of one *woman* under a roof means *peace*," I offer.

"True. And a pig under a roof means . . ."

"*Home*."

"Just remember, we women exist to give a man heirs and feed, clothe, and amuse him. Never forget that."

While my brother recites simple poems, I work on my embroidery. I hope I'm successful at hiding my disappointment. I know Miss Zhao wasn't the only one entertaining my father and his friends. Yifeng was also being shown off. Now, when he forgets a line, Respectful Lady glances at me to complete it for him. In this way, I'm learning what he's learning too. I'm older, so I'm much better at memorizing. I'm even good at using words and images from poems in my thoughts and when I talk. Today, though, I stumble on a line. Respectful Lady purses her lips. "You will not take the imperial exams or become a scholar like your brother," she points out, "but one day you will be the mother of sons. To help them in their future studies, you must learn now." It stings to disappoint her when, on a good day, I can recite poems from the *Book of Odes* and read aloud from the *Classic of Filial Piety for Girls*. Today is not one of those days.

In the late afternoon, my mother announces it's time to move to the studio. Yifeng and I follow Respectful Lady at a proper distance. The folds of her gown billow, and her sleeves are picked up on the breeze—just like in a painting. The air moves enough that we are awash in the odor that comes from her bound feet. A special aroma will eventually come from my own feet, my mother likes to remind me when I cry during my binding, and it will fascinate my husband. Today, the scent from my mother's feet is far from pleasing. I swallow hard as a wave of nausea washes through me.

I have no memories of ever being outside our compound, and I may not pass through the main gate until I'm in my hair-pinning days and am taken to my husband's home in marriage, but I don't care. I love our home, especially the studio, with its whitewashed walls, simple furniture, and shelves filled with books and hand-scrolls. My mother sits on one side of the table; my brother and I sit across from her. My mother watches as I grind the ink on the inkstone and mix in water to achieve the perfect density and blackness. I hold my brush in one hand and with my other hand pull my sleeve up and back so it won't get stained. Respectful Lady has said that each calligraphy stroke must be fluid, yet bold. Beside me, Yifeng tries his best, but his characters are wobbly. Checking his work causes *me* to make my second mistake of the day. Instead of my stroke thinning like the end of an eyebrow, I make a blot on the paper. I lift the brush but keep my face down, staring at the mess I've made and waiting for my mother to say something.

The silence continues, and I glance up. She gazes out the window, oblivious to me, my mistake, or Yifeng's wiggling. When she's like this, we know she's thinking about my two older brothers, who died on the same day five years ago from heavenly flowers disease—smallpox. If they'd survived, they would be ten and twelve years old. And if they'd lived, my father might not have brought in Miss Zhao, I wouldn't have Yifeng as my younger brother, and my mother wouldn't have a ritual son.

My maid, Poppy, enters, and Respectful Lady gives a small

nod. Without inspecting my work, she says, "That's enough for today. Poppy, please have the children change and then bring them to the library to see their father."

Poppy takes my brother to Miss Zhao, and then the two of us continue to my room. Father bought Poppy for me on the occasion of my birth. She's fifteen, with big feet. Her eyes are set wide on her face, and she has an obedient disposition. She sleeps on the floor at the foot of my bed and many times has comforted me when I've been awakened by a nightmare. She helps me to dress, wash, and eat. I don't know where Poppy comes from, but she'll be part of my dowry, which means we'll be together until whichever one of us dies first.

Having sat nearly all day, I'm antsy, but Poppy will have none of it.

"Yunxian, you are worse than your brother," she scolds. "Stand still so I can brush your hair."

"But—"

She holds up a finger. "No!" She gives me a stern look, but it quickly turns into a grin. She spoils me. It's true. "So, tell me what you learned today."

I do my best, reciting the usual things: "When I marry, I will respectfully serve my father-in-law. I will not look at him when he speaks to me. I will not address him, ever. I will listen and obey."

Poppy noisily sucks her teeth to let me know she approves, but my mind is chewing on something Respectful Lady said earlier today. *Always remember your place in the world.* I was born into the Tan family. My given name is Yunxian, which means Loyal Virtue. Medicine has been in my family for generations, but my father chose a different path. He's an imperial scholar of the *juren* level—a "recommended man," who has passed the provincial exams. He works as a prefect here in Laizhou, which is close to the ocean but hundreds of *li* from our family's ancestral home in Wuxi. For longer than my lifetime, he's been studying to take the next and highest level of the imperial examinations, which take place every three years. The geomancer has already chosen a date for Father to travel to the capital, where he'll complete his final studies before the testing begins. If he succeeds, the emperor himself will read my father's essay, announce that he's achieved the level of *jinshi* scholar—a "presented scholar"—and award him his title. I don't know how our lives will change if that happens, except that our family will have taken another step up the ladder of life.

What else can I say about my place in the world? I am eight years old, young enough that I still wear my black hair in ribboned tufts. Respectful Lady has told me that my complexion is as fine as the flesh of a white peach, but that can't be true since she has Poppy apply ointments to the three pockmarks—one high on my forehead and two side by side on my right cheek—that are visible reminders that I survived smallpox while my brothers didn't. My feet make up for these defects. They are perfect. Today I wear a pair of silk slippers embroidered by my mother with flowers and bats for good luck.

Poppy nudges me. "And your relations with your future mother-in-law?"

"Yes, yes," I say, snapping back to my maid. "When she sits, I will remain standing. I will rise early, but I won't make any noise that could disturb her sleep. I will prepare and serve tea to her—"

Poppy pats my bottom, satisfied that I'm ready to be presented to my father. "That's enough. Let's hurry now. We don't want to upset the master."

We retrace our steps, picking up Yifeng from the room he shares with Miss Zhao. The three of us walk hand in hand. The rain has finally started, but we're protected by the colonnade. The drops hitting the tile roof sound comforting, and already the air feels cleaner, lighter, as the humidity is washed out of it.

In the library, my parents sit next to each other in simply carved chairs. An altar table rests against the white wall behind them. A summer orchid blooms from a bronze pot. Respectful Lady's hands lie folded in her lap. Her feet are propped on a brocade footrest, and her slippers, as small as my own, peek out from under her gown. Respectful Lady is always pale, but today her skin appears almost translucent. A light sheen of sweat glistens on her forehead and upper lip.

My father seems unaffected by the odor coming from my

mother's feet. He sits with his legs spread and his hands on his thighs, so his fingers point inward and his thumbs rest outward. He wears the long, layered robes of his rank. The sleeve guards that edge the hems of his tunic are heavily embroidered. A mandarin square, also embroidered, covers his chest and tells all who see him his grade within the imperial system of civil servants. He motions for Yifeng to come to him. Poppy drops his hand, and Yifeng darts across the floor and jumps into our father's lap. I would never do that. I lost the ability to run when my feet were bound, but even if I could run, it would be inappropriate for me to act so recklessly. My father laughs. My mother smiles. Poppy squeezes my hand reassuringly.

After five minutes, the visit ends. My father has not said a word to me. I'm not hurt. We've both behaved in the proper way. I can be proud of that. Poppy retakes Yifeng's hand. We're about to leave when my mother suddenly rises. She sways like a stalk of young bamboo in a spring wind. My father glances at her questioningly. Before he can say a word, she collapses to the floor. Apart from her hands, which lie splayed and limp, and her face, which is as white as a full moon, she looks like a pile of discarded clothing.

Poppy screams. My father leaps from his chair, lifts my mother into his arms, and carries her outside. As he trots down the colonnade, he shouts for other servants to come. They arrive from every corner, including a man and a boy of about twelve. They are only the fifth and sixth males I have ever seen. They must live here, but I've been isolated in the inner chambers, where I've been protected from the eyes of boys and men apart from my father, Yifeng, and the two brothers I barely remember.

"Take my horse and fetch the doctor!" Father orders. "Bring hot water! No! Bring cold water! Compresses! And find Miss Zhao!"

The old man and the boy break away, as do the cook and the kitchen scullery maid. When Father reaches my mother's room, the remaining servants and I follow him inside. Respectful Lady's marriage bed is big and spacious—like a little house, with three small rooms—to give utmost privacy. A moon-shaped archway leads to the sleeping platform. Father lays Respectful Lady on the quilt, sets her arms by her sides, and straightens her gown so the silk drapes over her feet. Then he smooths the tendrils of hair that have come loose from her bun and tucks them behind her ears.

"Wake up, Wife," he pleads. I've never heard him speak so tenderly, not even to Yifeng. He glances back at the rest of us crowded into the marriage bed's first antechamber. "Where is Miss Zhao? Get her!"

A couple of servants run out, while others enter with hot and cold buckets of water.

At last, Miss Zhao arrives. She touches Father's shoulder. "It's best if you leave." She turns to the servants. "All of you too, except for Yunxian."

My father regards me. I see in his expression something new, but I'm unsure what it is.

"Maybe I should take the girl," he says to his concubine.

"Leave her here. She needs to learn." Miss Zhao puts a hand on the small of his back. "Let us know when the doctor arrives."

Once everyone has left, Miss Zhao looks at me squarely, which is yet another thing that has never happened before. "I suspected this would happen," she says. "We can hope that by fainting Respectful Lady has given us time to help her."

"But what's wrong?" I ask timidly.

"I've been told your mother took great care with your footbinding, choosing to do it with her own hands. Too often a mother can turn sentimental when her daughter cries, but not Respectful Lady. She did everything correctly, and not once did your feet become infected. Now you know how to take care of your feet—"

"Poppy helps me—"

"But you understand that maintenance is required."

"Unbind the feet every four days," I begin to recite, knowing these rules are no less important than those for the stages of my life or how to behave toward my future mother-in-law. "Wash them. Trim the toenails and sand down any places where a bone might break through the skin—"

"Whether toenails or a shard of bone, if the skin breaks, you must take extra care to keep the wound clean. Otherwise, you will get an infection. If you ignore it, the bound foot—unable to find fresh air—will begin to fester. Some mothers take this risk when binding their daughters' feet." Some of the pride I feel in my feet falls away when she adds, "The person who bound my feet allowed this to happen and was able to break off my dead toes. This is why my feet are so very small, and it is something your father appreciates."

Now is not the time to crow, but I can't possibly say that to Miss Zhao.

"My point is," she goes on, "infection can set in, and if a mother isn't vigilant, then her daughter will probably die. But little girls aren't the only ones who can perish. Adult women who don't properly care for their feet can also succumb."

With that, Miss Zhao pulls Respectful Lady's gown up to reveal the embroidered leggings that cover the unsightly bulge of the bent heel and crushed arch. This lump of useless and unappealing flesh is supposed to remain hidden, and seeing it reminds me of something Respectful Lady told me during my binding: "Our feet don't shrink or disappear. The bones are simply moved and manipulated to create the illusion of golden lilies."

Miss Zhao unties one of the leggings and pulls it free to expose fiery rivers of red that streak up my mother's leg. What startles me even more is the look of her calf. It is as thin as rope, far more slender and formless than mine. I reach out to touch what looks so clearly wrong, but Miss Zhao grabs my wrist and pulls me back. She picks up one of my mother's feet. It looks tiny in her hand.

"Our legs become emaciated because our feet cannot carry what lies beneath the skin," Miss Zhao states. "This is nothing to worry about. The problem is, your mother has an infection."

I struggle to make sense of this. Respectful Lady is respectful in all ways, including in the care of her body. She would never ignore her feet.

"I'm going to unwrap her foot," Miss Zhao explains. "Are you ready?"

When I nod, Miss Zhao slips off the shoe and hands it to me. The smell worsens. The concubine swallows, and then proceeds to unwind the three-meter length of gauze binding cloth. With each layer removed, the smell of decay gets stronger. When Miss Zhao gets closer to the skin, the cloth comes away stained yellow and green. Finally, the foot is naked. A jagged sliver of bone protrudes from the left side of the midfoot. Freed from the bindings—and I can't imagine the pain my mother must have been experiencing—the foot swells before our eyes.

"Get the bucket."

I do as I'm told. Miss Zhao gently moves my mother's leg so it dangles off the side of the bed and places her foot in the water. My mother stirs but doesn't waken.

"Go to Respectful Lady's dressing table and bring me her ointments and powders."

I do as I'm told. My father's concubine shakes some of the same astringent Poppy uses on my feet into the water. It's made from ground mulberry root, tannin, and frankincense. By the time the doctor arrives, Miss Zhao and I have patted dry my mother's foot, sprinkled alum between the toes and over the injury, and set it on a pillow. My mother has stirred each time we've moved her, but she has yet to open her eyes.

"You stay here," Miss Zhao says. "I'll talk to your father to see how he wants to proceed. A male doctor may not see or touch a female patient. A go-between is needed. Often the husband is chosen, but I will volunteer."

As soon as she's gone, my mother's eyes flutter open. "I do not want that woman in my room," she says weakly. "Go out there. Tell your father that she cannot be the go-between."

I step into the corridor. It's still raining, and I gulp in the fresh air. Even so, the smell of my mother's rotting flesh clings to the back of my throat. My father and Miss Zhao speak to a man who must be the doctor. I have now seen my seventh male. He wears a long robe in dark blue fabric. His gray hair laps at the curve of his stooped shoulders. I'm afraid to approach, but I must. I walk up to my father, pull on his sleeve, and say, "Respectful Lady is awake, and she asks that I be the go-between."

The man I take to be the doctor says, "Prefect Tan, it would be proper for you to do this duty." But when my father's eyes brim with tears, the doctor turns to Miss Zhao. "I suspect you have some experience with the ailments that afflict women."

I am only a girl, but I must honor my mother's wishes. "Respectful Lady wants—"

My father slaps the back of his hand against his other palm to stop me from saying another word. Silently he weighs the possibilities. Then he speaks.

"Doctor Ho, you will use my daughter." Father looks down at me. "You repeat exactly what the doctor says to your mother and what your mother says back to the doctor. Do you understand?"

I nod solemnly. His decision reflects his love for my mother. I'm sure of it.

The adults exchange a few more words, and then my father is led away by Miss Zhao.

The doctor asks me a series of questions, which I take to Respectful Lady. She answers, "No, I have not eaten spicy foods. You can tell him my sleep is fine. I am not suffering from excessive emotions."

I go back and forth between Doctor Ho in the colonnade and my mother in her bed. The questions—and the responses—seem to have little to do with my mother's infection. That she doesn't volunteer these details puzzles me.

After the doctor is satisfied, he writes a prescription. The scullery maid is sent to a pharmacy to pick up the herbs for the formula. The cook brews the decoction, and a few hours later, when it's ready, it's brought to my mother's room. I lift the cup to her lips, and she takes a few sips before falling back on her pillow.

"It's late," she says in a soft voice. "You should go to bed."

"Let me stay here. I can hold the cup for you."

She turns her head to face the wooden panels on the back wall of the marriage bed. Her fingers press against one of them, idly wiggling it in its frame. "I will have finished the drink by the time you've washed your face."

I go to my room, change into bedclothes and sleeping slippers, lie down, and nestle between the goose-down-filled mattress and a cotton quilt. I'm drained by all I've seen and find myself drifting off to sleep. I don't know how much time has passed before I'm awakened abruptly by the sound of people running. In the gloom,

I see Poppy sit up and yawn. She lights the oil lamp. The sputtering flame casts dancing shadows on the walls. We quickly dress and go out to the corridor. The rain has stopped, but it's dark. The birds singing in the trees tell me dawn is coming.

Just as we reach Respectful Lady's room, Cook rushes out and turns so swiftly that she nearly crashes into us. I totter on my bound feet, thrown off-balance. I place a hand on the wall to steady myself. When she sees me, she wipes tears from her cheeks with the backs of her hands. "So sorry. So sorry."

The household is thrown into more commotion as Miss Zhao crosses the courtyard with Doctor Ho behind her. Without pausing, they enter Respectful Lady's room. I start forward. Cook says, "Don't go in there." But I slip past her and through the door. The smell is something I will never forget.

A curtain has been hung over the front of the third chamber of my mother's marriage bed. My father sits on a stool before it. My mother's bare arm rests in his lap, the palm facing the ceiling. Doctor Ho tells my father to wrap Respectful Lady's wrist in a linen handkerchief. Once my father finishes this task, the doctor steps forward and places three fingers on the cloth. He closes his eyes to concentrate, but how can he feel anything through the handkerchief?

I look away and glimpse the cup I held up to my mother last night. My heart thumps in my chest as I realize she never took another sip.

Over the next two days, the entire household is busy. Servants come and go. More herbs are brewed for "invigorating" teas. I'm once again sent in to ask Doctor Ho's questions and return to him with Respectful Lady's answers. Nothing helps. Respectful Lady continues to weaken. When I touch her hand or cheek, I feel burning heat. Her foot, still balanced atop the pillow, has grown to the size of a melon. Rather, a cracked melon that oozes foul-smelling fluids. A prized characteristic of a perfectly bound foot is the cleft formed when the toes come back to meet the heel of the foot. Ideally, it should be so deep that a large silver coin can slide into the crevice. Now bloody goo drips from the slit, while the red streaks have continued to climb up her leg. As the hours pass, Respectful

Lady becomes less interested in the words that shower down on her, turning her face to the back wall of her enclosed bed. I'm allowed to stand next to her, to comfort her and let her know she's not alone.

She mumbles names. "Mama. Baba." When she cries out for my brothers who died, my index finger seeks out the heavenly flowers scars on my face.

On the fourth night, Father, Miss Zhao, and Yifeng enter. Tears stain Miss Zhao's powdered cheeks. Even when her face shows sorrow, she is still beautiful. My father chews on the insides of his cheeks, reining in his emotions. Yifeng is too young to understand what's happening and gallops toward the bed. My father scoops him up before he can disturb our mother. Respectful Lady raises an arm and touches my brother's boot.

"Remember me, Son. Make offerings for me."

After the threesome leaves, only Respectful Lady, our two maids, and I remain. The lamps are trimmed low. The gentle *plink-plink* of rain on the roof fills the room. My mother's breathing slows. A breath, then a long pause. A breath, then a long pause. Again, the names of those gone fall from her lips. I don't know if she's looking for them or if she's responding to their calls to her from their home in the Afterworld.

Suddenly she turns to face me. Her eyes open wide. For the first time in hours, she's fully *here*.

"Come closer." She reaches for me. I take her hand and lean in to hear. "I lament that life is like a sunbeam passing through a crack in a wall and that I won't live to see you become a wife and mother. We won't have the sorrows of partings or the joys of reunions. I won't be able to help you when you have disappointments or rejoice with you in moments of good fortune."

She once again closes her eyes and lets her head fall away from me. She doesn't release my hand. Instead, even as she murmurs the names of the dead, she squeezes it and I squeeze back.

"To live is to suffer," she mutters. This is her last coherent sentence. She cries, "Mama, Mama, Mama." She mumbles my brother's name. "Yifeng. Yifeng. Come!" She does not call for me.

I'm exhausted, but I continue to stand vigil despite the ache I feel in my feet. As tired as I am, I want to share in her pain. Mother to daughter. Life to death.

In the deepest darkness of the night, Respectful Lady takes her last breath, having reached twenty-eight years of age. I'm nearly overwhelmed by feelings of helplessness and guilt. I should have *been* more—a son of Respectful Lady's own blood who would be worth living for. I should have been able to *do* more to help her.

The Threshold Is High

Respectful Lady is barely in the ground when the long-appointed day for my father's departure to Beijing to make his final preparations before taking the next level of the imperial exams arrives. Miss Zhao, Yifeng, Poppy, and I are to be sent to live with my paternal grandparents in Wuxi. My father has arranged for most of the journey to be by water, and he's hired two bodyguards to protect us. I'm allowed to choose something to keep that belonged to my mother. I pick her red wedding shoes. Crying servants pack our furniture, clothing, and other household items, which are taken away on mule-drawn carts. My mother's personal servant is sold to a salt merchant. The cook and the scullery maid will stay until our last meal is served, but my father has sold them to . . . Who? Where? I'm not told. We are in mourning. I do not recite poems or the rules for girls. I do not practice my calligraphy or play the zither. Instead, I sit with Miss Zhao as she supervises my embroidery. In bed at night, after Poppy falls asleep, I hold my mother's shoes and weep.

Miss Zhao, Poppy, my brother, and I leave six mornings after my father's departure. Miss Zhao gives Yifeng and me pieces of candied ginger to suck. "It will help with movement illness," she says. We step over the threshold and into the street. A part of me aches to be leaving the only place I've ever been, but another part is excited to see what's outside the gate. Not much as it turns out. Miss Zhao and my brother enter a palanquin, the door is closed, and they're carried away by four men. One of the bodyguards opens the door to the second palanquin. Poppy gives me a gentle nudge. I climb in. "I'll follow on foot," she says.

The palanquin jiggles as the men lift it, and we're on our way. This is the first time I can remember being inside a palanquin. No window allows me to look outside, and the air inside is stale and hot. The box sways and bumps, responding to the individual footfalls of the bearers. I immediately feel sick to my stomach. I suck harder on the ginger. I have nowhere to settle my gaze. Outside, I hear vendors calling for customers, the creak of wagon wheels, the brays of a complaining donkey. Odors seep into the palanquin. Some I recognize—food cooked on open braziers, sewage, and something that smells like the padded fur jackets we wear in winter. I feel even more queasy.

The palanquin jerks to a stop and is lowered to the ground. The door opens. Poppy reaches in a hand to help me out. What I see is more than my eyes can take in or absorb. So many people. And they're doing . . . *everything*. I must be standing with my mouth agape, because Miss Zhao waves her hand in front of my face and says, "Your mother would have preferred that you keep your eyes on the ground. Please act properly to honor her. Now come. Follow me."

She leads me through the bustle of the dock. With my eyes down, all I see are Miss Zhao's flowing skirt, Yifeng's black shoes, and the two sets of boots belonging to the bodyguards. Once on deck, we're escorted to a room with four pallets on which to sleep. The room is also outfitted with a pitcher of water, a honeypot to do our business, and a bucket with a lid. The walls have no decoration, not even a window to look out of. The palanquin was hot and close, but this room feels worse.

The next six days and nights are miserable—far, far, far beyond what the soothing qualities of candied ginger can remedy. Poppy gets sick first, which is when Miss Zhao tells us the purpose of the bucket. I get sick next. Then the three of us take turns lifting the lid to the bucket. Only Yifeng remains unaffected.

Just before dawn on the seventh morning, the pitching lessens. Miss Zhao, who in recent hours has propped her forehead on the crook of her arm against the edge of the bucket, lifts her head and announces, "We've turned up the Yangzi. Soon we'll veer onto the Huangpu to reach Shanghai." A hint of a smile lifts her lips for the first time in days. "The city that abounds in everything." Without asking a single question, I'm learning a lot about my father's concubine. She clearly had a life before she entered our home. She has been as considerate of me on this journey as she has of her own son. And she seems to have respect for my mother.

Too fast to see much of anything, we're escorted to a sampan. The bodyguards take our traveling bags to the shelter where we're to spend the journey, but Miss Zhao doesn't follow.

"How long will it take us to reach Wuxi?" she asks the boatman.

"If the wind gives us more strength than the current, then maybe a couple of days," he answers.

Miss Zhao closes her eyes in response. I understand. I'm still unsteady from our ocean journey, and the bobbing of the sampan isn't calming my stomach one bit. When the bodyguards emerge from the shelter, she sways over to them. They're supposed to be protecting us, but they back away as though they're being approached by a fox spirit.

"I don't know that I'll be able to stand more days in a windowless space," she says to them in her melodious voice. Then she gestures to Yifeng and me. "And I don't think they'll be able to either. Please let us remain outside, where it will be more comfortable."

The bodyguards deny her request, insisting that they need to protect us.

"Even if a farmer or another boatman glimpses us," she replies, "in a moment we will have sailed past."

"We don't want to get in trouble," one of the bodyguards says. "Prefect Tan—"

"Need never know," she finishes. "We can keep this a secret between us."

After a bit more back-and-forth, she settles an arrangement by placing coins in their hands. Poppy and I exchange glances. We aren't supposed to like the concubine, but in this moment we're both grateful to her. As one guard takes a position at the front of the sampan and the other stands at the rear with the boatman, Miss Zhao herds Yifeng, Poppy, and me to seats under a canopy. The boatman pushes us away from the dock. Now I can see everything. The buildings, the people, the activities on the shore all help to distract me from my nausea. After an hour or so, the boatman steers us onto the Wusong River, which is far smaller than the Huangpu. We're still going against the current, but the shift in direction also means a shift in the wind. It comes from behind us now, and we glide over the smoother waters. The boatman maneuvers the oar rhythmically as we pass *li* upon *li* of rice paddies. No walls hide the view or limit the sky. When Yifeng needs to relieve himself, Miss Zhao holds on to him so he can do his business right into the swirling waters.

"Time to eat," the boatman announces as the sun peeks through the clouds. He ties the sampan to a tree growing on the bank. He gives Miss Zhao a basket filled with rice balls rolled in sesame seeds, which she hands out to each of us. After lunch, when the boatman takes Yifeng ashore to run off some energy, Miss Zhao says, "You've now gone many days without studying. I wanted you to have time to let your feelings settle."

My breath catches. I don't want to talk about my grief with her.

"And, of course, there was the horror of the ocean voyage . . ." She shakes her head as if to push the memory of it from her mind. "But now it's time to begin again, don't you think?"

"Respectful Lady was my teacher."

Miss Zhao looks at me with such sympathy that I have to fight back tears.

"She was a wonderful teacher to you and Yifeng. Could there be a better way to honor her than to continue what she started?"

The rice balls feel like rocks in my stomach. I swallow hard.

"Maybe you think because I'm a concubine that all I know is how to be beautiful for your father and provide him with amusements," she goes on, "but he wouldn't care for me if I didn't have other skills. I can read and write. I've studied the classics. So let's see what you know. Tell me, what are a wife's main duties?"

"To give birth to sons, uphold rules, and perform rituals that will guarantee a family's success," I mumble the list.

"And a concubine's main duty, once you put aside everything

else, is to provide a son if the wife is unable. I did that for your mother."

I lift my eyes. I'm almost too scared to ask my question. "Are you going to become Father's wife now?"

"This is not the time for you to worry about that," she answers. But she can't hide the longing in her voice when she adds, "Even if your father chooses me to become his wife, I know I could never replace Respectful Lady in your heart. For now, let's open a book. I would love to hear you read."

Yifeng and the boatman return to the sampan. We spend the rest of the afternoon drifting along a canal. I read aloud, and the others listen. If I stumble on a character, Miss Zhao leans over my shoulder to help me figure it out. When one of the guards points out a curiosity on the shore or Yifeng suddenly yips his delight at seeing something for the first time, Miss Zhao allows me to close my book and look too. Respectful Lady would never have done something like that, but I can't fault Miss Zhao since she isn't a real mother.

As the sky ripples pink at the end of the day, the boatman pulls to the shore and moors the vessel for the night. He makes us a simple meal of rice, braised bean curd, and sautéed river fish with soy sauce and green onions plucked from a nearby field. Miss Zhao, Yifeng, Poppy, and I go inside to find two pallets. Poppy will sleep on the floor by my feet as she usually does. Miss Zhao and Yifeng snuggle together. I have a pallet to myself. My entire body aches for my mother, and I'm pretty sure I'll never be able to fall asleep. Then, shockingly, I feel a hand on my back. It can only belong to Miss Zhao. She begins to hum softly and rub my back in small circles. I stay as still as possible, because I don't want to let her know that I know it's her . . .

We leave early the next morning. Hours slip by, but not once am I bored. There's so much to see—a nearly naked boy sitting on the back of a water buffalo, farmers stooped in fields, willows draping long tendrils into the river. Sounds enchant my ears—the quacking of a flock of geese tended to by a pair of giggling girls about my age, a group of children with barrels tied to their backs to keep them afloat as they splash in the water, the boatman singing a country song. We glide on rivers, ponds, and small lakes, and finally along ever smaller and narrower canals. When I glimpse Miss Zhao gazing at the sights with the same intensity as I am, I realize she's doing what I'm doing—taking in as many images as she can to preserve for later.

Finally, we reach the outskirts of Wuxi. "I'm told you are to be taken to the Tin Mountain district," the boatman says. When Miss Zhao nods, he goes on. "We are close to Lake Tai. Have you heard of it?"

"When I was younger, I used to go to the dragon boat races on the lake," she answers.

I know of the Dragon Boat Festival, but I never went to the activities in Wuxi. First, I was a baby and too young. Then my feet were being bound. I could have gone last year, but I had a fever and had to stay in bed. My father took Respectful Lady and Yifeng. How they talked about the fun they had—describing the decorations on each boat, the colorful costumes the rowers wore, and the strategies the boatmen used to win. I remember as well how upset Miss Zhao was that my father hadn't let her join the party and how quietly pleased my mother was to see the concubine sulk. This year, my father took Miss Zhao, which left my mother more melancholy than usual.

Miss Zhao turns to me. "Maybe we can go together next year."

I can tell she's trying to be nice to me—and I've always wanted to go—but does she think she can buy my favor as easily as she bought the bodyguards? I keep my answer short. "Maybe."

She draws in her chin and looks away. After a long silence, she says, "We don't know what awaits us at your grandparents' home. I am not your mother, and it seems you don't want me as a friend either, but you might want to reconsider that. When we step over this new threshold, you will know only three people—Poppy, your brother, and me. It's important for women—and girls—to find friendship and steadfastness where they can. I can be those things for you if you'll let me." She holds up a hand to keep me from speaking. "We're almost there. I'll gather our belongings."

Suddenly I'm scared. Everything the concubine said is true. My entire life has been turned upside down, and now we're about to enter a strange household where we won't know a single soul apart from each other.

The boat turns onto a new canal just as Miss Zhao comes back onto the deck. Both banks are lined with walled enclaves from which roofs sprout like small villages. The boatman steers the sampan to a stone dock, which looks like a floating pavilion with its upturned eaves and stone balustrades. My grandparents' home is called the Mansion of Golden Light. The gray walls that protect the property stretch down the road that parallels the canal in both directions. The main gate rises proudly, with the family name carved in the plinth at the top. A pair of stone lions stand guard, one on either side of the heavily carved wooden doors. The gatekeeper calls to someone inside, "They're here! They're here!"

I take a last look around me, positive that once I step over the threshold and into the Mansion of Golden Light I won't leave it again until my wedding day. Then I give myself a little shake and return my gaze to the gate, still nervous after Miss Zhao's caution.

The threshold is high to show the importance of the family, and Miss Zhao and I must be careful as we step over it. To the right and left, servants' rooms edge against the protective wall.

I won't let myself be separated from Poppy, and I pull her along with me as we continue into a courtyard. A woman with bound feet greets us. She's slender and pretty but no match to my mother or Miss Zhao. She addresses Yifeng—the lone male in our group. "My name is Inky. I manage the day-to-day affairs in the Mansion of Golden Light. I will make sure your needs are met." She runs her eyes over each of us from top to bottom. When she sees Poppy's big feet, her forehead crinkles in clear disapproval. Then she straightens her narrow shoulders and gestures around her. "There are five courtyards here. Your grandparents have asked that you stay in the rooms at the back of the compound, where our inner chambers are located. We hope you will find them satisfactory."

We quickly pass through the second and third courtyards. Covered colonnades fringe the sides. The beams and rafters are carved and painted. The buildings themselves are impressive, with tile roofs that look like fish scales and upturned eaves with glazed guardian figures protecting the corners. Each courtyard is grander than the last, but Inky doesn't tell us what they're for or who lives in them. When we enter the fourth courtyard, she stops to explain, pointing to her right. "Those are the rooms where Master Tan and Lady Ru see patients." She gestures to her left. "Here are Master Tan's bedroom and study. Your grandmother has the rooms next to his. Do not bother them when they're seeing patients." Inky considers what she's said, then adds, "Do not make noise of any sort." She looks at my brother. "This means you especially."

We reach the fifth courtyard. As in all households—even a smaller one like where I lived with Father and Respectful Lady—the rooms farthest from the main gate are considered the safest, so they are where all the unmarried girls, including the concubines, reside. Inky dips her head politely in my direction. "Please wait here." Then, "Miss Zhao, follow me."

My father's concubine takes two steps, then turns back to make sure I'm watching where she's going. I nod to let her know I am.

Poppy and I stand together, surrounded by grandeur neither of us has seen before, while Inky escorts Miss Zhao and Yifeng up a step, across the colonnade, and into a room. I quickly count the doors on that side of the courtyard. Her room is the third from the left.

Inky returns, and Poppy and I follow her up a step across the courtyard from Miss Zhao's room. A door stands ajar. "We've been waiting for you," Inky says, "and everything has been prepared. We hope you will find your quarters satisfactory."

The space is probably four times the size of what I had back home. A table and chair are positioned before one wall. Porcelain brush holders sprout calligraphy brushes in every size and shape. Books and handscrolls fill shelves behind the desk. My zither has been placed against another wall. Instead of the kang on which I've slept my whole life, my mother's marriage bed rises before me—a room within a room. Seeing it, I feel as though a sword is driven through my chest.

Inky stares at me sympathetically. "Your grandmother thought you would want to be close to the one who brought you into the world."

I blink away tears.

When I don't say anything, Inky turns to Poppy. Instructions are given. Things are pointed out. I absorb none of it. I miss my mother.

Later, after Poppy has bathed me and dressed me in clean clothes, I'm brought to meet my grandparents in the Greeting Hall. My mother and father are so much in my mind that I'm startled to see my grandparents seated as my parents were in their paired chairs on the night Respectful Lady collapsed. I drop to my knees and put my forehead on the floor.

"Please rise," Grandfather Tan says. "Step forward so we can get a better look at you."

I feel my grandparents' eyes on me as I move.

"Lift your face," Grandfather Tan orders.

He wears a long silk underrobe of deep blue silk, with an embroidered hem, a belt with a jade buckle, and a tassel that hangs to the side. He has a wispy mustache, and a thin beard sprouts from his chin. He winds the tail with his fingers so that it curls down midchest. His eyes look kind, and his hands appear smooth and pale. Wrinkles like bird tracks in sand run from the corners of his eyes. The word to describe Grandmother Ru other than old is plump. She should have wrinkles, but her face is smooth and unaffected by her years. Pearls and jade pieces decorate her tunic, which is embellished with embroidery on the hem, sleeve edges, and neck. Her hair is still black, piled high on her head, and held in place with jade pins and other gold ornaments.

After what feels like an eternity, Grandmother Ru comments, "She looks like her mother."

With that, I start to cry.

"Bring her to me," Grandmother Ru says.

Before I can begin to take in what's happening, Grandfather Tan has picked me up and put me on Grandmother Ru's lap. She wraps one arm around my waist to hold me close, while her other hand goes to the back of my head to bring me to her shoulder. "There, Child. Let the tears come."

Grandfather Tan gently pats my back. He makes comforting cooing sounds, and then says, "This is your home now. Don't worry. We will take care of you."

No Mud, No Lotus

"*Guan, guan* cry the ospreys," I recite, "on the islet in the river. The beautiful and good young lady is a fine mate for the lord."

Grandfather Tan laughs as I come to the end of the first stanza of the "Air of the Fish Hawks" from the *Book of Odes*. He likes to listen to me recite poems or chant from the classics, especially in the evenings, when he treats himself to cups of wine. Now he turns to Grandmother Ru, who sits on the other side of the tea table. "Does this poem tell the story of a young noble finding a kind and lovely maiden? Is it a criticism of the government, an allegory about Queen Tai Si, who was the ideal and idolized wife of King Wen, or an example of how people should behave in relation to bedroom affairs?"

She waves him off. "Do we need to discuss these things in front of Yunxian? She's too young."

"But she's smart!" He pinches his beard between thumb and forefinger.

"You praise her too highly and with such glowing words," Grandmother teases. Both grandparents adore me, but I spend the most time with my grandmother. While propriety would dictate that we maintain physical distance from each other, she likes to keep me close. Her hugs and kisses go against everything I've been taught, but I love them just the same.

"I waited a long time to have a granddaughter," he responds. Even though it's just the three of us, he's dressed to show his status. The square on the chest of his outer robe is embroidered with a purple mandarin duck, signifying to the world that he's a Gentle-man Scholar of the seventh rank. The body of his hat is made of black silk with a dome of ruby-red silk.

"You mean one who can entertain you."

Grandfather nods, admitting she's correct.

Grandmother smiles at him indulgently before returning to the book she's been poring over. We're in the pharmacy, which smells of herbs. Three pearwood medicine chests the color of warm amber, each with dozens of small drawers and three large drawers along the bottom, sit side by side within arm's reach. Characters in fine calligraphy describe what herb, mineral, or bone each drawer holds. Floor-to-ceiling shelves lined with earthenware jars, bas-kets, and tins occupy a side wall. On the opposite wall, anatom-ical drawings show meridians from the front, sides, and back of a body, head to foot. Beneath these, a row of chairs stands in a straight line for patients who come for treatment. A high table in the center of the room allows my grandparents to stand when they weigh and mix formulas. The tea table is small, but it's where they spend most of the day. They share love, respect, and work, with no cross words between them.

"I'm thinking about your nephew's wife," Grandmother says, officially changing the subject. "Lady Huang is pregnant for the sixth time, but she's been bleeding and she's having trouble pass-ing urine."

Lady Huang. I'm not sure who she is. Like all married women, including my grandmother, she goes by her natal family's name.

"Are you positive Lady Huang is with child?" Grandfather asks.

"Men think it's difficult to diagnosis pregnancy, and some-times it is. But two months ago, just to make sure, I gave her a tea made from lovage root and mugwort leaves." Grandmother juts her chin. "The lady drank it, and the baby moved as it was supposed to."

"Leave Lady Huang alone to grow and deliver her baby in peace," Grandfather declares. "It is my belief—and that of other scholar-physicians—that birth is best when it is natural. *When the blossom is full and the melon is round, they drop of their own ac-cord.* We see this in gardens, but we also observe it in animals.

One never hears of monkeys dying from difficulties in giving birth. Therefore, this should not occur with women. A complicated birth happens only when others try to manage, control, or hurry it."

Grandmother sighs. "Only a man who has not endured labor would say that."

"Perhaps a formula to cool her qi—"

"Cool? For a woman having trouble in her child palace? Rarely."

It is said—truthfully, I've been told—that Grandfather married Grandmother because she came from a family of hereditary doctors. After all, everyone benefits when a wife can see to the medical needs of the women and children in her household. As an imperial scholar, Grandfather also had an interest in medicine. Just as every wife must give her husband at least one son, it is a man's duty to ensure the family line. The best way to accomplish this is to see that wives and concubines not only get pregnant and give birth but also survive. Grandfather, even as a young man, liked to read ancient medical texts. When he served as Grand Master for Governance, he worked in the secondary capital of Nanjing, where he was an official on the Board of Punishments. He continued his personal studies even as he spent years away from home, traveling to perform his duties—just as my father might if he passes the next level of imperial exams. When Grandfather returned from his years in Nanjing, he was recognized as a *ming yi*—a "famous doctor"—in the tradition of literati physicians. His learning comes from reading books; Grandmother Ru's training comes from following her parents, who learned from their parents, who learned from their parents, and so on.

"Then what do you suggest?" Grandfather asks. He is not just a man of distinction but also the headman of our clan. His word rules, and we are all to obey. That said, he respects Grandmother's expertise and often follows her advice.

"I'll examine her first before I decide," she answers.

Grandfather nods slowly.

"In a few days, Midwife Shi will come to see Lady Huang," Grandmother adds.

At this, Grandfather pauses and looks sternly at Grandmother. "You know I don't approve of midwives." When he turns to me, I know I'm about to be tested. "Tell me why."

I don't want to answer, because whatever I say will irritate Grandmother. But what else can I do? "There is no place for the Three Aunties and Six Grannies in a gentry family's home," I recite, my head down so I don't have to see Grandmother's reaction.

"And who are they?" he asks.

I stare at my slippers, torn between the two people who care for me. A finger lifts my chin. Grandmother says, "Answer your grandfather."

"The Three Aunties are Buddhist nuns, Taoist nuns, and fortune-tellers. The Six Grannies are matchmakers, shamans, drug sellers, brokers, procuresses, and midwives." I recite the list from memory without knowing what some of those on it are.

"Respectable families don't allow religious women into our homes because we follow Confucian ideals," Grandfather says. "As for the others, they are snakes and scorpions to be avoided at all costs."

"Husband, you know perfectly well that—"

"Beyond this," Grandfather grumbles, "midwives are linked to wicked deeds like abortion and infanticide. Who hasn't heard of the sort of midwife who, when confronted by a baby who refuses to leave the child palace, cuts off its arm so she might bring it into the world?"

Grandmother shakes her head. "This happens on the rarest occasions and is done only to save a mother's life—"

"Their standing is further lowered," Grandfather continues, "because they're often called upon to check a woman's virginity in court cases and perform corpse inspections in instances of un-natural deaths—"

"Husband!" Grandmother snaps. "This is too much for Yun-xian to hear." She turns to me and modulates her voice. "Child, look at me," she says softly. "Respect your grandfather in all things but know as well that midwives are a necessity. A more pleasing phrase we use for a midwife is *she who collects the newborn*." Her eyes glide back to Grandfather. "You do not touch blood. I do not touch blood. We consult from afar. I might attend to a woman in labor—giving her herbs to speed delivery and make the baby slippery—and after birth provide the decoctions that will rebuild her vitality, but I would never try to catch an infant—"

"Confucius made clear that any profession in which blood is involved is considered to be beneath us," Grandfather agrees. "A midwife's contact with blood places her on the same base level as a butcher. Furthermore, midwives are disreputable. They are too much *in the world*."

"Perhaps." Grandmother sighs. "But since we physicians acknowledge blood as corrupt and corrupting, then how can a woman give birth without the aid of a midwife?"

"Peasant women—"

"Work in the fields all day, have their babies in the corners of their shacks, and then cook dinner for their families," Grandmother finishes for him.

"So—"

"So nothing!" Grandmother is starting to lose her temper. "Have you seen that with your own eyes? Maybe those women have a mother-in-law in the household who helps them. Maybe there's a midwife who works in the village. Maybe—"

Grandfather holds up a palm in an effort to make peace, but Grandmother isn't done.

"Do men die in childbirth?" she asks. "No, they do not! Even the empress is attended by a midwife. So don't tell me that a woman can just give birth by herself! If giving birth is so easy and painless—"

"I never said it was painless—"

"If giving birth is so *natural*," Grandmother continues, "then how is it fated that labor and delivery put life at risk? A woman is the only animal on earth who should not deliver her offspring alone, because the baby comes out facedown, making it nearly impossible for a woman to pull it out by herself. A midwife is indispensable, whether you like it or not."

"Indispensable," Grandfather echoes.

"And midwives can receive great rewards—"

He nods, finally giving in. "If one is lucky enough to attend to imperial women in the Forbidden City, she is rewarded on a level even men like me can envy."

"Land, gold, titles—"

Still trying to make peace, he adds, "We could also say that two families cannot be joined without the consultation of a match-maker." But, since he's entitled to having the last word, he can't stop himself from finishing with "That doesn't make these women any less unsavory."

Grandmother gives him a quick look but remains silent. Feeling he's won, Grandfather brightens. He once again addresses me. "Tell me about qi."

I recite in the same way I do poems, couplets, and the rules by which a girl should live. "Qi is the material basis and life-sustaining force of all existence within the body—"

"A parrot can say words," Grandmother interrupts, still irritated, it seems, by Grandfather's views on midwives, "but does it understand their deeper meaning?"

I try harder. "Everything in the universe has qi. Mountains, stars, animals, people, emotions—"

"I like to say qi is the *pulsation* of the cosmos," Grandmother comments, "while the body is a *reflection* of the cosmos—all governed by yin and yang."

Hearing Grandmother's hint, information I've memorized since I came here rushes from my mouth. "Yin and yang are dark and light, down and up, inner and outer, old and young, water and fire, Earth and Heaven."

Grandfather encourages me to continue. "Yin is—"

"The source of death," I finish for him.

"Yang is—"

"The root of life. Yin is shadowy and female, while yang is positive and male."

Grandfather nods his approval, and I smile back at him. He directs his next comment to Grandmother Ru. "This girl is intelligent. We should not restrict her to ordinary needlework. We should allow her to study my medicine."

In the last three months I've heard him say something like this many times, and each time a spark of hope ignites inside me. My father and uncle didn't want to become doctors, and I hear they both have ambitious plans for their sons that don't include medicine. Even now, my brother is learning the discipline required for studying for the imperial exams. That leaves me. I so wish to learn from my grandparents. Everything they say opens new pathways in my mind. And, if I could become a doctor one day, then I might be able to help the mother of a girl like me. Grandmother, however, has yet to be convinced.

"Today I've spoken of blood, but the more important substance is Blood," she says, ignoring him. "They sound like the same word, but how are they different?"

This is a simple question with an easy answer. "We have the blood we can see when our skin gets cut," I say, "but Blood is a bigger essence. *In women, Blood is the leader*. It is what allows a woman to become pregnant and feed a fetus. It turns into mother's milk upon her giving birth."

"Exactly. You must put aside the idea of function," Grandmother Ru explains. "We are not concerned with veins and arteries, muscles and bones, or organs with specific occupations. We are looking to find how illnesses arise from imbalances in the bodily form of yin and yang. They interact like night flowing into day and winter into summer. One is always rising and one is always falling, never stopping. In the process, they are repairing and transforming each other. As physicians, we aspire to bring yin and yang into balance so the life force is strong. What else can you tell me about the body as the universe?"

And on it goes, with Grandfather and Grandmother asking me questions and me trying my best to please them with my answers. When I'm with them—even though they are constantly testing me—I can almost forget how much I miss my mother, my father, our home . . . Just everything . . .

———

During my time in Wuxi, I've been mostly confined to the women's quarters with concubines and wives, toddlers and children, and older girls who are preparing for marriage. Infants are usually elsewhere with their wet nurses; boys over seven are no longer allowed in the women's quarters; and some women are too "indisposed"—physically or by their emotions—to gather for embroidery and gossip, cardplaying and petty arguments. I'm the only girl my age, and the older girls have no interest in me. I don't have a friend, but this is no different than when I lived in Laizhou. I'm thankful for Miss Zhao, who oversees my daily lessons. I think she's grateful to me too, since she's having a hard time being accepted by the other concubines. She's a good teacher—more patient than my mother but no less demanding.

When I want to be alone, I go to my room and climb into Respectful Lady's marriage bed. It has a roof, windows covered with silk paintings showing scenes of poetic life, and a canopy over the entrance with wooden tassels that hang down as decoration, all carved from rosewood, pearwood, and boxwood, and fitted together without a single nail. There are two antechambers—the first is where a maid sleeps on the floor, and the second is a dressing room. The third room holds the raised sleeping platform. On one of my first nights here, I remembered the loose panel Respectful Lady liked to touch. I wiggled it free and found a secret shelf. For a moment, I hoped she'd hidden something there for me, but no. She knew it existed, though, and to keep my connection to her I set her silk-wrapped shoes on the shelf and fit the panel back into place. Now I often lie in the exact position Respectful Lady did when she had her face to the back wall, her hand playing with the panel. I'll touch the wood, knowing what's behind it, and cry for the loss of her. Around the other women and girls, I try to act happy.

I'm slowly becoming familiar with the Mansion of Golden Light. Forty family members live here, and another twenty people— housemaids, kitchen help, and gardeners—attend to our needs. The family entertains guests in the second courtyard, which has a hall large enough for the entire household to gather for rituals and banquets, and smaller rooms for drinking, poetry writing, and the like. Tan grandsons, uncles, and nephews live with their wives and families in the third courtyard. I'm also growing accustomed to the furnishings and decorations that show the age and elevation of my natal family: the paintings, the wall hangings, the vases, and elegant tables and chairs. Handwoven rugs cover the floors in nearly every room. Couplets written in the running-script style of calligraphy hang on the walls in the main halls, encouraging each and every one of us to live by the highest standards. *May the jewel of learning shine in this house more effulgently than the sun and the moon; may every book read buoy you on the river of life. A mountain of books has a way, and diligence is the path; the sea of learning has no end, and hard work is the boat.*

Today, Inky, the household's top woman servant, whom I met when I first arrived, fetches me from the inner chambers after my formal lessons with Miss Zhao are done. "Follow me," she says. "Your grandmother wishes you to come to Lady Huang's quarters for a consultation." As usual, I totter between excitement and nervousness. Grandmother will use this time to teach me an important lesson. If I make a mistake, I worry she won't invite me to watch her care for a patient again.

We pass through the fourth courtyard, where my grandparents live and see patients. When we reach the third courtyard, Inky guides me to a room. It's not unlike my own quarters, but with a simple bed—open with vestibules—a desk, and a dressing table with a mirror. Lady Huang lies propped against pillows. She is much farther along in her pregnancy than I would have guessed from my grandparents' conversation the other day. But what surprises me most is the presence of a woman and a girl. I can tell they don't live here, because their dress is too showy to be worn by a wife, concubine, daughter, or servant in a family such as ours.

"Yunxian," Grandmother says, "this is Midwife Shi and her daughter, Meiling. Midwife Shi has delivered all of Lady Huang's babies. Still, I always think it best for Midwife Shi to spend time with the woman who will give birth. After all, *ten babies will arrive ten different ways.*"

"Which is why there is comfort in knowing the person who will have her hands between your legs," Midwife Shi says to Lady Huang. The words and sentiment are coarse to my ears, but they don't bother my grandmother.

Grandmother and the midwife begin to question Lady Huang.

"Have you eaten crabmeat?" Grandmother asks.

When Lady Huang shakes her head, Midwife Shi says, "Good, since it can cause a baby to be born in the transverse position, because crabs walk sideways. What about sparrow meat?"

"I've made sure that Cook has not prepared sparrow in any form," Grandmother says, "since it can result in a baby being born with sparrow spots—black freckles."

"Worse, eating sparrow can cause a baby—boy or girl—to grow into someone with no morals," the midwife adds.

If one day I hope to become a doctor, then I should pay more attention, but honestly, I can't stop looking at the girl. I've never been in the same room with another girl my age. This Meiling is astounding to me. She has big feet, but otherwise her features are delicate. Her complexion is smooth and beautiful, without a single smallpox scar.

"Hello," I say shyly.

"Hello." Her voice is pretty too, and it matches her name perfectly. Meiling means Beautiful Chime.

The midwife, who's bent over Lady Huang, leans back on her heels and swivels toward me. "*Aah.*" The sound is gravelly and low but pleasant in its peculiarity. "So here she is." She glances at my grandmother. "I see what you mean."

Grandmother Ru laughs, although I have no idea what's so amusing. Then to me she says, "Step toward the bed. I want you to see what Midwife Shi is doing."

I edge forward. Lady Huang is red in the face, but I don't know how she usually looks.

"Come closer," the midwife beckons. "You too," she adds, motioning to Meiling.

We move to stand together by the side of the bed. We are the same height. I cast a quick glance at her. She dips her chin to peer at me. Her lashes are long. I wonder what she sees when she looks at me.

"We physicians perform the Four Examinations," Grandmother says. "I've listened to Lady Huang's pulses, which are thready. I've examined her tongue, which looks as dry as a desert. You can see she's flushed, showing internal Fire." She turns to Lady Huang. "Tell me, have you had headaches?"

"My head is always throbbing," the woman answers, "and I'm thirsty—"

"And your emotions? Do you feel at peace?"

Lady Huang goes another shade darker, which gives my grandmother her answer.

"You're angry," Grandmother says. "You and I can talk about why later. For now, know I can treat all these symptoms with Drink to Quiet the Fetus, which will help bring your qi back into harmony. Heat is a necessity in the child palace, but sometimes there's too much warmth as appears to be the case here. When Heat is cooled, Blood will return its attention to the fetus. A midwife has physical techniques that can help as well."

Midwife Shi clicks her tongue to get our attention. She doesn't look like a granny. She's not that old. "Meiling knows this already, but it is always good to review," she begins. "This is Lady Huang's sixth baby. She has not had problems before."

"This is true," Lady Huang mutters, shifting uncomfortably against her cushions.

"Sometimes a fetus is not at home in the child palace," the midwife says. "Sometimes the fetus is breech or sideways. If we find this now, then we can help move it into a happier location before labor begins."

I nibble the edge of my thumb as the midwife massages Lady Huang's belly, stopping now and then to inquire if she's causing pain.

"No," the lady answers. "I'm already feeling better. I can breathe again."

The midwife continues to squeeze and manipulate the belly. With each passing minute, the redness in Lady Huang's cheeks fades. I should be paying closer attention, but all I can think about is Meiling's sleeve against my sleeve. Her breath goes in and out as though she's timed it to match my own. She shifts her feet and her fingers brush against mine. For a moment, it feels like my heart stops beating.

"That's enough for now," Grandmother says. "You girls may go. Yunxian, please take Meiling to the kitchen. Ask Cook to give you something to eat."

Hearing these words, Meiling takes my hand. My spirit could jump out of my body. Once we're outside, I try to wiggle loose, but she tightens her grip.

"I've been here many times," she says, "but I'm always afraid I'll get lost. I don't want to end up somewhere I shouldn't."

"I feel the same way."

"How old are you?" Meiling asks.

"I'm eight."

"Me too. Then we were both born in the Year of the Snake."

I correct her. "The Year of the Metal Snake."

She nods, then raises her hand, with mine still in hers, to rub her nose. "A Snake is a yin sign," she says. "The most beautiful women in the world are said to be born under this sign. We can't help but be lovely."

Who would say something like that, as though she were entitled to loveliness when she's only the daughter of a midwife?

"You're the prettier one," I admit. "You haven't had smallpox."

"My mother made sure I wouldn't get it." In answer to my questioning look, she asks, "Didn't your mother bring in the smallpox-planting master when you were little?"

"I don't know who that is."

"He travels from village to village, trying to stay ahead of the disease. He carries with him scabs from those who were sick. For me, he wrapped two scabs in cotton, stuck them in my nose, and then sealed it for a day and night with wax."

"Disgusting—"

"It's better than dying!" She falls silent. Then, "Mama says that since I'm free from scars I might be able to marry well."

This sets my mind to wondering. My mother must not have hired a smallpox-planting master for my brothers and me. If she didn't, why not?

Meiling continues. "Is your family already talking to a match-maker?"

The thought is frightening. Of course I'll be married out when I turn fifteen, but how will a matchmaker—one of the grannies that Grandfather so dislikes—find out about me? Will Father come home to negotiate? Or . . .

"Don't be scared," Meiling says. "We all have to do bedroom affairs."

"I'm not worried about that." I bristle. "I already know about bedroom affairs. They are a wife's duty and the only way to produce a son. You can't get pregnant without doing that thing." What I don't say is that even the idea of going to my husband's home scares me. I've lost my mother. My father is far away. To be separated from Grandmother and Grandfather—and Miss Zhao and my brother—will be added cruelty.

We reach the kitchen. Cook gives us tangerines, which we take back outside. Together we walk to my favorite courtyard—the one with my grandparents' pharmacy. The entire outdoor space is taken up by a pond dotted with lotus pads. Meiling and I cross a miniature stone bridge over a stream that connects one side of the pond to the other and the south side of the courtyard to the north. Koi lift their snouts out of the water, begging to be fed. We sit on a bench shaded by a cassia tree, peel our tangerines, and pop the segments in our mouths. Birdcages hang from branches, and birdsong fills the air. It's now fall, and the leaves have turned yellow, orange, and red to match the season. The dappled light that filters down through the trees makes the world shimmer around us.

"Have you seen the lotus in bloom?" Meiling asks. When I nod, she adds, "A lot of babies are born in this household, so I've seen them many times. I'm learning at my mother's side so that one day I can take her place."

I bite my lip, searching my mind for something to say that will show my education and that I'm not alone in the world. It comes to me. "My mother always said, *No mud, no lotus.* Do you know what this means?"

Meiling's eyebrows squirm like caterpillars as she considers the aphorism. I hurry on before she can figure it out.

"It means that goodness can grow from difficulties. Adversity can sprout into triumph—"

"From mud, the lotus will bloom." Her eyes light with understanding. "I know mud. I don't have a father, which is why my mother is teaching me to take care of myself."

"You're the lotus, then?"

"I guess so," she says, her cheeks pinkening.

Her admission forces me to look inside myself. It's hard to see how the mud of my mother's death will turn me into a lotus.

The koi swim toward us, their tails swishing back and forth and their mouths opening and shutting. Meiling leaves me to skip down to the pond's edge. I try to imagine what her calves must look like to carry her thus, while mine have been growing slimmer by the month. She kneels in the soft moss and extends her fingers down to the fish. They nibble at her fingers, and she giggles.

"Come! You have to feel this!"

I'm much more tentative as I walk down the bank, because the moss feels dangerously slippery under my bound feet. I kneel beside Meiling. Dampness immediately soaks through my tunic and pants. I can't imagine that Poppy is going to be happy with me.

Meiling giggles again. "It tickles!" When I still hesitate, she says, "Don't be scared. They don't bite." Now she fully laughs. "They *do* bite, but it doesn't hurt."

I don't want to appear a coward in front of a midwife's daughter. I reach my fingers into the pond. Some of the koi swim to me. Nip, nip, nip, nip. Little titters escape my mouth.

"You see!" Meiling exclaims, her eyes bright.

I'm just beginning to relax when she jumps up, runs along the bank to scoop up fallen flowers and leaves, and scampers onto the bridge. "Come up here! I have an idea for a game."

But I can't run. I can't scamper. I barely know the idea of play, although I've seen my boy cousins chase each other, even kick a ball back and forth. I look around to make sure no one is looking. I get up off my knees and brush at the silk of my pants, which does nothing to erase the moss stains. I slowly pick my way across the uneven ground, onto the pebble walkway, and meet Meiling on the bridge. She hands me some of the flowers and leaves.

"Let's see whose fall the fastest and whose float the best. We'll start with a single leaf." She holds one out over the balustrade, and I do the same. "One, two, three, and away."

We let go of our leaves and watch them swirl down in slow circles, hitting the water at the same moment. The leaves glide against each other, push apart, and come together again as they're carried along by the gentle current. They float toward us and then under the bridge. Meiling grabs my hand and pulls me to the other side. We lean out over the balustrade, waiting for our leaves to appear.

"Look! Mine's first!" she cries. She raises her eyebrows. "But yours is close. Shall we do it again?"

I completely forget myself as we drop flower petals and leaves off one side of the bridge and rush to the other side to see whose will come through first. Sometimes Meiling wins; sometimes I win.

The sounds of voices interrupt our fun. Grandmother Ru and Midwife Shi stand together in the colonnade. Suddenly I'm aware of just how dirty I am—my hands, my clothes. I look down and see that my embroidered silk shoes are ruined. The midwife grins. My grandmother frowns. Then the two women lean their heads together and speak in low voices.

Meiling once again takes my hand. "My mother and I will be back to see Lady Huang. If you don't find me, I'll come looking for you."

Her boldness inspires me. "I hope so," I say. "I really hope so." Then she skips down the bridge and runs to her mother.

"You could try to act more like a lady," the midwife says.

The message received and understood, Meiling walks carefully and slowly, as though she were a girl of high standing. At the last minute, she glances back at me. I feel something pass between us. As Meiling and her mother step out of sight, I miss her already.

Grandmother claps her hands. From somewhere—the shadows it feels like—Poppy and Inky emerge. They must have been watching Meiling and me all along.

"Give her a bath," Grandmother orders. "Then bring her to the pharmacy." To me, she adds, "We will discuss what you learned today and other things too."

An hour later, I'm seated across from my grandmother. "Do you want to help me make Drink to Quiet the Fetus?" When I nod, she says simply, "Good." She opens drawers and cabinets, pulling out things I don't recognize. "This is special large-head atractylodis from Hangzhou," she says, holding up something brown and dried. "We're going to soak it in rice water, which will help the healing properties enter Lady Huang's body through her Spleen and Stomach meridians to dry the Damp, harmonize the Stomach, and prevent miscarriage. Here's another herb that we'll prepare in vinegar. It helps to remove toxic Heat, invigorate Blood, and control pain."

I don't fully comprehend the things she says, but I'm able to follow her directions. She lets me pour the rice water and later the vinegar. She shows me how to gaze into the liquid to judge its strength by the depth of the color. She asks me to hold the sieve as she pours both mixtures into an earthenware pot. I'd like her to tell me more about what the different roots and herbs are and their purpose, but her thoughts are elsewhere.

"Having babies is central to every woman's life," she says. "But every pregnancy is a crisis of life or death. Will the mother survive and continue to run the household? Will the baby survive to become a descendant?"

When we're done and Inky has taken the formula to Lady Huang, Grandmother directs me to sit across from her. "Your grandfather has spoken about teaching you *his* medicine. I look at it differently. Your mother died because no male doctor could properly examine or treat her." She silently taps her fingertips on her thighs, seemingly struggling with what to say. "It is not the custom to teach hereditary medicine to a daughter, who will eventually marry out and take her knowledge with her. Your grandfather's type of medicine is different. It can be learned from a book, by anyone."

"But you learned, and you married out."

"I did," she admits, but doesn't expand on how that came to pass. Her fingers give a decisive thump on her thighs. "I cannot say if you will be a good student or not, but I am willing to teach you *my* medicine. Doctors, whether male or female, call it *fuke*— medicine for women. Are you interested?"

My mouth spreads into a wide smile. "Yes, Grandmother Ru."

She hands me a small book. "This volume contains formulas and treatments more than two hundred years old. Start by memorizing the first three formulas. Once you can recite them without mistake, you will come to me ready to enumerate the problems for which they are most efficacious and how best to employ them."

I take the book and read the title: *Excellent Prescriptions for Women* by Chen Ziming. Still beaming, I draw the volume to my chest. "Thank you, Grandmother."

"Don't thank me yet. When I was your age, I was already helping my parents in their practice. We have much work to do, so stop grinning! Nothing is assured. We will have to see how well you learn. Ultimately, *I* will decide if you are worthy of absorbing all I know."

A Slippery Birth

I can now get around the Mansion of Golden Light without help from Inky or another servant. The same cannot be said for the inner chambers, where I feel lost and out of place. Each wife's position is set by how close her husband is by blood to Grandfather. Higher-placed wives treat the wives of Grandfather's second cousins as though they were rotten turtle eggs. The concubines are even more biting. Grandfather alone has three of them. I don't know what names they were given by their families, but here they are called White Jade, Green Jade, and Red Jade. White Jade is the most treasured, because white jade is the rarest and most beautiful form of the stone, but all three are higher placed than Miss Zhao, whom they all seem to enjoy taunting. She is new to the household and vulnerable despite being Yifeng's birth mother.

When White Jade asks, "Now that Respectful Lady is dead, will you become the wife?" Miss Zhao blushes. She wants this very badly.

Green Jade is even more direct. "If your master truly cared for you," she observes, "then he would have elevated you already. Like all of us, we belong to the man who bought us. We live where we're told to live, and we do what we're told to do."

I try to block out the conversation by chanting to myself the formula I'm supposed to be learning: *Decoction of Four Gentlemen—ginseng root, large-head atractylodis rhizome, licorice root, and poria mushroom. We call licorice root the Emperor of Herbs, because it mixes well with other ingredients and fights against poisons in all forms, whether metal, stone, or herb.*

Red Jade cuts through my concentration. "You might think you're better than we are, but you aren't. Can you tell me you weren't born to a poor family? Can you say that your father didn't sell you to a Tooth Lady so you could become a Thin Horse when you were still so young you'd have no memories?"

Miss Zhao stiffens. "I remember my parents."

Red Jade snorts. "But can you pretend you weren't raised in a stable filled with other Thin Horses? The Tooth Lady fed and sheltered you. She taught you to write poems, sing, and play instruments. She bound your feet. You were told that if you did well, you would be sold to become a concubine or a courtesan."

White Jade nods knowingly. "Yes, like all of us, you are from Yangzhou—the city said to have the most beautiful women in the world. We share something else as well. Whether animal or woman, we are a man's possessions."

Soon enough bitterness bubbles from the lips of other concubines in their circle.

"I've given birth to three children, but not one can call me Mama. That is reserved for the wife—"

"My husband's wife could kill me, and she would not be punished by anyone in this household, let alone by the courts—"

"Just you watch, Miss Zhao," White Jade needles. "Your master will bring someone new home with him—younger, prettier. It happens to all of us."

With that, Miss Zhao leaves abruptly, making excuses as she walks out the door. I feel for her, in a new home, with no friends, and my father away in Beijing. As soon as she's gone, though, the gossip really gets going.

"She's skinny."

"I don't care for how she paints her lips."

"Her gowns are lovely in their own way, but they reveal too much of where she came from."

I try to focus—*the Decoction of Four Substances: angelica root, lovage, white peony root, and . . .*—but it's hopeless.

While the three Jades happily unite to torture Miss Zhao, they are even meaner to each other. It seems Grandfather has been spending recent evenings with Red Jade, leaving his other two concubines feeling irritable and insecure.

"I serve him food I make with my own hands," White Jade boasts.

Green Jade brags, "He likes the way I play the pipa."

Then they shift to arguing over who looked the prettiest when Grandfather took the three of them to the Dragon Boat Festival earlier this year and whom he might select to take with him next year. Each is sure she will be his only companion. And all this happens in front of Grandmother! She ignores them until the fighting becomes too much.

"My husband does not visit your bedchambers for the quality of your food or music. As for who will go to the Dragon Boat Festival next year, that is for me to decide." Grandmother glances at me and explains in a low voice, "I never go, and I don't allow the wives to go either. I'm a doctor. I'm already doing something outside what is considered acceptable. But by staying home with other wives and their daughters, I show the world that we are Confucian women above reproach."

I'm disappointed I won't get to go, but I can't miss what I haven't experienced. The same cannot be said for Miss Zhao, who I bet will be saddened to learn that she will not attend the festival unless my father returns to take her. In any case, life will carry on in the inner chambers. Tomorrow will bring different squabbles, and the jostling for position will continue.

———

With my mother, I used to learn poems and passages from the classics. Now I do that with Miss Zhao. When we're done, I practice memorizing symptoms, formulas for treatments, and the details of individual cases that famous doctors of the past have, as Grandmother puts it, chronicled across the millennia. I've come to understand the Five Concepts—Water, Fire, Wood, Metal, and Earth—which help to explain phenomena happening in the body. As Grandmother first instructed me, I've put aside the idea of function of different organs to focus instead on the Five Depot

Organs—the Spleen, Heart, Kidney, Lung, and Liver. The Spleen warehouses energy from food; the Heart is the captain of Blood; the Liver stores Blood; and the Lung regulates qi through breath.

"Most important for women is the Kidney, for we are by our natures connected to water and darkness," Grandmother explains to me when I join her in the pharmacy in the late afternoon. "We are also governed by the Seven Emotions of elation, anger, sadness, grief, worry, fear, and fright. Of the Five Fatigues, three specifically target women: fatigue from grief brought on by losing a child or husband, fatigue from worry about finances, a wayward husband, or an ailing child, and fatigue from trying to lift her family to a higher status. If women are prone to the Five Fatigues, then men are apt to fall victim to the Four Vices of drink, lust, desire for riches, and anger. Now, tell me about the Five Deaths."

"They are from childbirth, fright, strangulation, nightmare, and drowning."

"Very good. And how do we diagnose an illness?"

"We use the Four Examinations." I hold up fingers one by one. "Looking, asking and listening, smelling, and pulse taking."

Grandmother nods her approval. "At every moment, you should be looking for patterns of disharmony. With my eyes, I can see withering or blooming of the skin. Is it shiny and moist, as it should be, or is it puffy, bloated, lusterless, red, white, or yellow in tone? With my ears, I hear groaning, sighs, and sounds of desperation, but I also listen for strength, weakness, and high and low pitches. With my nose, I can smell the scent of disease, that something is as off or as turned as rotten meat. I ask my patients questions in hopes of having a soul-to-soul encounter. Of the Four Examinations, the art of taking a pulse will be the primary diagnostic tool you'll use in the future."

She reaches for one of my hands and pulls me to her.

"Before we visit Lady Huang," she says, "we will review how to read the primary pulses. Place three fingers just below my left wrist bone. There are three levels that you will learn to feel—light, medium, and then with deep pressure. You will do this on each wrist, to gather a total of six readings."

She moves my fingers to the depression below the joint of her wrist bone and the place from which the wrist bones lead to the pointer finger. "We call this location the Fish Border. It is on the Lung channel." She presses lightly on my fingers so I might feel deeper. "You are now on the Liver pulse. You can ascertain a woman's constitution if you take what you're feeling deep within yourself. In time, you will learn to identify twenty-eight separate and distinct types of pulses. With experience, you may learn even more." She pauses. "Tell me, Yunxian, how do you identify a hollow pulse?"

"A hollow pulse feels like the stem of a scallion," I answer. "It's hard on the outside but empty inside."

"And what does that tell you?"

"Deficient Blood."

"What about a wiry pulse?"

"It's tight like a string on an erhu. It shows stagnation in the body."

"And what do you feel on my wrist?"

I stare at her. I can recite but I can't yet discern.

She pulls my fingers off her wrist. "Enough of that for today. Learning to read the pulses will take months, if not years. Let us take up another subject—symptoms. It is said that strange symptoms are as numerous as the spines on a hedgehog—"

I have been trailing my grandmother for more than a month as she treats our female relatives and their children, all of whom live with us. They suffer from common ailments—colds, coughs, and sore throats—and Grandmother is always keeping guard for signs of smallpox.

"Every baby brings fetal poison with him or her into the world," Grandmother tells me. "Fetal poison is a product of the pollution found in the child palace long before birth. Sometimes it comes because mother and father were drinking when Essence met Blood, or the mother ate too many spicy foods, but it can also result from labor when a fetus's excrement, hair, or the clotted blood of a mother finds its way into the infant's mouth. It can flare up at any time. For boys, it often arrives with the onset of those dreams that come to them when they've reached twelve or thirteen years. But the most common eruption of fetal poison is smallpox. The disease sweeps across our great land every three years, when the smallpox goddess emerges from hiding to spread her heavenly flowers. The best way to keep the pestilence outside the gates is to invite in the smallpox-planting master."

"Does he really glue scabs from the sick inside children's noses?" I ask, making a face.

"It's called variation, and we've done it in China for centuries," Grandmother answers. "There are other methods too. Some smallpox-planting masters collect the matter that oozes from the sores and then spread it on a cut, or they apply a dab of the pus to the bottom of a nose. Sometimes the smallpox-planting master grinds dried scabs and then uses a reed to blow the powder—from a distance—into a child's nose. Sometimes, when a mother can't afford to hire a smallpox-planting master, she dresses her child in clothes worn by another child who died from the disease. None of these techniques is without danger. A child can get sick with a mild case of smallpox. Some end up with scars. Some even die. But if they endure these days of discomfort, then most reach adulthood with no further problems. Always remember that prevention is the most important form of medicine."

I'm about to ask why my brothers and I didn't have variolation when Grandmother steers the conversation in a different direction. "The smallpox-planting master visited me when I was a girl, so I've been able to treat patients with the disease over the years. If smallpox ever enters your household, here's what you should do . . ."

A few minutes later, she goes in yet another direction. "Boys and girls, and men and women, are essentially the same—both get skin rashes, upset stomachs, gout, and the like—except when it comes to the importance of Blood in women's lives—menses, pregnancy, birth, and the postpartum period." Seeing my cheeks redden, Grandmother adds, "There is no place for embarrassment in medicine. These are natural things that occur within women. As you will learn, most of my cases have to do with ailments below the girdle, because we are more susceptible than men to being invaded by pernicious elements. It is up to us to help the women in our household."

I smile. It boosts my confidence whenever she says *us*.

Grandmother picks up a handful of sachets and an earthenware jar filled with a brew. "Nothing is more vital than giving birth to sons. Let us now go to Lady Huang's chambers. I've requested that Midwife Shi join our consultation since the day is coming when Lady Huang's baby—as does every fetus—will become an enemy in her body, fight to get out, and need to be expelled."

Grandmother's lessons continue as we walk through the colonnade. The humidity is so heavy today that the plants look like they're sweating. "It is widely acknowledged that doctors would rather treat ten men than one woman. I disagree. Just as a general knows to use barbarians to attack other barbarians, we can employ the strategy of a woman doctor to heal other women."

She touches my shoulder to make sure I'm paying attention. "Never forget that multiple lives are at stake during childbirth. The baby—or babies, in the case of twins. The mother. The father and all those left behind in the family, who will no longer benefit from a wife who can manage a household. And the midwife, for if anything goes wrong, she will be blamed and her reputation harmed. Most doctors don't attend births, but I feel it is my responsibility to be in the room for labor and delivery and to keep the potential cascade of tragedies behind a dam. I do this by putting my best efforts to the well-being of the mother. This is not easy. The words passed down to us by a Han dynasty official more than fifteen centuries ago still hold true. *In women's central affair of childbirth, ten women die for every one that survives.*"

The aphorism clamps around my chest, squeezing out my breath. It can't possibly be true, because that would mean too many babies without mothers. Then I think of my own mother. She survived my birth, but I didn't have her long enough. Her death, while not from childbirth, caused the ripple effects of which Grandmother spoke. Like seeds on a dandelion, every person in our home—from the cook to me—was blown in a new direction when she died.

Before I can push my sadness aside, we arrive at Lady Huang's quarters. She's in her second week of "entering the month," when the baby could come at any time. She now must stay in bed. Her husband has sought another place to sleep to prevent them from doing bedroom affairs. Although the announcement of the beginning of labor is under the guidance of Heaven—and not humans—many women in the household have been given chores designed to help with the birth. The concubines, who are skilled at painting and calligraphy, have written couplets with positive sayings to hang on the walls. Inky has assigned two servants to bring in fresh straw when labor begins and then take it away to be buried after the baby is born, because it's taboo for bedclothes bloodied by childbirth to be washed and dried in the sunlight. "If such a thing should be seen by evil spirits," Inky has explained to me, "then they'll be tempted to harm the baby and hex the mother." Grandmother has been busiest of all, preparing decoctions and pills to create an easy birth.

"Some believe a woman full with child should eat raw eggs and sip sesame oil to make her baby slippery," Grandmother tells Lady Huang. "Yes, these things are slick, but who could think of putting them in your mouth when pregnant? A man! That's who." She sniffs indignantly. "Mallow seed can also make a fetus slippery, without the slime." Grandmother then asks me, "What have I taught you in this regard?"

"That all women pray for a slippery birth," I answer absently. I wonder why Meiling and her mother haven't arrived yet.

"I don't mean that," she snaps. "I'm talking about men and what they think about women."

Ah, she wants the usual rules about girls and women, so I begin to recite. "*When a girl, obey your father—*"

"No! I mean, yes, of course. But I'm thinking of another saying. *You must speak if you wish to be heard.*" Her features soften, perhaps because she realizes she's been harsh. "I'm not angry at you," she says. "I'm irritated with men. I'm lucky to love your grandfather, but most men—other doctors, especially—don't like to see us succeed. You must always show them respect and let them think they know more than you do, while understanding that you can achieve something they never can. You can actually *help* women."

Midwife Shi and her daughter enter. I'm struck again by how pretty Meiling is. Today she concentrates on her walk, deliberately trying to make her feet seem smaller. Then we stand side by side as we usually do, while Grandmother performs the Four Examinations, and the midwife palpates Lady Huang's belly. They each ask us questions designed to test what we've absorbed these past weeks. My education continues to be about balancing the cosmos within the body and harmonizing that body to the vast cosmos that surrounds us, while Meiling's studies are centered on the physical mechanics of getting a baby from the child palace to this world.

Once Grandmother decides Meiling and I have learned enough for the day, she dismisses us to go outside. We're playing our leaf-racing game when a couple of boys run into the courtyard, over the bridge, and into the colonnade. My little brother trails behind them like the last in a line of ducklings. The boys push and whoop.

"Really, boys are such a nuisance," I say to Meiling.

Green Jade and White Jade enter the colonnade. They walk arm in arm, supporting each other as they sway side to side, their long gowns swirling so that I catch glimpses of their bound-foot slippers. One of the boys bumps into Green Jade. She teeters. White Jade tries to steady her, but they have no way to regain their balance. Together they topple, falling into a heap of silk and bangles. One of them screams. The boys don't even look back as they dash through the moon gate that leads to the next courtyard.

Meiling drops the leaf she's holding and runs to the women. I wish my feet could do the same, but in all circumstances— especially in an emergency—I need to mind my steps. When I reach Meiling, she's bent over the two women, pulling away layers of cloth to see who is who and what is what.

Green Jade pushes Meiling away. "Don't touch me."

Meiling draws her hands back as though she's been singed. "I was trying to help."

"I don't want your help." Green Jade turns to White Jade. "Are you hurt?"

"My leg," White Jade cries.

When Green Jade feels White Jade's leg, the concubine screams and goes the color of the stone for which she was named.

I kneel next to Meiling and ask White Jade, "Will you let me look?"

White Jade shifts her anguished gaze from me to Meiling and then back to me. She bites her upper lip and nods. I carefully pull up White Jade's gown, revealing her lower leg. Instantly I'm in my mother's room after she collapsed and I saw her naked limb for the first time. But instead of having red streaks running up the calf, White Jade's leg is bent at an unnatural angle.

"It's broken," Meiling says.

Indeed, one spot has bulged into the shape of a steep mountain. The bone looks like it could break through the skin at any second.

"Poppy," I call, knowing she must be nearby. She steps into view. "Go get Grandmother. Hurry!"

"And my mother as well," Meiling adds. "Bring them both."

White Jade whimpers. "It hurts . . ."

I sit back on my haunches, trying to figure out what to do. "Maybe we should try to pull it straight," I say to Meiling.

"I once saw a bonesetter do just that," she agrees.

Hearing this, White Jade whimpers again.

"I'm scared that if we don't do something, the bone will tear through the skin." My mind goes again to my mother, and I add, "If that happens, infection will come. But if we pull the bone—"

"You will do no such thing!" Grandmother's voice comes out as sharp as cut glass. "You two girls step away right now!"

Meiling and I scramble to our feet and back away. Midwife Shi kneels next to the concubine, but Grandmother keeps her distance. "This is not the type of affliction physicians like your grandfather and I treat."

"I know," I say. "We just—"

"I don't want to hear a single excuse. I've sent Inky to find a bonesetter. Now all we can do is wait." With that, Grandmother turns away—disappointed or angry with me, maybe both.

When the bonesetter arrives, Midwife Shi scoots behind White Jade, wraps her arms around the concubine, and clutches her opposite wrists with each hand drawn across her chest. The bonesetter cups White Jade's calf with one hand and, without telling her what he's going to do, quickly pulls her ankle with his other hand. White Jade screams, but the bone is once again—to my eyes at least—in place. I exchange glances with Meiling. He's done exactly what we'd planned to do.

As he wraps the concubine's leg in a support made of cloth and bamboo, Grandmother steps forward.

"Servants will carry you to your quarters," she tells White Jade. "As soon as you're settled, I will come with a tea to help ease your pain."

Sweat glistens on White Jade's forehead. She reaches her hand out to Grandmother, who doesn't take it. "What will this mean for me?" she asks. In these words, her deepest fear is revealed: about her future ability to entrance Grandfather with her beautiful lily-foot walk.

"I cannot say," Grandmother answers.

———

A few hours later, Lady Huang goes into labor. Grandmother still hasn't commented on what Meiling and I almost did to White Jade, but she allows me to go with her to Lady Huang's room anyway. She reminds me that most doctors leave the supervision of labor and delivery solely to midwives, as there is too much blood involved in these activities, and that doctors are typically called in to help only if something goes wrong.

"Personally, though, I like to assess the situation from the beginning," Grandmother says, while we wait for the midwife and her daughter to come back to the Mansion of Golden Light. "Lady Huang has pain around her waist, which is the most obvious sign, but we can also discover labor's arrival in a woman's pulse. Here." She places my fingers on Lady Huang's wrist. "See how erratic it is? We say it feels like a bird pecking at grain or water leaking through a roof."

For months I've been struggling to find the subtle characteristics of the different pulses, but now I can feel that it's just as Grandmother says. I feel the jittery *tat-a-tat*. Since I'm still in trouble, I have to hide my smile. I've crossed another threshold.

Midwife Shi and her daughter enter. Meiling keeps her eyes

down. I wonder what words of reprimand fell on her ears when they got home, but there's no opportunity to ask. In another break with traditions followed by male doctors, Grandmother doesn't sit behind a screen. The two of us sit on chairs in a corner of the room, while the midwife and Meiling hurry back and forth across the chamber on their big feet, sorting and arranging the things needed for the birth—a knife, a roll of string, a basin filled with water, and a portable brazier. Just as there are rules about what a woman can and cannot do during pregnancy, there are guidelines to be followed during labor. The first is that only three people should be in attendance, but that seems to apply only to those who are actively assisting the laboring woman: in this case, the midwife, Meiling, and another woman who has arrived to help and really does look like a granny.

Two servants enter, quickly spread a bed of straw in a large bronze basin, and then just as quickly leave. We wait as Lady Huang suffers through spasm after spasm, until finally Midwife Shi says, "It's time." She helps Lady Huang move from her bed to a squatting position above the basin. Lady Huang reaches for the rope that hangs from the ceiling. She holds tight as the place between her legs bulges. She closes her eyes and moans. Meiling and the old woman support Lady Huang on each side of her waist. Midwife Shi moves behind Lady Huang, with her hands underneath the childbirth gate, ready to catch the baby.

"Tell me if the good lady starts to droop," the midwife requests of those in the room. "We cannot let any part of her touch the straw. Why is this, Meiling?"

"Bad influences can creep inside her," Meiling answers. "She could get infant-cord rigidity."

I glance questioningly at Grandmother, who explains, "'Squatting on straw'—by that I mean labor—is a time for death to visit a woman. Her body is forced open as she gives birth, allowing Cold and Wind to invade her. If infant-cord rigidity creeps inside a woman, her back will become stiff and eventually bend backward like a bow. Her jaw will lock until death relieves her agony. You will recognize the symptoms if you see them."

Lady Huang grunts and groans. What's happening at the

childbirth gate doesn't seem all that slippery to me. Just the opposite. Several times I have to shut my eyes. The head comes out face toward the back, looking up at Midwife Shi. Meiling and the other granny keep their hands firm on Lady Huang's waist as she pushes out the baby's shoulders. The rest of it slips out, finally, in a *whoosh*. I can't see if it's a boy or a girl. Grandmother doesn't inquire as to the baby's sex, and neither does Lady Huang. Grandmother warned me about this ahead of time. It is taboo for anyone in the birth chamber to ask this question for fear that evil spirits will hear the answer and swoop in to harm the infant.

Lady Huang continues to hang on to the rope. Midwife Shi keeps saying encouraging words. As soon as a big red blob of something falls out, Midwife Shi cuts the cord and ties it with string. Meiling lets go of Lady Huang's waist and pushes the basin aside, managing to get some blood and other goo on her hands. Another basin is filled with warm water so Midwife Shi can wash the baby.

Meiling turns toward me. "Did you see how I helped?" She sounds proud of herself, but I'm torn. She did a good job, but polluted blood got on her. I can't imagine it. "You and your grandmother helped too," she says. "Mama told me that Lady Huang was heading toward bad circumstances before your grandmother's remedies calmed her spirit and brought her health back into balance. Even I could see that."

I can't stop myself from bragging. "We were trying to create a slippery birth."

Grandma's snort and Midwife Shi's gravelly laugh bring such warmth to my face that I think I might die. Meiling comes closer to me, reaches out, and puts her fingers on my cheeks. I should flinch away, knowing the filth that recently covered her hands, but her fingers are cool and comforting. Then I feel eyes on me. It's Grandmother. I'm afraid she might scold me for the second time today, but she doesn't.

"I will return every day while you're doing the month," Midwife Shi tells Lady Huang. Only then does she open the blanket that swaddles the newborn and reveal to us that he is a boy.

A Contract Between Two Hearts

Lady Huang is "doing the month," which will unravel over the dangerous four weeks following birth. Her son's umbilical cord has been dried, ground, and formed into a paste with cinnabar powder and licorice, which Grandmother has wiped across his palate, giving him some of his own root of existence to protect him from fetal poison and lengthen his life. Grandmother and I visit Lady Huang every morning to make sure she isn't affected by noxious dew—old blood and tissue that refuses to leave the child palace. The new mother spends several hours a day squatting over a basin so that this pollution can leave her body. Grandmother and I watch for fever, convulsions, or for Lady Huang to become pensive in her emotions. We bring with us different warming medicines, and Grandmother has been strict with Cook to make sure Lady Huang is offered warming foods only. Her Blood has transformed into milk, and the baby suckles well.

Grandmother writes a summary of the case in a notebook. "Sun Simiao, the great physician of old, tracked his own illnesses and compared them to those of his patients to improve his understanding of the efficacy of different treatments," she tells me. "By recording my cases and their outcomes, as he once did, I can look back on patients I've treated over the years to clarify what might work or not work in a given situation." She shows me her entry about Lady Huang: her troubles during pregnancy, what was prescribed, what the midwife did, and how healthy the baby was when he was born. "You could keep a notebook too," she suggests. "Your first entry could be about White Jade."

"But I shouldn't have done that. I should have waited for the bonesetter." I hesitate before adding, "And we still don't know the outcome."

"All true. Still, the important thing is to learn from your successes *and* your failures." Seeing the doubt in my eyes, she adds, "Just consider it."

But I don't feel comfortable writing about what happened.

Midwife Shi and Meiling come every midday to make sure Lady Huang is healing well and that her bleeding is normal. When Meiling and I are allowed to go outside to float flower petals and race leaves, I tell her Grandmother's idea and ask what she would do.

"I would never have that problem, because I don't know how to read or write."

My brow rises in surprise. "Then how will you teach your sons?"

She doesn't answer my question. Instead, she wordlessly drops the flower petals balanced on her palm. Each one takes flight, floating down in individual concentric circles to the stream below.

———

Midwife Shi and Meiling continue to visit to care for Lady Huang, always heedful to avoid any places in the Mansion of Golden Light where they might encounter the men of our household. Every time, Meiling and I get to go together to the garden in the fourth courtyard, just the two of us. I've never had a friend, and I treasure these visits. I think Meiling does too.

I don't see much of either of my grandparents because they've been devoting hours each day to the negotiation of a betrothal for me. I have officially entered the period of the Three Letters and Six Etiquettes that are part of the deal making which will settle whom I'm to marry, the bride price the groom's family will pay, and what my dowry will be. I'm not allowed to be a part of these conversations, but Inky, who serves tea and sweetmeats to the matchmaker when she calls, is hardly discreet. At night, she comes to visit Poppy in my room, and they pick apart each candidate and consider every detail.

"Your mistress is descended from the highest class of literati," Inky whispers loud enough for me to hear. Poppy rests her chin on her hands, listening as though the words are of utter importance to her. I suppose they are. She will come with me when I marry out. My good fortune will be her good fortune. "A poor man with an auspicious future can be a good match for a wealthy girl, but that would not be appropriate in this situation," Inky continues. "Many men in the Tan family have served as officials. They've enjoyed hereditary advantages and have been promoted to the loftiest levels of society. Little Miss's great-grandfather was awarded Gentleman Scholar for those of top rank."

Poppy nods as though she understands what that means.

"He was Investigating Censor in Nanjing," Inky goes on. "He spent years away from home, traveling to Hunan, Hubei, Guangdong, and Guangxi. They say he was a good and fair investigator and judge. It is through him that the family was awarded this compound as a gift from the emperor. And have you seen the scroll depicting the dragon in the clouds which hangs in the Greeting Hall? That was given by the emperor upon Master Tan's retirement from office."

How is it, I wonder, that she can know so much more about my family than I do? Maybe it's because, as for Poppy, her life depends on my family's lineage and prosperity.

Inky speaks about my father's older brother, Tan Jing. His second son is Lady Huang's husband. I have yet to meet Uncle Jing, but he must come home enough that his wife has given him five children, while his concubines have produced another seven offspring. He is Secretary and Manager in the Ministry of Revenue—another exalted position. Inky then lists my grandfather's titles and my father's accomplishments, adding, "And you know that Little Miss's father will triumph in the next round of exams and be elevated even higher than he already has."

"So Little Miss must be matched family to family," Poppy says in understanding.

"Yes! But that could mean position to position, or position to landholdings, money, or connections to the emperor."

By the time Lady Huang finishes doing the month, the betrothal negotiations for me have intensified. I learn about some of the offers of marriage, each one coming with a letter that lists a family's ancestors going back three generations, along with all titles that have been bestowed. Grandmother rejects a literati family in Hangzhou because they live too far away for easy visiting. Grandfather turns down an extremely wealthy family when he learns the son was born in a year not compatible with a Snake. My grandparents are looking for a young man whose birth year is in affinity with mine. Anyone born in the Year of the Boar is dismissed without consideration. Snake is a Fire sign, while Boar is a Water sign. Fire and Water will never get along.

Sometimes when I hear Inky and Poppy gossiping about all this, I curl up in my mother's bed with my face to the wall. Poppy is loyal to me and brags about my good attributes as a female Snake, since we are known to be good daughters, practical wives, and natural caretakers as mothers. "But our Little Miss will be even better than most," Poppy claims, "as she will take special skills into her new household."

Inky, who's seen more of life, has an opposite view. "She can read, write, and recite from the classics, but no one would say she has exceptional talent in this regard."

"That's because she spends her time studying with her grandmother—"

"Medicine is a waste of time for a girl! Tell me how memorizing a formula will increase her abilities to compose poetry to entertain her husband or paint landscapes to add to the amusements in the women's chambers."

"But—"

"Her spinning, weaving, and embroidery abilities are uninspired too. These skills show diligence and discipline. They can also bring in money if her future family should fall on hard times."

Inky's assessment makes me feel insignificant. I need to try harder to build my woman talents in order to learn all I can to help my sons become scholars, train my daughters so that one day they'll be marriageable, and please my husband so that he'll appreciate me, while still studying medicine with my grandparents. I'm also mindful of not being like the parrot Grandmother mentioned. I follow her like a shadow and ask her questions nonstop. Late at night, I often slip out of bed, light a lamp, open a book to a formula, and recite it to myself, searing it into my memory. Slowly, slowly, I'm coming to understand the deeper meanings of what Grandmother is teaching me, and I think I might be catching up to where she was at my age, but sometimes I feel like I'm drowning from the expectations and responsibilities that have been placed on me.

It's a lot for me to worry about, and I get a stomachache and fever. I don't want to eat, and I can't sleep. Grandmother diagnoses my condition as childhood depletion. She orders me to bed for a week and brings special foods and tonics to my room. Miss Zhao also visits every evening to check on me. One night, after she and Poppy think I've fallen asleep, they sit beside the brazier and sip tea. They discuss my prospects, of course, but soon their conversation turns away from the topic that has obsessed the household. It turns out they came from the same town.

"When I was five years old, a Tooth Lady came to see my father," Miss Zhao quietly confides.

Tooth Lady. I remember the other concubines teasing Miss Zhao about that.

"That happened to me too," Poppy confides, "but I have no memory of it."

"She brought me to Yangzhou, where I lived in a house with other girls training to become Thin Horses—"

"I wish we could have been in the same house," Poppy says, her voice quavering.

"It wasn't so bad for me, and I hope it wasn't terrible for you either," Miss Zhao replies.

"I worked hard, but when I turned seven—"

"They decided on a different future for you. You're pretty, but your feet . . ."

"They are my failure," Poppy admits. "Every time the Tooth Lady wrapped them, I peeled off the bindings when no one was looking. My bones never broke." She glances at her feet in disgust. "Look how big they are!"

"If I'd been there, I would have helped you, encouraged you."

"Maybe I was destined to be a servant, plain and simple." Poppy sighs. "My training shifted to childcare and learning to attend to a lady."

I slow my breathing. I've learned more about Poppy in these few minutes than I've learned since my birth.

"But you were lucky in the end," Miss Zhao says comfortingly. "Even though you didn't become a Thin Horse, you weren't sold to become a woman who solely lies on her back for men."

At this, Poppy wraps her hands around her shoulders. "I'm still a plaything for the boys and men here," she whispers. "If I stop getting my monthly moon water . . ." She squeezes her shoulders a little tighter as though protecting herself from the world.

I had been following along, but now I'm completely lost.

"Don't worry about that," Miss Zhao responds. "There are things you can take to keep from becoming full with child." After a moment, she says, "Instead, let us do what we can for Yunxian. Without a mother, she must rely on her grandmother, you, me, even Inky, to set her on a good path. We are the circle of good that surrounds her."

Until tonight, I have never thought about where Poppy came from or even about her feelings, although she knows everything about me, having bathed me, emptied my honeypot, held my forehead when I've vomited. I've always thought of her as being just my servant—always with me. Now I see she is more than that. As for Miss Zhao . . . Her words—a circle of good—remain in my mind. I must try to open my heart and sympathies to her too.

———

Once I recover, Grandmother stuns everyone in the inner chambers by inviting Midwife Shi and her daughter to visit us in the pharmacy. Meiling and I are told to sit next to each other on two pearwood stools. Both of us fold our hands in our laps. We wear pretty outfits and ribbons in our hair. Mine are of finer quality, of course, but the midwife has taken great care to make Meiling look like a girl of high standing. The two women sit at opposite sides of a teak table, a porcelain teapot and cups between them, with a bronze vase holding a single orchid set to the side.

Grandmother begins the conversation. "I want to propose an idea—a more formal relationship between your daughter and my granddaughter." Meiling and I exchange glances. This is a totally unexpected announcement. "I realize the two girls are from different classes—"

The midwife, who can't hide her distrust, interrupts to state the obvious. "My daughter has big feet. Yunxian has bound feet."

Grandmother acknowledges this mismatch with one of her own. "Yunxian is studying to be a physician, while Meiling will get filth on her hands when delivering babies."

"My daughter carries my family name, for she has no father. Your granddaughter is descended from—"

"We could continue listing all the reasons not to formalize something that many people, including my husband, would find unsatisfactory, but may you and I consider the positives instead? Both girls were born in the Year of the Snake, specifically the Year of the Metal Snake. A Metal Snake can be gifted with a calculating mind and enormous willpower—"

"Or a Snake can be a scheming loner," the midwife says, still unwilling to list a good attribute.

"A Metal Snake craves luxury and easy living, which Yunxian was born to," Grandmother goes on.

"A Metal Snake without these comforts can have an envious streak, find it difficult to face failure, and will seek to settle scores."

"Which one is Meiling?" Grandmother asks.

Midwife Shi responds with a question of her own. "What does it matter if both girls were born in the Year of the Snake? Their natures can be nothing less than different, with the potential to cause many conflicts." When Grandmother doesn't argue the point, the midwife continues. "For as long as anyone can remember, a beautiful face has been acknowledged as a window into a girl's inner character. It shows her to have a 'beautiful' nature—to be kind, generous, and diligent. It can also change a girl's fate, allowing her to improve her status through marriage."

Grandmother visibly perks up. "Have arrangements been made for Meiling?"

Grandmother loves me and is doing everything she can to give me a good future, but it hurts to realize that when the subject of beauty arose, she assumed the girl in question was Meiling.

"A matchmaker has completed the arrangements for Meiling," the midwife answers. I'm surprised. A midwife's daughter has had her betrothal settled before I have? "My daughter is to marry the son of a tea merchant—"

"In Wuxi?"

"I would not marry out my daughter to a family far away, no matter what the bride price."

Grandmother nods her approval.

"Lady Ru, why do you seek a special friendship between your granddaughter and my daughter?" Midwife Shi asks bluntly.

Grandmother doesn't answer the question. Instead, she says, "The girls never should have touched White Jade."

"Agreed. That task is for bonesetters alone."

"But they did," Grandmother says. "Fortunately, no blood was involved."

"I would say what is more fortunate is that they called for you and they caused no harm."

Grandmother takes another sip of tea. Then, "For now, we can say that the girls did not panic or run away. Not only did they not hide their faces in our skirts but they had the correct idea about how to treat White Jade."

Midwife Shi quietly waits. I dare to peek sideways and find Meiling staring at me.

"My husband—all men—would say these two should be kept apart," Grandmother continues. My breath catches at the thought.

"And yet they have become friends," Midwife Shi points out.

"Indeed."

"But you are considering another factor."

"We live in a world of contradictions," Grandmother says. "Midwives have lowly reputations, while doctors are respected. Midwives can get rich, while doctors can acquire fame—"

"You aren't telling me anything I don't know already."

"What I'm saying is that, in my experience, it isn't a matter of either-or. Both things can exist at once."

"So?"

"I see something special in my granddaughter, but I also see something special in your daughter—"

"Meiling learns quickly." Midwife Shi smiles. "With the right connections, she could go very far as a midwife."

"I agree." A long silence follows. Finally, Grandmother speaks again. "I have not known my granddaughter long, but I've learned she has certain physical frailties. It would give me peace to know that a midwife could look in on her from time to time when she moves to her husband's home. Your daughter could do that for me."

"I see." Midwife Shi quietly thinks this over. "I am not opposed," she says at last, "but one girl's reputation could be stained by the girl below her, while that girl could reach for riches, ideas, and position, only to be disappointed that she can never attain them."

"It is a risk, no doubt." Grandmother laces her fingers together. "And there's the issue of the other work your kind does." She lowers her voice, but I can still make out the words. "I'm speaking of the help you give the coroner."

Midwife Shi lifts a shoulder as though this were insignificant. "Would you prefer female victims be examined by men? In death, especially by violence, I'm the last person to touch a woman or girl. I usher her to the Afterworld with dignity."

"But you also check for chastity in court cases! Those are living girls!"

"Can you tell me that your husband would not want to prove the state of a servant's childbirth gate if your son were accused of—"

"This would never happen!"

"It happens all the time." Midwife Shi visibly bristles. "Look. You're the one who invited us here. You're the one who, from the beginning, encouraged this friendship."

An uncomfortable silence falls over the two women. Midwife Shi has been insulted, while Grandmother seems to be weighing the wisdom of her plan. I glance at Meiling to see how she's reacting to all this. Her expression confounds me.

As is typical when she's considering something, Grandmother's eyelids fall to half-mast, and she strikes a beat on the arm of her chair with the nail of her right index finger. *Tap, tap, tap* . . .

"*Friendship is a contract between two hearts. With hearts united, women can laugh and cry, live and die together,*" she recites. "Despite the various barriers and potential problems, I still believe there could be benefits for both girls, as well as for the two of us, if we go forward with my proposal."

Midwife Shi's loud and gravelly laugh fills every corner of the room. Hearing the coarseness of it, Grandmother looks away. After a sip of tea to regain her composure, she says, "My granddaughter lost her mother. Who knows how long I will remain on this earth? Your daughter never knew her father. You are in good health, but we can agree that your fortunes are forever precarious, depending on the outcomes of childbirth and the good words that pass from family to family about your skills—"

"The same can be said for a doctor of women's medicine."

"Exactly."

The two women regard each other silently.

"There is one more thing," Grandmother says at last.

"Another one?"

Grandmother ignores the barb.

"As women," she says, "we can hope that Yunxian and Meiling will marry into families that are kind and generous, but who knows what fate has planned? You and I do not always agree on treatment methods, yet I believe respect exists between us. I want Yunxian to have someone she can trust and who will stand by her for years to come, whether or not her mother-in-law, sisters-in-law, or—"

"All those other women who cohabitate in a household such as this," the midwife finishes, gesturing vaguely with her hand, not quite able to control her impatience.

"Even the richest woman on earth must live under a mother-in-law," Grandmother says.

"Forever true," the midwife agrees.

"I want Yunxian to have someone who can share in the care of women and offer comfort when things go wrong."

"No one likes to lose a baby or a mother in childbirth," the midwife admits.

"I do have one condition. There is to be no talk whatsoever coming from your daughter on aspects of your profession unrelated to midwifery."

Midwife Shi gives a single curt nod.

———

Not long after this, the terms for my bride price and dowry are settled. The Letter of Betrothal arrives, announcing that the conditions between the two families are equal and that a geomancer has determined that the year, month, day, and hour of my birth are compatible with those of my future husband. In seven years, I'm to be married to Yang Maoren, the only son in a wealthy family that owns mulberry groves, silkworms to eat the leaves, and several silk factories in and around Wuxi. The Yangs live in a mansion-compound called the Garden of Fragrant Delights. My husband-to-be has three younger sisters. I'm told he is one year older than I am. Therefore, he was born in the Year of the Dragon—the most powerful and admired of all signs. Nevertheless, this is not a match of an official family to another official family. Rather, I'm to be married out to a merchant family.

I try to hide my disappointment, but Grandmother, who has a lifetime of training in reading expressions and emotions, sees the truth on my face. "Like you, a Dragon will never give up," she comforts me. "You will find your husband to be naturally ambitious. He will surely succeed at his exams and will no doubt take a high position as an official like your father and grandfather. If the two of you play your parts well and according to the rules of civilization, then you will, as a couple, reap many rewards."

Almost immediately, the Letter of Gifts is delivered, listing the number and types of items to be sent as part of my bride price, which will include a whole roast pig, sweetmeats, and cakes to be shared with all who live in our household, as well as money for my father and grandparents to pay them back for their care of this future daughter-in-law. In addition to gold ingots, jade carvings, and jewelry, the Yang family will provide bolts of silk of different weaves so seamstresses can begin to sew the gowns, leggings, capes, and tunics I'll eventually take to my new home. Not long after Grandfather receives the Letter of Gifts, the bride price is delivered. Tradition says that certain gifts must be returned. I find the first one easily when I open a cloisonné box and discover fresh lotus petals, which symbolize having many children. But after that, I struggle. The Yang women must have had fun hiding these things, because Grandmother and I spend hours looking through everything to uncover them.

"I found the scissors!" I exclaim on the second day of our search. Scissors symbolize that a man and wife will never separate. In the same trunk I find the ruler, which sends the message of thousands upon thousands of *mou* of land. Grandmother and I pack these three gifts in a red lacquer box, and the matchmaker takes them back to the Yang family. With this, the first two of the Three Letters and four of the Six Etiquettes have been completed. Now the two families will enter into the period of the Fifth Etiquette with each side meeting with a geomancer to begin looking for an auspicious wedding date, when I will be as perfect and fresh as a flowering plum branch in spring rain.

I'm grateful to my grandparents for taking such care with my betrothal, but it's in my nature to worry. I'm eight; Maoren is nine. I don't know who I'll be in seven years, let alone what he'll be like. What if Maoren doesn't pass the imperial exams? What if his family sees my lack of womanly skills as a problem? What if I don't give birth to a son? Will my husband bring in a concubine or many concubines? No matter what I do or where I go, I must live as a proper Confucian woman: *When a girl, obey your father; when a wife, obey your husband; when a widow, obey your son.* My entire life will be limited to a total of three places: the house where I lived with my parents, the Mansion of Golden Light, and my future in-laws' compound and garden.

———

Weeks later, White Jade—who Grandmother and the bonesetter agree is healing well—is abruptly sold by Grandfather. She is simply gone one morning. By day's end, a new White Jade arrives.

She's seventeen, and her beauty rivals that of the other two Jades. Only time will reveal who will climb to be Grandfather's favorite, while the first White Jade has provided a lesson to all the girls and women in the Mansion of Golden Light, no matter their age or status: Our golden lilies are both a gift and a peril. We must prize and care for them but also be watchful with every step we take. Our tottering and swaying on our spindly and weak legs make us appealing to men, but a single misstep or fall can change our futures.

The next time Meiling comes to the compound, Grandmother says I can take her to my room. When I notice my friend looking curiously at the carved wooden tassels that hang from the rosewood canopy of my mother's marriage bed, I take her hand. We step through the antechamber, where Poppy sleeps at night; through the second space, which was once my mother's dressing room and is now mine; and then through the moon-shaped archway into the third and largest room, which houses my bed. I pull Meiling up onto the raised platform to sit on the soft mattress.

"This is bigger than where Mama and I live," she says.

She must be teasing me.

She gets up on her knees to look at one of the silk paintings that covers a window. It shows a husband writing poetry with brush and ink to his wife, who sits nearby. Meiling then edges along the bed's side walls, examining each window painting. To me, they seem ordinary, showing a wife in a flowing gown playing an instrument for her husband's pleasure or the two of them walking by a stream, but Meiling is entranced.

"They're so pretty," she says with a sigh. "And look at these. What are they?"

Her finger touches a tiny carved piece of boxwood about the length of one of my feet in height and nearly twice as wide. This part of the bed has twenty of these carvings, but I've never paid much attention to them as, once again, they simply show the grace of leisure days—in miniature—that were so much a part of Respectful Lady's own life. But what has always seemed commonplace to me beguiles my friend. I rise to my knees and scoot to her side. Now that I look, I see that the details are amazing. Even on such a small piece of wood, the artist has found ways to bring out every drape or fold of a garment, the movement of water over rocks, and the uniqueness of the clouds in the sky. Soon enough, Meiling and I start to pretend we're the characters captured in the carved tableaus. I even pull out a couple of tunics and scarves to change Meiling from the daughter of a midwife into a girl like me. We laugh and giggle, going from the dressing room back to the bed, where we lie on our backs, hold hands, and laugh some more.

"This is even more fun than racing leaves," Meiling says.

"Here, let me show you something." I wiggle the panel to the right of where I rest my head at night. "See how it's loose. I can pull it out—"

"Don't do that!"

"I can put it back in again." But I don't. Instead, I remove a small bundle.

Meiling sucks in air.

"No one knows about this hiding place or what I keep inside." Slowly I fold back the silk. Meiling's eyes widen when she sees Respectful Lady's red wedding shoes. "They belonged to my mother."

Inspired by the moment, I ask her to share something with me. "It doesn't have to be a secret. Just something we can have between us—as forever friends."

"Forever friends. I like that," she says. She peers up at me through her lashes. Her cheeks go pink when she confides, "My biggest secret is my wish to learn to read and write."

I smile. "I can help you with that. I will teach you." I leave the marriage bed, go to the table, and pat the back of a chair, inviting her to sit. "I'm going to show you how to write ten basic characters. The next time you visit, I'll teach you another ten."

But when she doesn't come right away, I realize I've caused her to lose face. I can't act like I'm above her just because I can teach her to read and write. I rub my chin, thinking. Then I return to the bed's entrance. "I shared something with you, and you shared something with me. I can give you something, but you need to give me something back."

"But I have nothing to give."

"Yes, you do. Would you give me what I can't see?"

She cocks her head. "You know there are things I'm not allowed to talk about."

I shake my head. "No, no, no! I don't mean anything like that!" Although I most definitely do. *A Snake can be gifted with a calculating mind.* That would be me. I want to hear the stories about corpses and all the other things too. *A Snake can be gifted with uncompromising willpower.* That would be Meiling. Grandmother Ru and Midwife Shi may have agreed to this friendship, but it will take time for Meiling and me to build trust between us. I'll need to work slowly to get the secrets she's supposed to keep from me. "Just tell me about the outside," I suggest. "What's it like beyond the gate? During the New Year's Festival, my father made offerings to our ancestors, we got new clothes, and had a banquet. He set off firecrackers on New Year's Day, but I don't know how other people celebrate. During the Lantern Festival, we released lanterns in our courtyard, but what is it like outside? I'd love to see lanterns coming from houses all across Wuxi." I pause to take a breath. "I've never been to the marketplace. I've never—"

"I can tell you about all those things." She grins. "For every ten characters you teach me, I'll give you back word stories."

"Good!" I exclaim, but I wonder if she realizes I'll be receiving much more than I'll be giving her. "Now let me show you how to grind ink on the inkstone . . ."

———

Not long after this, Grandfather receives a letter from the capital informing him that my father attained a high level in the imperial examinations and is now a *jinshi* scholar of the fourth rank. As such, he was presented to the emperor, who personally read Father's essay. Already the Tan family—through my great-grandfather, grandfather, and great-uncle—is an established part of the provincial elite. Already our family holds enormous power and prestige. That my father has become a *jinshi*—having never needed to repeat an exam—gives him status in his own right, while building the family's glory. To add to his triumph, he's entered the rank of Lesser Grand Master of the Palace and has been appointed to a position on the Board of Punishments in Nanjing, as my grandfather was. It's a great honor, but it will require him to travel from county to county to investigate and rule on crimes. It's all wonderful, but it makes me sad too, because it means he'll continue to be far from the family. My grandparents can't stop smiling, though.

"We must have a celebration of this accomplishment," Grandfather announces. "I'll consult with the geomancer to find an auspicious day for our son to return home."

Grandfather arranges for musicians to accompany my father to the Mansion of Golden Light from a distance of five *li*, so our neighbors and their servants can celebrate our family's good news. Grandmother sends Cook to buy ingredients for a banquet and orders the gardeners to rearrange pots filled with hibiscus, orchids, and cymbidiums so the courtyards are filled with color.

On the appointed day, everyone in the household—including women and girls who've been given the rare treat of being allowed to join the menfolk—gathers outside the main gate to await my father's arrival. Miss Zhao has taken great care with her appearance and that of my brother. She's even combed my hair and chosen my clothes to show what a good caretaker she's been in my father's absence. Despite the teasing she's received in the inner chambers, she's acted as a good wife since my mother died. As if to prove this to my father, she holds my brother's and my hands so we look like a wife and children who've faithfully waited for the master to return.

I'm eager to see my father, but I'm also excited to be outside the gate, having believed this wouldn't happen until my wedding day. Before I can begin to soak in my surroundings, though, the air fills with the sounds of clappers, cymbals, and drums; the braying of pack animals; and the clank and jingle of the metalwork on their harnesses. The noise grows louder until the procession comes into view. At the front, three pairs of men carry red banners mounted on tall poles. I see my father in a sedan chair, riding high above those who carry him. This will be his life from now on, for a *jinshi* is so elevated in position that his feet should never touch the ground unless absolutely necessary. Behind him, a palanquin and several carts follow.

My father steps down from the sedan chair. He wears his scholar's hat, a straight-cut loose robe belted with a black sash, and leather boots. An elaborately embroidered square patch has been sewn to the chest of his tunic. It shows a pair of wild geese, which announces to anyone who sees it—peasant or nobleman—that he is an official of the fourth rank, which Grandfather has told me is just four levels below the emperor himself. My father brings his hands together until they are hidden beneath his sleeves and then bows formally to Grandfather Tan and Grandmother Ru. He watches as servants present gifts to his parents, Yifeng, and me. But this is not all. As box after box of goods are unloaded and brought through the gate, the door to the palanquin opens and a young woman steps down, gracefully holding up the hem of her skirt to reveal a slim stockinged ankle and a bound foot in a shoe of emerald-green silk embroidered in a pattern of subtle delicacy. Her gown is the color of bamboo sprouting in spring but embroidered with the white chrysanthemums of fall. Blue sapphire earrings hang from her lobes. Her complexion is as white as goose fat. Her makeup accentuates her fine brows, and her hair is swept up not in the fashionable style of a concubine but in the elegant combings of a wife.

Miss Zhao's hand tightens around my own as the woman makes obeisance to my grandparents. Then my father takes her by the elbow and introduces her to the relatives that matter the most. Finally, Father brings her to us.

"Daughter, Son," he says, ignoring Miss Zhao, "please meet your new mother. You will call her Respectful Lady."

I'm the first of the three of us to lower myself to the ground to show deference to my father's new wife. As my forehead touches the stonework, words the original White Jade once spoke enter my mind. *Whether animal or woman, we are a man's possessions.*

PART II

HAIR-PINNING DAYS

The Twelfth Through Thirteenth Years
of the Chenghua Emperor's Reign
(1476–1477)

A Selfless Heart

I turned fifteen a month ago, and my hair was pinned up to show everyone I am ready for marriage. It has been seven years since my family received the Letter of Betrothal, and I am one day away from going to my husband's home. My mother's bed has been dismantled and sent ahead with Lady Huang—as a highly valued and fertile woman in our family—to "make up the room," supervising as men piece each window and decorative panel back together. She'll watch as they roll out rugs and position my wardrobe, desk, and chairs. She'll put away my clothes, cosmetics, and jewelry. She'll personally adorn the bed with the wedding linens and pillows I've embroidered over the years, so that all will be ready when my husband and I reach the bridal chamber.

A simple bed has been brought to my room for me to sleep on tonight, making me feel like I am already a guest in my family home. I tell myself that I'm fully prepared to enter the second stage of a woman's life. I've attained the Four Quintessential Attributes for a woman: virtue, elegant speech, proper comportment, and diligent work habits. I've struggled to improve my embroidery skills and labored for two full years creating pairs of shoes to be presented to my mother-in-law and the esteemed aunties in my husband's home. I was diligent in the sewing and embroidering of my bridal shoes, knowing that the quality of the stitching and design will be especially judged. (I hope no one looks too closely. I plan to walk as daintily as possible, so my shoes never peek out from beneath my bridal skirt.) Naturally, I'm familiar with the idea of bedroom affairs from having helped Grandmother treat women with issues below the girdle these past years, but I've also received instruction from Meiling, who was married out six months ago and has confided more about what happens in the bedchamber, and from the illustrated books Miss Zhao has given me to study.

The day begins with a visit to Grandmother in the pharmacy. She turned sixty-one this year, but to my eyes she looks no different than the first day I met her. I expect her to relate more details about what will happen under the bridal quilts. I'm wrong.

"When you turned fourteen, your yin qi welled up within your body and you started having your monthly moon water," she begins. "Until you are pregnant or go through childbirth, this will be your greatest connection to other women. You understand within your own body what it means for another woman to have stagnating or congested Blood, when women are suffering from depletion of energy, headache, or sorry emotions."

"I'm more concerned with how I'll fit into my husband's home."

Grandmother responds in her own way. "Excessive joy can cause the yang within to disintegrate. Excessive anger can cause yin to snap. Too much sorrow can lead to exhaustion. These things happen not just to wives but to concubines, maids, and servants too. Stay aware as you take your place in your husband's home."

"I'll try."

"Although you've studied with me for seven years, you are still a novice doctor. Confine yourself to treating girls if the opportunity should arise. Promise to write to me with your ideas for treatment before you attempt anything. I'll either write back with my approval or tell you to think harder. Don't forget you're still learning. In time, when you're older and have more experience, wives and concubines will seek you out. Trust me on this."

She pauses to let me absorb what she's said. Then, "Please take care of yourself. Don't let ill health or pensive feelings overcome you, no matter how your husband or others treat you. I have lived as the principal wife. You must do the same. If you fulfill your duties, you can have control over who your husband brings in. But remember, as long as your mother-in-law lives, even the pots and pans will report what they hear."

I do not find these words reassuring.

Grandmother motions to Inky and Poppy, who are carrying a chest, which they set on the table. It's made of red lacquer with an image of elegant ladies sitting in a pavilion limned in gold.

"Some believe that everything in a bride's dowry becomes the possession of her husband and his family," Grandmother says. "Others say the dowry belongs to the bride alone. I hope the Yang family follows the latter custom so you might use your dowry as you wish. You could spend it on yourself, but a good woman—a good wife—will be selfless and think of others. If your husband should need better tutors to finish preparing for the imperial exams . . . If he doesn't pass the exam and needs to have a title or civil position purchased . . . If floodwaters come, food becomes scarce, and your husband's family should be hungry . . . A good wife will let her husband or her father-in-law sell or pawn her dowry if ever they should fall behind in their taxes or want to build a new pavilion. A selfless heart will help in all these instances."

"I wish to be as good and kind as you, Grandmother."

"Thank you, Child, but I'm not finished. Sometimes a woman needs to look after herself. If you should become a widow and your husband's family decides to sell you or discard you to the street, you'll be able to provide for yourself." Her eyes fill with emotion. "I could say that you'll always have a home here, but your grandfather and I won't be on this earth forever. And who knows where your father will be at any given time? I'm not suggesting you can't count on him . . ."

But that's exactly what she's saying.

"If something unforeseen should happen, you need to be prepared," she goes on. "You might not leave your husband's home with your bed, clothes, or any other possessions. And even if you did, these things are not always easy to pawn. This is why we give a bride jewelry. This is your cash." She smiles, adding, "It also makes you look and feel beautiful." She lifts the lid of the chest. "The Yang family sent some pieces at your betrothal, and your father has provided even more items for your dowry, but what's in here comes from your mother. Your father put these pieces aside for you after she died." She cocks her head as she observes, "He could have given all of it to his new Respectful Lady." She pulls out a gold bracelet with intricate filigree work encircling the band and set with a carved piece of jade. "Your grandfather and I gave this to your mother as part of her bride price. When you wear it, think of her."

One by one, she brings out hairpins, necklaces, earrings, and bangles in gold, jade, sapphire, and emerald. There are pearls of every color and shape. The pieces made from kingfisher feathers of iridescent blue are my favorites.

————

Miss Zhao comes next for a private visit. "Hair-pinning days are the shortest and most precious time in a woman's life, for a girl is like a camellia—perfect for one moment before it drops from the branch at the height of its beauty," she says by way of greeting.

Miss Zhao has helped me in many ways these past years. While I still don't care for embroidering, the quality of my stitches improved under her watchful eyes. I don't remember a time that she was ever cruel to me, and she's always doted on Yifeng, who's eleven now and already devoted to his studies. He'll never be considered her son, because he belongs to my father's wife as her ritual son, and she'll never be my true mother, but we have become close.

After she sits, Miss Zhao begins with an abrupt statement of fact. "I hear that the Yang family's home is much larger than this one."

"The family is said to be wealthy," I agree, "but it's hard to envision a house grander than the Mansion of Golden Light."

"When I was a little girl, I couldn't imagine anywhere bigger or better than my parents' home." She falls silent, perhaps remembering the time before the Tooth Lady bought her to become a Thin Horse and how her life changed after that. "When I joined your father in Laizhou, I believed I'd landed in paradise. Then I came here. There is always a place that's bigger and better . . . But let me tell you something, Yunxian. Your surroundings will mean nothing if you don't fit yourself into the rhythms of the household."

Miss Zhao passes on the gossip she's heard about those who inhabit the Yang family's inner quarters. "Don't worry too much about the concubines," she counsels. "Even as a new bride you will have higher standing than they do. Your husband's younger sisters should concern you, though. Their envy will come from the understanding that you'll remain forever in the home where they were born, while they will marry out. They will leave behind certain comforts, position, and the love of their mother. They may struggle with you for having for the rest of your life what they are losing for the rest of theirs."

"Thank you, Miss Zhao," I say. "Thank you for always giving me good advice."

She puts a hand over mine. "I hope I see you again."

"I'll be back three days after my marriage—"

"For the traditional visit, but after that? Who knows?"

"Surely I'll be allowed to call on you," I say, alarmed. "You and Grandmother will come see me too, won't you?"

She hesitates before speaking. "Even if you're allowed visitors, who says I will be one of them? I'm fortunate that your father has not sold me. He could still summon Yifeng to Nanjing for Respectful Lady to raise."

I'll never become accustomed to hearing my father's wife being called Respectful Lady, but what Miss Zhao says is true. She is many years past the perfection of a camellia. Since my father remarried, he could have sold or traded her. He could also have bought one or more additional concubines. (For all we know, he has done that and keeps them in his official residence in Nanjing. If so, we have heard of no sons coming as a result.) Miss Zhao is still lovely, no question, but beauty fades. The words I offer are not just for comfort but because I believe them to be true.

"I will do my best for you, if I'm able, but you can always rely on Yifeng. He loves you very much. You are the only mother he has known. You are *his* Respectful Lady."

———

The next morning, my wedding day, I rise early so I can light incense at the family altar and bid farewell and give thanks to my ancestors in the Afterworld, particularly my mother, for always protecting and looking out for me. I visit my grandparents to serve them tea as a matter of respect, to offer a formal goodbye, and to thank them for taking care of this unworthy girl, and they reward me with the traditional responses. When I return to my room, I find a table laid out with dumplings, fruit, and other treats for those who'll assist me to bathe, put on makeup, comb my hair, and help me dress.

Meiling arrives first. She has grown more beautiful with each passing year. She's sensitive in the use of powder and pastes to color her cheeks, which only accentuates the fullness of her lips and the elegance of her cheekbones. Although she spends time in the outside world, she's been able to maintain a pale complexion. Her waist is slender and her shoulders slope in such a way that her gown, which today is the color of water under a cloudless sky, drapes with the fluidity of mercury. She wears satin shoes in a deep apricot color. I remember how long she spent embroidering the white peonies that blossom across the tops and sides of the shoes, trying to create the illusion of smallness. As Grandmother has said on many occasions, if Meiling had been born into a better family and had her feet bound, then she surely would have been matched into a good family. Grandmother's acceptance of Meiling, it must be said, is what has allowed her to visit me today.

Meiling touches the soft indentation where her collarbones meet. "I wanted to get here before everyone else—"

"So we could be alone," I finish for her.

After seven years, my relationship with Meiling is unlike any other I've witnessed between sisters, between concubines, and certainly between wives and concubines. Grandmother wanted Meiling and me to learn from each other, and we have. Although Meiling struggled to absorb the skills necessary for reading and writing—her calligraphy will never be as refined as mine—she's mastered enough characters to write simple letters and poems. In exchange, she's told me about the carnivals and festivals she's attended, with a lot of detail about food: the candied taro stand where Midwife Shi takes Meiling to celebrate a successful birth, the mooncakes they buy at a shop in Wuxi's main square, the special pork and mushroom dumplings the two of them make to celebrate the Dragon Boat Festival. My strategy to get her to give me these innocent descriptions of the outside world as a way to lull her into talking about forbidden subjects worked. Over the years, I've been able to pry from her many of the unseemly aspects of a midwife's profession—helping coroners examine women and girls whose deaths are questionable and finding the answers by looking for clues that remain on their bodies. How to determine which poison was used to kill a concubine; whether a woman found in a well died from suicide, murder, or accident; if a girl's childbirth gate has been violated. My grandparents are correct that this is filthy work—something that no follower of Confucius would *ever* do—but the stories of particular cases have captured my imagination and helped me understand aspects of life and death not taught to me by my grandparents.

What has continued to tie Meiling and me together is our study of women's medicine, she from the perspective of a midwife's apprentice and I from the perspective of a doctor in training. I've been in the room with Midwife Shi and Meiling when they brought new cousins into the world. We shared joy when Lady Huang's first daughter-in-law gave birth to twin boys. We've listened to Meiling's mother and my grandmother discuss fertility issues, miscarriages, and difficult births. We sat quietly when Grandmother Ru and Midwife Shi debated how to treat Red Jade, who became pregnant when my grandfather was away in Nanjing for several months. Grandmother diagnosed a ghost pregnancy, which, as the world knows, can last as long as five years. It did not come to that. Midwife Shi oversaw the miscarriage, and Grandmother allowed Red Jade to remain in the household. The concubine's loyalty to my grandmother will last until death, and we've seen the many ways Red Jade's eyes and ears help Grandmother to this day—revealing intrigues in the inner chambers, helping keep track of when monthly moon water comes for each and every girl and woman in the household, and, most important, informing on a concubine, wife, or daughter who might succumb to the wiles of a demon or ghost as she herself once did. And Meiling has recounted cases from other households where she and her mother have worked with male doctors. Through her stories, I've learned how those doctors treat women, and the power they wield over women in labor by letting them suffer "as nature intended," by refusing to prescribe herbs to alleviate pain or make a baby slippery.

If I have a deeper understanding of women and their bodies from watching and listening to Meiling, the same can be said for her observations of my grandmother and me as my knowledge has expanded not just in treating the common ailments of women and children but also in the medicine specific to below the girdle. But our connection goes far deeper. I held Meiling when she cried after she and her mother brought a stillborn into the world. She held me when I learned my father wouldn't be coming home for my wedding. I comforted her when she learned whom she would marry: a tea merchant, older than she is by ten years, named Zhang Kailoo. She's comforted me each year when I weep on the anniversary of Respectful Lady's death.

With only a few minutes alone together before the other women in the household come to help me dress, I hurry to share my feelings with Meiling. "I may be going to my husband's home, but you will never be far from my heart."

"We are so close, no one could slip a piece of paper between us," she agrees.

"I wish you and your husband could be a part of today's celebration. It is a sorrow for me that you can't."

"It's not possible," she says, accepting. "You're going into a household of note. A modest tea merchant and an old granny would not be suitable guests."

"Old granny!"

We laugh as we always do when she refers to herself this way, but today the laughter is a show of bravery on both our parts.

Meiling tips her head and casts her eyes down in the demure way she has since we first met. "Yunxian, I'm forever grateful to your grandparents for buying tea from my husband to be a part of your dowry. When you prepare it for your mother-in-law, think of me."

"I will."

"I hope as well that you'll have many hours alone with your husband so that the two of you might get to know each other as Kailoo and I have. On those nights when I'm not assisting my mother with a delivery, Kailoo and I sit under a camphor tree in a nearby square, drink tea, and talk. I hope you and your husband will be as happy as we are."

"Grandmother says my husband and I have been well matched."

"A perfect match and great happiness should bring you many children."

I take the blessing into my heart even as my friend sighs. A half year has passed since her wedding, and she's still not pregnant. I worry about this for myself, and I know there's only one way to make a baby . . .

Meiling takes my hand and asks, "Are you afraid about what will happen tonight?"

"I'm more informed than most girls," I answer, acting as brave as I can about something I'll do tonight with someone I have yet to meet.

"I've told you before I can help you. I learned the trick from my mother." She holds up her index finger, mimes wrapping cotton around the tip, and then makes a stirring motion.

The skin along my scalp crawls. The method used to test a girl's virginity in accusations of rape or in betrothals that may have been betrayed is the same as what Meiling is suggesting to ease the pain of my wedding night.

"Thank you, but no," I say.

She smiles as she drops her finger. "I grew up hearing my mother refer to what a husband and wife do as bed business. She always says it's a woman's duty to do this business for her husband. I prefer the way your family has talked about it. Bedchamber affairs can bring a woman great joy, if you let them."

"Grandmother says it's a husband's responsibility to make sure his wife has the happy moment, which helps to unite Blood and Essence to make a son—the ultimate happy moment."

Meiling tucks her chin. My nervousness about what tonight will bring has caused me to touch her most painful failure—not getting pregnant.

"I didn't mean to—"

"You're leaving everything and everyone behind." Her words

come out sounding melodious, but they cut to *my* most vulnerable place. "Your grandmother, Miss Zhao, Inky—"

"This is the sad truth for every bride on earth," I say. "But couldn't it also be said that it is the true start of life? We're taught that a girl is raised by her natal family until it's time to go to her true family—that of her husband."

"Stop reciting all that!" Her eyes widen at the sharpness of her own voice. "I'm sorry. I don't mean to be harsh. You and I are different in so many ways. This is what I love about our friendship. But we must always be honest with each other." She nibbles at her bottom lip, hesitating.

"Go on," I encourage.

"At first I was disappointed to be married to someone so much older than I am, but Kailoo turned out to be a good man, and I don't wake to serve my mother-in-law or have to steer through the intrigues of the inner chambers. Not only does Kailoo allow me to travel freely to attend to laboring women, he encourages it. He's proud of me. He says I am a true Snake." She recites, "*If a Snake lives in the house, then a family will always be free from want.* I'm bringing in money and raising our status. I do this by getting to see my mother nearly every day as we go from house to house to bring babies into the world."

She walks to the table, where the clothes I'll be wearing today have been laid out. She runs her fingers across the gold ornaments on the headdress. "In your married life, you will have wealth and privilege," she says at last.

I can't help but smile. "*A Snake can be jealous for no reason—*"

"This is not a case of a toad in a pond wishing to be a swallow in the sky. I am not jealous." She turns to face me. Tears run down her cheeks. "What if this is the last time I see you?"

Startled, I bring my hand to my mouth. How could I not have thought of this? My eyes well and overflow, but before I have a chance to speak, Grandmother enters.

"Finally!" she exclaims. "The bride weeps as she should."

Miss Zhao comes next. She's followed by Lady Huang and her daughters, the three Jades, and a few of the higher-level servants, including Poppy and Inky. As the room fills with the gay chatter of the women who love me, Meiling edges toward the wall. Her presence is still frowned upon by some, but my grandmother is allowing her to remain with the family until Grandfather hands me off.

Grandmother claps to get everyone's attention. "It's time to dress the bride!"

I'm helped into a silk skirt and tunic the color of cinnabar. The skirt is embroidered with good luck and fertility symbols. The tunic is embroidered with a dragon and phoenix in gold and silver threads. My lips are painted the color of red lotus petals and my cheeks dabbed with white cream. Grandmother places the phoenix crown on my head. Charms in gold filigree, jade, and other precious and semiprecious stones dangle, their tinkling bringing birdsong to mind. From a distance, we hear clanging cymbals, beating drums, and squealing horns.

"The *Book of Odes* tells us that a young woman at marriage leaves her parents and siblings far behind," Grandmother says. "It does not mention grandparents and others who love her." Her voice catches. Then, "The groom has come to fetch the bride. It is time for your veil."

I'm encircled by the women in my family. A chorus of good-byes enters my ears. I seek individual faces, trying to memorize each unique pair of eyes, sharpness of cheekbones, or delicacy of chin. Together Grandmother and Meiling lift a red veil embroidered with peonies and set it over my crown. The cloth is opaque, so now I can see only by looking down the front of my bridal tunic and skirt to my shoes.

"On this day alone, you dress as an empress," Grandmother says, "while your husband will wear the costume of the ninth rank. Live up to the emblems and you should both be happy."

With that, Grandmother takes one arm and Meiling the other to guide me through the courtyards. The whole way Grandmother whispers words of advice and love.

"We're at the last threshold," she announces. "Lift your foot here."

Outside the compound, I sense movement around me. I imagine what everything looks like: Decorated palanquins lined up for my relatives to ride in. The rest of my dowry—from the smallest sewing needles to large pieces of furniture—is wrapped in red silk or packed in red chests brightened with gilt and loaded onto carts and litters to be paraded to my husband's home so that the world can see the wealth I bring with me.

"Greetings, Master Tan" comes a male voice. "We have come from the Yang family to present the Letter of Wedding Ceremony."

"I will accept your letter," I hear Grandfather say.

A few minutes pass as Grandfather silently reads it. In my mind, I imagine him nodding as he makes sure all is in order, including acknowledgment of my father's gift to the Yang family of thirty *mou* of land, which was earlier conveyed by deed.

Meiling tightens the crook of her elbow around mine and whispers, "This is it. Goodbye, dear friend."

"Meiling—"

"Neither of us knows what the future holds, but promise to write—"

"And promise to visit me."

Meiling's arm slips from mine, and Grandfather's firm grip replaces her gentle one. A proper bride is expected to shed tears to show her reluctance to leave her family. This is not hard for me nor is it something I do out of duty. I sob as my grandparents guide me through the crowd. Looking down, I glimpse different pairs of feet. I recognize Miss Zhao's blue satin shoes embroidered with snowflakes and my brother's leather boots. I see the slippers belonging to the different Jades. I spot Poppy's big feet; she'll be walking alongside my palanquin as she did when we left Laizhou. Later she'll tell me what she saw: how many people lined the road to watch our procession, how grand were the houses we passed, and if there were clouds wisping across the sky. I don't see Meiling's apricot shoes.

I'm helped into the palanquin. My body trembles. No matter how much I've prepared for this day, leaving everyone and all I know is sad. My emotions are so jumbled that I barely notice the discomfort of the ride. The discord of the cymbals and other instruments accompanies every step and jostle. The trip takes about forty-five minutes, but the bearers could be carrying me in a circuitous route so that I'll be unable to find my way home on my own.

The drumming and cymbal crashing become even more frenetic. The pop of firecrackers and loud cheering announce that I've reached my destination. Voices shout orders and instructions, which tells me that already men are unloading my dowry. I wait in the palanquin, nervous as a fly up a water buffalo's nose. This moment is called "the great coming home," for it is said Heaven has preordained this union, but how can I feel anything but anxious—and scared—to see the place, family, and husband that have been set for me by destiny?

The door to the palanquin opens and a hand reaches in. Green cloth has been laid for me to walk on, so I can avoid contact with the filth and dangers of the earth. My escorts, by tradition, are widows. The hands that hold mine are spotted with age. I try to imagine the faces that go with the quavering voices that tell me to raise my foot over a threshold, be ready to take two steps up, or beware the slight incline of a garden bridge. Their voices are nearly drowned out by the clanging of instruments and the raucous greetings from others who live here. One more threshold and I'm inside a room. I'm guided forward until my red slippers are positioned next to a pair of man-sized shoes embroidered by me. They belong to my husband-to-be. I sway, and my sleeve brushes against his sleeve. Instinctively, we both pull away. Still, I'm aware of his presence—the warmth of his body next to mine, his breath nearly as ragged as my own.

Then things happen quickly. A voice asks us to bow three times: "The first is in worship to Heaven, Earth, and the revered ancestors of the Yang family. The second is in respect to Master Yang and his wife, Lady Kuo. Now bow to each other to show you will always be loyal and courteous—husband to wife and wife to husband."

With that, I am a married woman. I no longer belong to my natal family; my relatives and ancestors are now entirely of the Yang lineage. Hands take my arms once again, and I'm escorted back outside and through more courtyards, twisting and turning. Perhaps this puzzle of a journey has also been designed to make me feel lost. Finally, I step over a threshold and into a new room. Children laugh and giggle, squeak and squeal. I don't have to see them to know they're jumping on my marriage bed—my mother's bed—to encourage the mattress, linens, and woodwork to bring me the greatest fertility.

"Come away now," a woman's voice—stern and authoritative—commands. This must be my mother-in-law, because the children obey without a single complaint.

I'm guided to the bed. My husband sits next to me. His hands rest on his thighs. They show no signs of work other than holding books or a calligraphy brush. The traditional banter begins as strange fingers tuck red dates in the pleats of my clothes.

"Soon you will give birth to many children," someone says, because the words *date* and *son* sound the same.

"May your life together be sweet," another voice calls from across the room, because dates are sweet.

"May you have five sons and two daughters."

"May you have a long life and many sons."

"May your stamina never dissipate."

"May your candle never go out."

These last quips for my husband are met with rowdy guffaws, but that's as far as that sort of teasing goes.

Lotus seeds shower down on us. The written characters for *lotus seed* and *children* share a radical, while the sound is a homophone for another word meaning *in succession*. So again, wishing us many children but without intimate teasing about Blood and Essence joining. I'm handed a goblet of wine. A red string is tied around the stem, and it leads to the stem of the goblet held by my husband. Voices cry out. "Drink! Drink! Drink!" I take a single sip, but then a hand pushes on the base of the goblet, tilting it up until I have no choice but to gulp down the rest of the rice wine. It burns as it travels to my stomach. Even as the liquid begins to transform my mind and emotions, a thumb and forefinger lift an edge of my veil. A pair of chopsticks bearing a half-cooked dumpling moves toward my mouth. I don't want it, but what can I do? The word for *raw* sounds similar to *bear children*. The texture is mushy, but I can tell the meat is fresh.

Just as the banter starts to turn coarse, the woman I presume to be my mother-in-law speaks again. "It is time to leave these two to commence their married life. The rest of us will go to the banquet."

In moments, everyone departs.

"Are you ready?" my husband asks. When I nod, he gently lifts my veil. The glow from a special dragon-and-phoenix candle is not enough to light the room, but it does reveal my husband's face, which is as round and as pale as the moon. He is even more handsome than I'd dreamed.

"Let the candle's luminosity drive away bad spirits—"

"And bring us good luck," I finish for him.

"May we be like a pair of mandarin ducks."

Again, I complete the phrase. "Paired for life in unreserved loyalty and love."

It's not long before I discover how lean he is, how strong his shoulders are, and how gentle he can be. As the sounds from the wedding celebrations continue to come to us from a distance, I finally understand, in a way no words or drawings could teach me, about bedchamber affairs. When it's over, I draw my legs up, with my feet flat on the mattress, and pray that a son is being made.

———

The room is dark when I wake the next morning. The dragon-and-phoenix candle has burned to its base. Poppy didn't sleep in the antechamber of my bed, so she was unable to rise early and open the heavy brocade draperies to bring in light. I shift in the bed, bump against my husband, and immediately pull back as if I touched a hot brazier. I slip off the bed, step through the two antechambers, and into the main room. In the shadowy light, I find my wardrobe, where Lady Huang has placed my folded skirts, vests, tunics, and jackets in drawers according to the season. I dress, comb and pin my hair, and wash my face. I drape myself in my finest rose-cloud cape—rosy in color and voluminous like a cloud—and quietly pad to the door. I open it to find Poppy waiting for me. The sky is just beginning to turn pink. I must hurry . . .

"Good morning, Little Miss," she says, handing me a cup of scented tea so I might cleanse my mouth as my mother taught me. "I've learned where to take you. Follow me."

As I look back over my shoulder to close the door, the morning sun sends a wedge of light into the room. My marriage bed, which by any measure is significant in size, seems small in the large space. Through the dimness I see the outlines of embroidered wall hangings and pearwood furniture set just so. I turn back to Poppy, and for the first time meet the grandeur of the Garden of Fragrant Delights. This single courtyard is probably four times the size of the one where I lived with my mother and father. I don't have time to explore right now. I follow as swiftly as I can behind Poppy through courtyard after courtyard, turning this way and that.

Poppy holds open a door, and I step inside. My mother-in-law and father-in-law, both formally dressed, wait for me. Poppy has already arranged for the hot water, cups, and teapot.

"Father. Mother," I say as I drop to the ground and put my forehead on the floor.

"Very good," Master Yang says. "You may continue."

It is a new wife's duty to serve tea to her in-laws. My hands shake, but I'm comforted to see the gift from my grandparents—the canister of loose tea leaves. I know the tea will be of the highest quality. I brew tea, pour it, and, with my head bowed in deference, offer the first cup to my father-in-law. Once I hand the second cup to my mother-in-law, I sit back on my heels.

"A family's fortune can be foretold by whether or not its members are early risers." My mother-in-law's tone is no less gruff or demanding than when she shushed the children in the marriage chamber last night. "Rise before dawn and do not retire until my son is ready."

"Yes, Mother—"

"I would prefer you call me Lady Kuo."

I'm not sure how to feel about this desire for formality. Does she not see me as part of the family? I will need to work hard to win her approval.

"I will rise earlier tomorrow," I promise, keeping my gaze lowered.

"So be it."

And that is that. They dismiss me. I haven't even had a chance to see their faces. By the time I get back to my room, my husband is gone. My eyes fall on one of the decorations hung on the walls. It shows two birds perched together on a peony branch. This image sends the message of happiness and longevity to newlyweds. Red characters written in flowing script unfurl down the right side of the painting: *White-haired, growing old together*.

———

Three days later, as tradition requires, my husband and I go to my family home. As I suspected, the palanquin transporting me to the Garden of Fragrant Delights had taken a roundabout route. In fact, my grandparents live only fifteen minutes away. I could walk there if I had to. Without any hesitancy, I can send Poppy to deliver letters to my grandparents and brother, but also to Grandmother to give to Meiling.

My grandparents host a banquet for our family, but now I am only a visiting guest. Over the next two days, I barely see my husband, who spends his time with Grandfather. Perhaps they are discussing Maoren's upcoming examinations or what position he might take once he passes, *if* he passes. I stay in the inner chambers.

"Was your husband kind on your wedding night?" Miss Zhao inquires.

"What does the house look like?" Lady Huang probes.

"Tell us of your father-in-law," White Jade urges.

"Will your mother-in-law make a place for you in the household?" Green Jade wants to know.

"Or in her heart?" Red Jade asks, even more pointedly.

I answer that my husband was kind, but I have no one and nothing else to compare my wedding night to. The Garden of Fragrant Delights is too big for me to grasp, let alone explain. My father-in-law seemed nice enough, but I have no idea when I'll see him again. As for my mother-in-law . . .

"I don't think she likes me," I say.

"Give her time," Grandmother Ru says. "Mothers-in-law are

by their natures demanding. It might be different if *her* mother-in-law were still alive, because Lady Kuo would then be the second-ranked woman in the household. But she isn't, which means she controls everything within the gates of the compound, including you. Lady Kuo can make your life miserable, or she can accept you. Just remember that as women we have nowhere to place our emotions except inside our bodies, where they burrow and fester. As a woman born in the Year of the Snake, you must be especially heedful. Snakes are blessed with lovely and smooth complexions, but inside they roil from stress and turbulent emotions. Be careful, dear girl. Be very careful."

A Container for the Universe

"*Start teaching your son when he is a baby,*" Lady Kuo recites, seemingly to the air. "*Start teaching your daughter-in-law when she first arrives.*"

I close my eyes for a moment. What my mother-in-law has said is true, but I take her words as criticism of me. I've tried in every way I can think of, using every method I've been taught, to please her. I rise every morning one hour before sunrise. I bring her tea and breakfast. I wash her hands and face. Sometimes I pin up her hair. But in these past seven months I have not done the one thing I'm supposed to do, which is get pregnant with a grandson who will guarantee her husband's direct line and provide for her when she goes to the Afterworld.

I open my eyes to find her assessing me. What have I done wrong today? Is the tea too strong or too weak? Has someone in the inner chambers complained about me . . . again?

"You look thin, and your color is not fine," she observes.

"I'm sorry."

"Don't be sorry. Eat. Pinch your cheeks."

She tightens her jaw in her usual show of impatience with me. Her in-laws—my husband's grandparents—died from typhus five years ago, elevating her to top woman in the household at the young age of twenty-nine. Her forehead is naturally high, but she piles her hair in overlapping buns to accentuate that creamy expanse, sending the message that what is inside is always working. She's given birth to one son and three daughters, but her figure is slim.

Her fingers are long and tapered, but she rules with an iron fist, because, in addition to the usual responsibilities every mother must bear, she keeps the household accounts, tracks the moon-water cycles of every female inhabitant in the Garden of Fragrant Delights, and maintains strength and power in the inner chambers. Poppy tells me that the servants respect her, because she has never once beaten a maid, wet nurse, or kitchen helper so badly that she could not do her job the following day. Scolding, however, is a different matter—whether toward lazy servants, misbehaving concubines, or someone irksome to her, like me.

"What do you have to say?" she asks irritably.

"I'll try harder."

"I'll try harder. I'll try harder. I'll try harder."

My cheeks burn crimson at the way she mimics me.

"Pour me a little more tea, then you may leave," she says in a softer tone. "I will see you later."

The liquid flows into her cup without a single drop lost. Then I begin to back out of the room, holding up my skirt so I don't trip.

"Yunxian," she says before I reach the door. I stop, waiting for a new critique.

Will it be that I'm not friendly enough in the women's chambers? That my poetry skills aren't amusing? That I set a bad example for her daughters and other unmarried girls with my inability to laugh and gossip along with the others?

"I came here as a bride myself," she says. "I know what it's like to be on the bottom rung of the ladder, but you must think ahead to when you're on the top rung."

She clearly means to encourage me, but all I feel is despair.

"Thank you, Lady Kuo," I say, but I don't have her skills and can't imagine ever becoming adept at them. I miss Grandmother and the purpose I felt at her side. I miss Miss Zhao's quiet encouragement. I miss Meiling in too many ways to count. In our parting words, I asked her to visit, and she asked me to write. She has not visited. I've written many letters but have not received a single reply.

I walk through a colonnade in the direction of the women's rooms at the back of the compound. It's still early enough that the servants have yet to dim the wicks that burn in the silk-gauze lanterns that hang above my head. I'm passing through the fourth courtyard when Second Uncle comes hurrying in my direction. As Master Yang's second brother, he is the second most important person in the household, tasked with many duties and responsibilities. I lift my sleeve to cover my face and avert my gaze until he's gone past. I don't say a word and neither does he, but his forceful strides stir the air, causing my sleeves and skirt to billow. Not for the first time I wonder what it would be like to be a man, moving with determination, going beyond the gate, when I'm not permitted to peek through a crack in the wall, if one were even to be found.

I hold on to the balustrade to steady myself. My mother-in-law was right in her assessment of me. I have lost weight. I am pale. My loneliness is a black chasm within me, and I feel weak and sad. I should continue to the inner chambers, but the prospect fills me with gloom. The women there don't like me. I let my mind drift to my natal home and my grandmother.

"The human body is a small Heaven and Earth," she tells me. *"Whatever happens in the body as a whole is also happening in each appendage and organ. Never forget the deleterious effects of yin on women. We can be invaded through our orifices by Wind, but we also leak and drain from those same openings. Not only are our bodies troubled by Damp, but our emotions are as well. Men have physical cravings for food and bedchamber affairs, but we women ooze affection and desire, love and hatred, envy and jealousy, nervousness and vindictiveness, bitterness and revenge—"*

"Yes, Grandmother."

"What are the ingredients for the Decoction of Four Substances, and why are they important?"

"Angelica nourishes Blood, white peony root supports Blood, the rhizome of lovage moves and breaks up Blood, while rehmannia root inspires the qi and balances the cooling properties of the other three ingredients."

"Always remember, in women, Blood is the leader."

I take a breath, hold it, and then slowly release it. I'll go to the inner chambers, but first I'll visit the Garden of Fragrant

Delights—the garden for which the mansion is named. I shouldn't wander off alone. If someone sees me, I'll say I'm seeking inspiration for the afternoon's poetry contest. I continue through the covered colonnade, keeping my face down, trying to make myself invisible. The Yang compound has many large courtyards, mini-courtyards, wings, and structures. Each family group has its own quarters, with a kitchen, dining hall, and private courtyard. There are buildings for washing, storing grain and other foodstuffs, and housing the lesser servants. The Yang family even has its own live-in weavers. Sometimes I hear them singing, but I have yet to follow the sounds to the rooms where they make silk damasks, silk satins, and common raw silk cloth.

When I get to the Courtyard of Whispering Willows, I step through a gate and enter another world. Generations ago, the emperor gave a large plot of land abutting the western side of the mansion to a Yang ancestor who'd served the empire well. That ancestor built a protective wall around the property and then set about creating the Garden of Fragrant Delights. I can't know what it meant to him, but for me the garden is a refuge. It is, by my guess, even larger than the main compound where we all live.

Pavilions dot the landscape. A stream meanders around rare stones brought from the bottom of Lake Tai, where the waters have riddled them with holes and fissures, giving them a delicate appearance. Strategically placed portals and lattice windows provide the visitor with vistas of the natural world miniaturized. Moon gates lead from one part of the garden to the next, each one giving a perfect view of a twisting tree branch or a spray of orchids. Gingko trees that stood here long before the garden was created cast dappled shade. Flowering trees—the red-petaled peach, the rose-tinted crabapple, and coral-blushed quince—burst forth with splashes of color in different seasons. Vines creep and cling to balustrades and walls; some hang from branches or eaves and wave gently in the breeze. The walkways are inlaid with stones to massage the bottoms of the feet. If the body replicates the cosmos and the ear is a reflection of the entire body, then the garden is a container for the universe. Rocky grottos evoke mountain ranges. Ponds and streams bring forth the idea of lakes and rivers.

Male voices float to my ears from one of the pavilions, and I stay as far away as the paths allow. My father-in-law and other men in the household like to meet there with friends to drink, play cards, sing songs of the mountainfolk, and be entertained by a concubine chosen for her particular skill. That they are still here at this early morning hour tells me that last night's revelries were particularly enjoyable. I pass the Three-Way Moon-Viewing Pavilion, where I've spent precious hours with my husband on the nights of the full moon, observing that silvery orb in the sky, in the reflection of the pond, and in the mirror mounted at an angle above the lounging couch. We've tried hard on those nights to make Blood and Essence mingle to create a baby. How could the beauty and romance of this spot continue to fail us so?

I reach a whitewashed building called the Hermitage, which rests in the middle of the garden's largest pond. I cross the zigzag bridge and step onto the terrace that surrounds the structure. Resting my elbows on the carved marble railing, I gaze down at the water lilies and lotuses that float on the pond's surface. It's early enough that the koi are still nestled in the mud. The pond is so shallow, I could probably walk across it and get wet only to my knees. This terrace is my place to contemplate, to wonder, to dream. The garden, where every instance of wildness is manicured and controlled, is a reminder that I—like every man and woman on earth—am insignificant in the face of nature. I try to let the melancholy in my head flow down my arms, out my fingertips, and into the rippling water. As I breathe in the scented air, images of my grandparents, my brother, Miss Zhao, and Meiling come to mind. *Think of me. Remember me. Love me.*

Fortified, I retrace my steps, leave the garden, and go to the inner chambers at the back of the compound. The women who live in the Garden of Fragrant Delights—including me—are among the most fortunate in the land. This also means we're kept the most secluded. *A good woman should not take three steps beyond the gate.* As a result of this belief, some of the concepts found in the garden can be seen in the main gathering room. A miniature stone from Lake Tai sits on a stand. Incense gives off a woodsy scent. Lacquerware screens present tableaus of women watching an opera and attending a dragon boat race—things Lady Kuo would never allow us to do. Brush-and-ink paintings depict a deserted bridge after a snowstorm, a branch of cassia stretched over a pond's still waters, and a towering mountain range with a small temple inhabited by a lonely monk. A pair of ancestor scrolls hang on one of the walls—the eyes of my husband's great-great-grandparents keeping watch on us.

Second Uncle's wife beckons to me in a solicitous voice. "Yunxian, would you care to join our circle today?" Although she is just a year younger than Lady Kuo, tiny lines of bitterness blossom out from around her mouth. She sits with her two sisters-in-law in a corner of the room where a library—with inkstones and brushes of every size, cupboards filled with books, and hand-scrolls to entice the imagination—has been set up. My husband's uncles—all younger sons—have schemed over the years to assume control of the family and its vast holdings of money and land. Second Uncle in particular. He won't succeed, because the direct line is set by Heaven and birth order. (That is unless death befalls both my father-in-law and my husband.) Even so, everyone in this room wants *more,* as if there weren't enough for everyone.

I respond with a respectful nod. "Perhaps later, if Lady Kuo permits it."

My answer is a clear no. I can't be seen trying to align myself with Second Aunt, who exchanges scornful glances with her cohort.

"Come on," Third Aunt entreats, patting a spot beside her. "We're discussing the best ways to keep a husband happy. A young bride like you could learn from us."

I'm reminded of the line from the *Book of Changes* that says, "*Be a hidden dragon. Do not act.*" Most people interpret this as an admonition for a woman to be quiet and compliant. Grandmother taught me something different: hide my feelings, harness time, and when I'm ready I will leap, swim, or fly, and no one will be able to stop me. For now, though, I gaze modestly at the floor, trying to achieve Meiling's demeanor when she does this.

"Thank you so much," I respond, "but Lady Kuo has been instructing me on bedchamber affairs."

This is untrue, but my answer solidifies my alignment with her.

I think the matter is closed, but Fourth Aunt offers a variation on Third Aunt's invitation. "There's more to being a wife than bedroom affairs. A married couple should seek harmony—"

The others don't try to hide their snickers.

"We hear the way you berate your husband," Second Aunt gibes Fourth Aunt. "You're a tyrant! No wonder the poor man stays in Nanjing. Every time he comes home he must face a barrage of insults."

"Poor Fourth Uncle," adds Second Aunt in pretend sympathy. "Whenever he catches sight of you, he runs away like a beaten dog."

"What about the time she smacked him about the ears?" Third Aunt asks, her mouth spread into a broad grin. "Fourth Aunt is lucky she has sons. Otherwise, her husband would have deposited her on a riverbank."

"Oh, how I wish for that. I could finally get a good night's sleep!" Second Aunt says.

Low laughter bubbles from others in the room. You could look at this exchange as teasing or the truth. I feel like it's a bit of both, for I doubt there's a person here who hasn't heard the sour complaints Fourth Aunt hurls at her husband when he's in residence.

"*Waaa!* I know a story that touches on this very problem." This comes from Spinster Aunt, who sits across the room with a group of widows and other older women. She's the last surviving sister of my husband's great-grandfather. Her husband-to-be died before marriage, but she's remained chaste and loyal to him to this day. Her hair is completely white. She has the roundness that comes from not having had monthly moon water for many, many years. She's known to have the best embroidery skills in the household, but it can also be said that her mind is even more nimble than her fingers. Although not a mother herself, she's often called upon to bind feet if a mother is susceptible to her daughter's tears, and she has assisted at the births of most children in the household. "Shall I tell it?" she asks.

This is greeted with a chorus of yeses, although I notice that Fourth Aunt looks far from enthusiastic.

Spinster Aunt begins. "There once was a woman who beat her husband so badly that he ran to the bedchamber to hide. 'Come out! Come out!' she hollered. But he didn't—"

"The husband believed he had the will of a tiger. He cried, 'No, no, no!'" This comes from Lady Kuo's great-aunt, whose face is as wrinkled as a salted plum. The family she married into died out, leaving her nowhere to go. That Lady Kuo and Master Yang took her in is considered a great benevolence. "He was insistent, yelling, 'When a brave man says no, he means no!'"

"His words were indeed formidable," Spinster Aunt agrees. "But wait! What is that mewling?" She leans forward and cups a hand to her ear. From around the room come the plaintive mews and whines of kittens. "The wife narrowed her eyes and opened her ears. *Ah!*" Spinster Aunt exclaims. "The sounds were coming from under the bed. It turned out that the brave tiger was nothing but a kitten when faced with his wife's venom. Is there a man anywhere who does not quail before a woman who has become a terror of the back apartments?"

The end of the story is met with appreciative laughter. The positions of these old ones are tenuous, but today they have earned their keep. They live, even more than I do, under the rule of Lady Kuo, and I do not have a place among them.

"Yunxian, you want to know how best to please a man? Come sit with us. We know every wile and ploy." The speaker is Miss Chen, Master Yang's newest concubine and current favorite, which gives her a surprising amount of power over the other concubines. She's my age and flawless in her beauty and comportment. She and the other concubines paint their faces, dress in elegant gowns, and nibble from trays laden with pears, nuts, dates, and persimmons. She has nothing to gain from having me join her circle, but her offer is even less appealing than sitting with the high-ranking wives.

I look around for the final category of women who live here and find them sitting together in a corner. My husband's three sisters have their heads together as they embroider bound-foot shoes for their future husbands' mothers and revered aunties. Miss Zhao's warnings about them could not have been more accurate.

I'm lucky when they ignore me. Too often I've been the target of their pranks, which they cleverly disguise as accidents. Several times they've motioned for me to sit on a particular stool, only for me to find my bottom layers soaked through with water. "Oh," the oldest always says in fake surprise, "however could that have happened?" The other two sisters barely contain their giggles when I have to leave the inner chambers with my clothes looking like I couldn't make it to the honeypot. The oldest sister is fifteen and will marry out later this year. The youngest sister is nine. She'll be married out in six years. I'll be counting the minutes until all three of them are gone.

As I stand alone in the middle of the room, it hits me that it will be difficult—maybe even impossible—for me to make a friend here whom I can trust or to whom I can confide my loneliness. This leaves the boys under seven and the girls still in their milk days for company.

"Auntie Yunxian." It's Yining, the eight-year-old daughter of Second Uncle's first concubine. She slips her small hand into mine.

"I was hoping you would come for me," I say.

I let her pull me to a low kang covered with cushions that sits in an empty corner of the room. We've been spending time together these past weeks, as I hold a low position in the household, and so does she. I've been ailing, and so has she.

Yining opens *Analects for Women* to the page where we left off yesterday and gives the book to me. "I've been practicing my memorization," she says. "Will you listen?"

"Of course. But first tell me how you're feeling."

"I had to sit on the honeypot many times in the night," she reveals shyly. She looks wistfully at the other girls her age who sit in a circle playing a game. "The aunties don't want me by their daughters. They don't want me to pass on my illness."

Yining and I lie back against the pillows. I hold the book with one hand so I can follow along as she recites. The fingers of my other hand sneak to Yining's wrist to feel her pulses. A few months ago, when her stools turned watery and white, Doctor Wong, the physician to the household, was brought in to treat Yining. He diagnosed diarrhea brought on by malnutrition. Of course, he didn't *see* Yining. He only examined her from afar, sitting behind a screen, as is customary. Nevertheless, Doctor Wong gave her mother a prescription to be filled at a local pharmacy. I think he was wrong in his diagnosis and wrong in his treatment, which is why Yining has weakened further.

Lady Kuo knows I was training to be a doctor, but she's been adamant that I not pursue medicine or treat anyone. "You have one job," she's said on more than one occasion, "and that is to become full with child." I don't know what will happen if I disobey her directly, which is one reason I've done nothing to help Yining. The other reason is that Doctor Wong is in charge of the case. He's an important man, I've told myself, and must know more than I do. But I can't sit by any longer. Like me, Yining has lost weight and her lips grow whiter each day. Her smell is sweet—too sweet. She has a common enough childhood ailment, but it doesn't come from a lack of food. The girl suffers from excessive love. She's the only child of a concubine and overindulged in every way—from being dressed in silk to having every petition granted. She's pampered with too many sweets and rich delicacies. As a result, she suffers from food damage, which has caused her digestion to cease working properly. If I can cure the dampness in her Spleen-Stomach qi deficiency, I feel sure she'll recover quickly, and I can write to Grandmother of my success. But if something isn't done soon, then Yining will continue to waste away until death steals her.

"*When your mother-in-law is sitting, you should stand,*" she recites just as Lady Kuo enters. My mother-in-law parks herself on a carved teakwood chair placed in a prominent spot in the room. She's like the sun, and every woman and girl is arranged about her, each one leaning her head ever so subtly toward Lady Kuo's radiant power. Fortunately, she doesn't insist on the admonition against my sitting when we're in this room. I suspect that in her own way she's worried about my physical weakness but that her goodwill could change if she's irritated by indigestion, if she sleeps too little or too much, if Maoren complains about me. "*When your mother-in-law gives you an order,*" Yining continues, "*carry it out right away.*"

"Very good." I praise the girl, but I'm only half listening. I wonder what will happen to Yining when her mother's face starts to show its age. Will they both be thrown out? Will Second Uncle keep the girl to raise as an amusement for the boys in the household or sell her to a Tooth Lady? Neither of these futures will come to pass if the girl dies. "Would your mama let you visit me in my room tomorrow?"

"I think so."

"Why don't you ask her?" I encourage.

I bet that Yining used to love to run, because even with her feet bound I sense restrained eagerness in her steps as she walks to the cluster of concubines. Second Uncle's first concubine smiles when she sees her daughter. Her manner—even more than Yining's pulse—is proof of my diagnosis.

While Yining implores her mother, I place my fingertips on my wrist. Grandmother has always said that only a fool is a doctor to herself, but what else can I do? I read the three levels of pulses and come to the same conclusion I did yesterday and the day before that. My qi and Blood are growing more deficient. With a sigh, I let my fingers fall back to my lap.

As the hours spool out, some women switch to painting, while others compose poetry. I've never been good at these pursuits. In the late afternoon, women begin to retire to their own chambers—the wives to make sure their children are fed, and each concubine to prepare in case she's to be her master's chosen one tonight. As soon as Lady Kuo leaves, I go to my room. Until Maoren comes for dinner, I'll be alone.

In the mornings my thoughts go to Grandmother and our lessons. This time of day I spend with Meiling. In my mind, I transport myself back to my bedchamber in the Mansion of Golden Light. I see her before me clearly. I can smell her hair and the jasmine tea we were drinking. We are thirteen years old. She's had her first monthly moon water; I haven't. I've just listened to her read to me and watched her practice her calligraphy. Her voice was even in her reading, and her written characters showed improvement. When our secret lessons are finished, we go outside to our favorite spot—the bridge overlooking the stream in the fourth courtyard.

"*There were acrobats and archers, storytellers and puppeteers,*" Meiling recounts, her eyes wide as she tells me about a festival she and her mother attended to celebrate cherry-blossom season in the hills above Lake Tai.

I ask my favorite question. "*What did you eat?*"

"*Scallion pancakes and grilled meat from a stand. So tasty!*"

"*What else did you do?*"

"*Mama and I walked to the pagoda.*"

I take her hand and hold it over my heart. We stay this way in quiet companionship, listening to the trickle of water over rocks in the stream and the breeze soughing through the trees.

"*It's been a while since our last visit,*" she says at last. "*Are you ready for me to feed your nightmares?*"

"*I never have nightmares!*" I protest, although her stories do make my imagination spin.

She laughs. "*I'm just teasing you.*" And then she begins. "*A servant was found hanging from a beam in a building outside a compound not far from here.*"

"*Life is difficult for servants,*" I say. "*I bet many want to escape.*"

"*That's what her master said, but what someone says and what is physically left behind can be quite different. Mama and I helped the coroner cut down the body, but not before he showed us what he found. If the servant had killed herself, the rope would have stayed in place when she dropped. Instead, the dust on the beam on either side of the rope was disturbed.*"

I consider the detail. "*This told you that she'd been moved after her death and her body lifted to the beam, which caused the dust to shift.*"

"*Correct! It turned out the family rehung the girl outside the gates to distract from what had happened inside the gates.*"

Meiling and her mother studied whether the victim's eyes were found open or closed, the hands in tight balls or loose, the tongue pressed against the teeth or protruding from the mouth.

"*All this helped us to determine if the girl had indeed died from suicide, if someone had strangled her, or if there was an entirely different cause of death. What do you think occurred?*"

Again, I put my mind to work . . .

I remember that day clearly and how each time Meiling told me a story like this, it brought me closer to her. Our minds were linked, even though we led very different lives. Perhaps this is what Grandmother wanted all along. For my intellect to be sparked, to stretch beyond the walls of a compound, and to learn to use the Four Examinations not just for medical symptoms but in all facets of life—whether in dealing with murder or suicide or in navigating the complexities of life in my husband's home. I sigh, missing my friend with my whole heart. I'll try writing to her again . . .

I sit at the table, dip the tip of the brush in ink, and bring it to the paper.

> *Dear Meiling,*
>
> *You said you would visit me, but I have yet to be honored by your presence. Perhaps a baby now lives in your child palace, and you are staying safe at home. If this is so, I hope you are feeling well. If you are not and need anything, please send word to either Grandmother Ru or me.*
>
> *I've written to you many times these past months, but not once have you replied. Your silence is like rain on my worries, feeding and growing them. I cannot conceive of what has happened. Have I done something to hurt or anger you? Do the worries of which you spoke on my wedding day still trouble you? If you could know—truly know—how lonely I am, you would come to me. I'm sure of it.*
>
> *I'm confused. I feel myself swirling down, down, down.*
>
> > *I will forever be your friend,*
> > *Yunxian*

I reread the letter, making sure I haven't written a character Meiling won't recognize. Next, I write to Grandmother, telling her that I'm well—I don't want her to be concerned about my welfare—letting her know how I'd like to treat Yining, and including a list of the ingredients I'd like her to send so I can make a formula, if I'm correct, and some extra herbs for me that won't alert Grandmother to my condition and will confuse Lady Kuo if I'm caught.

"Poppy," I call, "take these to Grandmother. She'll get the letter to Meiling."

I anticipate that Poppy will return with a note from my grandmother saying the usual things—that all is fine, that Miss Zhao has been helping her in the pharmacy, and that Yifeng is studying hard—along with the herbs I requested. But will she bring a letter from Meiling?

———

A husband is Heaven to his wife. I want to please Maoren. I want to make him happy. I want us to create a life that parallels all the scenes of marital bliss that are in the silk paintings and tiny carvings that surround my bed, but Maoren and I don't spend much time together. He's busy during the day with his tutors. Many nights he continues his studies in his library and doesn't come to me at all. And soon Maoren will leave the compound for his final push before taking the municipal exam to become a scholar of the *juren* level. Although our hours together are scant, I believe in my heart that he likes me. I like him too. In time, our affection will grow, I hope, into the deep-heart love the concubines are always talking about.

Tonight, since Poppy has yet to return from her errand, I serve my husband a simple meal of a soup, duck glazed with kumquat, water spinach sautéed in ginger and garlic, and tofu with black mushrooms and pickled turnip. When I pour his wine, he touches my hand.

"Sit with me tonight," he says. "Let me feed you."

It's hardly proper. Wives don't eat with their husbands, but no one is here to see what we're doing. He uses his chopsticks to lift a sliver of duck. With his other hand cupped beneath the morsel, he guides it to my mouth. The way he watches me chew causes my cheeks to flush, which seems to please him even more. I'm equally fascinated by him: the precision with which he picks up a slice of mushroom, the gentleness with which he places it between my lips, the look in his eyes as he takes in my features. He's the first man, apart from my father and grandfather, with whom I've spent time alone; I suspect—but can't be sure—that I'm the first woman with whom Maoren has enjoyed the luxury of soaking in every mark of beauty and every flaw. When we're like this, I feel more exposed than when we're naked together.

Poppy returns in time to clear the dishes. When Maoren disappears into my marriage bed, she gives me a letter and a packet from Grandmother, which I tuck in a drawer. Then she removes the layers of my daywear, holds up my favorite silk sleeping gown for me to slip my arms into, and then ties the sash loosely at my hip. Last, Poppy helps me change into a pair of bound-foot slippers on which I've embroidered lilies in bloom. Poppy leads me to the bed, supporting me as I step into the first antechamber. As I cross through the dressing room, Poppy reaches in to place a lantern on the bench.

"I'll be right here, Little Miss," she says with a bow. By the time I'm under the quilts with Maoren, Poppy has rolled out her bedding in the first antechamber and lain down. I do not know—nor do I want to know—what she thinks of the sounds Maoren and I make as we begin to perform bedchamber affairs.

He takes one of my feet in the palm of his hand. He caresses the silk. He admires the embroidery, saying, "When I see the beautiful petals you stitched, I'm reminded that in every step you take your golden lilies bloom beneath you." He brings my slippered foot to his nose so he can appreciate its aroma. But mostly it's as I've always been told. My feet are physical proof of the pain I suffered to give him this treasure so dear to him. He'll never see them naked, but he knows from the books that taught him about bedroom affairs that hidden beneath the binding cloth is the deep cleft formed where my toes meet my heel. I could not have known this when Respectful Lady told me about the importance of this attribute when I was a girl, but now I understand that the shape and depth of this fissure are titillating to my husband.

I have not yet needed to twist myself into the strange positions I saw in the books Miss Zhao showed me before marriage, but Maoren must have seen or read some of those same volumes, because he's attentive to my desires and makes sure I find pleasure.

Afterward, as we lie curled together, our Blood and Essence mingled, I have the courage to ask, "Would you allow me to invite my friend Meiling for a visit?"

He answers as he always does—with patience and the exact same words: "That is for my mother to decide."

Tonight, I press him further. "I miss sharing confidences with Meiling. For many years, our hearts beat together as one."

"My mother would say that now your heart should only beat with mine," he says sympathetically. After a moment, he adds, "But I will speak to her."

———

The next morning, I complete all the usual rituals for my mother-in-law and then return to my room. I take the package Poppy brought to me from my drawer. Grandmother has written a short note: *You are correct in your diagnosis and plan for treatment. Proceed.*

I mix the ingredients and set the pot on the brazier to brew. The medicinal smell that fills the room instantly carries me to my grandparents' pharmacy. The aroma both lightens and deepens my homesickness. I return my attention to the other items I requested from Grandmother. By the time Yining enters, I have everything ready.

"I want to share a secret with you," I say. "I'm a young doctor."

She giggles. "That's not a secret. Everyone knows."

This must mean Lady Kuo has forbidden others to talk to me about this or seek my help. That makes me nervous, but I won't be deterred. Yining will benefit from my medicine.

"I plan to attack your illness from different directions," I tell her. "First I'd like to do moxibustion. Do you know what this is?" When she shakes her head, I hold up a small cone made from pressed ground mugwort. "I'm going to place these on your body and burn them."

Her eyes widen.

"I promise moxibustion doesn't hurt," I say, but she remains unconvinced. To soothe her, I add, "I only want what's best for you."

I take her to the kang I use during the day for lounging and reading. She sheds her tunic and lies on her stomach. I place five cones on spots on her back known to help with digestive disorders and light them as I would incense. A new, and to me familiarly wonderful, aroma now blends with that of the remedy percolating on the brazier.

"Are you all right, Yining?"

"It feels warm . . ."

"That warmth is opening meridians that will stimulate your qi." She rests quietly as the cones burn down. Before they reach her skin, I pluck them off and place the remains on a saucer. She sits up and puts on her tunic. I give her Pills to Preserve Harmony, which are made from seven ingredients. Of these, three are the most beneficial in this situation. Poria, an herb thought to be in union with the pine tree, will tranquilize Yining's heart and pacify her restless spirit. The fruit of the forsythia will dispel Heat, remove toxins, and disperse the accumulations that have so plagued her. The essence of radish seeds will promote Yining's digestion and strengthen her stomach.

"You're going to feel better soon," I assure her, "and your constant visits to the honeypot will end."

Just as the girl swallows the pills, the door flings open. Lady Kuo enters. Her arms are folded across her body with her hands hidden up her sleeves—the model of calm and decorum—but her expression is as wily as that of a fox that's cornered a rabbit. Poppy comes in behind her and drops to the floor in a position of absolute and total obeisance.

"What is that stink?" Lady Kuo demands.

"I'm making a remedy for myself," I answer, rising from the kang and bowing my head in respect.

"Doctor Wong takes care of the women in this household. He is a brilliant man—the first in his family to become a physician. Even if he wasn't the Yang family physician, I would never allow a daughter-in-law, especially one as young and inexperienced as you, to make her own medicine."

"But my grandmother taught—"

"Stop speaking! In this household you are a daughter-in-law, not a doctor. Do you understand?"

I don't, because I thought my skills were among the attributes that made me a good prospect as a wife for her son, but I nod anyway.

In the silence, Lady Kuo takes in Yining. "I heard you were here. I came to see for myself."

Yining is an insignificant child so has probably never been addressed by Lady Kuo. Still, as the daughter of a concubine, Yining understands her lowly place and the importance of keeping secrets.

"I like to visit Auntie. She's been helping me with my lessons." She answers so smoothly that she's almost believable. *Almost . . .*

When Lady Kuo sees the remains of the moxibustion on the saucer, her cheeks go ten shades darker. To Yining, she says, "Get out." Once the girl leaves, my mother-in-law focuses on me. "You treated a child?" When I don't respond, her eyes narrow as she continues to scrutinize me. "And you treated her without asking her mother?"

"I didn't ask the concubine directly. No."

Lady Kuo's breath flows through her teeth. She could beat me. She could deprive me of the privilege of leaving this room.

"You should know," she says as she seems to regain control, "that I did not come solely to see if what the gossips said was true."

She slowly pulls her right hand out from her left sleeve. She holds a packet of letters. I recognize them as the missives I've written to Meiling during the months I've been here. Seeing them, my vision goes black, and my legs begin to tremble.

"Your maid has been bringing them to me," Lady Kuo says, putting into words the only possible explanation.

From the floor, Poppy weeps her misery.

"I didn't think I would ever have to show them to you, and eventually you would stop writing them," Lady Kuo continues. "But today you left me no choice. You need to learn the ways of this household. You will never again use my son to supplicate on your behalf. Furthermore, a midwife is not the kind of person to be a friend to my son's wife. This is even worse than a wife using her husband to beg or a wife trying to practice medicine. You will not write to the midwife again. Do you understand?"

She is my mother-in-law, which leaves me only one response. "Yes, Lady Kuo."

With that, she turns and leaves. I stare at Poppy on the floor. It's devastating to know she betrayed me. I tighten my grip on the back of the chair. I want to scream. I want to cry.

"Poppy," I manage to say. "Get up. I need you to fetch . . ." My mind is so clouded by emotions that I can't think of a single thing that will help except to have her out of my sight. "Just go."

As soon as she's out of the room, the black wooziness returns. I sit. I put my elbows on the table and my forehead in my palms. I've lost Meiling, and I won't be able to do the one thing I'm good at?

Still unsteady, I go to the shelf where I keep my books and other papers. I find an empty notebook and return to my writing table. I stare at the first blank page, hesitating. I think of my grandmother and the form and structure she uses when recording her cases. Then I begin to write:

A girl eight years old from an elite family suffered from . . .

When I'm done, I take the notebook to my bed, edge across the mattress to the far side, wiggle the loose panel free, tuck the notebook in with my mother's shoes, and then secure the panel back in position. A wedge has been placed between my husband and me. I have been betrayed by Poppy. I am without friends, and I am ailing. My mother-in-law has forbidden me to write to Meiling or help the women and girls in the household. I can survive most of these blows, but I will not give up who and what I am—even if that means hiding my actions by practicing medicine in secret.

Go Back Home

"How lucky we are to live during the age of the Great Ming," Miss Chen, Master Yang's concubine, comments. "Our country suffered through centuries of Mongol rule, but Zhu Yuanzhang drove them out, and became the first Ming emperor. Even the word itself—*ming*—tells of light, brightness, and the radiance of virtue. May the first hundred years of the Great Ming continue for a thousand years and gloriously on to the end of time."

I'm across the room, reclining on a kang, feeling so tired I could doze off, though it's morning still. I force myself to a sitting position and pick up my embroidery. I send my needle down through the silk, pull it up and through the cloth, and drag the fuchsia-colored thread along the edge of my flower-petal design. I pretend not to listen, but my ears strain to hear the conversation between the concubines, who know so much more about the outer world than wives ever will.

"The first Ming emperor asked the populace to embrace Chinese ways once again. Men have gone back to wearing traditional Han dynasty styles, while women like us"—Miss Chen's hand flows through the air from her hair ornaments to her gown, her fingers trailing like silk gauze lifted by a breeze—"dress in styles that call to mind the elegance of centuries past."

Lady Kuo speaks from her circle of wives. "Life is not just about gowns and jewelry. We are fortunate not to know war—"

"Yes, we have relative peace," the concubine interrupts as she stretches toward a platter of dried fruit and nuts that have been painstakingly arranged into a pattern of butterfly wings. She pops a melon seed in her mouth, spits out the shell, and looks from face to face to confirm that cutting off my mother-in-law has escaped no one's notice.

"My husband has told me of marauders from the north," Lady Kuo says, proving that Master Yang confides news of the world to her as well. "We can be grateful that the Hongzhi emperor continues construction on the Great Wall to keep out barbarians."

The conversation, which is taking an increasingly competitive turn, is suddenly interrupted by squealing laughter.

"Yining!" Second Uncle's first concubine calls out sharply. "Quiet!"

"Yes, Mama," the girl answers obediently, but she can barely contain her exuberance. She's become the child I suspected she might be—full of sass and giggles. It will be a matter of only minutes before her boisterous ways get the better of her again. For now, though, the exchange between the concubine and her daughter has brought an end to what could have turned into another quarrel between Lady Kuo and Miss Chen. Oh, but I wish they'd continue their bickering, since the events of which they speak—though far removed from my life—are interesting to me.

I return to my embroidery. At one time different women tried to lure me into their particular circles—every person here wanting to gain strategic advantage—but ever since the incident three months ago with Yining and my letters to Meiling, I'm so clearly an irritant to my mother-in-law that I should be avoided at all costs. *Should be avoided* is not the same as avoiding, however. Several women have noticed Yining's recovery, while my mother-in-law does a good job of pretending not to see any difference in the girl's health. As Grandmother predicted, once others saw my skill, a couple of wives and concubines have quietly sought advice on how to treat the ailments that strike their children, and Spinster Aunt has asked what to do about her insomnia. For any and all these requests, I write to Grandmother first with my ideas for treatment. And I continue to be careful—very careful—not to get caught.

I'm getting by even as I continue to be lonely. Late at night, when my husband is asleep or if he's returned to his library to study,

I like to stand by an open window to pass the solitary hours. I've learned to recognize the singing voices of individual concubines, the honeyed tones insinuating themselves through the courtyards. Now, when one of those women approaches me during the day, I have a face to put to the voice. I'm still not fully myself, but I have recovered from what ailed me when I first arrived, although I have new symptoms, all of which have gone unnoticed by the wives and concubines. Sometimes we see only what we want to see and what will serve our own purposes.

Second Uncle's first concubine drifts across the room toward me. "May I sit?"

"Yes, of course."

"I'm pleased with how well Yining is doing," she says. "And I've continued to follow your advice about her diet, but what shall I do about her unruliness?"

I smile. "Her Blood is vigorous at this moment. It will settle in time." I put a reassuring hand on the concubine's sleeve. "Later, when she's older, it will return again. With so much vitality, she and her husband will easily produce an heir."

"*Hmmm . . .*"

It's then I realize she hasn't come to speak about Yining. My suspicion is confirmed when she glances in the direction of the circle of concubines before asking, "Miss Chen is also demonstrating boisterous Blood, wouldn't you say?" She pauses. Then, "She would like you to confirm her condition."

I assume Miss Chen thinks she's pregnant. I can understand why she wouldn't want to tell Lady Kuo, because the news might not be met with good cheer.

"Perhaps Miss Chen would like to join me this afternoon for tea," I suggest.

"She would be forever grateful."

Later that day, after my mother-in-law leaves to review the number of bags of grain and other foodstuffs in the storage room, I retire to my room. It's not long before Miss Chen arrives. She has the same pale look that I see when I gaze in the mirror.

"May I feel your pulse?" I ask. She wordlessly extends her arm. My fingertips seek an answer for her. Once I have it, I release her wrist. "I was looking for what we call striking yin and salient yang. This occurs when the pulse thrums against my fingertips. These two unique features tell me that Blood and Essence have successfully combined. You are with child."

Miss Chen blinks. "What should I do?"

"Your first responsibility is to tell Lady Kuo." When Miss Chen hesitates, I ask, "Would you like me to go with you?"

She's a smart one, and I can see her weighing what my offer might mean. From her perspective, she came to me, which is bound to upset Lady Kuo. I also gave the concubine a diagnosis when Lady Kuo has explicitly ordered me not to use my medical skills. Of the two of us, Miss Chen must think Lady Kuo's anger will fall on me, because she says, "I would be honored and grateful for you to accompany me."

Early the next morning, Miss Chen meets me outside my room so we can go together to Lady Kuo's chambers. My mother-in-law tries to hide her surprise when the two of us enter, but she remains silent as I pour her tea. Then I position myself next to Miss Chen. The concubine tucks her hands up her sleeves, and I do the same, so we look like a pair of matching puppets.

"Miss Chen would like you to know that a resident is dwelling in her child palace," I announce. My mother-in-law flushes. I suspect she's angry. Before she can start to yell, I add news of my own. "I too am with child."

Lady Kuo startles. "You're full with child?" She gives me a flinty look. "How do you know?"

"I have not had my monthly moon water in three months."

"Three months!" She flushes another shade darker. "And you're only just telling me?"

"I wanted to be sure," I say.

Lady Kuo looks flustered. "Only one person determines who is pregnant in this household," she says unsteadily, "and that is Doctor Wong." She motions to Sparrow, her servant. "Send for him."

A shiver runs through me as I recall Grandmother warning me about the methods male doctors use to confirm this diagnosis. This is Miss Chen's first child and she was not raised by physicians, so she must not be aware of the procedure, because she says, "I will do whatever is required."

Lady Kuo regards the concubine. "And how long have you kept your secret? Or have you already told my husband?"

Next to me, Miss Chen sways ever so slightly.

"Answer me!" Lady Kuo snaps.

Tears well in the concubine's eyes. I hold on to my elbows deep within my sleeves. Miss Chen may have thought my presence would benefit her, but I had read the situation differently and planned accordingly. I cannot say my motives were pure of heart. I wanted to put myself in a better light. My chance came a couple of weeks ago, when I first suspected that Miss Chen was pregnant. I just had to wait. I would not like to call myself devious, but I needed both to be sure of my own condition and to present the news in such a way that my mother-in-law might look kindly on me. Maybe *kindly* is the wrong word. I *hoped* Lady Kuo would be pleased to learn her only son's wife was with child; I *believed* she wouldn't be able to hold back her usual criticism of me. That pattern is too resolute in her. I thought that by orchestrating the announcement to unfold this way, I would direct Lady Kuo's ire at her husband's concubine instead of me. I hoped as well that I might find an ally in Miss Chen, and we could go through our pregnancies together.

Doctor Wong arrives that afternoon to see Miss Chen and me. He sits behind a screen in my quarters. I try to visualize what he looks like from listening to his voice as he instructs Poppy on how to brew raw Sichuan lovage root and mugwort leaves. I'm accustomed to the medicinal odors of potions stewing on a brazier, but Miss Chen's complexion turns white then green then back to white.

"Drink the tea," Doctor Wong says from across the room. He sounds older—distinguished and confident. I imagine him stroking a graying beard when he adds, "If you feel movement like a butterfly in your belly, then you are pregnant."

I don't feel anything, and I don't think Miss Chen does either. Nevertheless, I announce, "The butterfly is busy."

"Then you will indeed have a baby" comes Doctor Wong's affirmation of what I already know.

Next to me, Miss Chen hesitates.

"Tell him you feel a butterfly," I say in a low voice.

"But I don't," she whispers back.

"Do you need a man to confirm what your body is already telling you to be true?" I ask.

She ignores my question to speak to him directly. There's familiarity between them. "Doctor Wong, you know me. Have you helped me become full with child?"

What an odd question, I think, but his laugh is jovial and surprisingly warm. "Of course! But we want proof, don't we?"

From the other side of the screen, he orders Poppy to add honey locust fruit to the existing tea.

"You're pregnant," I murmur. "You don't have to drink that."

I'm trying to warn her, but Miss Chen is stubborn. "You're no older than I am. What do you know?"

When Poppy brings the brew, I ask her to fetch a bowl as well. Then I form a placid expression on my face and silently watch as Miss Chen drinks the concoction. When she starts to retch into the bowl, I pull her hair away from her forehead. Hearing the horrid sounds, Doctor Wong proclaims, clearly pleased, "This is no trifling illness. This is proof of pregnancy." It is also the beginning of what will be weeks of morning sickness for Miss Chen. I wish I had the ingredients to make Drink to Quiet the Fetus, but perilla, with its subtle flavors of licorice and mint, is not something I have stored in my room or can easily acquire from the main kitchen. I do suggest that she suck on preserved salted plums, which every household keeps on hand to calm upset stomachs.

———

I've helped Grandmother with many pregnancies, but I'm not above having the same concerns of any woman with child. To give birth to a son is paramount. After that, the goal is to have a slippery birth. But what if a baby is breech or transverse or labor lasts longer than three days? *In childbirth, for every woman who lives, ten die.* Obviously this saying can't be true, but it reflects the way people interpret the inherent dangers of giving birth. Protective rituals have been handed down for generations, and I follow all of them. This means no lifting of anything heavy—whether with my arms or with my mind. I'm careful not to ingest rich foods, because they might build Fire inside my body. I don't eat rabbit, because it may cause my baby to be born with a harelip. I don't eat sparrow meat either, because those small birds are known to have night blindness, and I don't want my baby to be born with the same affliction. Oh, sparrows. They cause many problems.

I had hoped to have Miss Chen as my pregnancy companion, but even now household rules keep us apart. "She's a concubine," Spinster Aunt tells me. "You're a wife. You don't want her frivolous ways seeping into your baby." I suspect Miss Chen might take a different view. I'm too boring for her.

Of course, there's much discussion in the inner chambers about whether Miss Chen and I will deliver boys or girls.

"This is a matter of yin and yang," Spinster Aunt instructs us all. "If you are carrying a boy, then you will feel him flutter at four months, because yang is ascendant. If it is a girl, she won't make her presence known in your body until five months, for it is in the nature of yin to be tardy."

Both Miss Chen and I feel our babies move at four and a half months, which elicits a new set of probabilities from Spinster Aunt. "Now we can determine sex by where the babies reside within their mothers. Let's feel their stomachs! If the stomach is soft, that means it's a girl, hiding her face against her mother's spine. If the stomach is hard, well, then, it's a boy, because he's ready to face the world."

Daily, Miss Chen and I have our bellies prodded. Women argue about whether there is a son or daughter inside. Some women make bets. My feeling? Miss Chen's stomach feels no different from my own—neither soft nor hard, just growing.

My husband seems happy, and that makes me happy. When I reach seven months, my grandparents send a flower-covered basket filled with good-fortune buns and painted duck eggs, wishing me luck with my coming ordeal. I'm filled with such gladness that I'm emboldened to ask my mother-in-law when Midwife Shi will come to call.

"I know her and her daughter already," I say, as if Lady Kuo weren't already acquainted with this fact. "But it will be helpful for Miss Chen to meet in advance the women who will catch her baby."

"We do not use Midwife Shi in this household," Lady Kuo responds. "Even if I had not already forbidden you to have contact with the young midwife, I would still insist that we use the granny who has brought all the Yang children into the world. Her name is Midwife Lin. You will meet her in plenty of time." She pauses. "And you already know Spinster Aunt, who will assist at the birth, as is the custom in our home."

I try to remain calm, but I am heartsick. I *need* Midwife Shi and *want* Meiling.

———

When I "enter the month," my husband moves out of our room so we won't be tempted by bedchamber affairs, which are said to be harmful to a fetus at this time in the pregnancy. I feel alone and fearful, but Spinster Aunt, who visits each day so we might become more familiar with each other, tries to convince me otherwise.

"You have Poppy," she reminds me during one of her morning visits.

"It's not a secret she betrayed me—"

Spinster Aunt nods, then says, "Never forget that, but what else was she supposed to do? She had to do what Lady Kuo asked of her."

"I accept that, but it's hard for me to trust Poppy now."

"And yet you should."

"I'll try harder." After a pause, I add, "I still feel you are the only person here who truly cares for me."

Spinster Aunt laughs. "You are wrong! Your husband cares for you. Master Yang is looking forward to a grandson. The women in the inner chambers ask after you every day. You are more well liked than you imagine."

I notice that she has not included my mother-in-law on her list.

I enjoy Spinster Aunt's company. She likes to gossip, and her stories are usually filled with humor. She also has a wealth of information about pregnancy and unborn infants.

"Now that you are big, we can determine the sex without doubt," she opines during another visit. "If your baby moves on the left side of your body, then it is a boy. If it moves on the right side, then it is a girl." This doesn't tell me the sex, since my baby likes to kick and punch me on both sides, but it reassures me that he or she is healthy and strong.

At last, Lady Kuo brings Midwife Lin to my room to introduce us. To me, she appears as wide as she is tall, with a face like a rotting apple. Under my mother-in-law's watchful eyes, the midwife palpates my abdomen and declares that the baby will arrive within days. The servants are pulled into action, bringing all the things that will be needed when labor starts: the birthing basin filled with straw to catch the pollutants that will flow out of me, coal in a basket by the brazier for heating water, a rope tied to the roof of my bed for me to hang on to when I'm ready to expel the baby. They also set out toweling to clean the baby once it arrives, swaddling to keep it warm, and a container to hold the placenta. Four nights later, my baby announces its desire to leave the child palace. Spinster Aunt is roused from her bed and brought in to assist. Midwife Lin lays out the most important tools of her trade: a knife, string, and a special basin for washing the baby once it comes out.

I've attended many births. I know what to expect, and it's not this. The contractions get stronger, but the baby refuses to complete its journey. Hours pass. I hang on to the rope, letting the weight of my body encourage the baby to come down, while at the same time pulling myself up so that my open parts never touch the straw beneath me. Spinster Aunt positions herself in front of me so I can lean against her when the spasms come. Between contractions, she rubs my back, massages my stomach, and whispers, "Relax. Rest. Breathe." Nothing helps. More hours pass. I'm exhausted.

As expected when difficulties arise during a labor, a doctor is summoned. Doctor Wong arrives and takes a position behind a screen. He proposes different tactics to help things along. "We will have her eat raw egg whites, which will help the baby to slip out," he orders. I swallow the slimy contents of a small cup and promptly throw it up. He has me ingest the brain marrow from a rabbit. "Rabbits are fast," he says. For me, the rabbit concoction is a lot faster on the way out than it was on the way in. I feel in my body that whatever Doctor Wong suggests will have a bad outcome. Still, I hear him behind the screen talking to my mother-in-law as he changes strategy once again, saying, "Sometimes it's best to let these things happen on their own."

On the morning of the second day, I'm so worn out and my thighs so cramped from the squatting position that I collapse. Spinster Aunt wipes my forehead. Midwife Lin murmurs encouraging words, but the look on her face tells me she's worried. I roll into a ball when the next contraction hits. The pain is so great that it slices into my head as cleanly and as sharply as a streak of lightning. When the spasm retreats and my mind can focus enough to send words from my mouth, I say, "Bring me tea."

Poppy shuffles forward with the pot and a cup. "No," I say. "It's not for me to drink. Pour it on my hand."

Everyone knows that drinking tea is better than water straight from a well. One can make a person sick; the other doesn't. I don't know why. Maybe it's the astringency in the leaves. I think these things as the fluid stings my hand. Then I take a breath and use my wet fingers to explore the childbirth gate. I feel something, and it's not a head. I groan as I pull out my hand.

"What is it?" the midwife asks.

"The baby is coming leg first," I answer.

Midwife Lin draws the back of her fist to her mouth and sits back on her haunches. Spinster Aunt moans her distress. From the other side of the screen, my mother-in-law demands that someone inform her of what's happening. This is followed by a similar request from the doctor. I can see in the midwife's eyes that this situation is beyond her.

I scream when the next contraction hits—from the pain as my baby's foot exits the childbirth gate and touches air, from the knowledge that I'm going to die, and from the sadness that I doubt the midwife has the knowledge to cut the baby from my belly once I'm gone so that he or she can live.

I don't know how much time passes. The stabbing pains in my

body are excruciating. Every time another contraction batters me, my mind goes white. Then, a voice . . .

"Yunxian, we're here."

From the chasm where my mind has been hiding, I try to swim back.

"Yunxian, open your eyes. I'm here. My mother too."

"Meiling . . ."

"Yes, it's me. You can thank Poppy later. Now, try to relax. Let Mama and me look."

Another spasm. I drift on a black sea as the three midwives talk.

"I did what I could," Midwife Lin confesses plaintively.

"I thank you for keeping her alive," Midwife Shi says. "Now all energies must be put to getting the baby out. Extreme measures must be sought."

"Poppy, can you bring ink and a brush?" Meiling asks.

Doctor Wong's garbled shouts swirl on the sea around me. "You must listen . . . I am the doctor . . . Lady Kuo wants . . ."

Another contraction. Will it be seconds or minutes before the next one?

Meiling puts her lips to my ear. "I'm going to write a message on the sole of your baby's foot. Just three characters. *Go back home.*" I have no awareness of her doing this, but I know she's finished when she speaks loud enough for all to hear. "What Mama will do next will not hurt the baby, but you will feel it. We're going to lift you up. Take hold of the rope. Yes, it's hard, but you can do it."

Two pairs of hands help me back into position. I grab the rope. Spinster Aunt's soft belly cushions my left side. Meiling's familiar arms embrace my right side. Midwife Shi holds up a pin for me to see.

"Your baby has received our message on his foot. What I do next will encourage him to obey, but it must be done with great precision or the baby will be tempted to reach up and grab your heart."

Meaning I could die.

"*No mud, no lotus,*" Meiling says encouragingly. "You're in pain now, but soon you will cradle a son in your arms."

I tighten my hands on the rope. Four arms support me. Midwife Shi pricks my baby's foot with the pin. I scream when my baby yanks its foot and leg back up into its longtime home. For the next hour, Midwife Shi massages my abdomen until the baby is moved into the proper head-down position. Suddenly, as if all the hours before have not occurred, the baby whooshes out. Without a word, Midwife Shi wraps it and carries it behind the screen to Lady Kuo and Doctor Wong. The infant cries, which tells me it's alive, but I don't know if it's a boy or a girl.

I hang from the rope until the placenta comes out. I want to lie down, but the two pairs of arms hold me upright.

"Let all the noxious dew run out of you," Meiling urges.

When my mother-in-law swishes into view and out the door, I understand that I've given birth to a girl—a terrible disappointment for the family, a letdown for the doctor and his reputation, and a failure for me. My next sinking thought is that I'll have to go through all this again. And again. And again. Until I birth a son.

———

For the next twenty-eight days, I must remain secluded while I "do the month," so I'll be protected from the eyes of those who harbor unfriendly thoughts toward me and from any demons who might want to cause trouble in the form of illness or death to me or my daughter. "You may not wash your hair or bathe, because you shouldn't be exposed to the yin effects of those activities," Spinster Aunt cautions me the morning after I have given birth. Then she tells me that Doctor Wong has dismissed Midwife Lin, blaming her for the difficulties of my labor, and that Midwife Shi has been pulled away to deliver a baby in another household. "Lady Kuo has asked Midwife Shi's daughter to come this afternoon to check on you." It is a welcome surprise for which I'm extremely thankful.

My baby is asleep on the bed beside me when Meiling arrives. I expect to see my friend, but she is here to perform her duties. Her tone is serious as she asks me basic questions about how I'm doing. When she's satisfied with my answers, she says, "Nothing is more important than cleansing you of your noxious dew. Here, let me help you into position."

Her hands hold me steady as I lift my gown and stoop above a low bowl so that what's still inside me can drain out and be disposed of along with my other birth pollutions. To help things along, she massages my belly with a roller. She takes breaks from this activity to hold a cup to my mouth so I might drink a mixture of vinegar and ink, a combination well known for its efficiency and thoroughness in breaking up blood clots. She pulls away the cup and stares into my eyes. At last, we are soul to soul. I begin to weep, revealing my disappointment to the one person who fully understands me.

"Thank you for saving my baby, but why did it have to be a girl? Why isn't it a son?"

Meiling glances at my daughter before returning her gaze to me. "The women in your grandparents' household and the women here—if they live to reach forty-five—have at least six children. Many are pregnant ten or more times—"

"I wanted a son. I *needed* a son—"

"Only to lose their babies in miscarriage or labor," she continues, speaking tenderly over my disappointment. "You'll get pregnant again. The next one will surely be a son. For now, embrace this creature who came from your body. Look at her face. Let her bring you joy."

I hang on to the rope with one hand so I can touch my baby's cheek. Despite her difficult journey into this world, she's nicely formed. But when I look at her, all I see are the dangers that lie ahead. "Even if babies manage to breathe the air of this world," I say, "many will die from a summer fever, never reaching the age of seven—"

Meiling's hands stop moving. "Just listen to your ugly words! Have you ever heard a woman sound so sorry for herself? At least you have a child. I've been married longer than you, and I have yet to become pregnant. You can still hope for a son, but day by day my dreams of having children are turning into despair."

Her anguish cuts through my preoccupations. I ask, "Have you sought Grandmother's advice?"

"I have, but my mother has sent me to other doctors as well. What is natural for most women is not coming naturally to me."

I'm about to question her on the herbs she's taking and ask if I might feel her pulses when the door opens and Lady Kuo enters with a woman I guess to be twice my age. I'm still balanced above the basin, but they push into the first vestibule of my marriage bed without regard for my embarrassment.

"I've brought a wet nurse," my mother-in-law announces, without greeting me or acknowledging Meiling's presence. "I've hired her many times."

I run my eyes over the woman. Wet nurses are common in elite households, and most women use them. This one certainly looks healthy enough, but my limited experience tells me that the best way for babies to attach to their mothers is through their nipples.

"Thank you, Lady Kuo," I say. "But I will feed your granddaughter myself."

Her response surprises me. "I'm happy to see this show of motherly devotion."

The wet nurse looks disappointed, though. I've deprived her and her family of income.

On the third day, my daughter is washed in water invigorated with special medicines and then taken away to be presented to the entire family. Spinster Aunt tells me that Maoren has named our daughter Yuelan—Moon Orchid. My heart lifts, knowing he's sending me a private message about our nights together in the Three-Way Moon-Viewing Pavilion. "Yuelan may be a girl," Spinster Aunt confides, "but your husband couldn't stop smiling." I wish I could see Maoren to find out if this is true, but we can't be in the same room until I've finished doing the month. Still, I'm heartened.

The next day, Meiling comes again. I don't know why Lady Kuo is allowing her to attend to me, but I'm not about to question anyone about it.

"How are you feeling?" Meiling asks. "Where do you hurt?"

I hover my hands over my chest. "Everything here is hard and swollen. The milk wants to come, but it's as if the spout of a teapot is clogged."

"Alleviating this problem is a granny's specialty," she says.

To help my milk come in, Meiling presses warmed stones against my aching breasts and massages them with a cooling rub. I feel something inside loosen. My daughter grabs hold of my nipple and suddenly she has milk dripping from the sides of her mouth.

———

As the days pass, my bleeding dwindles and finally ends. The better I feel, the more I'm reattuned to Meiling, and I sense a barrier between us. I had taken her reticence to be a manifestation of her profession: she was the midwife and I was a first-time mother. She was coming in daily contact with my blood—something I was trained to find repellent. But now I see the distance between us has nothing to do with those things. Rather, it's emotional. She's too polite to say what's bothering her, but I think I know what's wrong. On Yuelan's twelfth day of life, I find the courage to bring it up.

"I wrote to you many times," I begin, expecting it will take time before she opens her heart to me. I've read her incorrectly, because she blurts, "Not once did I receive a letter."

"That doesn't mean I didn't write them."

I go on to recount what happened with Lady Kuo, but my explanation isn't enough for Meiling, who says, "You could have sent Poppy with a note to say what had happened."

"But it was Poppy who betrayed us! She gave the letters to Lady Kuo!"

"You could have sent Poppy to deliver a message with her mouth," she presses. "This is how women like you have communicated with women like me for all eternity."

That hurts.

"I was afraid of my mother-in-law—"

"Who isn't? No. This is just an excuse."

I look inside myself to find my faults and mistakes. I see them clearly, but I once again put the blame on my maid. At this, Meiling shakes her head impatiently.

"Poppy snuck out of this compound and came to tell my mother and me about your labor," she says. "Poppy probably saved your life, and she did it at great risk to herself."

Again, I question myself. Is it a measure of how weak I still must be—or how self-centered I've always been—that I haven't questioned how Midwife Shi and Meiling so magically appeared at my side? Still . . .

"But tomorrow and the next day?" I ask tentatively. "Can I trust Poppy to take a letter or even a spoken message to you?"

"Now? I doubt it," Meiling replies. "Poppy belongs to you, but she lives here. She's a servant, but she still has to consider her own fate and destiny."

So no letters or messages can be sent.

I take Meiling's hand. "I'm sorry I hurt you, but I hope you can understand I was hurt too. You promised on my wedding day that you would visit—"

"I tried, but the guards wouldn't let me in. It was easy for them to turn away a midwife."

"But you're here now. I'm glad we've had these days together, even if I haven't been the best company."

Meiling's shoulders soften. "I hope they can continue after you've finished doing the month," she says, our eyes meeting for the first time this visit.

"My father-in-law's concubine will be having her baby soon. Maybe we can see each other when you and your mother come to help Miss Chen while she does her month."

Meiling raises her eyebrows as she considers this. "The decision to hire my mother belongs to Lady Kuo and Doctor Wong, but they should be pleased with how her skills helped you deliver."

I prefer to think that success will nurture more success and that Meiling and her mother will become regular visitors to the Garden of Fragrant Delights, as they have been for many years to my grandparents' home. For now, I hope I've begun to mend the rift between us. My parting words to her express what I feel.

"Even when we're separated, my thoughts are with you. The ties that bind us have been knotted even tighter."

But the smallness of Meiling's smile tells me we haven't fully resolved things between us. Then, before I can inquire further, she's gone.

The next day, Spinster Aunt comes to visit. Although she's never had a child herself, she knows about mothering. She's taught me how to care for my nipples when they become sore and cracked and has offered to spend the night in my room so she can take care of Yuelan when she's awake and I can get some sleep. She's advised me on what oils are good to use to soothe the childbirth gate when Maoren and I resume bedroom affairs. Best, she makes me laugh. Today she drags a stool into the dressing room of my marriage bed and sits on it. She takes my baby in her arms, looks at me, and begins the day's lesson.

"You must protect your daughter against drafts and dampness, because a baby's qi is, by its nature, young and weak." I know this, but it reassures me to hear it repeated. "Her bones are soft and not fully formed, which means you must handle her carefully. Keep the protective band tied around her belly so Wind and other venomous elements don't enter through her healing umbilicus."

I repeat something my grandmother taught me. "Every infant— whether a boy or a girl—is like a bubble floating on water or a wisp of cloud in the sky, easily swept away."

Yuelan burbles, and Spinster Aunt gently rubs her tummy.

"You should start making bound-foot shoes for the girl," she suggests.

"Her binding is still years away," I say.

"Ah, but you must make many pairs! She'll need new shoes for each stage of her binding." Spinster Aunt extends a gnarled finger. "I'm going to teach you how to make a proper shoe—from mixing the paste and layering the soles to sewing on the decorative outer covers. But first, while you're doing the month, you can start by learning embroidery skills that will elevate your standing as a wife and mother . . ."

My mind drifts, imagining Yuelan and me making offerings to the Tiny-Footed Maiden, imploring her to make my daughter's feet as perfect for her future husband as mine are to Maoren. Spinster Aunt's voice jolts me back to the present. "We'll begin today as though you've never before set a needle through cloth."

She leaves the marriage bed, hands the baby to Poppy, and returns with embroidery supplies. I prop myself up against some pillows and listen to her instructions.

"I plan to teach you how to embroider a bat to look like it's flying." Spinster Aunt nods to herself, pleased with the idea. "And how to make a peach look as though it's freshly picked."

I smile. *Fu,* the word for *bat,* sounds like *good fortune.* But a bat is not just a symbol of happiness and good luck, it also embodies the male principle, especially when paired with a peach, which represents the female principle. Spinster Aunt is encouraging me to begin looking forward to my next child.

An hour later, we're still working quietly together, with Yuelan napping against my thigh, when my mother-in-law enters. She stands at the entrance to my marriage bed and holds up a hand.

"You don't need to stand," she says. After I bow my head in thanks, she goes on. "The young midwife told me you are nearly recovered. I'm glad to see her assessment is correct."

"My heart lifts to hear that you've been speaking to Shi Meiling. I hope she's proven herself to you," I say.

"She has, and her mother too." Then she makes a brusque announcement. "At Doctor Wong's suggestion, we will begin to use them to care for the pregnant and laboring women in the Garden of Fragrant Delights."

Which means Meiling and her mother will become regular visitors. I brighten at the news.

"However, the fact remains that a friendship between the two of you cannot be allowed." Lady Kuo turns her gaze to Spinster Aunt. "Since Yunxian is doing so well and you have so much experience, you can finish seeing her through doing the month." Before I can object, Lady Kuo addresses me directly. "There will be no arguments. I gave you this temporary gift, and you should be grateful. Now you will turn your gratitude to Spinster Aunt. She is fully capable of tending to you now that your bleeding has ended."

Later, Spinster Aunt shows yet another side of herself when she comforts me as I cry. Meiling and I haven't even been given a chance to say goodbye to each other.

Three days later, on Yuelan's sixteenth day of breathing the air of this world, I'm awakened by her birdlike cries. Poppy brings her to me, and I open my gown so my baby can nurse. When she latches on and my milk lets down, I suddenly start to shiver. By the time she's finished with my first breast, my temperature has shifted and I'm sweating. I have a moment of panic, thinking I might be developing infant-cord rigidity, but my back is fine, my jaw remains loose, and I haven't been attacked by convulsions.

When the baby's done nursing, I have a desire to get up and walk with her as I burp her. It's my first time out of my marriage bed since my labor began. I feel surprisingly weak. Again, heat rises in me, and I begin to sweat so fast and so much that the room swims around me. I quickly give Yuelan to Poppy and stumble back to the bed.

"You're supposed to stay in bed when you do the month," Poppy chastises me as though I'm still a little girl.

I start to shiver. "I think something's wrong," I say. "Can you get Spinster Aunt?"

Poppy nestles Yuelan in the crook of my arm and then runs from the room. She returns a few minutes later. "Miss Chen's baby is coming. Spinster Aunt is with her."

I lift my head off the pillow, momentarily filled with hope. "Did Midwife Shi come? Is Meiling here?"

"Midwife Shi is with Miss Chen. Meiling is delivering a baby— by herself—in another part of Wuxi."

"By herself," I echo. This is Meiling's first time to catch a baby unsupervised. I'm proud of my friend and happy for her, but I wish she were here. "Let me know what's happening with Miss Chen. After her baby is born, ask Spinster Aunt or Midwife Shi to visit me."

"Doctor Wong is here—"

"I would prefer to talk to a woman."

All day I wait. I can't eat, and I don't want to drink. I feel my qi ebbing. I'm a doctor. I should do something. But I feel too awful to think properly. I drift in and out of sleep. Poppy has to shake me awake to feed my baby. While Yuelan sucks, I try to do the Four Examinations on myself. Fever, chills, lack of appetite . . . I give Yuelan back to Poppy and immediately I fall back asleep.

The crackling sounds of firecrackers jolt me awake. I hear cymbals, drums, and raucous cries too. Poppy hovers above me. "Miss Chen had her baby. It's a son. Master Yang is joyous. He's named the child Manzi. The entire household is celebrating."

I'm pommeled by dark thoughts. This son of Miss Chen's . . . What will Manzi's presence mean? Will my mother-in-law claim him as a ritual son? If so—and in my fevered state I can't be sure—I think this would mean that he'd be next in the line of succession should something unforetold happen to Maoren. And my condition is worsening, but everyone is occupied elsewhere.

Spinster Aunt visits in the early evening. I should tell her how I'm feeling, but she's so subdued I'm afraid to trouble her. If I were feeling better, I'd inquire about Miss Chen's labor and delivery, but I don't. Spinster Aunt volunteers nothing about it either, although in ordinary circumstances she might have revealed that the concubine hollered about the unfairness of her fate, cried that her childbirth gate might never resume the happy state that once captivated Master Yang, or—and this is the worst in my imaginings—that she rejoiced at bringing a son into the world when I only gave birth to a daughter.

"You don't seem yourself tonight," I manage to say. "Can I have Poppy pour you a cup of tea? Would you care for some watermelon seeds? I know they're your favorite."

"Don't worry about me," she replies. "This is a time when all concern should be directed to you."

Except that she seems oblivious to my physical state. This tells me her mind is truly troubled. Ignoring my own symptoms, I reach inside myself to see if I can help her.

"You've done so much for me," I say. "Is there something I can do for you?"

Keeping her eyes down, she worries the edge of her tunic.

I force myself to ask, "Did something happen during Miss Chen's labor?"

Spinster Aunt's eyes flash for a moment, but all she will say is "Finish doing the month, and then we'll talk."

I attempt two more times to get her to reveal what's bothering her, but she evades my questions. I don't feel well enough to keep trying, and I don't want to trouble her by confiding how bad I'm feeling. For her part, she's too distracted by whatever is bothering her to notice that something is wrong with me.

After a few more minutes, she slowly rises. "I'll come to-morrow."

The next morning, I open my eyes early enough that Poppy is still asleep in the first antechamber of my marriage bed. The light coming through the shuttered windows is muted, telling me the sun has not yet risen. I'm neither hot nor cold, which is good. I shift on the mattress. I feel wetness between my legs. I pull back the bed linens and find them stained with blood. It's too soon after Yuelan's birth for the first arrival of monthly moon water, and it's too late after the birth for it to be noxious dew. I shouldn't get up. I shouldn't walk. But I need to find padding.

I slide to the edge of the bed, swing my legs to the floor, and step quietly and carefully over Poppy. After I take care of myself, I stand in the middle of the room. I'm still not supposed to leave my room, but I long for a breath of fresh air. It's early enough, and no one will see me. I find a shawl, draw it over my shoulders, and walk outside. Above me, the sky is just turning pink. The air is still. The greens of the plants refresh my eyes. I find myself lured from the colonnade down into the courtyard to a spray of orchids as white as frost on glass growing at the base of the stone bridge that crosses the pond.

I'm extra careful as I pick my way down the pebble path slick with dew. My fingers graze along the tops of the azalea bushes, which are so grand in size that they temporarily block my view of the orchids. I sway around the shrubs to find a pair of legs stretched akimbo on the ground. I draw a breath and fall backward to the earth. Frightened, I crawl forward and peek around the azaleas. The legs are still there, and they end in bound feet. I recognize the fine embroidery on the shoes as coming from only one person's fingers.

"Spinster Aunt," I whisper.

The strange position of her legs . . . Her trousers sopping wet . . . Something is terribly wrong. I edge around the bush, follow the legs up, and see the upper half of Spinster Aunt's body submerged facedown in the pond. I scream. I scream and scream. I scream until women in this courtyard—sleepy and still in their nightclothes—come to see what's happened. They're followed by maids and other servants. And then they're all screaming too.

A Circle of Good

Two days after I found Spinster Aunt's body, my father-in-law and husband come to my room unannounced. Their visit is highly unusual, especially because I am still doing the month. I haven't had a chance to dress or do my hair, but they don't seem to care about the improprieties or my appearance. Master Yang addresses me directly, perhaps for the first time since my wedding. "If you'd been more discreet, then the servants wouldn't have become distressed. You should understand by now that we have eyes and ears—spies—in our midst and that word of your hysteria would find its way beyond our walls. If you'd acted with decorum, then the family could have handled Spinster Aunt's death with dignity and privacy. Instead..."

He tells me that news of a woman found dead in the Garden of Fragrant Delights snaked its way to the local magistrate, and now an inquest has been ordered to determine if Spinster Aunt's death was the result of an accident or wrongdoing. Doctor Wong will testify that he pronounced Spinster Aunt dead. Midwife Shi and Meiling will report on the autopsy on behalf of the coroner, who is busy elsewhere.

"And, as the person who discovered the body, you will be called as a witness," Master Yang continues, his voice stern. "None of this would have happened if you'd obeyed the basic rules of motherhood by staying inside while doing the month."

My husband is even less sympathetic, and it hurts even more that he doesn't see the obvious physical changes in me. "Your actions have embarrassed me before my family."

Their attitude is disappointing, and it reminds me of the case of the servant girl found hanging that Meiling once told me about. That family also tried to protect its reputation and avoid scandal, only to make matters worse in the end.

The next day, Poppy helps me dress. While she does my hair and applies my makeup, I drink tea, hoping it will invigorate me. Despite these efforts, the person who stares back at me in the mirror looks wan and lacking in vigor. With so much going on in the household, I haven't had an opportunity to ask to see Midwife Shi, or Doctor Wong either. I sigh as I rise. I have one last task to complete before I can leave the room. I change my padding and hope it lasts through the inquest.

At least I don't have far to walk. Everyone has gathered in the colonnade of the fourth courtyard, so we can view where the death occurred, as is the custom. The men sit together on the left side of the aisle. The three most important men in the household are together in the front row: my husband to Master Yang's left and Second Uncle to Master Yang's right. I haven't seen the three of them side by side before, and it strikes me how strong Yang blood is in them with their full-moon faces, and identical heights, builds, and even the fall of their hair. I also see Doctor Wong for the first time. He's not at all as I'd imagined. He's far younger—in his mid-thirties, with high cheekbones, and perfectly formed brows that draw attention to his eyes. He's clean-shaven, like my husband, and dressed simply but elegantly. I'm on the right side of the aisle with Lady Kuo and a few of the women who rushed to the courtyard in response to my screams. I see Midwife Shi, but Meiling is not in attendance, although I expected her to be here as part of her apprenticeship. Spinster Aunt lies on a table under a sheet of muslin. From my position, I can see the white orchids that beckoned me three nights ago.

A man sits at a small table facing us, with his back to the courtyard. He wears a long robe bearing the embroidered insignia of his rank. A black cap rises high on his head with two wings extending over his ears. A sparse beard covers his chin with two long forks of hair like a serpent's split tongue reaching down his chest. He begins by introducing himself. "I am Magistrate Fu. I am the sole investigator. I can make an arrest. I also serve as the judge and can pronounce the sentence if wrongdoing is found." He pauses to regard us. Then he continues, speaking deliberately. "I expect truth, and I will order one of the three accepted methods of torture to assure it—beating with a stick, ankle squeezers for men, and finger squeezers for women—if need be. Those who lie or falsify evidence will receive one hundred blows from a heavy rod as set forth by the Board of Punishments."

The magistrate falls silent to let us absorb this information. Then, "All inquests must take place in front of the assembled family and the accused, if there is one, so that good and evil can meet face-to-face, without secrets, without bureaucracy, without opportunity to shield parents, grandparents, siblings, or servants, or allow the guilty party to avoid the results of his or her actions." He pulls on one of the tails of his beard. "Nothing is more serious than a capital case, if this indeed turns out to be one. No piece of evidence can be treated lightly. If even one tiny mistake is made, the repercussions can stretch ten thousand *li.*"

He proceeds with official language to note the date, the province, the prefecture, and the names and titles of those in attendance. He then reads from a paper on the table before him. "We are assembled today to determine what led to the death of Yang Fengshi, known by her family as Spinster Aunt. From the honorific by which she was addressed, I understand she was never married. She was seventy years of age."

Yang Fengshi. How could I not have known her given name?

Magistrate Fu peers at the gathering to see if anyone needs or wants to make a correction. With no reaction coming, he continues. "Every official in my position follows the rules set forth more than two centuries ago in *The Washing Away of Wrongs* by Song Ci, the first person in the world to develop and record the forensic process. We will follow his example and begin with examining the scene where the death occurred. This is especially important in cases of drowning. We will inspect the ground to see if the victim lost her footing or was forcibly pushed into the water. I ask Master Yang and Doctor Wong to accompany me."

The three men make their way to the path I walked the other

night. Doctor Wong has a determined, yet surprisingly graceful, stride. After a few minutes of mumbled discussion behind the azalea bushes where I found Spinster Aunt's body, they return to the colonnade. Once the men are seated, Magistrate Fu speaks:

"Was the ground disturbed at the water's edge? Yes. If the victim had been a man, I would suspect that a struggle had occurred, for the dirt and mud in the area has been greatly agitated, but the victim was a bound-footed woman. As men, we admire the sacrifice and pain our women endure to give us this beauty to enjoy, but it leaves them unstable. I'm afraid this wouldn't be the first case I've encountered where a woman lost her balance, fell, and met with death. Older women are particularly vulnerable."

His words hang in the air before he continues. "The next question we must ask ourselves is, did the woman drown? In ordinary circumstances, I would say the depth of the water is too shallow. Wouldn't you agree, Master Yang?"

"Yes," my father-in-law accedes with a nod.

"And you too, Doctor Wong?"

"I'm in full agreement with the magistrate."

I am as well, since I bet I could wade across the pond and get wet only up to my knees.

"Let us now turn to the evidence given to us on the body," Magistrate Fu says. "Midwife Shi, please step forward and take us through what the coroner found during his examination."

I've always been intrigued by the stories Meiling told me about autopsies, but what once may have been entertaining cases to be solved take on a very different meaning when the case is about someone I knew and liked. Nevertheless, Midwife Shi has done this many times, and her manner and tone convey the same authority she has in the birthing room. As she speaks, I learn more details than I would ever have wished to hear. And I see more too, when Midwife Shi pulls back the coverlet to reveal Spinster Aunt's naked body. The women gasp, while the men go utterly silent. This may be the tradition at an inquest, but it's shocking. The tea I drank churns in my stomach, and I have to close my eyes to gather myself.

"You can see that I removed her clothes and hair ornaments,"

Midwife Shi explains. "These items have been wrapped in rice paper and will be preserved by the family. Usually, I would wash the corpse with a mixture of hot water, wine, and vinegar, but the coroner felt it was important to show you the markings of mud and pond water on and in the body. In all cases of drowning, water seeks a home in the belly, which he found through palpation."

I consider this, and it seems in accord with things Meiling has told me in the past.

"The question then is, *why* did she drown?" Magistrate Fu asks.

Midwife Shi hesitates.

"Go on," the magistrate urges.

Midwife Shi glances at Doctor Wong, who nods his encouragement. It surprises me that she would defer to him, but the only other time I saw Midwife Shi in the presence of a man was during my labor, and that was Doctor Wong too.

"If Miss Yang fell," she says at last, "then we would expect to find her hands open. If she jumped in—say, in an act of suicide—then her hands would be clenched and her eyes closed. If someone held her under the water—"

A new round of startled gasps interrupts the midwife's recitation. Heat flushes through my body, and yet I feel cold.

"We looked to see if mud was present under her fingernails or in her mouth or nostrils," Midwife Shi continues. "This would suggest she was held down to the bottom of the pond. We did not find these things."

But from where I'm sitting, Spinster Aunt's hands and mouth seem well coated with mud. I wonder if other people have noticed this discrepancy as well.

"You're leaving out an important fact, are you not?" Magistrate Fu asks.

Midwife Shi slowly nods. "The body has been positioned so those in attendance will not be disturbed by the indent on the left side of her head, where it is likely she hit her head when she fell."

Although I want to honor Spinster Aunt by following—and questioning—every detail, the slight burst of energy I got from the tea has ebbed. I feel light-headed and feverish again. Plus, it's time to feed my baby, so my breasts ache . . . Spinster Aunt . . . I'm grateful I didn't see this damage when I found her.

"In your opinion was Miss Yang a victim of violence?" Magistrate Fu asks.

"In cases like this," Midwife Shi responds evenly, "the coroner and I always consider the facial expression. We discerned no fear. Miss Yang looked at peace."

My eyes reluctantly return to Spinster Aunt. Grandmother taught me to look as part of the Four Examinations, but she also said issues of anatomy and death were to be avoided.

"Can you confirm she was a virgin?" Magistrate Fu asks.

I don't see what this has to do with Spinster Aunt's death, but Midwife Shi answers anyway. "I performed the proper examination. The gate of childbirth was unharmed."

To think of Spinster Aunt having protected her childbirth gate her entire life only to be violated by Midwife Shi's finger in death . . . I'm not the only one to be upset. Two women seated behind me faint, and servants carry them inside. The magistrate lets none of this deter him.

"To be clear. No knife was inserted there to penetrate the vitals?"

Midwife Shi shakes her head.

"I need a verbal answer," the magistrate reminds her.

"No knife was inserted. No foreign object or human has ever entered her childbirth gate as far as I can determine."

"So we can assume she didn't commit suicide as a matter of saving face or to protect a secret lover," the magistrate declares.

These ideas are appalling. Why isn't Master Yang stopping this line of questioning?

"Correct," Midwife Shi responds. "And it is unlikely she was held underwater by someone."

Magistrate Fu doesn't question Midwife Shi about the injury to Spinster Aunt's head, which, as he said earlier, seems like an important fact. Instead, he dismisses the midwife and calls on me to be the next witness. When I rise, I'm nearly overcome by dizziness. Once everything stops spinning, I slowly walk up the aisle and take a seat. I must look awful, but maybe everyone thinks that's to be expected as I'm a woman, naturally frail, unaccustomed to being in such a public situation, and further diminished from the ordeals of childbirth.

The magistrate inquires as to the circumstances by which I discovered Spinster Aunt. I keep my answer simple and to the point.

"I walked outside and found her."

I expect him to question me in detail about the position of her body and what else I might have seen, but he goes in a different direction entirely.

"I've been told you were close to Miss Yang," Magistrate Fu says.

"I was."

"And you know the ways of the Garden of Fragrant Delights."

"I'm recently married in, so I'm not all that knowledgeable."

"But you understand the rules for elite women."

"I was raised in accordance with the *Analects for Women* and the *Classic of Filial Piety for Girls*."

"Am I to understand that Miss Yang had no knowledge of the outside world?" he asks.

"Spinster Aunt lived her entire life within these walls, never venturing out," I answer.

"Would she wander the grounds alone late at night?"

"No."

"But apparently she did." He pauses to consider this incongruity. "Let me ask this in a slightly different way. Would she fall on a path she'd walked on since childhood even if it was at night?"

"Spinster Aunt grew up near ponds—whether in this courtyard or elsewhere in the compound, especially in the Garden of Fragrant Delights itself. But any bound-footed woman can fall."

"The pond is shallow. A man would have simply stood up and walked away, but she was a woman. Perhaps she panicked."

I remember Spinster Aunt's calm when my labor was going badly. "She was not the type of person to panic. But if she hit her head, maybe she lost consciousness."

The magistrate pulls on the twin tails of his beard. "And maybe she wished to die," he says, seemingly wanting to cover all possible explanations. "It is hard, after all, for a woman not to fulfill the womanly duties that are required of her."

"If you're suggesting suicide because she was a spinster, then you are mistaken." The sharp tone of my voice provokes grumbling from the men. I glance at my husband. His face is lowered, humiliated by my boldness. I should refrain from saying more, but I can't stop myself. "Spinster Aunt visited me on the night she died. We made a plan to meet again the next morning. And there was something she wanted to tell me after I finished doing the month—"

"So again, you think this was an accident?"

"I'm only a woman. It's not my place to form a conclusion," I say, hoping to make amends to my husband and his family for having left my room, polluted myself by finding Spinster Aunt, and embarrassed the clan by responding with screams and calling the attention of others.

Magistrate Fu dismisses me. When I stand, I feel blood gush into my padding. I freeze. This shouldn't be happening so long after Yuelan's birth. Aware of everyone's eyes on me, I try to keep my pace steady as I walk along the aisle toward my seat. I pass it and continue on, hoping I can get to my room before blood can spot my gown. Behind me, I hear Magistrate Fu. "As there are no other witnesses to call, I will proceed to my decision." I force myself to keep walking. I reach the colonnade and use the balustrade to steady myself. "I believe Yang Fengshi slipped, hit her head, and spent her last moments unconscious and breathing water," the magistrate says. "Therefore, I am labeling this an accidental death. If circumstances should change and new evidence is revealed, the family is welcome to order a re-inquest."

———

Funeral arrangements are quickly made. Because Spinster Aunt was an unmarried woman—a worthless branch on the family tree—the rites are simple and private, held just one day after the inquest. I can't attend because I'm still doing the month. But even if I weren't, I wouldn't be able to go because I'm much too ill. I should try to analyze my symptoms, looking for some type of infection, but after the added strain of the inquest, I'm too sick to think properly. Someone—Poppy?—must finally notice and inform Lady Kuo, because I'm vaguely aware that servants enter and set up a chair and screen in a far corner of my room, which tells me that she's summoned Doctor Wong.

When they enter, I have my second glimpse of Doctor Wong. I've spent little time with men in my life, and again I'm struck by how different he looks from my scholarly father and grandfather or my father-in-law and husband. Doctor Wong is taller than any of them. His shoulders look as though they could bear a great weight. He quickly disappears behind the screen and sends questions to me through my mother-in-law. I answer as best as I can. Over the next two days, he tries different remedies, and I must take them. He first prescribes a drink made with wine and a boy's urine. Then he has me inhale vinegar fumes. Neither treatment relieves my symptoms. On the third day, he writes a prescription, which Poppy brews for me to take. It doesn't help. My condition declines. The room is dimmed. I'm ignorant of the passage of time, but my breasts turn hard, then soft because my milk dries up. The wet nurse I initially rejected is brought in. Then one day a beautiful face appears above me. It's either a fox spirit or a ghost. I shiver, close my eyes, and turn away.

"Yunxian," the specter calls to me. "Yunxian. Open your eyes. It is I. Meiling."

I lift my lids. The creature is too flawless to be real—with cheeks like sunlit clouds, eyes as black as obsidian, and hair that reflects the light like moonbeams on a pond at midnight. It cannot possibly be my friend.

"You are more slender than the stem of a flower," the creature proclaims, dropping by the side of my bed. She glances over her shoulder. I follow her gaze and see my mother-in-law standing at the entrance to my marriage bed. "She needs her grandmother. Lady Ru is the best doctor in all Wuxi at addressing below-the-girdle ailments that afflict women."

Lady Kuo doesn't stir. "That won't be necessary," she says. "I will ask Doctor Wong to return. He is our family doctor and the one I trust most in the women's chambers."

"I'll fetch Lady Ru anyway," the wraith says. As she walks toward the door, I look for the fox tail to peek out from under her gown. It doesn't.

My room is once again prepared for Doctor Wong's arrival. This time he brings Maoren. It's my husband's second visit to my room while I'm doing the month. He shouldn't be here, and his presence fills me with distress until a new and even more disturbing thought enters my mind. Maybe I've completed the month and don't realize it.

Doctor Wong and Maoren keep their voices just low enough that I can't make out their words. Maoren steps across the first antechamber and sits in the vestibule next to my bed. His spine is rigidly proud. Becoming a father has turned him into a man, and yet all I see is worry in his eyes. When he says, "The doctor has questions he wants me to ask you," I remember when I acted on my father's behalf—and my mother's wishes—as the go-between for her and her doctor. I didn't understand what I was asking, so I had no embarrassment, but my husband goes red to the roots of his hair when he asks the first question. "Doctor Wong would like to know if the blood coming out of you looks like the white part of scallions, like water in which rice has been washed, or like meat that's rotted in the summer sun?"

"Rice water," I answer. This symptom would suggest excess Damp.

Maoren leaves to report this to the doctor and returns to probe further. "Does it flow like water, dribble like flaxseed oil, or come out in clots?"

"A little of all three."

This answer confounds the doctor as it's perplexed me.

My husband comes back to me with yet another inquiry. "Are the fluids that leave your body as dull in color as chrysanthemum petals that have dropped in fall or shiny like fish brains?"

"Fish brains."

Again, this answer seems to baffle the doctor, who comments just loud enough for me to hear, "Some of her symptoms indicate Cold, but shininess suggests Heat. These things should not coexist."

"Maybe we should have the midwife come again," Maoren proposes tentatively.

"*Only fools and idiots entrust their wives to the hands of grannies.*" The doctor casually recites the aphorism.

I recall a saying from the *Book of Rites*. *If a doctor does not have three generations of medicine, do not take his drugs.* I could never say this aloud, but I do tell Maoren I would like to see my grandmother.

From across the room, the doctor says, "A woman doctor is not much better than a granny. She can see and touch during the Four Examinations, but what does she know *really*?"

"Neither my wife nor her grandmother is a granny," my husband says.

The doctor laughs lightly, as though he's been joking all along. The next thing I know a curtain is hung from the ceiling of my bed, my wrist is wrapped with a length of cloth, and I'm told to extend my arm through the curtain.

"Please rest assured," Doctor Wong says, only his pledge is not for me. "I can feel your wife's pulses without touching her flesh."

Again, my mind spools back to when Respectful Lady was dying. Since the doctor couldn't see my mother, he couldn't examine her form or her qi, her luster or color. Nor could he truly feel her pulse through the linen handkerchief. The same must be true for Doctor Wong.

"Physicians like myself must consider a woman's emotions, how they caused the affliction, and how they might affect treatment," he tells Maoren. "Your wife is not thriving . . ."

But he doesn't ask why. And he's thinking backwards, but I have a fleeting moment of clarity. There's a big difference between how emotions might cause a woman to fall sick and how they will affect treatment and looking at the organic symptoms first. Once the symptoms are understood, then we should consider how emotions may have aggravated the ailment and how they should be addressed when looking for a cure. In my case, the bleeding and fever have been exacerbated by my sadness at having failed to produce a son, my loneliness in a household that still doesn't accept me, and the stress of Spinster Aunt's death. Not the other way around.

"While I'm finding Cold, the root of your wife's suffering is too much Heat," the doctor says. "Have the two of you engaged in bed-chamber affairs in the month before or since your wife gave birth?"

"Not once!" Maoren exclaims indignantly.

"Then she must have been eating things that produce Heat—chilies, peppers, fried foods. These often cause a difficult labor," he adds pointedly. "You're lucky the fetus did not die within her belly. Yes, too much Heat. I will give her cooling medicines to boost her yin," he announces in his determined voice.

But I'm quite certain Doctor Wong is wrong in his diagnosis, which means his treatment plan won't work. I'm so weak, though, and my mind so clouded that I can't figure out what to do or even how to speak up for myself. As happens to many women after giving birth, I retreat into darkness.

———

I'm dozing when I feel fingers on my wrist. I open my eyes to see Grandmother Ru. My mother-in-law, Miss Zhao, Inky, and Poppy hover behind her. The person I thought was a fox spirit—Meiling—is also present. I ask the obvious question.

"Am I dying?"

Grandmother snorts. "Absolutely not! But you are not well either." Her expression is stern when she asks, "How could you have let things go so far? You know better."

"I've been very worried about her," Lady Kuo says before I can answer. "I personally made sure she took all the formulas Doctor Wong prescribed."

Grandmother ignores my mother-in-law and speaks to me. "What you need is the Decoction of Four Substances, which will help with your Cold depletion. It's the best strategy for regulating Blood and emotions for nearly every female disorder—from rashes to post-childbirth woes. Angelica root, lovage, white peony root, and rehmannia will warm your center and inspire stagnant Blood to leave your body and new Blood to come into being, thus replenishing your qi."

Miss Zhao once spoke of creating a circle of good to protect me. A circle of women surrounds me now. Poppy and Inky take turns standing by the door so they can let us know when someone is approaching. Grandmother and Miss Zhao bathe me, feed me, position me above the honeypot, and help me with my clothes. Grandmother reads my pulses at least five times a day. Miss Zhao unwraps my bindings and cares for my feet, since I'm too ill to perform this most basic task. It's difficult not to think of my mother in these moments.

Slowly I regain strength, and after ten days I'm able to dress myself and walk around the room. I'm allowed to hold Yuelan, and I hope the thread that bound us when she lived inside me can be knotted back together. It hurts every time I return her to the wet nurse.

Although I'm recovering, Grandmother gives me a warning one day when she and Miss Zhao come to visit. "I don't want what happened to your mother to happen to you. She was haunted by sad yin emotions. This frailty allowed evil influences to take root in her body."

I have to contradict her. "You weren't there. She died from an infection in her feet."

"I did not treat your mother. I only know what Miss Zhao and Poppy have told me." Grandmother thrums her fingers on the table. "The point is, Wind has found your body. Now Wind knows just how easy it is to invade you. This susceptibility has made you vulnerable to the Six Pernicious Influences, especially Cold."

She's right, of course. I became ill when I first moved here, and now this. It's to be expected that Wind will be seeking me from now on. It's a discouraging thought.

"We're lucky Meiling came to get us," Grandmother says. "When you didn't recognize her, she came straight to me. We are even more fortunate that you are like a pearl in your grandfather's palm. He sent us here to find out what was happening." After a long moment, she adds, "It is a good thing we came when we did."

I don't like to think I was close to death, so I ask, "And Miss Chen? How is she doing?"

"It's so like you to think of others," Miss Zhao comments.

"Midwife Shi performed her duties without incident. Both mother and son are doing well," Grandmother says.

A son . . . I had hoped that was just an ugly dream.

"And," Grandmother goes on, "Doctor Wong has decided to use only Meiling on his cases going forward. People are to call her Young Midwife now."

This news is unexpected. I thought Lady Kuo told me Doctor Wong wanted both Midwife Shi and her daughter. Grandmother must sense my confusion, because she says, "You've been ill, so I guess no one has yet told you about Midwife Shi."

"Is she all right?" I ask.

Grandmother's response is opaque. "These male doctors—all devout followers of Confucius—recite their sayings about treating women and how many women will die in childbirth, but they have no understanding of what that means."

I can tell she's trying to avoid upsetting me. "Grandmother, please tell me what's happened."

"First Doctor Wong told people that Midwife Shi forced a woman to push too early, which resulted in the baby's death, but I've watched her deliver many babies and she's never done something so careless. Doctor Wong was there when another baby came out with a head plump with water. The girl died two days later, which all considered a blessing. Still, it was another death. Then a baby tried to enter the world with the cord around its neck. Midwife Shi told me she did everything possible to slip the cord over its shoulder. In the end . . . Never mind! You don't want to know these things. They will distress you. And you shouldn't discuss them with Meiling." Grandmother sighs. "Babies and mothers die all the time, but one, two, three fatalities in a row? Is this fate, destiny, or bad fortune? I cannot say, but it's a well-known fact that in cases of the death of a mother, fetus, or both, midwives are always blamed."

"Then why would Doctor Wong use one at all?"

"You know the answer. Doctors like us don't touch blood, and someone has to catch the baby. Even your grandfather grudgingly accepts these truths."

"And maybe Doctor Wong is showing his benevolence in helping Meiling."

"Maybe."

After a moment, I ask, "Can't you do something about Midwife Shi?"

Grandmother folds her hands and sets them in her lap. "You should know one more thing. Performing the autopsy on the spinster is another black mark against the midwife. Doctor Wong has labeled Midwife Shi too polluted to attend a birth in any elite family, including this one."

"But inspecting the dead is not a new trade for Midwife Shi."

"Of course it isn't," Grandmother admits. "But news of what happened here has spread like spilled grain, which rats have taken to every corner of Wuxi. For now, Midwife Shi has lost her reputation. No husband wants to risk his future son's life. No doctor wants to be associated with bad results. Not even me."

"All on Doctor Wong's say-so?"

"Yes, on his say-so." Grandmother stares into the middle distance. "My main responsibility is to the health and well-being of the women in our family. If I now used Midwife Shi for one of your aunties or cousins and there was a bad result, how could I face your grandfather?"

"Why haven't Midwife Shi's failures stained Meiling?" I ask. "It seems no household would risk using her either."

"I agree. Gossip and suspicion are as sparks and tinder," she answers. "But Doctor Wong is telling people he appreciated the way Meiling handled the difficulties of Yuelan's birth. The written message on her foot saved both of you. How fortunate for Meiling that you taught her to write basic characters."

I'm unsure how to interpret this. Is she praising Meiling for learning to read and write? Or is she criticizing Doctor Wong for his poor performance during my labor?

"I don't care for Doctor Wong, as you may surmise," she rasps. "But we must be grateful to him for giving Meiling work. I'll use Young Midwife too. And you should be happy, since this means she'll now be the midwife to this household—"

"Someone's coming," Inky hisses from the door.

"So tell me, Yunxian, does your husband prefer to eat chicken or duck?" Grandmother asks, quickly changing the subject.

———

After another week, Poppy informs me that my husband is to visit. It will be our first time seeing each other since the embarrassing interlude with Doctor Wong. I dress in an embroidered silk tunic over an underskirt of fine silk gauze that will wisp behind me when I walk. I brush my hair, twisting it into a high bun decorated with gold and jade pins. I comb my bangs to fringe across my forehead like cormorant feathers. Grandmother and the others compliment me on how lovely I look, and then they depart to allow me time alone with my husband. I cradle Yuelan in my arms. She's almost seven weeks old, and I'm grateful to the wet nurse for how pudgy she is. Maoren enters and sits next to me. He gazes at us with eyes of love, but when he speaks, his words shred my spirit.

"You've been ill a long while," he says, "so you may not be fully aware of how much time has passed. In three days, I will leave the Garden of Fragrant Delights to take up my final months of study in Nanjing before the municipal exams."

I close my eyes so tears can't escape.

"I'll miss you," I say.

"I'll miss you too." He brings one of my hands to his lips and kisses the palm.

"I'm sorry I brought you a daughter."

"Please don't apologize. You'll have a son next time."

I must be brave, as my mother was when my father traveled for his work, as my grandmother was when my grandfather was stationed in Nanjing, and as Lady Kuo is when my father-in-law sojourns to the countryside to check on his land, crops, factories, and all the people who labor on our behalf.

"I suspect you'll need books to help in your studies," I say. "Will you let me buy them for you?"

Maoren smiles. "Father has purchased everything I need, but your offer tells me not only that you're a good and proper wife but that we truly are a pair of mandarin ducks."

"Floating together side by side. Mated for life." For me, these are no longer words simply to be recited. The sentiments are real.

"I bring other news," Maoren says. "Your grandfather is here."

My heart leaps.

"He's with my father right now," Maoren goes on. "Instead of being sad at my parting, please be happy that you will see your grandfather shortly."

Maoren stays a few more minutes. He sips tea. He tells me

that our baby is pretty. He gives his regrets that I've been ailing. "It hurts me that we have not been able to be together again as man and wife, but Doctor Wong says this is how it must be until you've completely recovered."

Then he rises, squeezes my shoulder, and departs. I check myself in the mirror, add a bit more color to my cheeks, and pat my hair to make sure every strand is in place. A short while later, Grandmother enters. Her lips rise at the corners when she sees me.

"So you've heard."

"May I see him?" I ask eagerly.

"He's waiting for you on the terrace of the Hermitage."

By the count of days, I've more than fulfilled doing the month, but this is my first time leaving the fourth courtyard since giving birth. Anticipation and joy buoy me, but I don't go far before my legs—unused to walking beyond the confines of my room—begin to tremble.

My eyes moisten when I reach Grandfather. He holds my face in his hands and wipes my tears with his thumbs. I could do the same for him. I've never before seen a man be so affected by yin emotions.

"I would bring you home if I could," he says at last. "But this is not possible. *A wife only follows her husband.* But I've made arrangements that should help you. I've spoken to Master Yang."

I try to imagine what that must have been like. Master Yang has far more property and money than my grandfather, who, in turn, outranks my father-in-law in officialdom by many, many degrees. It also surprises me that he has gone above my grandmother, who should have been the one to speak—woman to woman—to my mother-in-law. This, more than anything, tells me how much my grandfather loves me, even though I'm married out.

"Let me explain," he goes on. "In situations like this, a girl's natal family can send strings of cash or give another *mou* of land to secure a favor. But our family has something even better—connections. I reminded your father-in-law that my father, my brother, my son, and I have all been presented to the emperor through our achievements in the imperial exams."

A shiver runs through me. If Master Yang is anything like his wife, he will not have taken well to the suggestion that he is *less than . . .*

Grandfather stares out across the pond. Koi have gathered below the pavilion, and they gape at us, their mouths begging.

"You've never questioned me about what I did when I worked on the Board of Punishments," Grandfather remarks after a long pause.

And I never would have asked, because the world knows this is one of the most powerful positions in government and also one of the most despised.

"People like me follow the Great Ming Code to determine sentences," he explains. "We consider what method of torture will be used to extract the truth. We decide if the guilty will be punished with military service, be forced to wear a heavy cangue around his neck, or be placed in shackles in the public square. And for how long. Will someone be banished to a distant province or will his miseries end quickly by decapitation?" As I listen, I sense his anguish. "Your grandmother and I have taught you about the balance of life through yin and yang—dark and light, death and life. Everything I did, while necessary for society to function and flourish, came from the shadow side of existence."

"Is this why you became a physician?"

He nods. "Following your grandmother in her practice was the opposite of all that. Medicine keeps people aligned with the cosmos."

Another silence falls over us. I'm aware of birds twittering, the trickle of the stream that meanders through the garden, the water cascading over the grotto, and from the other side of the wall the distant noises of the outside world.

His eyes meet mine. "We don't know how well your husband will do in the first level of exams, and he'll have many years after that to study before he'll be trained enough to see if he might pass the exams to become a *jinshi* like your father and me. Not all rewards come from merit, Yunxian. Some people benefit from hereditary titles. Some men advance through connections. I told Master Yang I will help his son—"

"Maoren will be able to do it on his own—"

"Many men have lofty aspirations, but few achieve them,"

Grandfather states matter-of-factly. "Not every man is talented enough to wear the cap, robe, and badge that tell all who see him of his abilities. Not every man—even if he passes the imperial exams—can immortalize himself by leaving his mark on our civilization. Your husband is a decent man, but he is hardly a Dragon in spirit. His father is willing to make some concessions now to guarantee a future for his son."

His words land in my stomach like a sack of stones. If Maoren was so unworthy, then why did Father agree to match me to him? And why did Grandfather and Grandmother go along with it? But it's not my place to ask these questions.

"So-o-o-o . . ." Grandfather draws out the syllable. "I have never cared for midwives and their kind, as you know, but I cannot allow you to go without companionship. Meiling, as Doctor Wong's chosen midwife, will come to see you every day until you are completely well. After that, I've suggested that she check on you periodically so she can report back to your grandmother and me. Furthermore, I will send a palanquin to bring you to the Mansion of Golden Light once a month. I've told Master Yang that you must be permitted to continue your studies with your grandmother. Last, I've been promised that the women in the inner chambers will be kinder to you."

"Grandfather, thank you."

The words seem small for the gifts he's given me, but he waves them off as though what he's done is minor. We visit for a while longer. We sip tea. We watch the koi—gold in color, silvery in sparkle, as they swim in and out of the shadows. Finally, he rises.

"If the things I've negotiated are not provided, tell Meiling. If they don't let her in . . ." His features soften. I fight to control my emotions. "If they don't let her in, find a big-footed maid you can trust and send her to me." From his pocket he pulls out several silver coins, places them in my palm, and folds my fingers around them. "Pay whatever she asks."

———

As promised, Meiling comes to see me every day, bringing formulas from my grandmother. After I've fully recovered, Meiling's negotiated visits drop to once a month, but sometimes we're able to speak to each other after she attends to another woman in the household. Today we sit on the terrace of the Hermitage, where we can converse in private. The more time I spend in the garden, the more I discover. The way light reflects on the pools of water. How the butterflies love to dance above blossoms. The sounds of birds that sing of their journeys and the relentless whine of cicadas. All this has a calming effect on my baby, lulling her to sleep in my arms, which only adds to the peaceful atmosphere.

Meiling has brought letters from my grandmother, grandfather, brother, Lady Huang, and Miss Zhao. I have missives for her to take back to the Mansion of Golden Light, but I sense some reluctance from Meiling as we pass the envelopes. Now that I'm close to being myself again, I have the fortitude to ask, "Are you still upset that I didn't write to you? I told you Lady Kuo took my letters."

She shifts her gaze to a far corner of the garden. "Don't worry about what's behind us."

"But something still bothers you." I wait for her to speak. When she doesn't, I ask, "Aren't you glad we get to spend time together?" I laugh lightly. "We now see each other more than we did when we were girls."

"But it isn't the same."

"We don't race leaves, if that's what you mean. But we can still trade confidences—"

"We can," she says, but I hear no happiness in her voice.

"Meiling?"

"This past year has changed us both. You're now a fine lady, and I'm still just a midwife. This is like asking a pig and a tiger to get along."

"I don't see it that way at all. We're both Metal Snakes," I remind her.

"With differences—"

"Yes, Grandmother and your mother once discussed those, but they agreed we're the same in the ways that matter—"

"The ways that matter," she repeats. "Now you're rich—"

"And you can still go where you want whenever you want."

"You came here with everything that once belonged to your

mother—her gold and jade," she goes on. "Your dowry may be controlled by your mother- and father-in-law, but these things *belong* to you." She gestures to the splendors around us. "But weather and human life are unpredictable. Some families go up. Some families go down. There may come a time when your belongings will help save these people."

I notice the way she says "people" and not "your family" or "your husband."

"What you're saying isn't fair or correct. First you say I'm different because my husband's family is rich. Then you say I've always been different because I had a good dowry. After that, you imply that the Yang family could lose its standing and fortunes. I don't understand."

"No, you don't," she replies, her voice trembling with emotion. "I've been coming to see you off and on since your baby's birth, and not once have you inquired about my mother. You've not asked about my husband either. Have you no interest in me? Do you suppose I live in a courtyard house or in rooms above my husband's tea shop? How do you think my mother is surviving now that no one will hire her?"

"Oh, Meiling, I've been selfish . . ."

She gives me a sad smile. "You aren't hearing me even now. This isn't about your emotions. I'm a working woman. I've always had to get by on my own. I know the cost of food, firewood, cloth, housing—"

I hold up a hand to stop her list from growing any longer. "What's wrong, and how can I help?"

With that, she buries her face in her hands and starts to weep. Slowly, she begins to tell me of her life. Her husband is struggling with his business. They do indeed reside in rooms above his shop. Her mother—with no elite families hiring her—has come to live with them.

"Kailoo is kind, and we like each other," Meiling confesses, "but three of us living together in two rooms is not the same as dozens of people living in a courtyard home such as this. I long for a child, but it's hard to make one when my mother is never more than two body lengths away."

I don't have the knowledge or experience to imagine what her life must be like. "All these years, I've thought you were the lucky one," I say. "When I think of the things you've seen—"

"The things I've seen," she echoes. "Yunxian, you would not believe what I've seen even if I told you. Orphaned children begging on corners . . . What giving birth to ten or more babies does to a woman who has not one servant . . . The ugliness of autopsies . . ."

The torment of these experiences scrapes at the beauty of her features, and I'm reminded for perhaps the ten thousandth time of the nature of yin and yang and how it's woven into the fabric of every aspect of our lives—from the intimate details regarding two women to the way they affect the cosmos. When one person rises, the other sinks. When one person is happy, the other falls into despair. Meiling's and my natures may ebb and flow, but our friendship makes us part of a single whole. I feel it's my duty to help lift her out of her chasm as she helped carry me from the brink of death. I would not be able to call myself Meiling's friend otherwise.

PART III

RICE-AND-SALT DAYS

The Third Through Fifth Years
of the Hongzhi Emperor's Reign
(1490–1492)

The Wife Is Earth

Rice-and-salt days may not be the longest period in a woman's life, but they are the most important and most arduous. For a wife and mother, one day can feel like a year. I begin this day by writing the results of a case in my notebook.

A fifteen-year-old scullery maid suffered from scrofula and endured more than thirty sores and lumps, reddened and bruised, on her neck. Burdened by heavy work, especially in summer, the lumps multiplied, and she experienced both fever and chills. I detected Lung and Kidney deficiencies, exacerbated by taxation and Summer Heat. I burned mugwort moxibustion on the tips of her elbows and on seven other points. The lumps suppurated and have since vanished, with no recurrence.

I list all eight moxibustion points for future reference, but I don't write the girl's name or that she resides in the Garden of Fragrant Delights. I always keep this information private. I set down my brush and put away my notebook. Just before leaving my room, I tuck a small ball of tea wrapped in rice paper in my pocket. Meiling brought it to me from her husband's tea shop the last time she visited. A few minutes later, I tap on my mother-in-law's door and enter. Lady Kuo still sleeps, but her maid, Sparrow, has risen from her pallet, dressed, added fuel to the brazier, and set a pot of water to heat.

"Good morning, Lady Tan," Sparrow says in a low voice.

"Good morning," I reply. "Did Lady Kuo sleep well?"

"The same as usual," Sparrow answers uncomfortably, glancing at an empty wine pot.

This accounts for the sour smell that hangs in the room—the same kind of rankness my husband brings home with him after a night of drinking with friends. That is, when he's here in Wuxi.

"What kind of tea have you brought this morning?" Lady Kuo asks sleepily as she pulls herself to a sitting position. I watch as she reaches for a cup on her bedside table and spits into it. Over the past year she's developed a cough. It's not bone-steaming disease, which reveals itself slowly, with a patient coughing and losing weight and energy until he or she begins to hack up blood. Those cases, if untreated, end horribly, with the patient dying as blood gushes from the mouth. What ails Lady Kuo is something else entirely. As the day progresses, she'll repeatedly clear her throat—*keeck, keeck*—and then spit her saliva into the cup she keeps nearby at all times. Doctor Wong has provided remedies, but nothing seems to help. I have my suspicions of what could be causing her such distress, but Lady Kuo would never let me treat her.

"Are you going to answer my question?" Lady Kuo asks.

I pull the ball from my pocket and carefully open the paper wrapper. Inside is a small, perfectly formed, dried type of citrus called a mandarin. Lady Kuo stares at it with interest. I motion to Sparrow, who brings a pot filled with hot water, an elegant porcelain teapot, and a single cup on a tray.

"Far from here in a small village in Guangdong province, farmers grow this mandarin, which is unique in all China," I explain. "They make a little cut at the top as you would to remove the stem from a gourd or melon. Then, without damaging the peel, they scrape the fruit from inside, dry the peel until it hardens, pack the interior with tea, put the top back on, and then let the whole thing dry some more until it looks like this—flawless and unblemished."

"As if it came right off the tree."

I make a small sound of agreement, pleased she appreciates how exquisite it is. Lady Kuo watches as I crush the fruit in my palm to reveal the leaves inside. I drop everything into the porcelain pot, pour the hot water over the leaves and peel, let them steep for a few seconds, pour the fragrant brew into a cup, and offer it to my mother-in-law. Lady Kuo takes a sip and says, "I taste the citrus blossoms on the day the sun opened them." Her pleasure lasts a moment, and then she regards me with distrust. "It's not medicine, is it?"

"Of course not. I hoped you'd enjoy the taste."

Lady Kuo takes a few more sips, then *keeck, keeck*. She reaches for her spittle cup and dismisses me with a peremptory nod. I bow and return to my room. I have two shelves behind my writing table where I keep a small selection of herbs that any wife would have in her home to treat her family. I gather together a few ingredients, step back outside, and walk along the corridor to my second responsibility of the day.

I've lived in the Garden of Fragrant Delights for fourteen years, during which the ancestors have continued to reward the family with prosperity and good health. As Lady Kuo frequently points out, "The ancestors provide for us, but the only way to keep them happy is by making offerings, and the only person who can make those offerings is the eldest son." Master Yang currently performs the ancestral rights as the head of the family. When he dies, this duty will skip over Second Uncle and pass to my husband in keeping with the direct line of succession. It's my obligation as Maoren's wife to provide a son who'll see to these responsibilities when he dies. Extra sons won't hurt. But I need to give birth to that first important son, who'll carry the burden of protecting the family and guaranteeing its future for generations to come.

I've reached twenty-nine years, a year older than my mother was when she died. I've fully grown into the grace that bound feet bring to a woman. I'm the mother of three girls—a terrible disappointment. I haven't given birth to an heir, nor have I been pregnant again in the last six years. This has not been lost on my mother-in-law. How many times have I heard "If you were as clever as you think you are, then you would be full with child again"? Too many times to count, but it's hard to make a baby when one of the people is occupied elsewhere. Not long after Yuelan was born, Maoren passed the first level of imperial exams and became a "county scholar." Three years later, he succeeded at the provincial exams and became a *juren*—a "recommended man." Although Maoren is studying to take the final exams to reach the *jinshi* level, I suspect he won't pass. Grandfather made good on his promise, however, and found my husband a position on the Board of Punishments in Nanjing. It's several days away, so Maoren rarely comes home. When he's here, we try hard to make a son, but we have not had luck yet.

I enter the room my daughters share. The two oldest girls are already up and dressed. My youngest daughter, Ailan, is still in bed, and she calls weakly, "Mama." Even from across the room I can see tears glistening on her cheeks.

"Sit up," I say. "You know what we have to do today."

"We clean and tighten every four days," she whimpers.

Yuelan bites the inside of her cheek. Chunlan turns away, picks up a comb, and—with her back to us—runs it from her scalp down to the ends of her black hair.

"Daughters, you need to help. This is the only way you will learn."

Reluctantly, my two older girls come to the bed. Yuelan is now thirteen. Her betrothal has been arranged, and the match will be beneficial to both families. I'll have her for two more years. Chunlan, whose name means Spring Orchid, has reached ten years. She carries a lot of her father in her. Her face is round and pale. She has a sweet disposition, but I'm vigilant in my efforts to curb her tendency toward laziness. Her marriage has also been set.

"I see Poppy has assembled everything we'll need today," I say, displaying calm when I feel turmoil about what I must do. I wish I could explain to them that while I take pride in what I've accomplished with their footbinding, I despise this chore with equal measure. Who among us would wish to inflict agony on her child? We say we want sons to continue the family line, but sometimes I wonder if what we're really saying is that we'd rather have a son than do this.

I offer a few words of comfort in advance of what is to come. "You have pain but remember footbinding teaches you to tolerate physical distress and trains you for the rigors of childbirth." I caress Ailan's cheek. "Are you ready?"

She nods solemnly. Ailan, Love Orchid, turned five this year. I worry about her frailty and vulnerability. She's my only child not to receive variolation from the smallpox-planting master. The last time he came to town, Ailan was sick, so she couldn't have the procedure. I tell myself not to worry, because during the time I've lived here we haven't had a single case of smallpox. Similarly, we've had no deaths as a result of footbinding, when typically one out of ten girls dies during the two years it takes to complete the process. I will not allow Ailan to become the Yang family's "one."

I turn to the table where the things I need have been lined up: scissors, needle, thread, two rolls of clean binding cloth, two ceramic pots, and an earthenware jar. On a shelf behind the table a row of shoes—all embroidered by my own hands—wait to be fitted to Ailan's feet. I reach for the jar and pour some of the tonic Grandmother taught me to brew into a cup and hold it to Ailan's lips.

"Take a few sips. As I've told you before, it will frighten away your pain."

The medicine acts swiftly, but even before Ailan's eyes start to dull, I have Yuelan and Chunlan each unwrap the bindings from one of their little sister's feet.

"You are both gentle," I praise them as the long lengths of cloth unspool and pile on the floor. By the time they're done, the medicine has fully taken effect. Ailan's naked feet are red, bruised, and swollen, but not so much that I can't see that they're taking shape. The big toe remains in its natural position, while the four smaller toes have already been rolled under the foot. The arch is still in the process of bending. It will be a while yet before her toes reach her heel.

"What is the size we want?" I ask.

Yuelan recites the answer. "The length of a mother's thumb."

"Your feet will bloom like golden lilies," Yuelan encourages her little sister.

"This is how Mama shows her love for us," Chunlan adds.

I set Ailan's feet in a basin to soak in warm water mixed with mulberry root, white balsam, tannin, and frankincense. I leave the drying to my daughters. "You need to get into every crack and crevice," I instruct. "You must check the toenails and make sure they're short enough they can't break the skin." When they're finished, I massage Ailan's feet. No amount of mind-numbing medicine can fully remove the sensations that sear through my daughter as I press my thumbs as hard as I can between the bones of her feet, stretching the tendons and muscles.

"It will be over soon," Yuelan soothes her sobbing sister.

"I promise to bring you a plum," Chunlan coaxes, "if you can endure awhile longer."

Their kindness pulls at my heart. One day they'll be good mothers.

After I finish working on Ailan's arch, I rub alum over her skin to help keep the foot dry and inhibit swelling. Next comes a powder I made from crushed herbs—to soften the bones, minimize pain, and prevent infection. Last, I pull a packet from within my tunic and hold it up for Ailan to see. "I brought you something special today. It's what I use for my own feet, and I think you'll like it." I sprinkle the powder on a roll of binding cloth, releasing a pleasant scent of clove, cinnamon, and flower petals. Then the binding begins. Usually I like to use damp gauze because the cloth will tighten as it dries, but not today. Ailan has earned a tiny reprieve.

I wrap one end of the cloth over the top of her foot, pull to fold the four small toes as tight as I can toward the heel. Ailan whimpers. The cloth comes back up, around the heel, across the top of the foot, and under the arch, both securing the big toe and creating as best I can a pointed shape. On I go, moving the cloth in the design of infinity until all three meters are used. Without being asked, Ailen places an index finger on the end of the cloth to hold it in place, while I thread a needle. I make my stitches small and knot each one so Ailan won't be able to pull apart the bindings over the next four days.

"We're done," I say after I've completed the process with her other foot. "Today you'll wear a pretty new pair of shoes." I sprinkle more of my special powder on the insides of the shoes and slip them on her feet. I worked especially hard on the design. This pair is made of dark blue silk, and the embroidery was inspired by what I've observed from the terrace of the Hermitage. A duckling floats down the side of the shoe toward a water plant that blooms at the tip. Koi swim across the top. Three butterflies dance together on the back of the heel. Ailan can't help but smile at their beauty.

I dab her wet face with my handkerchief. "You are brave," I tell her. "We have yet to know the ultimate outcome, but I feel confident about what we've accomplished so far. I'll make sure to place extra offerings for Spinster Aunt for the guidance and care she provides us from the Afterworld."

I turn to my two older daughters. Their eyes are misty. I sympathize. In my heart I ache for Ailan as I've ached for each of my daughters during the hard months of footbinding.

"Instead of going to the inner chambers, let us stay together here awhile," I suggest.

Yuelan straightens her spine and folds her hands in her lap. "Grandmother Kuo wanted to test us today on the *Classic of Filial Piety for Girls*."

I keep my face as calm as the surface of a pond on a wind-free night, but my stomach churns in agitation. *I'm* their mother. I've been teaching them from the classics just as Respectful Lady taught me. Mirroring my oldest daughter, I lengthen my back and allow my hands to find rest on my lap.

"You girls are fortunate to have a grandmother who shows you such love, but let us stay here for a time as I proposed. You can perfect your memorization, and your little sister can have a few minutes to recover."

Yuelan weighs what I've said. Her thoughts are as clear on her face as if she'd spoken them aloud: *Obey my mother or obey my grandmother?* Yuelan has not yet had her first monthly moon water, and she's still two years away from going to her husband's home, but I find the transparency of her emotions worrisome.

Chunlan makes the decision for all of us when she begins reciting. "*The husband is heaven. The wife is earth. The husband is the sun, which makes him as constant as that bright sphere. The wife is the moon, waxing and waning, strong but inevitably weak.*"

Yuelan chimes in with the next section. "*Heaven is honored, residing in the sky above us, while earth is lowly, dirty, and trod upon.*"

None of my daughters has shown interest in my medicine

beyond learning the basics for how to treat a child with an earache or upset stomach. This has been a disappointment, but maybe it's understandable. I was inspired by Grandmother Ru. While I've taught my daughters what they need to learn to become proper wives and happy mothers, the influence of their grandmother Kuo, head of the household, has been strong.

After a peaceful hour, Poppy appears and gives me a nod.

"I wish we could stay together like this until the evening meal," I say to my girls, "but this is the day I visit my grandmother, while surely yours awaits your arrival." I put a hand on one of Ailan's knees. "You need to walk today," I remind her. "It will be hard, but you have your sisters to help you."

Ailan sucks in her lips. She must obey.

I address Yuelan and Chunlan. "Pay attention during your lessons with Grandmother Kuo, but make sure you find times to get Ailan up and walking." I hold up a hand to prevent any words of resistance. "Yes, it will hurt her. Yes, she will cry. But you are good sisters, and this gift you give Ailan will be something she'll carry with her forever." After a pause, I add, "In the afternoon, take her to the courtyard. She likes that."

The sun is still rising in the sky when I go to the front gate. The guard lifts the latch, I step over the threshold, and walk to where a palanquin and my bearers wait for me. My life is still mostly limited to the four walls of the Garden of Fragrant Delights. I have yet to go to the marketplace, let alone the Dragon Boat Festival. My grandmother's reason for not allowing the wives and daughters of the Mansion of Golden Light to attend the festival was tied to her position as a doctor. She felt that being a physician pushed the boundaries of what was proper for a woman. Lady Kuo has a different reason. "Let the concubines go," she says every year. "Tonight, when your husbands come home, take advantage of all they've felt during the day to unite Essence and Blood. Another son is the best reward for remaining inside the gate." So for me every trip outside the gate is an opportunity. At this time of year, when the weather is fair, only gauze covers the palanquin's windows, which allows me to see a filtered view of the town. Today the walkways are quiet.

When I arrive at the Mansion of Golden Light, I go straight to the pharmacy, where I find my grandparents seated at a table waiting for me. "Yunxian, welcome," Grandfather calls out. He recently turned eighty. His hair and beard have thinned and gone fully white. He motions for me to sit, and Grandmother pours tea. I inquire after their health, to which Grandfather responds, "We both are well." He takes a noisy sip from his cup and smiles appreciatively. "Tell us what you learned this week."

"I've been reading old texts about cases and medical theory," I answer.

"Which ones?" Grandmother inquires. She'll reach seventy-six on her next birthday. Her hair has been slower to change than Grandfather's, but streaks of gray run through it. "What can you tell us?"

And so begins an hour of instruction and discussion, including reviewing the small cases I treated this month in the Yang family compound: the concubine who complained of recurrent nosebleeds and headaches—conditions that, while mild, are dangerous for a woman who must rely on her beauty and health to protect her position; one of the old aunties asked for something to relieve pain in her hip; an eye infection that threatened to spread to all the children in the inner chambers but that I stopped at just three cases.

After the hour is done, Grandfather removes himself.

"Let me feel your pulse," Grandmother says, reaching for my right arm, taking my wrist in her hand, and letting her fingertips alight on the first level of my pulses.

"This isn't necessary," I say, gently, trying to pull free.

She doesn't let go. "I continue to worry about you."

"Grandmother, every mother gets tired."

"You have a long history of illness. You got sick when you first came to live here and then again when you moved to your husband's home." She pauses. "You nearly died after Yuelan's birth. Weakness that comes from something like that never leaves entirely."

"My second and third pregnancies and births were uneventful," I say.

"Because you had Meiling and me to look after you," she

points out as she presses a bit harder on my wrist to reach the second level of my pulses. "Some women have weakness in the Liver, which, when stagnant, can result in the disharmony of the qi that presents itself as aches, pains, frustration, and moodiness. Others are born with weakness in the Kidney, which can release feelings of not wanting or being able to do certain things, of wishing to stay in bed all day, in the dark—"

"Grandmother—"

"You must always be cautious, because, as a Snake, you are prone to these sorts of imbalances." Her fingers seek the third level of pulses. "A Snake is easily stressed. A Snake is susceptible to sicknesses of the mind. A Snake doesn't like to eat."

"I've been eating—"

"But have you been eating enough?" She doesn't wait for me to reply. "Snakes appear beautiful on the outside, but they have flimsy souls." She pauses. "What happened after Yuelan's birth cannot be allowed to happen again."

I smile to reassure her. "So what did my pulse tell you today? Was it floating, slippery, knotted, scattered, hidden—"

"Are you going to recite the twenty-eight types of pulses?" Grandmother bristles, finally dropping my wrist.

"If you want me to."

"It's enough for you to know I'm concerned." With that, she changes the subject. "Your brother is well. Yifeng's wife is pregnant again. Four sons in six years . . . The household is noisy with their mischievousness."

"The Tan family line is assured," I say.

"True, although it is a shame that your father's wife has not given him children."

"He's always traveling." I don't know why I feel compelled to make excuses for my father, a man I haven't seen since he triumphed in the imperial exams.

"That makes no difference!" Grandmother snaps. "This Respectful Lady sojourns with him."

Yes, this wife's experience is far different than what I have with my husband. "My father must care for her very deeply to keep her so close."

Grandmother sniffs. As much as I love her, she is a mother-in-law. She'll never be satisfied with her daughter-in-law.

"Tell me more about Yifeng," I say. "Are his studies progressing?"

"He hopes to take the next level of examinations in two years. He will surely do well."

I inquire after Grandfather's three Jade concubines—all fine—and Miss Zhao, whom my father has kept within the family so as not to cause Yifeng consternation—also fine.

Inky brings two bowls of soup noodles and more hot water for tea. After lunch, Grandmother tests me on the properties of herbs and other ingredients. She presents hypothetical cases and asks what course of treatment I would employ.

"A woman has a rapid pulse—"

"A sign of Heat—"

"She's also experiencing shortness of breath. Her complexion is red, and her body is puffy. She has no desire for food, and her tongue is pale and moist but swollen. Even though she wears a padded jacket, she can't stop shivering. None of this would suggest Heat."

"In this case, the rapid pulse, which ordinarily would tell of a Heat disorder, is a manifestation of extreme weakness. The patient is suffering from a Cold yin disharmony."

"Good," Grandmother says. She proceeds to present patients with three different types of coughs. "What does the sound of a furious cough emerging without warning tell you?"

"That would be a sign of Excess."

"A rasping cough, calling to mind desert sands?"

"Heat. Maybe Dryness."

"And a cough that is feeble and rattles wetly?"

"Deficiency."

And on it goes. My mind stretches to find the answers, knowing that in our medicine there are multiple ways to arrive at diagnosis and treatment. Two hours later, the inside of my skull feels as thick and heavy as rice porridge.

"Every year your knowledge and understanding grow," Grandmother compliments me, signaling the end of our session.

"But will I ever know enough? Will I ever be as skilled as you?"

"Never, and never!" Then she laughs. "*I'm* still learning! I suspect I'll still be learning on my deathbed."

This is something I refuse to contemplate.

"When was the last time you read Lao Tzu?" she asks.

"I don't remember."

"Read him again before you come next month. Be prepared to talk about his ideas about balance and harmony." She begins to recite. "*Being and non-being produce each other. Difficult and easy complete each other—*"

"*Long and short contrast each other,*" I continue. "*High and low distinguish each other.*"

"In life and in medicine, we always return to harmony and disharmony." Grandmother's eyes shine as she adds, "Yin and yang are always in movement—buoying and changing each other."

It's now late afternoon, and I still have another stop to make. Grandmother tries to get me to stay. "Come with me to the inner chambers. Everyone would love to see you, Miss Zhao especially."

I smile. "I'd like to visit with her too, but Meiling waits for me. Please give Miss Zhao my best regards and tell her I'll see her next time."

Inky waits outside the door to walk me to the front gate. Instead of going back along the quiet alleyways to the Garden of Fragrant Delights, my bearers carry me on roads crowded with carts, wagons, horses, mules, and camels to the center of Wuxi. As we cross the main square, I carefully lift the curtain and see four convicted criminals sitting in a row with their wrists and ankles immobilized in a wooden structure. I glimpse another man walking through the square with a cangue around his neck. It is also made of wood, but it spreads out wide enough that he can't possibly feed himself and is so heavy that he struggles to remain upright. I pull the curtain shut.

The palanquin hits the ground with a hard bump. I pay my bearers for the labor they provide for me and for their silence, and so far they've kept my visits to Meiling a secret. I hold my sleeve over my face—to avoid smells and especially to avoid detection— as I hurry the few steps from the palanquin into Grace Tranquility

Teas. The shop is even better stocked than the last time I was here. The wall to the left has tea cakes piled high. The most expensive tea cakes are propped on a shelf, each on its own display stand, facing out, so customers will be attracted to the woodblock images on the rice-paper wrappings. Kailoo, Meiling's husband, stands behind the counter, waiting on a customer. I nod to him and then go up the back steps to the second-floor apartment. I enter the main room, and there sits my friend, bent over a basin, washing clothes.

"Meiling."

She turns to me, wiping her forehead with her wrist. "I wasn't sure what time you'd come. I'd almost given up hope."

"Grandmother had many cases to discuss today."

"Sit." Meiling dips her head in the way she has since she was a child. "Have you eaten? Would you like tea?"

She ignores my courteous denials that I'm neither hungry nor thirsty and brings out a plate of snacks and sets water on to heat. She wears a tunic that hangs midthigh, with woven frogs that fasten the cloth at her neck, across her bosom, and under her arm. Her trousers come to just below her knees, exposing her calves, which are brown and strong. A scarf covers her hair and is tied at the back of her neck. All are made from common cotton dyed a deep indigo blue. The clothes are clean, without a single frayed thread. She is dressed like a working woman but still manages to look elegant. A melancholic aspect to her features makes her beauty even more limpid and pure. I suspect that since I last saw her, she's experienced her moon water again. Another month has gone by without the planting of a baby.

We sit together and enjoy the food and tea she's prepared. The hubbub from outside can be heard through the open window.

"This tea is delicious," I say after taking a taste.

"Everyone likes jasmine tea," she responds, "but most of it is made from spraying tea leaves with jasmine oil. My husband has procured *real* jasmine tea." She takes a sip, holds the liquid in her mouth to enjoy the flavor, and then swallows in such a delicate way that I can practically see the tea glide down her throat. "The farmer lays out tea leaves, then puts thousands upon thousands of unopened jasmine blossoms on top," she goes on, doing a good job of selling her husband's merchandise. "By morning, the blossoms have opened, sending their scent—their essence—into the leaves. Then the farmer and his family spend the next two days picking every blossom off the tea."

"It sounds like hard work. Time consuming, anyway."

"*Ha!* That's only the beginning! The farmer repeats this process another nine times! The tea absorbs the aroma of jasmine blooms for thirty days!"

"No wonder it tastes like this."

She leans forward. "I assume you would like some to take to your mother-in-law."

Naturally the tea is expensive, but I'm happy to pay the price. Meiling thanks me, adding, "That you share our tea with your household has given an endorsement of quality to our shop. Kailoo and I are forever grateful."

"I'm the one who's grateful to you. Your teas keep my mother-in-law from throwing me into the street."

We laugh at my joke, but it's true my tea purchases of Iron Goddess of Mercy, wild white peony, Dragon Well, and the Pu'er in the dried mandarin have pleased my mother-in-law over the years. Kailoo has capitalized on my patronage and that of other inhabitants of the Garden of Fragrant Delights. The reputation of Grace Tranquility Teas has grown, wealthy customers have come, and the business has expanded. Kailoo has become a well-to-do merchant, which has, among other things, allowed him to hire a maid for his wife.

"May I inquire after your mother?" I ask. "I haven't seen her in many months."

"Babies come when they come," my friend answers. "Important families no longer hire her, but poor women still need help."

Midwife Shi has not been able to recapture her reputation after all these years. It seems shameful to me, but I say, "I'm happy your standing continues to grow."

"My mother trained me well," she responds. "I know what I'm doing. Women trust me. No one is as capable as I am, I can assure you."

"Doctor Wong—"

"Has been good to me. If it weren't for him, I don't know what my mother and I would have done." Her jaw tightens under her flawless skin. "My husband is doing well, but if we want to keep improving our lives, all three of us need to work." She leaves unspoken *unlike you.* "I now attend to births in all the best families in Wuxi—"

"That's—" I try to interrupt to show my sense of joy for her, but her need to prove something pushes her on.

"Since I last saw you," she talks over me, "I delivered Magistrate Fu's son. You can't get much higher than that."

"That's wonderful! And I'm happy to see you reap the rewards of being a midwife with a good reputation. Grandmother and I are proud of you."

"I've received gifts of catties of meat, sacks of rice, and crates of coal." She takes a breath before continuing. "Furniture! Porcelain vases! Bamboo screens!"

Inside, I feel myself retreating. Her enthusiasm seems so mercantile, but then she and her husband have always been working people. The consequences of their labors can be seen in the shop, with its improved merchandise, and in this two-room apartment, where, over the years, I've noticed a nice kang purchased and set under the window for Meiling and her husband to sleep on, and a smaller kang in the other room for Midwife Shi.

"If I'm lucky," she comments, "one day a grateful family might honor me with a lavish funeral."

"That is the highest reward anyone can receive," I have to admit.

"Kailoo says that soon we'll be able to buy our own tea farm, expand the business, and . . ." She grins. "I've been eager to tell you that we're going to build a single-courtyard house."

"Oh, Meiling, this pleases me greatly!"

"None of this would have happened if not for Doctor Wong. A midwife needs male doctors if she's to fill the rice bowl."

That seems an exaggeration. But maybe it isn't. I know of only two women doctors—Grandmother and me. Grandmother is limited to caring for the female inhabitants in the Mansion of Golden

Light, and Lady Kuo is in charge of employing the physician in the Garden of Fragrant Delights. She likes Doctor Wong, and he uses Meiling.

"When I'm mistress of the Yang household," I say, "you and I will bring many babies into the world."

"I look forward to that." She reaches for a salted plum. "Have you seen Doctor Wong's book?"

"Hmmm . . ." This is something I don't want to talk about. Doctor Wong has published a book of his cases. It features standard remedies for common illnesses and recipes for "special formulas" to make perfumes, eliminate wrinkles, and glisten hair. But the most annoying, it seems to me, is that he chronicled solely the cases of the wealthy or illustrious. (Yes, that means he included cases from the Yang family.) Grandmother explained it this way: "Writing a book of this sort is a well-known shortcut to being named a *ming yi*—a famous doctor. The arrogance of it!"

Seeing my hesitancy, Meiling sighs. "Don't forget, it's thanks to Doctor Wong that you and I see more of each other when I accompany him to your home."

That's true. As the official doctor for the Yang family, he comes to the Garden of Fragrant Delights each month to offer his services first to the men and boys. Then he visits the inner chambers to check on the women, including me. Meiling and I don't get to spend much time together during these sessions, but we're able to look into each other's eyes while she relays Doctor Wong's inquiries to me and my answers to him.

"I'm grateful for anything that allows us to be together, however fleeting," I say.

But my words of conciliation are not enough for Meiling. "I don't understand why you don't have more respect for Doctor Wong. He and I have been in difficult situations, and they don't always end with a good result, but I don't know another doctor in the city who is as good at telling a husband that his wife has left this world. And did you see? He even included me in some of the cases he wrote about in his book. By name!"

I feel like she's run through the inside of my body with a rasp. Doctor Wong wouldn't have to tell a husband that his wife had died if he did a better job. More troubling, is Meiling becoming a person desiring the same kind of fame Doctor Wong is seeking?

I decide to change the subject to a topic that concerns us both. "Sometimes a husband and wife need help with bedroom affairs."

But I'm too clumsy, too abrupt. Meiling shakes her shoulders, as if brushing off cherry blossom petals falling in spring. After a moment, she says, "Kailoo and I enjoy bedroom affairs. That's not our problem. I sip this, he sips that, but we can't make one baby."

I reach across the table to take her hand. "I wonder if I could help."

She stares at me, her expression impenetrable.

"What are you thinking?" I ask. "Why won't you let me doctor you? Is it that I'm a woman? That I'm still too young?"

She swats away those ideas, but in that gesture—knowing her so well—I understand that she's keeping something from me.

"Is Doctor Wong giving you formulas to take?" I ask.

"Yes."

I'm hurt straight through to my marrow. Trying to cover my feelings, I ask, "What has he prescribed?"

Meiling waves a hand. "I don't want to worry you with that." Then, "Truly, I don't need assistance, but I know a woman who does."

"I only treat people in my family—"

"Other women need help too."

"I would have to ask Maoren's permission to visit another elite household, but he's in Nanjing," I say.

"The person I'm thinking of is not from an elite family." When I shake my head, Meiling says, "Your mother-in-law won't find out." After a pause, she adds, "Please, Yunxian. Would you let a woman suffer just because she doesn't live within the walls of your husband's home?"

"Bring her here the next time I visit—"

"That won't do. We need to go to her." Before I can argue, she's on her feet, opening cupboards and pulling out clothes. "You can't walk the streets looking like that. You'll need to change."

"Absolutely not!" I exclaim, but after her rejection of my

help, I feel I have to do this to show I love her still. Against all the wisdom I've acquired in life, I find myself slipping off my gown and pulling on the indigo cotton trousers and jacket Meiling gives me. The pants are longer than those she's wearing, so they cover my white, withered calves.

Three problems remain: the carefully applied makeup that marks me as a wife from an elite family, my hair piled atop my head and decorated with jade and gold ornaments, and my feet. Meiling uses a cloth to wipe away the cream, powder, rouge, and lip paint from my face. "I don't want to take apart your hair, because we won't have time to put it back together before you go home," she says, and then wraps a hand-dyed scarf over my bun and the adornments and ties the cloth at the back of my neck. We stand together to peer into a mirror. These simple changes make us look like sisters, but it also strikes me how only a layer of paint and a hairstyle can separate women by class. And our feet.

"Sit down," Meiling orders. I do as I'm told, while she rummages through more drawers and cupboards. She comes to me with clean rags and a pair of boots. She stuffs cloth into the toe of one of the boots. I slide my silk slipper inside. She prods the toe with her thumb, looks up at me, and says, "There's still too much room." I remove my foot, and she adds more rags. This time the boot fits. We go through the process for my other foot. I sit with my heels resting on the floor, my toes pointed toward the ceiling. My feet look disturbingly large.

"Try standing," Meiling says. "Take a few steps."

I wobble as I rise, and panic sweeps through me. "We shouldn't do this. If someone finds out—"

"No one will find out."

She holds my elbow as we go downstairs and slip out the back door into an alley. The boots, which seem huge and as heavy as anchors, make walking awkward. I lift each foot high and then deliberately set it down. Meiling naturally walks faster than I ever could, and she pulls me along at a quicker pace than is comfortable. We turn a corner and enter a busy pathway that edges a canal. We pass shops where customers bargain and negotiate. At an open-air teahouse, I see two men arguing about philosophy. Meiling puts an arm around my waist, hugging me close. She holds her other arm in front of her, washing it from left to right and back again, clearing people coming our direction from getting too close or bumping into us.

"Let's go back," I mumble. "This is a mistake."

She ignores me. "I told you that Kailoo and I are going to build a house. We've already visited a brickyard to place our order. There's a woman—"

"A *working* woman?"

"I'm a working woman," she replies impatiently. "Poppy, your cook, and all the other servants and concubines in your household are working women."

She's right, but that doesn't make what we're doing any less serious. If I'm caught . . .

It feels like we walk forever, but the wide bottoms of Meiling's boots support me quite well. We make another turn and veer away from the canal. What I see is much as Meiling described to me when we were girls. The colors are vibrant. Shops display their wares: bolts of silk and brocade piled high, fruit gleaming from baskets, and meat—red, sweating, attracting flies. It all manages to be beautiful and overwhelming at the same time. Storefronts gradually turn into rows of homes built side by side, with no space between them. Then the structures change again to factories that make baskets and other products, and process and spin silk. I jump when I hear a hard *thwack* from a blacksmith's stall, and the sound of grain being ground grates at my nerves.

We reach a gate, Meiling pulls the bell, and an old woman opens the door. She brightens when she sees Meiling. "Young Midwife! Welcome!"

"It's good to see you, Oriole. I've brought someone who might be able to help you."

The woman gestures for us to enter. It's beyond my comprehension that I could find myself in a brickyard. Oriole takes us to a shady spot under an overhang and motions for us to sit on some overturned crates. She pours tea, backs away as a servant might, and then stands with her head lowered and her hands folded.

"Please sit," Meiling says.

When Oriole hesitates, I add, "I can't examine you if you're over there."

She pulls up another crate and joins us. As Meiling engages Oriole in conversation, I take the opportunity to begin the Four Examinations. Looking: not surprisingly, her skin is leathery from spending her days under the sun in this courtyard, where she is also in constant contact with arid heat from the kiln. Despite this, I detect paleness lurking just under her skin. Her hands are rough, worn, and knobbed at the joints. She's thin in an unbecoming way. Instead of taking years off her life, as if she had the trim figure of a girl about to marry, her body looks as though it's consuming itself, wasting to dried flesh on bones. Most shocking, she wears straw sandals, revealing feet browned not just from the sun but from the dirt and dust of this place. Her toenails are long and dirty. Thick calluses edge her big toes and her heels. The sight is so unsettling that I shift my vision back to the woman's face. I take Oriole to be in her sixth decade of life. Smelling: she has the same aroma about her as my bearers do on a day such as this. It's the odor of hard work and garlic. Now for asking:

"What is your age?"

"I am thirty-eight," Oriole answers.

Grandmother and Grandfather taught me early on never to reveal my surprise when a patient discloses something disturbing.

"So you still get your monthly moon water?"

Oriole glances at Meiling, questioningly.

"The problem is not that she gets it," Meiling explains. "It's that it never stops."

"When and how did that start?" I ask.

"Once when I had my monthly moon water, my husband spent the day in town and I had to carry all the bricks myself. My labors didn't end until long after darkness fell. I had nonstop flooding for three months. This turned into nonstop dribbling for three years."

Three years?

My next question is an obvious one. "Has medicine helped?"

Oriole shakes her head, and Meiling chimes in. "How can medicine work if she hasn't been given a proper diagnosis?"

"Oriole, you are alone here today," I comment, hoping this might bring forth more information.

"My husband is often away," she says. "He sees to the delivery of our bricks. He likes to visit taverns too. And other places . . ." Her face turns a deep vermilion. Does she flush from embarrassment that her husband visits women who sell their bodies or from resentment and anger? "When he's away," she continues with emotion in her voice, "I'm left to carry and stack the bricks and tiles we make. Many nights I sleep alone."

I nod sympathetically. I too spend many nights alone in my marriage bed.

"May I listen to your pulse?" I ask. I've been studying medicine and treating women for years now. I feel confident, but I take my time, palpating to reach the three levels on both her wrists. Her pulse is as I expect. Thin, like fine thread, yet distinct and clear. I mull over her symptoms—the constant spotting, especially—and possibilities for treatment, knowing I can never ask Grandmother's advice on this case.

"You're suffering from Spleen qi deficiency and injured Kidney yin caused by taxation from toil," I offer. "This type of deep fatigue can come from too much work or from extreme mental doings like studying too hard."

"I sleep—"

"A single night of sleep will not allow your body to catch up. Taxation from toil is deep. Look what it has already done to you. If I write you a prescription, will you be able to fill it?"

"Oriole can go where she wants," Meiling answers on behalf of the brickmaker.

"Then here is what I would like you to do. First, please have the herbalist make you a Decoction to Supplement the Center and Boost Qi." I don't know if any of this will matter to Oriole, but I take the time to explain anyway. "This is a classic remedy from a book called *Profound Formulas*. My grandmother says she has the last copy in existence." Oriole's eyes widen as she absorbs this information. "The most important ingredient is one that we women rely on. Astragalus will help your fatigue and Blood prostration. I'm adding my own ideas to your prescription. Skullcap root purges Fire and inflammation. Nut grass rhizome not only has cooling properties, but it is well known to help with moon-water problems, weight loss, and sleep disorders. Japanese thistle is one of the best substances to stop runaway bleeding."

"Will it be expensive?" Oriole asks.

"There are no extraordinary ingredients here," I answer.

"You will be fine," Meiling adds soothingly.

"When you've finished this remedy, I want you to take Pill to Greatly Supplement Yin," I go on. "It includes among its many ingredients freshwater turtle shell and cork-tree bark."

"And I'll get better?"

"You will," I answer. "I'll send Young Midwife to make sure you're recovering. If you have other problems, she will bring me here."

I make this offer because I'm confident enough in my treatment plan to be sure I won't need to return. The pill is one I've used before. While it's known to quell Fire in the yin and supplement the Kidney, it also helps with turbulent emotions. Oriole is polite and hospitable, but her bitterness about her life radiates from her as the entire brickyard radiates heat. Her anger is far more deep-seated and difficult to treat than her weeping womb, but my remedy will work on this too.

Meiling and I say goodbye and retrace our steps to her home, where we're able to sneak back upstairs unobserved. I'm exhausted, and my feet are in more pain than when they were first bound. I bite my lips to keep from moaning as Meiling pulls off the boots. I struggle to compose myself as I change back into my clothes. The layers of underskirt, overskirt, tunic, and leggings feel suffocating.

The bearers do not regard me with suspicion when I step out the front door, which relieves my mind. Once we reach the Garden of Fragrant Delights, I step over the threshold and begin threading my way through the compound. I need tea. I need to change my clothes and put on fresh makeup. I need most of all to lie down and rest my throbbing feet. To do any of these things would cast suspicion on me, however. Each step sends streaks of pain up my legs, but I try to keep my expression placid.

I find the girls and women of the household in the last court-yard. Some are reading, others embroidering and painting. My mother-in-law sits with wives of her age but below her station. All of them sip rice wine from jade cups to help draw attention away from Lady Kuo's newfound need to quench the thirsty thing living inside her. From the pavilion comes the *click-click* of mahjong tiles; the aunties must be in another of their furious games. I pass the knot of concubines. I nod to Miss Chen, and she nods back. I'm a wife; she's a concubine. We are not friends, but we are polite to each other.

Miss Chen is Doctor Wong's greatest success, since together they have given the Yang clan a second heir. Manzi, now thirteen, attends the household school with other boys. My mother-in-law dotes on the boy, spoiling him with dates and sweetmeats. He's in position to become her ritual son. On some days, this seems like it has lessened intrigues in the inner chambers; on other days, Second Aunt can be particularly biting about the unfairness of it all. But tradition is tradition, and blood is blood. Succession is set by Heaven, and nothing will change for Second Uncle unless something happens to both my husband and Manzi. For now, though, Manzi has an elevated status. This being true, the matchmaker has already arranged a betrothal between Manzi and the daughter of a salt merchant of great wealth, solidifying both families' riches and power. All this has earned Miss Chen the position of empress of the concubines. She's also given birth to four daughters, the youngest of whom is not yet three years old. Her other girls—ages ten, nine, and seven—have exquisitely bound feet. (Who better to bind a child's feet than a Thin Horse? And, of course, they all have their mother's beauty.) All in all, Miss Chen has no cause for worry. She's so confident of her position that she's even allowed weight to gather around her waist—what little is left of it after birthing five children—and under her chin.

I spot Yuelan and Chunlan on either side of their little sister, walking her along a pathway embedded with pebbles. For men, the pebbles massage the acupuncture points on the bottoms of their feet; for women, the pebbles are cause for caution. A wrong step or a loss of balance can bring about a fall. For a girl undergoing footbinding, the pebbles push and prod her most painful parts.

"Mama," Ailan calls out when she sees me. The sheen of sweat on her brow and upper lip tell me of her anguish. Her bravery helps me to keep my own discomfort hidden.

I commend her for being so courageous and thank my older daughters for helping her. Then I ask, "Shall we play our special game? Yuelan and Chunlan, if you gather the leaves and flowers, I'll look after your sister."

I hold Ailan's elbow as she takes excruciating step after excruciating step along the pebble walkway and up onto the stone bridge. The two older girls join us, their palms held together like bowls, with petals and leaves piled high. The four of us line up side by side, our skirts swishing together. We each hold out a leaf. We let Ailan do the count.

"One, two, three, and away!" Our leaves swirl down, hit the water, and float under the bridge. Again I hold Ailan's elbow as we cross to the other side of the bridge. We're halfway across when I hear a loud *crack*. With a sudden intake of breath, Ailan pulls her leg up at the knee, then slowly lowers it to the ground. She wobbles, and I steady her.

"Another bone has broken," I say with pride. "Every day you make progress."

Her complexion goes as white as the underbelly of a fish. She swallows the hurt, steadies herself, and takes six more steps—each of which must be agony—to the balustrade. She grasps the stone handrail, leans over, and peers down to the water. She tries to hide her tears, but the current of the stream is calm enough that they hit the surface like raindrops. When the time comes, I'll make sure to tell the matchmaker that each tiny splash was a sign of the type of wife Ailan will become—diligent, uncomplaining, and obedient.

When her leaf appears first, she looks up at me. Her eyes have the faraway look that suffering brings, but the corners of her lips lift as she announces, "Look, Mama. I won."

Later that night, I write in my notebook about the brick-maker's case. I detail the basics, leaving out my feelings about the condition of her feet. I finish my entry as I usually do with the recipes for the basic prescriptions and the additions that will make them extra potent. When I'm done, I go to my bed. I look around at the tiny carved pearwood vignettes that capture moments of domestic bliss. Just the idea of playing an erhu by a stream . . . I finger the panel that has been loose since I was a girl. Jiggling it just so, I free it from its frame. I slip the notebook through the opening, set it on the small shelf with my mother's shoes, and then fit the panel back into place.

Finally, I can rest. My mother-in-law knows I'm continuing my studies with my grandparents. This is one more way she holds power over me—what keeps me obediently under her thumb. But if she knew I visited Meiling, she would put an immediate stop to it. I see no circumstance in which Lady Kuo would allow it, let alone the treatment of a working woman. But secrets exact an emotional price. So, in addition to the usual weariness brought about by a typical rice-and-salt day, my body and mind are utterly fatigued. For no reason that I can identify, the silent tears come.

The Hundred Pulses

"How will you greet your husband when you see him?" Second Aunt sounds cordial, but her bitterness about her aspirations for her husband to assume authority in the household has only grown over the years, leaving her face lined with resentment. "Will you be kind or—"

"Complain that he didn't bring you a bolt of silk—"

"Or a jade bracelet—"

"Or will you quickly take him to the bedchamber so he might give you a son?"

I glance at the faces of the women who sit together in their late morning circles in the inner chambers. The room fairly buzzes with anticipation. My husband is coming home for a three-month visit. He's bringing with him an official from the Department of Service in Beijing who is reported to be one of the richest, most refined, cultivated, and influential men in the capital. As such, he has powerful connections to the imperial palace. In the inner chambers, the women are surprised—and shocked—to learn that the official is bringing his wife and mother with him. The traveling party should arrive shortly, and we all have our ears perked, listening for the sounds of cymbals, drums, clappers, and horns that always accompany a high-ranking official's procession.

I tilt my head modestly, as I've seen Meiling do so many times. "I'm very much looking forward to seeing Maoren. It's been months since he was last here."

"It is in a woman's nature to be plagued by vitriol," Second

Aunt comments, "so plant a pretty smile on your face when you see him."

I take her advice to be as meaningful as a single grain of rice in a banquet cauldron. Nevertheless, I remain respectful in my response. "I will, Second Aunt."

"After all," she goes on, "who knows what our husbands have been doing and who they've been doing it with when they're away."

"You're speaking of jealousy," Fourth Aunt jumps in, as though every person here doesn't know that this is the very emotion that causes her to carp at her husband whenever he's home.

"Or envy," one of Second Uncle's concubines quips from across the room. "Who here hasn't heard you banging on my door when the master is visiting me?"

Lady Kuo holds up a hand. "That's enough!"

And it is for a few moments. But over where the widows and spinsters sit something's brewing. Those old ladies can be unpredictable. Great-Aunt, who moved here after her husband's family died out, can be especially nettlesome, yet her voice sounds casual when she begins speaking.

"A bevy of husbands was afraid of their wives." Heads swing in Great-Aunt's direction at the recognition of the beginning of the familiar story. "One day those men met in a tavern to discuss what to do. The first man said, 'I will beat my wife into submission. She will be as docile as a doe in springtime.'"

One of the other widows is ready with the next part. "The second man said, 'I will stop feeding my bride. Hunger will tame her bossiness.'"

"The third man said, 'I will tie my wife to the bed,'" Great-Aunt resumes. "'She won't be able to escape my charms then.'"

Listening to them, I miss Spinster Aunt. I think a couple of other women do too.

"All of a sudden, who should appear?" Great-Aunt asks in mock alarm. "Why, it was one of the Six Grannies! This one happened to be a crone who made her living as a fortune-teller. She warned the husbands. 'Look out! Look out! Your wives are coming!' Despite their earlier daring words, two of the men scattered like fleas from a dead cat. The third man stayed planted to his chair, proving he was the most valiant of men." She falls silent to let the suspense build. Then, much like Spinster Aunt did in the past, she leans forward to confide in a voice just loud enough for everyone to hear. "But when the other husbands regained their courage, they approached only to discover he'd frozen to death from fear!"

I join the laughter, but inside I'm as nervous as a bride. I'm lucky to love my husband and for him to love me in return, but sending letters back and forth over great distances by foot courier is not the same as sharing a bed.

Just then, we hear the first sounds of the procession. Lady Kuo raps her knuckles on the arm of her chair, signaling that she wishes me to approach. Standing before her, I feel every pair of eyes in the room on me. Poppy helped with my hair, brushing it until it shines, and inserting my best gold and jade pins to hold and decorate the upswept bun. The red paint on my lips and pink powder on my cheeks stand out even brighter and, I hope, alluringly, above my snow-white gown made of silk as thin and translucent as a cicada's wing. My mother-in-law would never offer a compliment, but on this day she can't complain about how I look.

"Do you think it will be better for you to be at the front gate, attend the banquet, or be in your bedchamber when my son arrives?" she asks.

There is only one correct response. "Though I long to see my husband and every minute apart has been a sword in my heart, I'll remain in my room. I hope his desires will bring him to me quickly."

Lady Kuo nods her approval. Then, "While my duty is to oversee the banquet for our guests, please be confident that I'll watch to make sure my son neither eats nor drinks too much. I want him active in the bedchamber."

I bow my head in deference, although it's hard to imagine what control she might have over my husband in this regard. She raps her knuckles again to dismiss me and then rises to address the room. "We don't often receive guests in the inner chambers. I expect everyone to be hospitable." After a pause, she adds, "I realize tomorrow is the day Doctor Wong and Young Midwife pay their monthly call. Their work is too important to cancel. I'll make sure you each have an opportunity to see them, but please remember that our men are making connections that can build the Yang family's wealth and reputation. We must do all we can to help by showing these traveling women"—those last words come out of her mouth as though she's speaking of ghouls—"that we live by the values Confucius and the emperor have set forth."

Not long after she leaves, I tell my daughters to keep working on their embroidery and then retire to my room. Listening to the distant sounds of arrival and greeting, and later the hum from the welcome banquet being held in the second courtyard, I keep returning to my wedding night and the anticipation I felt. The evening crawls toward midnight, but I remain still, so movement won't smear my makeup or push a single hair out of place. My gown drapes across my lap to the floor. I adjust the fabric so that the toes of my shoes peek out from the puddled silk as an enticement. I am like this—as sublime as a figurine of the Goddess of Mercy in meditation—when Maoren enters. My appearance has the desired effect.

"Tonight we will make a son," my husband says, pulling me into his arms.

———

The next morning, the visitors are already settled in the inner chambers when I enter. Everyone is in attendance, which means that Doctor Wong and Meiling have yet to arrive. My mother-in-law motions for me to sit next to her. It's the first time I've been positioned as the woman second in line of importance in the household. I should feel honored—and I do—but I'm distracted by the strangers among us and how different they are. Lady Liu, the wife of the visiting dignitary, tells us she's twenty-three years old. Her mother-in-law, Widow Bao, is fifty-one. Their clothes are fine but not as elegant as what we can have made in our province, where silk and dyes are superb and plentiful. Still, the simplicity of their gestures shows their refinement, while what I imagine to be big-city sophistication spills from their lips.

"The emperor has sent my husband to travel the length and breadth of our country. He is to find men and boys who would like to enter service as eunuchs in the palace," Lady Liu tells us. "Many husbands are gone for years at a time, and we women must accept our loneliness. My husband takes a different view. He wants his wife and mother to be with him in his journeys. In this way, we are not so different from the wives of the lowest *juren* scholars who accompany their husbands to remote postings."

"How admirable," Lady Kuo says, but to her this choice is as far from being admirable as the moon is from the sun.

"Knowing my son as I do," Widow Bao says, "I can tell you he is happy to have the women of his family around him when each day he's looking for other families willing to sell their sons—and grown men who wish to offer themselves—only to have their three privates cut off so they might be employed in the palace. My son's job is important, no question, but he profits from the hardship of many."

Lady Kuo purses her lips against such blunt words. Into the silence, Lady Liu tries to smooth the rough edges of her mother-in-law's comments. "Eunuchs are needed in the Forbidden City to care for the emperor, but their most important job is to watch over the women in the palace. Some emperors keep as many as ten thousand wives, concubines, and consorts."

"Ten thousand," someone across the room murmurs.

"In the right conditions, the son of a concubine can become the next emperor if the empress does not produce a son," Widow Bao adds innocuously. My mother-in-law glances in my direction to remind me that this situation could be in my future too.

"Every care must be taken that the empress and all other women in the palace are protected and saved—to a one—for the emperor," Lady Liu picks up. "This means—"

"No male arrows," Widow Bao finishes with a sly wink. "So we have eunuchs who can be trusted for their unique inability to perform their Confucian duty as men—produce sons." Her eyes gleam. "Knifers who do the cutting have shops and stalls just outside the Forbidden City. A man or boy walks inside with his three precious things attached. Once they're removed, they're sealed in a jar and stored on a shelf to be reunited with a eunuch's body upon death."

"And why should this happen?" Lady Kuo inquires, drawn in.

"To trick the demons in the Afterworld into believing he is still a man." Widow Bao allows herself an unladylike cackle. "If he is not reunited with his three precious things, he will be reborn as a she-mule."

A silence falls over us as we consider the indignity of such a fate. Widow Bao's tone changes. "Many things are different since the Hongzhi emperor ascended the throne two years ago. As we travel with my son, my daughter-in-law and I are looking for—"

Lady Liu interrupts, leaving me, and I bet many others, to suspect she doesn't want certain facts divulged. "The boy eunuchs are playthings. Toys, if you will, to keep women happy. They do not shy away from even the most private requests."

My mother-in-law looks uncomfortable, as though ants are crawling under her gown.

"Senior eunuchs often conduct the search for those who might like to join them in this life," Lady Liu continues, "but the emperor and those who run the Department of Service agree it is wise periodically to send someone who has all his parts and is without reproach to the local bureaus to make sure all is being conducted in a forthright manner. While it's not against the law for a poor father to sell a second, third, or fourth son into duty, my husband seeks to prove that the proper sums are not only changing hands but changing into the correct hands."

This room usually hums with conversation and activity. Not today. All the wives' ears are tuned to our visitors' voices. Such a novelty. Beneath the silence, I sense a deeper listening from the concubines, maids, and servants, each of whom probably followed a path similar to that of the boys who eventually became eunuchs, only the girls' fathers sold them to a Tooth Lady or some other procurer. For so many on the edges of this room, the worthless branch on the family tree gained value only when she was sold to help keep her family alive.

"We've been told there's a doctor in your household," Widow Bao comments.

"Ah, yes, he will be visiting today. Would you care to meet him?" Lady Kuo asks.

"I meant a woman doctor," Widow Bao clarifies.

"We only use Doctor Wong in the Garden of Fragrant Delights," my mother-in-law says stiffly. "I can guarantee he's a man."

"That's not what your son says. The first time we met, he said his wife has been training to be a doctor since she was eight years old." The widow glances in my direction. "I assume he was speaking of you."

A Dragon is always loyal to his loved ones. I am not the sort of woman to crow, however.

"Doctor Wong is known to be the best physician in Wuxi," Lady Kuo says. "He has published a book of his cases."

The widow sniffs. "We've seen it."

"He's clearly seeking a certain kind of clientele," Lady Liu comments. "Many people want to align themselves with the wealthy. The rich, in turn, want what they perceive to be the best money can bring them—"

"My concern is," Widow Bao interrupts, "he is not a doctor solely for women."

My mother-in-law bridles. "Doctor Wong has long overseen fertility issues in our household."

Our two guests listen politely: the younger one with twitchy energy, the older one with forced patience.

"Our party detoured to Wuxi to see . . ." Widow Bao slips a hand out from under her sleeve and rolls her wrist in my direction. "We're traveling with my son because we love him and don't want him to be lonely, but my daughter-in-law and I have other business. You could say double business. My daughter lives in Nanjing. We saw her when we were there. She's been quite ill."

"Her doctor says she might die," Lady Liu says, "but your son has given us new hope in the form of his wife."

"Do not take our request as simply women's folly," the widow adds. "My son insisted we come here, for he loves his sister very much and would like to do what he can to reverse the course of her illness. Great rewards can come to a family such as yours in gratitude for your hospitality, guidance, and good deeds."

Lady Kuo remains silent. I can't imagine her thoughts.

"Just think of the morality stories we've heard since childhood." Widow Bao holds out her right hand to give an example.

"A poor man helps a beggar by the side of the road. The beggar turns out to be a god or an emperor in disguise, and many gifts are bestowed on the poor man for his kindness and generosity when he himself had so little." She extends her left hand for her second example. "A family of great wealth and distinction, with storerooms overflowing, refuses to put even a single morsel in a beggar's bowl. Many years later, after the family has suffered from fires, drought, and bad luck at gambling, who should arrive in a grand procession? We all know the end of the story."

Lady Kuo clicks her fingernails against each other. I take this as an order to speak.

"I suggest you visit my grandmother. She is well known in Wuxi for her sublime treatments."

"We've heard of her," Lady Liu says, "but my mother-in-law and I agree that someone young might have fresher ideas. And your husband tells us you've had quiet successes."

"I've never treated a woman from a distance," I admit.

My mother-in-law settles the matter by saying, "Now you will."

"Then I'll try to do my best." I turn to our guests. "We can speak here, but perhaps you'd prefer to come to my chambers."

"Please stay. We would all like to hear what you have to say." Lady Kuo sounds solicitous, but our guests are not fooled.

"Your room sounds lovely," the widow says. "Let us retire there."

We walk slowly through the covered colonnades, stopping here and there so the visitors can enjoy the scent of jasmine and admire the plumes of a caged bird, while Poppy runs ahead to prepare. When we arrive, we settle, and Poppy pours tea.

"Please tell me about your daughter," I begin. "How old is she? What are her symptoms?"

Tears well in the widow's eyes, so Lady Liu speaks on her behalf. "My sister-in-law is thirty-five years old. When she hears people speaking, she becomes dizzy."

It's an odd symptom, no question, but it doesn't sound all that worrisome to me. However, we've reached the fifth month, when the growing heat and humidity can bring sickness and disease.

"Does she have a rash?" I ask.

"No cases of smallpox have been reported in Nanjing," Lady Liu answers.

Which is a relief.

"You asked for me because I'm a woman," I say. "I hope you don't mind if I ask some intimate questions." When both women nod, I go on. "Tell me about her stools and urine."

"She has fainted multiple times when sitting on the honey-pot," Lady Liu states.

"What does her doctor say?" I inquire.

"He says she's Blood and qi deficient," Lady Liu answers. "Now she coughs up blood."

They might have mentioned this symptom first, but hearing it, I say, "It sounds as though he's made the correct diagnosis."

"Is she dying?" Widow Bao asks, her voice quavering. "She's my daughter . . ."

"I can't do the Four Examinations from afar." I try to sound reassuring when I add, "Tell me more. Perhaps her doctor missed something."

"Ask us anything."

"Can you describe her disposition?"

"Until now, she's always been quick-tempered and impatient," the widow answers. "Now she stays in bed, weeping day and night."

This is another important symptom, but what is the cause? I remain silent, waiting for one of the women to tell me what brought about such sorrow. We each take sips of tea. Widow Bao's eyes fill again; Lady Liu gives one of those sighs known through the ages to convey loss of heart.

"My sister-in-law's daughter died ten months ago," she confides at last. "This is when she began to cry. Four months later, bandits killed her son."

Widow Bao openly weeps. When Lady Liu puts a comforting hand over her mother-in-law's, I wish I could have a relationship like this with Lady Kuo, but she has no interest and my desires are not what matter here.

"Widow Bao, I believe your daughter is suffering from a type of qi deficiency we call damage from weeping. You tell me your daughter was once quick-tempered. This is caused by qi constraint, which leads to Heat in the Liver, which, in turn, fires up Blood, which must be expelled by coughing. I don't have a full pharmacy here, but let me write out some prescriptions for you to take back to Nanjing."

The first remedy is Beautiful Jade Syrup, in which one of the ingredients—honey—is strained through raw silk. The second remedy is more complex, combining the Decoction of Six Gentlemen and the Decoction of Four Gentlemen. And third, I write an order for Calm the Spirit Pills to cool her Blood and help her sleep. I feel certain that Grandmother would agree with my approach.

"It may take a while for your daughter to regain her health," I say as I hand Widow Bao the prescriptions, "but she will."

"How long?" Widow Bao asks.

"You should see improvement within two weeks, but she won't fully recover for three months, maybe longer."

"You have much confidence."

"I have confidence in all my grandmother taught me and all who taught her."

"Then perhaps you can help me as well," Widow Bao says.

I suspected this might be coming. After so many years at Grandmother's side, I've developed the habit of examining the color and texture of skin, the vibrancy or dullness of hair, and the state of emotions of any woman or child I meet, whether they're asking for my advice or not. Grandmother says this is a good way for me to keep my diagnostic tools sharp, so that when I'm called upon for help—if Lady Kuo should one day ask me to treat her cough, for example—I'll be prepared.

The widow tells me that her monthly moon water is irregular. She has trouble sleeping and is plagued by bouts of sweating. She says she's always taken humble pride in being sharp of mind. "But now I can't remember a thing!" she complains.

I feel her pulse, which floats and surges. I diagnose qi and Blood deficiency.

"Like my daughter?" Widow Bao asks.

"Identical terms, with different results," I answer. "But you have no need of worry. I could do nothing, and your monthly moon water would probably stop entirely by New Year's Festival, but I hate for you to suffer from these aggravating symptoms."

Widow Bao's complaints are normal for a woman her age, which is why I have the necessary pills on my shelf. I pour some of them into a silk bag and pull the ribbon to secure them inside. "These will alleviate your troubles. You'll sleep better, and soon your monthly moon-water days will be behind you."

Widow Bao tucks the satchel inside her gown. "We mentioned we had double business to conduct on this trip. Let us discuss the second matter now. My daughter-in-law and I are also looking for midwives to bring to the capital. Your husband told us you have a friend who is a midwife. That surprised us."

"And made us curious," Lady Liu says. "She must be special to move comfortably around, and be accepted by, someone such as you."

"My grandmother recognized this quality in Meiling at a young age." After a moment, I add, "Would you like to meet her?"

"We would be grateful for that," Lady Liu says.

We walk to the last courtyard and into a room where we can see Doctor Wong positioned behind a screen to the left and a young wife perched on a kang, with Meiling on her knees before her, to the right. The doctor sees us, stands, then falls to the floor to perform obeisance. "Welcome. Welcome" comes his muffled voice.

"You may rise," Lady Liu says. "We've come to observe, if you don't mind."

"Mind?" The doctor scrambles to his feet. "It's an honor to have such esteemed ladies in Wuxi."

Lady Liu and Widow Bao must be accustomed to this sort of obsequiousness, because in synchronized movement they dismiss his words with the backs of their hands. They watch as Meiling pulls up three chairs next to the kang. She's dressed simply but elegantly today in one of my old gowns. She has tried to copy my walk since childhood, so her steps are delicate and graceful. I make the introductions, and the three of us sit across from the young wife, who is pale with nervousness. I touch her hand. "Don't worry. We're only here to listen."

Meiling serves as the go-between, bringing Doctor Wong's

questions from behind the screen and sending the young wife's detailed answers back to him. I'm proud of Meiling. Not only does she do a much better job at transmitting the messages than an embarrassed husband ever could, but she also carries herself well—showing equal respect to the doctor and to the patient.

The young wife recently gave birth. She suffers from severe itching on her ears, cheeks, and the nape of her neck. She sobs, hiding her tears with her sleeves. "I'm lonely. My husband doesn't listen to me. He pays no attention to my advice."

Meiling disappears behind the screen to pass on these words. Since Doctor Wong can't see the patient, Meiling also describes the young woman's red and scaled face and the patches where she's scratched so much the skin oozes. The two visitors and I hear her clearly when she adds, "As a midwife, I've seen cases of postpartum Wind itching many times. This happens when the childbirth gate is too long exposed during labor. Do you remember, Doctor Wong, how long her baby took to come out? Your good judgment saved two lives that day."

Silence falls over the room as Doctor Wong considers this information. Finally, he declares, repeating the diagnosis Meiling just gave him, "Tell the patient she suffers from postpartum Wind itching." He gives the same prescription I would have recommended to refill the empty spaces between the layers of the girl's skin, but he doesn't suggest anything to help with her itching.

From behind the curtain, Doctor Wong speaks again. "The goal of a male doctor is to see that a woman lives out her predetermined fate and destiny to have children. These things are controlled by Heaven."

"Thank you for that, Doctor Wong," Lady Liu says politely, but inside I burn. I rise and walk to the window, so our guests won't see the emotions cross my face. It may not be decorous to say aloud, but we women—rich, poor, educated, uneducated—are at the mercy of our bodies: the cycles of blood, the patterns of energy, the depth and complexity of our feelings. Heaven has nothing to do with any of that.

I compose my face and turn back to the room to find Lady Liu sitting on the kang next to the young wife, the two of them with their heads together as they whisper. Widow Bao and Meiling stand in the farthest corner of the room, also whispering. It seems both sets of women wish to share confidences away from Doctor Wong's ears.

I clear my throat and approach the kang. Lady Liu rises, and Widow Bao sways away from Meiling. We take turns leaning down to thank the young wife for allowing us to observe as Doctor Wong treated her. This is accompanied by separate messages from each of us spoken in tones that can't possibly reach him.

"It is a rare husband who listens to his wife, let alone takes her advice," Widow Bao says gently. "Don't let this trouble your mind any longer."

"Thank you for telling me about the birth of your daughter," murmurs Lady Liu. "Next time you'll have a son."

"I'll tell Lady Kuo how gracious you've been." Then, emboldened by the events of the day, yet remaining vigilant to possible listening ears, I lower my voice even further. "Come visit me in my room. I'll give you a special herbal wash. Use it for two weeks, and your face will be as beautiful as the day you wed."

We spend the rest of the afternoon in the inner chambers, where my mother-in-law pours rice wine for our guests, refilling her own cup more frequently than would be advised. I understand. The day has not gone as she planned, with more attention focused on me than she would like. She would be even more irritated to hear that her guests seemed particularly interested in Meiling and that she presented herself not just as an accomplished midwife but as a lady too.

That evening, another banquet is held. I'm not invited, but once again the convivial sounds of conversation and the weeping strains of an expertly played erhu reach my ears. I'm tired and wouldn't mind napping for a bit before Maoren comes to bed and we try again to make a son, but first I have three new cases to write in my notebook.

———

The next morning, the official announces that he and his family will return to Nanjing the following day and asks Maoren to travel with them. I had been looking forward to having three months with my husband. Now I have only one more night. Our bed-chamber activity goes well, but two weeks later, I learn that he has not planted a baby inside me. This news is met with a frown from my mother-in-law and a sly smile from Miss Chen. Six weeks later, a courier brings a letter letting me know that Maoren will return in another month's time. He doesn't say how long he'll stay nor does he inform me of Widow Bao's condition or that of her daughter. The former I can understand, but why wouldn't he let me know about the daughter? "You'd better hope nothing's gone wrong," my mother-in-law warns me, which only builds my concern.

On the day appointed for Maoren's arrival, I style my hair, apply makeup, and dress in a fine gown, hoping that his time away will have caused his body to dam his Essence, which will seek a flood of release. This time, though, I'm told to go to the Welcome Hall. When I enter, I find Lady Kuo in her chair, with my husband seated opposite her. She has always been forthright with me about her views on my fecundity, and I assume that all blame and responsibility will fall on me, but she surprises me by bringing Maoren into the discussion.

"Blood and Essence can't create a baby unless the husband visits the marriage bed," Lady Kuo begins, "which you, my son, do too infrequently."

"I'm in Nanjing—"

"It is also a husband's duty to make sure his wife experiences the same overflowing joy at the exact moment he does," she goes on. "Are you looking to bring your wife pleasure? Do you make sure that the hundred pulses arrive together?"

The tips of Maoren's ears turn red. No man wants to be questioned by his mother about whether he's able to orchestrate bed-chamber activities so that we both feel ultimate gratification at the same time. "I do everything *I'm* supposed to do," he mumbles.

I consider Maoren to be a good man—and he is by most measures—but Grandfather was right about him. My husband was born in the Year of the Dragon, and he's vexed by some of the Dragon's worst attributes—especially refusing to accept failure with grace. Sometimes, as now, he'll cast blame elsewhere. This is better than the alternative, which happens when he retreats into a cave of resentment because he hasn't gotten his way. It must be difficult, I realize, for him to have failed the next level of the imperial exams multiple times and have everyone know.

"Making a baby is an internal contest between yin and yang," Lady Kuo pointedly tells him. "It is up to yang to win over yin."

My husband stares at the floor. I doubt he's ever been so rebuked, but his mother isn't done.

"Taoist scriptures tell us that if you want a son," she reminds him, "then bedroom affairs must be conducted on the first, third, and fifth days after monthly moon water ceases. Please ignore the second, fourth, and sixth days, unless you want to sire another daughter. After that, you can forget all bedchamber activity, for the child palace will be closed for business."

I've heard this theory before, but in the inner chambers some women believe that performing bedchamber affairs just before the appearance of monthly moon water will guarantee a son. Personally, I've always held to Grandmother's advice: after the act itself, lie on your back with your knees up. To have a son, lean to the right so the baby may lodge on the yang side of the body; for a girl, lean to the left so she might nestle on the yin side of the body. Of course, I've followed these traditions and have yet to be given a son.

Before my husband can speak, Lady Kuo says the words I've been dreading. "Perhaps it's time to buy one or more concubines to give me grandsons."

I hope Maoren will dismiss this suggestion outright, knowing that a Dragon can be rude and rough in the way he speaks truth. Beyond that, custom says that if a man hasn't given his wife a son by the time he reaches the age of forty, then it's a wife's duty to select either a concubine or a secondary wife for him. But my husband is only thirty! That's far too young to bring in a concubine for this purpose. But when I glance at my husband and he refuses to meet my eyes, I see the other part of his Dragon personality come through. A Dragon likes things easy. A Dragon is privileged, spoiled, and used to getting his own way. He takes love and privilege for granted, because they are due to him as a Dragon.

"We must have a son to secure the family line," he tells me later as I undress, as though I didn't know this already.

We do what we're supposed to do. We do it every night for a week. A couple of times we pursue night sports by day. And then my monthly moon water comes. Dragons like to take credit, but if they don't win right away, they fizzle out. This is exactly what happens to my husband. Instead of coming to my marriage bed, he goes out to teahouses and taverns. There's a drinking party one night, theater the next. Whispers of gambling reach me in the inner chambers. My Dragon husband—in his disappointment—seeks pleasure rather than responsibility. A life of amusements is easily attainable for the small-minded man.

I skip my visits to Grandmother and Meiling. I don't want them to know my humiliation. I'm determined to hold on to Maoren and keep him to myself. I recall the illustrated books I saw before my wedding. On those nights that Maoren does come to my room, I surprise him with new twisting and turning. It's exciting and different, but my monthly moon water comes again. A profound disappointment . . . We go back to the usual ways of most husbands and wives. It's all so routine and sad that it takes a couple of weeks for me to notice that even my husband's fascination with my feet has vanished. Then he begins to sleep in his library, saying he wants to put his effort into his next attempt at the imperial exams. That's when I realize it's only a matter of time before my mother-in-law will do her duty and bring in a concubine.

I feel myself slipping into the syndrome my grandmother always warns me about. I keep up with Ailan's footbinding, but I lose interest in Yuelan's and Chunlan's embroidery and other domestic skills. Then the worst comes to pass. My mother-in-law finds a concubine for Maoren. I stay in my room, refusing to meet the girl. Poppy tells me she's fourteen and exceptionally beautiful: "She's called Snowpink, and her cheeks are as lovely as the pink of sunrise on freshly fallen snow." I curl into a ball. Despair. Failure. I have only myself to blame. If Snowpink has a son, I'll be able to adopt him as a ritual son, as Respectful Lady did with Yifeng and Lady Kuo might do with Manzi. But I want my own son, and I don't want to spend the rest of my life having to accommodate a concubine of elevated rank. In my mind, I try to fight back. Who knows how Maoren will react to his mother's gift? Maybe he won't like the girl. But my battle with myself is doomed, because what man wouldn't like someone fresh, young, obedient, and malleable?

A few days later, Maoren comes to my room in the late afternoon. He holds a letter sealed with wax. It's addressed to me, but he opens it and scans to the end.

"Lady Liu has written to you," he says. "She wants you to know that her mother is as mentally sharp as before her troubles began." He looks to me for an explanation, but I don't give one. "Lady Liu's sister-in-law . . . It says here she suffered damage from weeping?" Again he peers at me, but I'd never tell him about what I discussed with Lady Liu and Widow Bao. "I'm happy to inform you that the sister-in-law is much improved after three months, just as you said she would be. She also thanks you for introducing her to Young Midwife. She writes that there will be news forthcoming in that regard."

While this information lifts my spirits briefly, I'm too defeated to ask to see the letter myself. There's more to it, though. Maoren gives me a wide smile. "As a result of this good outcome—as well as the effort and consideration my father and I have given—good opportunities will be coming to our family in the form of imperial contracts to provide silk to the capital."

A Dragon can be cunning and manipulative, but I fear his ambitions and desires far outweigh his talents. Nevertheless, on this day, the letter has filled him with light, and we put aside thoughts of duty and responsibility and enjoy the gratifications of the flesh. In our most heightened moments, I feel sure he's forgotten about Snowpink.

A Snake Always Sheds Its Skin

Two weeks later, my husband's happiness and the warmth we've shared end abruptly when the news reaches us that Meiling has been chosen to go to the capital to join the Lodge of Ritual and Ceremony, which provides doctors, midwives, and wet nurses to the woman of the imperial palace. Until today, Maoren and I have had few disagreements, with never a raised voice. He's always preferred to follow the rules for a model husband: *Ascend the bed, act like a husband; descend the bed, act like a gentleman.* Not now . . .

"You were supposed to promote the family, not the midwife," Maoren says through clenched teeth.

"I did exactly what your mother told me to do. I was hospitable. I helped Widow Bao and Lady Liu. I took them to meet Young Midwife because they asked—"

"My father and I spent time and money hosting the official and his family here and entertaining them in Nanjing. How is it that the midwife is the one to be rewarded?"

I love Meiling, but I have to admit it stings that she's been selected for this honor. I remind myself that being called to serve women in the palace is the greatest honor a midwife can attain, and that the possibility of this outcome might have been something Grandmother saw in Meiling a long time ago.

"It's not my fault that the guests you sent to our inner chambers were looking for a midwife," I say. "But you must remember our visitors also sought guidance about Widow Bao's daughter.

My prescription helped. Your father should be content with the new silk contracts my good advice brought the family."

My comments could be interpreted as impertinent—truly, shouldn't he have known what Lady Liu and Widow Bao were looking for on their imperial tour?—and they don't go down smoothly. Maoren looks as though he's swallowed a lizard and it's trying to escape back up his throat. His Dragon scheming didn't work in the way he'd hoped.

"Go to her," he says, refusing to call Meiling by her name or her title. "Remind her where this opportunity comes from. Make her see how important it is to help the Yang family."

I don't know what he hopes I'll achieve, but he arranges for a palanquin to take me straightaway to Meiling's home—openly, without any secret ploys or tricks to deceive his mother.

When I arrive at Grace Tranquility Teas, Midwife Shi has her mouth set in a grim slit as she tries to wrangle a room filled with demanding customers. The news of Meiling's good fortune has already spread and is serving as an enticement to patrons who hope some of this family's luck will rub off. I slip through the crowd and up the back stairs to find Meiling and Kailoo in the main room, standing before an open trunk, surrounded by piles of clothes and shoes.

"I don't think anything I own is right for the palace," Meiling says when she sees me.

"They haven't requested you for the quality of your silks and brocades," I respond.

"That's what I've been telling her." Kailoo's face shines with pride.

"Perhaps I can help," I say.

Apparently, these are the exact words Kailoo has longed to hear, for he leaves the room in seconds. Meiling shakes her head and smiles. "I will miss him."

I approach and take her hands. "And I will miss you."

She draws away. "I'm scared."

"Of the trip? Don't be. You'll be on the Grand Canal for five weeks, maybe shorter, weather and conditions permitting. You remember that I once traveled—"

"I'm not afraid of the journey. They want me to care for women in the court!"

"So Maoren has told me." I pause, hoping my serenity will calm her. "You are the best midwife in Wuxi."

"But there are cities much larger than this one, where mid-wives must have greater skills—"

"Those midwives didn't meet the right people," I point out. "Even if they did, I doubt many would have your refinement."

"But what if I have to treat the empress?"

I laugh at the idea, and she joins in. Once I've collected myself, I say, "Even if this were so, does Empress Zhang have a childbirth gate different from yours or mine or any woman's across our great country?"

Meiling acknowledges this truth with a dip of her chin, but her worried expression remains. "If anything should go wrong—"

"They requested you because Lady Liu and Widow Bao saw you at work."

"I was only passing messages!"

"You gave Doctor Wong the diagnosis," I correct her. "Besides, do you honestly think their inquiries stopped after that day?"

"Emissaries came to speak with Doctor Wong," she admits. "He must have said good things about me—"

"Because your light shines on him too. The same people who spoke to Doctor Wong also visited Grandmother Ru. She told them that in addition to your skills as a midwife, you spent much time as a child in the Mansion of Golden Light. You learned how to dress and act around women of high standing." Her eyes probe mine until I add, "And I told them how you and your mother saved my life and that of Yuelan."

"Doctor Wong wishes he'd been appointed too."

"He would never be chosen, because male doctors are not per-mitted to enter the palace of imperial wives and concubines. Only the emperor can see those women."

"The eunuchs—"

"Some may be doctors, but they are not men."

"They could have hired Doctor Wong to take care of the men—"

"Meiling, stop."

With that, I turn to the garments she's strewn about. "Now what are you going to take? I've always liked those leggings. They hang long and cover—"

"My big feet."

"I don't think you'll need sandals—"

"Because I don't want to offend anyone," she once again finishes.

"Because it gets very cold in Beijing," I correct her.

"I won't be gone that long—"

"Summer is ending. It will take at least a month to travel north and another month to come home. And you don't know how long they'll keep you." I pause to let her consider this. "What do you have for the winter months? Boots? A fur-lined jacket?"

"My only boots are for walking through the mud after it rains. The ones you wore—"

"They'll have to do for now."

And on it goes as Meiling holds up pieces one by one—many of them my castoffs—and I nod or shake my head to give my opinion. She packs the indigo-dyed tunic and trousers that she dresses in when attending births but also includes the simple silk gown she's begun to wear for her monthly visits to the Garden of Fragrant Delights with Doctor Wong.

"This dress has brought me luck," she says.

"And it is elegant in any room."

We select nine hairpins, two necklaces, and eight pairs of earrings—the numbers of each considered most fortuitous for a Snake. We fill her embroidery basket, so she'll have something to keep her occupied during the trip up the Grand Canal and then during the days of waiting for women in the palace to go into labor. Last, we pack a selection of teas that Meiling will be able to brew on the boat and in her room once she reaches her destination.

"The taste and aroma will remind you of home and of all those who care for you," I say.

I'm thinking about all the women she helps, but her mind goes in another direction.

"I hope Kailoo misses me, but I doubt he will." She looks pained. "He's lost patience with my inability to give him a child.

Even a daughter would do at this point." Realizing she's touched my sensitive spot—that I have not been able to conceive a son—she adds, "You worry about this too. I'm sorry if I've hurt you."

"You could never hurt me." Seeing Meiling's eyes begin to mist, I take her hands once again. "Don't let fear attack you. Remember a Snake is descended from the Dragon. This gives you great strength and fortitude."

When I get home, I report nearly everything to my husband. He agrees to send several bolts of silk to Meiling, so she might make some clothes for herself during her trip, which will be a fine advertisement for the Yang family's products to the women of the palace. That night, he retires to Snowpink's room, and I sleep alone in my marriage bed. He leaves for Nanjing the next day.

————

The first three months of Meiling's absence pass quickly. The blossoms of summer have dropped completely, and the trees have turned gold. On a crisp autumn day, Maoren surprises us all with an unplanned visit. He sends a servant to request I come to his library immediately, which I do. I have news for Maoren, but before I can tell him, he brings out a scroll from his sleeve. It has even more wax seals than what secured the letter Lady Liu sent.

"The Lodge of Ritual and Ceremony has requested you go to the capital at once to treat a woman in the Forbidden City who is suffering from an eye infection," Maoren announces as he reads from the document. He looks at me. "I presume the midwife recommended you. You must thank her on behalf of the family when you see her."

I hold up a hand. "I won't be leaving home. Any doctor can treat an eye infection. I'm not needed."

"They aren't asking for *any* doctor. They're asking for you. As you say, this is a simple task."

I hadn't wanted to share my news this way, but I put my hand over my child palace and announce, "I'm pregnant. I can't go."

He lights up. "Will it be a son?"

"We won't know until he comes out," I answer, but my use of the word *he* does not go unnoticed.

Maoren beams, but I also see concern as he weighs this information. He taps the scroll. *"A wide sea lets fish jump; a high sky lets birds fly."*

"But—"

"We—*you*—cannot ignore an imperial request. You must obey. And who knows? Treat an eye infection one day and the next day you could be named a doctor to the imperial household. Think of the honor it will bring to our family."

He's right, but I don't feel honored. I feel irritation at Meiling for putting me in this position. Was it not enough that fate gave her an auspicious opportunity? Why not leave me to my own life—to my husband, my daughters, and the coming baby? But I can't dwell in my discomfort. There are too many other things to discuss and plan.

"I don't want you to travel alone," Maoren says.

"When I left my childhood home, my father provided bodyguards—"

"You will have bodyguards, but my father and I also want you to have a companion."

I look at him quizzically. "A companion?"

"As you had when you first came to Wuxi. My mother and father were informed of this trip at the time of our marriage negotiations. The matchmaker arranged a meeting with Miss Zhao. She confirmed there had been no opportunity for . . ." He looks away, embarrassed.

"I was only eight!"

"But pirates were on every ocean wave, and the countryside was thick with bandits. Your Miss Zhao was able to vouch for your—"

I put up a hand to keep him from saying another word. Until now, I hadn't known that Miss Zhao had been brought in to verify my virginity. And now Maoren wants her to certify my behavior while I'm gone?

"Miss Zhao is my brother's mother," I say. "I'll be happy to have her watch over me for you." I believe—I hope—that I've fully concealed my emotions.

"For my mother," he corrects. "For our family."

Maoren spends the night with me. He lies next to me, his stomach and chest along my spine, tucking his knees into the backs of mine, with one of his hands splayed across my belly. I know he loves me and cares for me and our family, but this decision will have consequences. When I'm away from the Garden of Fragrant Delights, he'll be able to spend as much time as he likes with Snowpink. She could get pregnant; she could already be pregnant. I could have a fourth daughter; she could have a son. An aphorism tells us *A clever man shapes his actions to opportunity,* but couldn't that be said about a concubine too?

———

Poppy, who'll also join the traveling party, begins to pack for me while I visit my grandparents to get their advice and to pick up a broad selection of herbs and other ingredients to treat an eye infection of unspecified cause that will probably be long gone by the time I reach the capital. Grandfather offers this guidance: "Even if the patient is the emperor's favorite concubine, don't forget that she is no different from any other woman—ten times more difficult to treat than a man." Only someone who's been married as long as my grandmother would have the audacity to bat at her husband's sleeve in dismissal—first, at the idea that I'd be called upon to help someone so exalted, and second, because of her intolerance for that ancient belief. Her eyes sparkle as she speaks the basic truth: "A woman is a woman whether born in the dirt or on silk."

My brother, Yifeng, wishes me luck, reminding me that what I'm doing will be good not only for the Yang family but for the Tan family as well. "My wife, our children, and I thank you," he says. He knows, though, that everything rests on the outcome of my treatments.

Miss Zhao has no say about whether she accompanies me, but then she's had few, if any, real choices in her life. I hope she'll enjoy the trip and that her past experiences will provide me with useful information.

The most difficult goodbyes are to my daughters. I tell my eldest girl, "You are of an age when temptations may come. Don't allow yourself to become a jade hairpin that falls in the mud." To which Yuelan laughs lightly and asks, "Where would I meet a stranger?" To my second girl, I say, "I'm relying on you to assure your older sister does nothing to stain her reputation so near to her marriage and to stick close to Ailan to make sure she walks each day." Chunlan nods, her expression solemn. And little Ailan? She cries and cries. "Don't leave me, Mama. Don't leave me." Her tears threaten to crack my composure, so my words are as much for me as they are for her: "Be brave."

The entire household comes to the front gate to bid me farewell. Poppy stands nearby, hopping from foot to foot, ready to run alongside the palanquin to the dock as she has for every important journey in my life. My trunks, boxes, and satchels have been sent ahead to the boat.

My husband and I act formally, as the occasion requires. I bow to him; he bows to me. And that's that.

Miss Zhao and the bodyguards are already aboard the boat when Poppy and I arrive at the dock. My father's concubine and I are to share accommodations, with Poppy sleeping on the floor. We open our trunks and lay out those items that will be useful during the journey—brushes, ink, and paper for writing, capes of different thicknesses for whatever weather we might encounter, jars with candied ginger in case of nausea.

"Do you plan on staying in our room for the entire voyage?" Miss Zhao asks. She is not the beauty she once was, but her acceptance of the passage of time exudes a quiet loveliness that to my eyes is both endearing and admirable.

"I do not, and I hope you don't either. I learned from you many years ago to travel with my own money. I'm prepared to pay whatever it takes to allow us to sit on the deck."

Miss Zhao smiles. "So we are to see the world again."

———

When we have favorable winds, the sails are hoisted. When the winds are against us, men on towpaths pull the boat upstream with ropes. In shallow waters, the boatmen use poles to propel us. If the water is deep, they rely on oars. We pass through locks that raise or lower the vessel to the required levels. We go day and night, covering about ninety *li* between sunrises. The greatest surprise is that the person who steers the boat is a woman. Her face is brown from the sun, her body wiry. She is, without doubt, lowly to have a position in which she works with her hands. As such, she sleeps under a lean-to on the deck.

Fall is upon us—the weather temperate, and the skies clear—which allows Miss Zhao and me to spend a lot of time on the deck taking in the scenery. Here in the south, we see abundance in every direction. Villages are well populated, with houses and other buildings made of brick, with tile roofs. Fields spread wide and lush with autumnal crops. Occasionally, we glimpse a woman drawing water from a well or pounding grain. Otherwise, it seems the land is so bountiful and rich that even the wives and daughters of farmers can remain inside to weave and embroider.

Miss Zhao engages me in conversation, inquiring about my daughters and husband. I'm truthful about my daughters and circumspect about my husband. Maoren and I are lucky to have love for each other, but I'm still hurt that he would send me from our home and my responsibilities to our daughters—and what I hope is a son inside me—in his pursuit of glories for the Yang family. Miss Zhao considers what I've said—and left unspoken—and makes a suggestion. "You should write to him." She would not have maintained her station, precarious as it is, all these years if she weren't sophisticated in the ways of men and their families. "You don't need to share endearments, although they won't hurt."

"But how would I send a letter? The mail system is for the emperor and government alone."

"You could hire a courier. Or you could wait to see if the palace will send a letter for you." She watches me consider these possibilities. "The main thing is to show your husband and your mother-in-law that you kept him in your heart despite the time and distance apart."

But when I try to compose a letter, I find myself at a loss for words because all I want to write is *I want to go home. I want my baby to grow well and safely. I want to give birth to a son.* I give up and don't write again.

Another time Miss Zhao asks if I'm looking forward to seeing Meiling. "You've always been close," she says. "This will be a way for the two of you to spend time together."

And because she's known us for so long, I'm able to confide my moment of jealousy about Meiling's appointment. Miss Zhao's expression is unreadable when she says, "I'm disappointed in you. You were born into a good family. Your only tragedy was the death of your mother. A hair off your arm is thicker than a man's waist when compared to someone who started out as poor as Meiling. You should be happy for her success."

Miss Zhao's words remind me of one of a Snake's worst attributes: envy. I feel color rising in my face, but she isn't finished.

"*A friend without faults will never be found*," she recites. "Many women call themselves friends, but one day the wind blows east and the next day the wind blows west. I never thought you would become a fickle or petty person. Especially not with Meiling."

For a moment I'm taken aback. *Who is a concubine to criticize me?* But of course I know the answer. Miss Zhao is the closest person I've had to a mother in my life.

"Thank you, Miss Zhao. You've reminded me of an important lesson. *Distance tests a horse's strength; time reveals a person's heart.* You've always been loyal and kind to me. Please know I'm grateful."

Her response is yet another lesson. "You've placed that aphorism on the wrong person. Perhaps you should think of it in regard to Meiling. When she was sent thousands of *li* away from home, who did she think of first to share in her good fortune?"

———

When we first began traveling north the changes in the landscape were gradual. Now, three weeks into our journey, each day the weather is colder and wetter. The few villages we pass look small and sad. There is little grass, and no evidence of the five grains planted. Poppy has become so bored with the scenery that she prefers to stay in our room. Not me, even though the rain pours down. I need fresh air. Miss Zhao and I dress as best we can against the weather and join the tiller woman under an oiled canopy, where she steers the boat. I'm surprised when she addresses me directly.

"I've overheard your bodyguards speak of you as a doctor," she ventures.

It's a strange turn of phrase. "Speak of me?" I ask.

The tiller woman raises a shoulder, conveying that the men were not talking about me with respect. She lets me absorb the wordless message, and then asks, "Would you ever consider treating a woman such as myself?"

I worry that the bodyguards might report me to my husband and mother-in-law and decide this would not be a prudent idea, but Miss Zhao says, "Of course she will. Doctor Tan looks at a woman and sees a woman—no matter her status. I speak from experience."

I'm not sure what touches me more—that Miss Zhao has called me Doctor Tan or that she appreciates the relationship we built after Respectful Lady died.

"I have no way to pay you," the tiller woman confesses.

Again, Miss Zhao speaks on my behalf. "You can thank her by giving us safe transport."

As I begin the Four Examinations, I realize I've taken in more about the tiller woman than I was consciously aware. This tells me that I'm observing and absorbing even when I'm not focused. Grandmother would be pleased.

My questioning reveals that the woman recently turned forty, so she is still in her rice-and-salt days, as I am.

"What's your main complaint?" I ask.

"I've had numbness in my hands for six years." She pulls one of her hands from the tiller, holds it up to my face, and squeezes it into a fist, then releases it, repeating the movement several times in a row. "I'm on this deck through every season. Sometimes I'm in the north during brutal freezes. Summer heat should bring relief, except that on most days I'm standing in the drenching rains of the monsoon."

"Has anyone or anything helped?" I ask.

She tightens her jaw. "I have seen street doctors only."

A couple more questions and a few minutes feeling her pulse

give me a possible answer. "The numbness in your hands is a Wind-Damp ailment. When we stop at the next station, come to my room."

The next time our vessel docks and the boatmen are occupied with bringing new supplies aboard, the tiller woman visits Miss Zhao and me in my cabin. The way she looks around at the modest accommodations suggests that she's never been allowed to enter a passenger's room, let alone sleep anywhere so nice. I have her lie down and treat her with moxibustion on eight points to warm her channels, dry her dampness, and stimulate her qi and Blood. When I announce that the treatment is complete, she sits up.

"I feel better?" That she asks this as a question—as if she doesn't believe the relief she's feeling—confirms for me that the treatment is already working. "How can that be?"

"*When there is pain, the body has no freedom of movement. Without pain, the body is free.* My grandmother taught me that."

The tiller woman stares at her hands uncertainly as she opens and shuts them. "Will it last?"

I lift my chin. *Of course.*

At the door, the tiller woman bows formally as if she grew up in a fine household. "*A woman who helps others helps herself.*"

To which Miss Zhao adds, "Our dear doctor has yet to take this lesson fully into her heart."

———

Five weeks after leaving Wuxi, we're rowed into Beijing as night falls. On the wharf, men and animals haul heavy loads. Guards in military dress carry torches, while others stand at attention with their spears and swords on display. They are far outnumbered by beggars, who crowd every cranny. The air stinks of manure and garbage. And it's brutally cold. Miss Zhao steps onto the dock, trying to conceal her distaste. I do not need the skills of a spiritualist to read her mind: *This is not Shanghai.*

An hour later, we're presented to Lin Ta, the eunuch in charge of the Lodge of Ritual and Ceremony. "You will answer to me when you are here or within the palace walls," he says. "Do you understand?"

Miss Zhao and I nod. Poppy is somewhere, already unpacking our trunks.

"Those of us who run the lodge not only select doctors, midwives, and wet nurses to serve in the Forbidden City but also dispatch punishment," he continues.

I keep my eyes lowered out of respect and because I'm afraid I would stare too hard at the eunuch. My few dared glimpses show me he matches the descriptions I've heard whispered about his kind. Without his three precious things, his voice is high. Although Lin Ta is tall and thin, his flesh hangs loose on his face and his opulent robes can't hide the layer of fat that droops from his waist as though he were a woman who has reached sitting-quietly days.

"Do not steal," he intones. "Do not lie. Do not gossip. Do not think too highly of yourself."

Miss Zhao and I don't say a word.

"Most important," he goes on, "do nothing that might inflame or arouse undesirable emotions in the ladies of the imperial household—"

"We would not do that." I'm not accustomed to being spoken to in such a dismissive manner, and the words have flown from my mouth before I could stop them.

Lin Ta ignores my outburst. "Punishments include expulsion from the palace, flogging, and beheading. Your family will be required to pay restitution, as well as reimburse the palace for all expenses accrued during your visit to the capital—whether you are dead or alive." He looks us over. "You are protected here, so your bodyguards will remain on your boat until I receive the order to send you back to Wuxi. Do you have any questions?"

Miss Zhao and I shake our heads.

"Tonight I will send food to your room," he says. "Tomorrow morning, you'll be taken to the Great Within—those rooms in the palace reserved exclusively for women. Please dress appropriately. Now follow me."

I've been told that eunuchs have a peculiar walk that makes them recognizable even from a great distance. This turns out to be true. Lin Ta leans slightly forward. He keeps his thighs close together as he takes short, choppy steps, with his toes turned outward. We women trail an aroma from our feet. Lin Ta smells of leaking urine.

Once he sees us to our room and closes the door behind him, Miss Zhao whispers, "I've heard that the Great Within has the largest private gathering of women anywhere in the world. The empress, the ladies of the royal family, and thousands of concubines all serve the Imperial Presence. The spoutless teapots guarantee that any child born in the Great Within is the emperor's alone."

"I'll never be as informed as you, Miss Zhao, but please don't repeat the words *spoutless teapot* again. Or *tailless dog*. Even I know these are the worst things you can call those creatures. Maoren says eunuchs are powerful—"

"They are watchdogs and spies!"

"So refrain from using either epithet while we're here as we don't know the punishment for insulting a eunuch."

"Your caution is well taken," Miss Zhao says.

The next morning, we wake to the quiet of snowflakes falling from the sky. Poppy helps us bathe and dress in our finest, most elegant clothes. Then Miss Zhao and I drape ermine-lined cloaks over our gowns and leave the room. Considering how many women must serve the thousands of ladies in the Forbidden City, the halls in the Lodge of Ritual and Ceremony are surprisingly silent. I peer at Miss Zhao out of the corner of my eye. She looks unsettled, telling me this is not what she expected either.

We step into the courtyard. I hate the cold, but I can appreciate the brutal purity of it. Snowflakes dance in the air, carried by the wind. Icicles hang like ivory chopsticks from the eaves.

"It's rare for snow to come so early here in the north," Lin Ta says in greeting. Crystalline flakes catch on his eyelashes as he looks upward. Then he returns his gaze to me. "I've had coal-heated foot and hand warmers placed in the carriage to make your ride more comfortable."

I appreciate the gesture, but the warmers do little to keep us from shivering. The windows in the carriage are covered by curtains, so we see nothing. We stop a couple of times. "Women for the Great Within," the driver says to those I presume to be guards. "Let us pass." We arrive at our destination, and a eunuch opens the door to the carriage. We're already inside the Forbidden City, surrounded by protective walls four stories high and painted the color of dried blood. Miss Zhao and I are escorted through gate after gate—each one guarded by a pair of elephants. *Live* elephants. We reach the Eastern Palace, where the women of the imperial household live. I see the usual marble terraces, except they are many times the size of those in the Garden of Fragrant Delights. Every beam and rafter is carved and painted. The courtyards don't have the lushness with which I'm familiar. Instead, they're paved and stretch wide and empty under clean white blankets of snow. Eunuchs are everywhere, many of them little boys. What surprises me most is that we see no women. Where are the ten thousand beauties we've heard rumored live here?

"Wait," the eunuch orders. He steps through a door. Miss Zhao and I seek each other's eyes. I reach out and touch her sleeve, trying to send the message that I'm glad she's with me.

The door swings open, and the eunuch motions for us to enter. We glide into a grand hall that could look austere in the severity of its architecture but for the embroidered hangings on the walls and the colorful silk carpets that unfurl underfoot. Perhaps twenty women sit in repose. Each is beautifully dressed in a long, flowing gown, with her hair piled high on her head and decorated with many ornaments and pins. They sit like open petals around a woman who presses a compress to her eyes. She must be my patient, who I see is also pregnant and farther along than I am. I suspect she might be an adored concubine. My vision next falls on Lady Liu and Widow Bao, each of whom nods in acknowledgment of my arrival.

A woman rises and begins to approach. She wears a gown of red damask and a black silk sleeveless jacket with scalloped borders. Her hair rises in an elaborate constellation of buns from which artificial flowers and kingfisher feathers sprout. Her steps are so light and ethereal it's as if she's floating across clouds. She looks radiant, as though she's swallowed a cupful of stars. Perhaps only a doctor such as myself would discern the signs that she's also full with child: the unique glow to her cheeks, the slight sway to her hips, the way she unconsciously keeps one hand on her belly as she walks. When she nears, I recognize who she is. Meiling.

A Snake always sheds its skin.

Meiling sees my confusion and smiles in greeting. "It's the custom for midwives and wet nurses to dress and be coiffed in the fine fashions of the court. Did you expect me to be in sackcloth? I would not be allowed to come inside the Forbidden City, let alone to attend to the empress."

The empress?

With that, Meiling opens her palm and glides her arm in the direction of the woman at the center of the blossom of the ladies of the court. "Empress Zhang, the Compassionate One."

Miss Zhao instantly drops to the ground to perform obeisance. I hesitate for a moment and see the woman I thought was a concubine languidly remove the compress from her eyes. In a second, I'm on the floor next to Miss Zhao.

A voice as mellifluous as water streaming over pebbles says, "The two of you may rise." Once we're on our feet, the empress speaks again. "Welcome to the palace."

The Great Within

I keep telling myself that the empress is no different from any other woman I might treat, but of course she is. She dresses in clothes embroidered with gold and silver thread. The decorations in her headdress are made of precious jewels. Her makeup is exquisitely applied each morning by a trio of young female artists. Everyone was wrong about how many women the emperor keeps in the palace. It is not thousands or even hundreds. The Hongzhi emperor has but one wife, and that is Empress Zhang. She spends most of her days in the special hall where I first saw her in the Great Within, but she prefers that I treat her eye infection in the privacy of her bedchamber, which is filled with furnishings made by the finest artisans in the land. I am to call her the Compassionate One, but I have not yet seen this aspect of her character.

"The Compassionate One's infection is much better today," I tell her this morning, my fifth in the capital. "It's a shame that it was allowed to fester for so long—"

"Many months," the empress says with a shake of her head. "But you've finally built the path to wellness."

"As soon as you're fully recovered, my party and I will return to Wuxi." I bow my head. "I'm grateful to have served you."

Empress Zhang smiles. "You will not be leaving so quickly." She smooths her hands over her belly. "As you traveled here, Lady Liu, Widow Bao, and the midwife all spoke highly of your skills in helping to create a slippery birth. As the mother of the next emperor, I listened. I would like you to stay."

"There are many fine doctors in the capital who I'm sure would be more capable—"

"Please don't be modest."

"I'm full with child—"

"And so is the midwife. The three of us can be pregnant together."

I remain silent.

"If you help to create a slippery birth, then I should have no difficulties during my labor and delivery." She pauses to consider. "I will put this another way. I am the empress. I don't expect to have *any* problems during labor, but I will be reassured to have a woman doctor, who has given birth herself, present as the next emperor enters the world."

I drop to my knees and put my head on the floor. "It would be a great honor," I say. Inside, however, I'm torn apart. I've done what I was summoned to do, and now I must stay longer? I fight myself to keep from crying.

After we're done with today's treatment, I follow the empress at a respectful distance as she walks to the main hall in the Great Within. When we enter, everyone—from the fine ladies down to the boy eunuchs—pays obeisance. After the empress waves them back to their feet, the women resume their activities, which are the same things we do at home—embroidering, playing chess, working with brush and ink. Widow Bao and Lady Liu smile in my direction. They look pleased with themselves, and I should be grateful for their recommendation. Meiling sits with them, staring at her hands. In addition to the dismay I feel about not being able to travel back to Wuxi, I'm hurt that she must have known this imperial order was coming and didn't warn me. I'm desperate to talk to her, but we have not had a moment alone together. Perhaps she's been avoiding me. Or not. Whatever the reason, for now I must keep my thoughts and emotions to myself.

The day unfolds as it did yesterday and the day before that with games, meals, music, and the empress telling stories. The hall is cold, and servants stay busy keeping the braziers going. We wear fur-lined coats or capes to stay warm. Meiling has built a strong connection to the empress, which is exactly how it should be. Meiling and I learned this custom on the day we met years ago in Lady Huang's chambers. Grandmother insisted that a laboring woman will always do better when she's comfortable with the midwife who will catch her baby. The difference between what happened in the Mansion of Golden Light and what happens in the Forbidden City, however, is great. Midwife Shi didn't dress to match Lady Huang. Here, Meiling is expected to attire herself to be in harmony with the surroundings. All her clothes, shoes, and hair ornaments have been given to her. But what's most impressive is that she moves comfortably among these women, including the empress, which shouldn't be surprising given that the two of us have spent so much time together over the years.

In the late afternoon, after the empress retires to her quarters, I wait for Meiling to say her goodbyes so we can ride back to the Lodge of Ritual and Ceremony together. As soon as we're seated in the carriage, Meiling takes my hands.

"I didn't know you were with child when I spoke to the empress about you. I never would have suggested you if I'd known. Please, Yunxian, don't be angry with me." She stares into my eyes. "I'm sorry."

As upset as I am, I can see she means what she says.

"I didn't realize *I* was pregnant until I was on the boat coming north," she goes on. "If I'd known, I wouldn't have come either."

"It is a sadness that your husband won't know your good news until you return home."

"Can we try to look at this another way? To see the positive in this situation? You and I appear to be at similar points in our pregnancies."

"Our babies should come about two months after the empress gives birth, so perhaps we can journey home before we enter our months," I optimistically suggest.

She lowers her voice and turns her gaze to the floor. "We can't do that. We'll need to stay here when the empress does the month."

She's right, of course. I try but fail to hide my disappointment. "I understand, and I understand what that means for us. By the time the empress finishes doing the month, we'll both be entering the month. We won't be able to travel home then. It would be too dangerous. We'll deliver our babies here and do our months in the lodge before going home."

Meiling sighs. "Again, I'm sorry."

I pull one of my hands from hers and pat her face. "At least we will be together."

———

After being in the capital for a month, I have a better sense of where I am. The Forbidden City is not yet one hundred years old, and every day I'm awed by its magnificence: the massive walls, the grand terraces, the imposing halls. Each courtyard has a colony of huts where eunuchs live and can easily be summoned. Boy eunuchs under ten years of age are considered "thoroughly pure," and I now understand Lady Liu's earlier reticence in talking about them. A woman of her delicacy would not want to discuss the intimate work they do for the women of the empress's inner circle. The boy eunuchs change the cloths the women wear during their monthly moon water, wipe their mistresses' behinds over chamber pots, and see to perfuming a woman's feet when she knows her husband will be seeking her company. Although the empress has offered several boys to serve me, I've declined. When you are carrying a child and hoping for a son, you do not want to think about slicing off those very items that make him a boy. Otherwise, I've grown accustomed to the comings and goings at the Lodge of Ritual and Ceremony, where midwives, wet nurses, and I sleep. Eunuchs no longer distress my eyes with their appearance or insult my nose with their smell. They are a nuisance, though, filled with a sucking need for power . . . and an appetite for corruption. Most of my interactions are with Lin Ta, who has requested that I meet with women who come to the lodge to seek positions in the Great Within.

Although I'm confined to the Great Within and the Lodge of Ritual and Ceremony, Miss Zhao, as nothing more than my chaperone, has been able to move with appropriate caution and transportation through the alleys and byways of the Central Borough—an area protected by its own walls and gates bracketing the Forbidden City's grounds. She has told me of boulevards lined with shops, food stands, teahouses, and wine emporiums—all decorated with red lanterns and signs in gilt. My father's concubine, who's seen far more of the outside world than I ever will, has said on more than one occasion, "Beijing is not as backward as I first believed. Yes, all that is unique or valuable comes from the south, but the people of this desolate outpost have made good use of our bounty." Almost daily, she has another insight: "Although the Hongzhi emperor is traditional in his thoughts and deeds, women have more opportunities in Beijing than where we come from. Here you can find women who are moneylenders and merchants. And the empress's doctor is a woman! You! And think of all the wet nurses and midwives who will benefit for years from the palace's beneficence."

It's true. As Grandmother used to say, a midwife can be rewarded with clothes, jewelry, position, and power that will visibly tell the world of her success. She might even end up with an aristocratic title. I will receive some of the same gifts, but this is a unique opportunity for Meiling. No wonder she's so happy. As for me, I miss my daughters and my husband. I even miss Lady Kuo and her *keeck, keeck,* Miss Chen and her selfish ways, and the other women of the inner chambers in my married home. Mostly, I wish I could have my baby within the safe walls of the Garden of Fragrant Delights.

Meiling saves me from my gloomiest thoughts. Each evening when we return to the lodge, we have dinner together—sometimes just the two of us, sometimes with Miss Zhao. We're both careful to eat all the correct foods and avoid those that could cause a girl to be born. After the meal, Meiling and I usually retire to her room. Over the years, she's had many opportunities to see how I live. She knows the carvings on my marriage bed. She understands the placement of the herbs I keep. Now it's my turn to see into her life. Her room is identical in size and furnishings to mine, but the differences in our Snake personalities are everywhere. A lacquer-framed mirror stands on her dressing table. Rouge-stained puffs of cotton lay across the tabletop in casual disregard. The fine clothes she's been given to wear in the empress's presence are treated no better than if they were made of muslin, but the way she drapes them over the back of a chair or across the bed looks luxurious, creative, carefree. She lights candles instead of oil lamps, setting the room in golden flickering hues.

As I do every night, I perform the Four Examinations on her. By my estimation, we are both about to enter our sixth month of pregnancy. Meiling's energy is high, and she seems to be thriving. She looks healthy—with color in her cheeks, her hair shiny, and the flesh along her arms moist and plump. Her pulse sounds strong at every level, signaling that both mother and fetus are doing well. She smells of perfume, but it's not there to hide sourness. I discern no rough waters in her emotions. I watch to make sure she drinks every drop of the Blood-warming decoction I've made for her. Once I'm satisfied, she loosens the sash that keeps her gown closed. I do the same. We move to the bed, where we rest against pillows, with a tea tray between us. We take down our hair and let it flow free past our waists. Our jade and gold hairpins lie scattered about us as though we were a married couple after bedchamber affairs.

"I wish we were home," I say.

"No mother wishes to give birth outside her own room," she admits. "But you can do this easily because you are brave. And you have me."

"Not brave. Not brave at all."

"If I'm not worried, then you shouldn't be either." Her voice is dreamy when she adds, "Fate spoke when it allowed us to become full with child at the same time. If it's our destiny to give birth far from home, then we must accept that. There are many midwives here in the lodge, and I won't be afraid if you're nearby."

She's right. More midwives reside in the lodge than Miss Zhao and I originally suspected, but not the number that would be required if the emperor had multiple wives and hundreds, if not thousands, of concubines.

The corners of Meiling's lips lift. "You've taken as good care of me as you have the empress."

"My concern for you will always be greater than for anyone else."

Meiling lifts the tea tray and sets it on a side table. Then she slides against me and rests her head on my shoulder. The heat of her body seeps into me. I wouldn't move for anything.

"This experience won't change your life," she murmurs, "but it's already changing mine. For once, you and I are equals."

"It is a great happiness—"

"Oh! The baby! Feel!" She takes my hand and puts it on her stomach. My baby has his favorite spot to torture me, but every night Meiling's baby entertains us with its pushing, kicking, head-butting, and who knows what else.

"If it's not a son who's already practicing running with a kite on a string," I say, "then it's a daughter who'll be as light on her toes as the Tiny-Footed Maiden."

"If it *is* a girl, will you help me bind her feet?" Meiling asks. "I want her to marry into a good family."

"Of course. And if you have a son, I will ask Maoren if the boy can attend our school in the Garden of Fragrant Delights. The tutors we employ are exceptional." I leave unspoken that it's not unheard of for a family such as mine to invite the sons of poor relatives or friends to benefit from a clan's generosity. "If I'm also given a son, then the two boys can become study partners from the first days of practicing their calligraphy until the day they arrive in the capital to take the exams."

"If we both have daughters, I hope they'll be as close as we have been."

"And will always be."

"If one of us has a son and the other has a daughter—"

"Are you already thinking about a matchmaker?" I say it lightly and hope she takes it the right way, because as much as I love Meiling, this match could never happen—not even if her daughter has a pair of perfectly bound feet.

"Let me dream, Yunxian. Let me dream."

Poppy, realizing I'll spend the night here again, arranges coals under the kang and feeds the braziers. She makes a little nest for herself with her satchel of clothes and the box she brought with her from Wuxi. (Sometimes I wake in the night and see her sitting over her belongings, going through them as though there'd be something I might be tempted to steal. Just the thought makes me smile.) Next to me, Meiling's body relaxes against mine as she drifts to sleep. Her breath deepens and her expelled air passes warmly down my chest and floats out over my hands. I should wake her, so we can change into our nightclothes. Instead, I run my fingers through the ends of her hair, smoothing the strands against my thigh.

I stay awake a long time, as I often do, and let my mind wander over the possibilities and improbabilities. Meiling and I may share similar status in the Great Within, and I only want the very best for her, but our lives are different. Nothing will change that, even if we wish it so. And I worry . . . Just as the phoenix rises from the ashes—and as Meiling has risen in status—there is another truth: *The higher you fly, the more crushing the fall.* I keep my eyes open just long enough for the first wick to burn out and for the golden light in the room and the sparks in my mind to dim.

———

Night follows day and day follows night. A second month has passed since Miss Zhao and I arrived in Beijing. Empress Zhang has entered the month and could go into labor at any time. Meiling and I will enter our months in another four weeks. I will spend my month not in confinement as a lady but as a working woman like Meiling. My emotions have continued to be in turmoil. I constantly remind myself of Grandmother's warnings about my weaknesses. Meiling is alert to them too. I struggle not to get despondent or sick, and I must thank Meiling for watching over these innate failings of mine just as I stay vigilant for anything that could cause harm to her or her baby.

Today we're gathered in the Great Within, and the empress is telling one of her favorite stories. Meiling sits nearby. She looks pale. Until last week, I'd never seen her look so happy or content. Then something shifted, and two days ago she began vomiting. We think morning sickness occurs only in the first three months, but for some women it can appear at any time—all the way up to and through labor. I'll adjust her formula tonight, but for now I must turn my attention to the empress.

"My husband is the only emperor in the long history of China to have just one wife and no concubines," she says in her usual elaborate way. She cracks a melon seed between her teeth, examines it, and then pops the morsel in her mouth. "Until the day he dies, I will be the only woman for him."

She likes to repeat the story, which means I've heard it several times since I arrived here.

"When my husband was a boy, his father kept thousands of concubines. His favorite was Consort Wan. The Chunghua emperor lost all interest in his wife, Empress Wu, who had already given him a son. Meanwhile, the consort struggled to get pregnant." Empress Zhang's voice lowers as she reveals what few outside the palace know. "Every time Consort Wan heard that another concubine was with child, she had that woman poisoned or secretly gave her herbs so she would miscarry. Empress Wu realized she and her son could be targets of the consort as well, and they went into hiding. Eunuchs and others protected them. When the emperor died, my husband ascended the throne. Consort Wan disappeared. No one has heard of her again."

While the story is from a previous generation, it's a reminder that Empress Zhang is attuned to palace intrigue and won't permit it. She looks around, taking in the women in her presence. "My husband is a follower of Confucius, Buddhism, and Taoism. He believes in rectitude and obedience. To honor his mother and all she did to protect him, he sets an example for the rest of the country—not just here in the palace. This is why today you find no concubines, consorts, or secondary wives in the Great Within."

Having the opportunity to oversee the empress's birth is without doubt a great honor, even if it doesn't come with the same rewards Meiling will receive. (This is as it should be. Meiling will be actively involved in the delivery, while I will attend only when the empress requests my presence or if a complication should arise.) I'll admit I wish I liked Empress Zhang more than I do. Although she can recite history and her place in it, I find her shallow. She's tantalized by a new purchase or gift, but her enchantment is short-lived. She immediately wants something else that's exotic or priceless—another multilayered headdress bedecked with jewels, a figurine of the Goddess Guanyin carved in ivory, a pair of life-sized marble lions. She enjoys the foods that come to the palace as tribute, but then needs my help with her resulting indigestion and sleeplessness. And yet . . .

She is still just a woman. She's as nervous about giving birth to her first child—who we all hope will be a son and the future emperor—as Meiling, a midwife with much experience. I'm a doctor, but I find both women look to me more for my personal experience, having gone through labor and successfully brought into the world three babies, albeit girls, than for the herbs they should take.

"Doctor Tan."

I shake myself out of my thoughts. "Yes, Compassionate One?"

"What ingredients does your family use for making mother's soup?" Empress Zhang asks. She's questioned me about this many times these past weeks, hoping, I believe, that I'll name something that will require her to dispatch men to find a rare ingredient. She is the embodiment of *One eye on the dish in front of her and one eye on the saucepan.*

"Everyone makes mother's soup a little differently," I answer. "Some add extra rice liquor to help bring in a mother's milk—"

"We have imperial wet nurses for that," she says with a sniff.

"Of course," I agree. "Others add extra ginger and nuts to the soup, which help a woman regain her strength after birth. I will make sure the cooks prepare a soup perfect for your particular needs."

But already she has lost interest. "Who wants to play a game?"

My baby pushes an elbow or knee against the inside of my ribs on the right side of my body. He likes this spot. (*He, he, he . . .* Maybe if I say it enough times, it will come true.) He's kicked or stretched on it so often that I feel sure the undersides of my ribs are black and blue. I push back against the bones with my palm and glance over at Meiling. She's lost in thought, with a hand on her belly.

Later, when I examine her, I'm troubled to find her pulse erratic. I review her formula. It is correct. I suggest that she stay in bed for a few days, which she does. On the fifth day, she rises, determined to return to the Great Within.

"I did not come this far only to fail," she murmurs. "You

know as well as I do that the empress must be comfortable with me when it comes time to catch her baby."

"Do you continue to have nausea? Any dizziness or pain?"

"I'm fine. Truly."

But she still looks pale to me.

———

During the empress's second week of entering the month, she goes into labor. To pass the time until she sends for me, I'm interviewing a woman who's applying to be an imperial wet nurse. She sits across from me, her soft white hands folded on the table before her.

"My husband is in the army and far away," she answers when I ask why she'd like the job.

"Your age?"

"I just turned nineteen."

"How many children do you have?"

"Three, and they have all nursed well."

Three children is the required number. In fact, she's met all the qualifications for a wet nurse: between the ages of fifteen and twenty, has proper deportment, married to someone in the military, has breasts that even through her clothes look plump with milk. She's quite pretty but would never be considered a threat to the empress for her husband's affections, not that the emperor is interested in anyone apart from Empress Zhang. Still, men are men . . .

"A wet nurse is considered a lifetime position," I say.

"I'd be honored to have this appointment. I don't know when or if I'll see my husband again. It's important that I provide for my family in case—"

"How lucky we are not at war," I say, but I've grown cynical enough to realize that the death of her husband is not what's on her mind. This assignment comes with even greater rewards than those bestowed on midwives and far more than are given to doctors.

Lin Ta enters, leans down, and whispers in my ear. I look at the woman across from me. "I'm afraid we'll have to continue this another day," I say, rising.

I hurry to my room to pick up the bag I prepared in advance of this moment. Then I follow Lin Ta as he leads the way to the carriage to take me the short distance to the Forbidden City. By the time I reach the Great Within, the empress's room has been emptied of everyone except for Meiling, two helper-midwives—Midwife Quon and Midwife Guo—and a few boy eunuchs to bring in water to heat on the brazier to help with the birth, make tea, and brew herbs, if needed. Empress Zhang nestles in the arms of the two helpers, her face constricting in concentration. She seems to be doing well, but when I glimpse Meiling's features, I sense something is wrong.

I kneel next to the women. My fingers seek the empress's pulse. It feels fine.

Meiling, sitting next to me, suddenly rounds her shoulders and hunches over her belly. She takes a breath and holds it. She keeps her lips sealed together in a reassuring smile, but the muscles in her face twitch with the effort it takes to maintain it. A few seconds pass. She exhales, and then says in a tight voice, "The empress has been in labor for six hours. She has done so well that she felt no need for you to come, but I thought you might like to attend anyway."

The empress grunts as a contraction hits her. As soon as it passes, she relaxes against the helper-midwives. I don't see anything out of the ordinary and am unsure why Meiling felt the need to summon me.

"This will most definitely be a slippery birth," Meiling says in that taut-as-string voice. "It won't be long before I ask the empress to get into position and grab the rope."

Again, Meiling bends forward. This time a hand goes to her stomach. I touch her shoulder to get her attention. She drags her eyes to mine. I see in them worry and fear.

"Compassionate One," I say, addressing the empress, "let me borrow the midwife for a moment so we can consult. We will return shortly."

I reach under Meiling's elbow and help her to her feet. Only with difficulty is she able to straighten. She smiles at the empress, but as soon as we turn away, her face twists in pain. I take her behind the screen that's been set up for me, and we sit on porcelain stools.

"You must be having teasing pains," I whisper reassuringly. "Many women experience these before a baby is due to enter the world. I did—"

"I'm a midwife. What I'm feeling is not that. My contractions are coming closer together. And . . ." She breathes in unsteadily. "They're getting stronger."

"Our babies aren't due for another two months," I say. "Let me take your pulse. You'll see. There will be nothing to worry about."

My fingers barely touch Meiling's wrist before I feel the galloping beat that signifies a woman already deep in labor. She closes her eyes as another spasm hits her.

"You need to go back to the lodge," I say.

Meiling shakes her head. "Never. Let me deliver the empress's baby and then we'll return to our rooms."

The empress groans. Meiling sets her face, rises, and returns to the empress. Breaking with tradition, I follow.

"Compassionate One," I say, "we are all women here. Although it's contrary to tradition, would you prefer I stay at your side? You are the empress and deserving of special treatment."

Empress Zhang nods, which means now I can watch over Meiling. I keep going over in my mind what could be wrong when her pregnancy has, until recently, followed a fortuitous path. The formulas I made for her were perfect. I'm sure of it. What she's experiencing now must be false labor. Once we get back to our room, I'll examine her and make adjustments to her herbs if need be.

After another three hours, Meiling stoops behind the empress. "Please grab the rope," she instructs. The empress, who is unused to obeying anyone apart from her husband, edges into position. In this moment, she's like any other laboring woman on earth—squatting, the space between her legs bulging, pain draining color from her features. I'm able to see the baby's head emerge, listen to Meiling's encouraging words, and watch as first one shoulder then the other push out, followed by a final swoosh as the torso, legs, and feet slip into the world. Meiling cuts the cord and carries away the newborn before the empress can see its sex.

"Is it the future emperor?" Empress Zhang implores.

Before Meiling can answer, she falters, still holding the baby in her arms. I hurry to her side and take the baby before her knees buckle.

"It's a boy," Meiling manages to get out before her body contracts into a ball.

The baby's arms jerk at their sudden freedom. His face twists into an expression of extreme unhappiness. His cry is healthy and strong. I quickly wrap him in swaddling, leave him on the table, and gesture for one of the boy eunuchs to come watch over the infant. The baby will be fine while I check on Meiling.

Across the room, the empress beseeches, "Let me see him. Let me see him," even as one of the helper-midwives catches the placenta before it hits the straw bedding. The boy eunuchs are uncustomarily quiet, and I realize it's because two of them have crept out of the room to relate the news of the birth to those with even bigger eyes and ears.

Meiling whimpers. She closes her eyes and shakes her head. "This isn't happening. Don't let it happen."

Her words are like fingers squeezing my throat. I was sure these were random pains . . . Maybe I should have insisted she stay in bed and keep her legs elevated . . . But she had to help the empress . . . There must be something I can do . . .

Meiling's struggles attract the empress's attention. "What are you doing over there?" Her voice obliges an answer, but I'm afraid to give it. "You! Find out what the fuss is about."

Midwife Quon crosses the room to us. She understands the problem immediately. "We need to get you out of here," she says as discreetly as possible. "Can you walk?"

"I'll try." But as Meiling rises, she screams as blood suddenly streams through her silk gown, and she collapses back to the floor.

"What is that commotion?" the empress demands.

Midwife Quon begins to pull away the layers of Meiling's clothing. I remember every caution my grandparents gave me about the polluting qualities of blood. I should recoil, but my concern for my friend has even greater force. Meiling screams again, and I take her hand.

"Don't let this happen, Yunxian," she moans. "Please, please, please . . ."

But there's nothing I can do to stop or even slow the inevitable.

"Help me sit up," the empress orders. "I want to see—"

Meiling cries out.

The other helper-midwife is attending to the empress, and the boy eunuchs have no duty to Meiling. Midwife Quon locks eyes with mine, wordlessly sending instructions. I support Meiling with my arms as her baby falls from the childbirth gate in a river of blood. It's a girl—a tiny blessing—and she is too small, too blue, and too still to be alive. I put a hand over Meiling's eyes, but she's already seen what cannot be unseen. Her body heaves with sobs.

Blood

Once we are back in the Lodge of Ritual and Ceremony, Midwife Quon insists that Meiling's childbirth gate be packed with clean gauze to stem the bleeding. I offer a roll of brand-new bindings made by the spinster aunts that I brought with me from home. "What a waste of something so precious," Midwife Quon comments when I hand her the untouched roll. Later, as I walk her to the door, I ask how she thinks Meiling is doing. The midwife looks away and says, "It's such a shame."

The next night when Midwife Quon stops by her lips stay clamped and she won't meet my eyes. I take this to be a bad sign. I think of all the times Meiling has taken care of me. Now it's my turn. She's lost a tremendous amount of blood, and her cheeks and lips have turned as white as marble. I dose her with a combination of herbs, trying to prevent infection and fever. Over the next two days, my fingers are constantly busy, monitoring the pulses in Meiling's wrists. I ask questions: Is she in pain? Is she hungry? Will she take a sip of tea? I get no response. Not a nod or shake of her head. Not a squeeze of my hand. She keeps her eyes closed even when I can tell from her breathing that she's awake. I don't sleep. I barely eat. I'm terrified that if I let down my guard for one minute, Meiling will slip away. And I still have no understanding of how this could have happened when I'd been so vigilant in my care of her.

"Meiling needs you to be strong," Miss Zhao says on the fifth day. "You should try to rest." I refuse, but Miss Zhao is insistent. "I'll be here. I'll watch over both of you."

I take Meiling's limp hand in mine and rest my head on the quilt. I'm drifting off when four men burst into the room. Two of them take positions with their backs to the door, spears planted on the ground. The other two come at Meiling and me. One of them pushes me aside. Then they grab Meiling by her elbows and drag her from the bed.

"What are you doing?" I scream, terrified, as Miss Zhao edges into a corner, her hands folded over her mouth.

Meiling tries to free herself, but she's small in stature and weak from all she's been through. From outside the room come cries of distress—the shrill tones from the eunuchs easily distinguishable from those of the midwives and wet nurses. Meiling's legs give out, and she sags in the guards' arms. The burlier of the two men motions to me and Miss Zhao. "You're coming too."

I can barely breathe, my fear is so great. Miss Zhao and I support each other as we're herded outside to two waiting palanquins instead of the usual carriage. Lin Ta stands with his hands hidden in his sleeves, his eyes averted. Meiling is pushed into the first palanquin. I'm about to follow her when one of the guards grabs my arm and holds me back. I don't dare try to shake myself loose, but I won't be separated from Meiling.

"Lin Ta," I say with a deep bow. "Please . . ."

He releases a hand from his sleeve and wordlessly waves away the guard. Before he can change his mind, I climb in next to Meiling, who's slumped against a corner of the palanquin. My body pulses, alive with an energy I've never experienced before, but Meiling is barely conscious.

By now I'm quite familiar with the journey that leads to the Great Within. This time we go in a different direction.

"Where are they taking us?" Meiling's voice is as insubstantial as a blossom left on a stone under the summer sun.

I shake my head.

The ride is extremely rough, with bumps and lurches, as if the bearers have intended to add to our suffering. When the palanquin lands with a hard thump, Meiling is nearly thrown from the seat. The door swings open, and a pair of hands reaches in and yanks her out. When I exit, I see we're in a courtyard before the entrance to a hall unknown to me. Miss Zhao descends from her palanquin and joins me as we follow the guards dragging Meiling. The back of her sleeping gown is blotted with fresh blood. She's too feeble to walk on her own, and the bare tops of her feet drag along the paving stones with her soles facing skyward. None of the men even bothers to glimpse at this profound nakedness, which tells me just how grave the situation is.

We enter the hall. Men in formal robes stand lined against the walls. In front of us on a raised platform are two thrones, one of which is occupied. The emperor . . .

Miss Zhao and I are pushed forward. When the man holding my shoulder lets go, I drop to the ground—Miss Zhao beside me—in total submission.

"I have striven to make the palace a place of good thought and proper acts." The emperor's voice is not at all what I might have imagined, *if* I'd ever given a moment's thought to it. He sounds like a regular man—like my husband or my grandfather—only the words he forms with his ordinary voice make my body shiver. "I have but one wife. Empress Zhang is the moon to my sun. One day long from now she will become the empress dowager, helping our son as he rules China. But you"—he lifts a finger to gesture at Meiling—"have offended her eyes with your vile act. I am outraged on behalf of the empress, who had to witness such pollution in the Great Within."

Meiling soundlessly weeps.

"I have discussed the offense with my counselors at the Board of Punishments, as well as with those who oversee the Lodge of Ritual and Ceremony," the emperor continues. "Together they have recommended that the offending party be immediately put to death. Since you are a woman, I see no reason to prolong your suffering in the ways that might serve as a caution to others. Decapitation will be swift and painless."

Just then a pair of double doors opens. The empress enters, followed by Lady Liu, Widow Bao, and some of the other ladies who provide company in the Great Within.

"Husband," Empress Zhang says with a formal bow. Then she mounts the royal dais and sits on her throne. One of the ladies arranges the empress's robes so they splay about her, making her look simultaneously small in the ocean of embroidered brocade and equal in dignity and power to the emperor. The other women fan out on either side of Miss Zhao and me.

"You should be with our son," the emperor says. "You should be doing the month."

"Yes, Husband" comes Empress Zhang's reply. "I have left my bed so I might appeal to you."

"Please continue."

When Empress Zhang begins, I realize she's about to reveal the side of herself known as the Compassionate One. I pray that it works.

"The midwife put the birth of the next emperor above the safety of herself and her child," the empress says.

"What does this matter when she insulted your eyes?"

"I beg you to show benevolence."

The emperor is not swayed. "I have made my decision."

Empress Zhang gestures to the line of women before her. "Each one of us implores you—"

With those words spoken, I find my courage. "I would like to say a few words on the midwife's behalf."

The emperor looks startled. Some of the men in their grand robes grumble their displeasure.

"Empress Zhang truly is the Compassionate One," I say. "And you are the Hongzhi emperor—the Emperor of Great Governance."

"Who is this?"

The emperor's question is not addressed to me, but I answer anyway. "I am Tan Yunxian, the doctor who oversaw the delivery of your son. I come from Wuxi. My father, grandfather, great-grandfather, as well as my uncle, have served the empire loyally for generations."

The emperor motions to someone, who approaches to receive instructions. This man then quickly scurries from the hall. I suspect he's gone to confirm all I've said, but I can't wait for verification before I'm allowed to continue speaking.

"I ask the Hongzhi emperor to consider this woman before you," I say, pointing to Meiling. "Imagine how she must have felt.

Imagine how the Compassionate One must have felt." I put my hands on my belly, and his eyes widen in recognition of what's hidden beneath the draping of my gown and robe. "See yourself as one of us in this condition. For one moment, imagine the creature inside ripping its way out of *your* body."

The emperor winces and looks away.

"That was happening to the midwife just as it was happening to me," the empress adds to stress the point.

"But the midwife continued her duties," I go on, "never once abandoning her responsibility to the empress. The midwife was prepared to give her life and that of her own baby. One did not survive. Do you now punish this woman who has already paid so much to do what was right and proper?"

The emperor has the grace to weigh my words, but I doubt they will change his mind.

Behind me, a small voice says, "Let the midwife live." I glance back to see who spoke and discover Lady Liu dropping to her knees and putting her forehead on the floor.

"Yes, let the midwife live." Widow Bao comes to her daughter-in-law's side. The widow is old. She has little to lose.

Then the other women are calling out. "Let the midwife live! Let the midwife live!"

A thin smile spreads across the emperor's face. Once silence falls over the hall, he says, "The midwife may live, but she must still be punished." He lets his words hang in the air. "She will be flogged thirty strokes. I also banish her from the capital for her remaining years. Last, the rewards she was to be given will be revoked."

The empress nods. "Let those transfer to Doctor Tan."

"You truly are the Compassionate One," her husband acknowledges.

As the guards drag Meiling away, Empress Zhang calls after them. "Be careful. Use a whip instead of a heavy rod. She is a pretty one. She has lost a lot and is about to lose even more. Let her keep her face."

Miss Zhao and I are returned to the lodge. Poppy brews tea for us, but the cups of liquid go untouched. Each minute feels like an hour. My body tenses each time I hear a footfall or a voice in the hallway. Finally, Lin Ta opens the door. A litter is brought in and set on the floor. Meiling is facedown, with her features hidden by long strands of hair that have come undone during her ordeal. Her right arm falls off the litter and lies lifeless on the carpet. The back of her gown, from her neck to her ankles, is saturated with blood in different shades and consistencies—from crimson to deep rust, from glassy wet where this precious life force continues to seep and ooze to lumps that are thick and clotted. Poppy, who knows the prohibitions about doctors touching blood, volunteers to remove Meiling's clothes.

"You can wait outside while I wash her," Poppy offers.

"I will do it," I say.

Miss Zhao hisses air through her teeth. Then, "I will stay and help too."

Meiling's gown is not just soaked. The whip shredded the silk. In some areas, the fabric needs to be pulled out of her flayed skin. As carefully as possible, Miss Zhao and I cut away the fabric, exposing the terrible wounds. The flesh is torn, with some gashes revealing glimpses of white bone. She's still bleeding badly from her miscarriage too.

"Poppy, we're going to need Midwife Quon," I say.

My maid disappears and returns with the midwife. She does not flinch or lose color. Blood is her business.

"Miss Zhao and I will see to Young Midwife's back," I tell her. "Can you—"

"Do you have more of those clean bindings?" Midwife Quon asks. "If we put her over a basin as we ordinarily would after birth, she'll bleed to death. I will repack her insides."

Poppy brings a bowl and fills it with boiled water. Miss Zhao's face is a mask of determination as she dabs at Meiling's back with a wet cloth. Each touch brings a whimper from Meiling. I open my chest of herbs, looking for ingredients to make teas, poultices . . . anything to help with her pain and prevent infection.

I return to the litter. All the silk has been removed. The damage to Meiling's back is the worst, but some of the lashes strayed down across her buttocks and thighs. It's too much for me to take in. I clench my jaw to fortify myself. I drop to my knees and use a finger to gently sweep the loose strands of hair covering the left side of Meiling's face. Not one part of the whip touched this cheek, and I can only assume the right side as well, for which I will thank the empress. But what startles me is that my friend's eyes are open, staring straight ahead. Respectful Lady lost the will to go on living when my two older brothers died. Now I see the same distance in Meiling's eyes.

I lean down and whisper in her ear. "You have a heart as strong as iron. You will survive. I will make sure of it."

———

When I was young, Grandmother told me stories of women who sliced pieces of flesh from their thighs to add nourishment to soups for ailing mothers-in-law or sickly sons. She spoke of wives so dedicated and loyal that they licked their husbands' festering wounds or sucked poisons from snake or insect bites. She praised the wife who stood in a snowstorm, freezing herself so she could lie beside her husband to relieve his fever. Those women used their bodies to show their loyalty. Now I use mine to prove my love to Meiling. Each morning I pierce a vein at my wrist, let the blood drip into a cup, add tea brewed with healing herbs, and hold it to her lips. During the day I keep my wrist bound with gauze. Even so, blood seeps through—like red ink stains—until evening, when I fully open the wound again and make Meiling another cup of tea enhanced with my life force.

I've received help from an unlikely person. Lin Ta came to me that horrible day and asked if I'd like him to send for a doctor who treats war injuries. "Not a bonesetter," he explained, "but a man familiar with wounds from spears, swords, and, yes, rods and whips." When I hesitated, he inquired about my knowledge of blood, exposed bones, and tattered skin and muscles. "How far down did the whip break through the soft parts on Young Midwife's back? Do you know how to reseal the skin? You need help."

The Hongzhi emperor has governed for just four peaceful years, so it wasn't difficult for Lin Ta to find an older man who'd treated men injured in battle. He cannot enter the Lodge of Ritual and Ceremony, but every night I meet him outside the back gate, where I share details of my patient's condition, and he instructs me. Of primary importance is what to do about Meiling's tattered flesh.

"You need to sew it back together," the doctor advises. The idea is appalling, but he gives me thread made from the fine fibers of white mulberry tree bark and a special needle to use. "For those areas too mangled to stitch, I suggest you search the corners of your room for spiderwebs. Keep them as intact as possible and lay them across the wounds. They work well to close that which does not wish to be closed."

The circumstances may be different between what happened to Meiling and what befalls a soldier, but I'm at war nevertheless. The fight I face is between healing and infection. I dab Meiling's back four times a day with astringent. When her flesh reddens or pus begins to ooze, I search my mind, looking for those herbs Grandmother taught me will help women in the most dismal of circumstances, knowing that despite the similarity of the injuries, a woman is not a man on a battlefield. She has cares and responsibilities a man will never know. I must also try to heal Meiling's emotions. Her mind is as scattered as grain dropped from a bucket. Some nights she's coherent; other nights she moans and weeps, sometimes crying out to imagined phantoms. More than once, she's grabbed my wrist and begged, "Let me die."

Between dawn and sunset, I leave Meiling in the care of Miss Zhao and Poppy so I can attend to the empress as she does the month. Empress Zhang proved she truly could be the Compassionate One when she saved Meiling's life, and I will be forever grateful for her actions, but she needs little from me and has shown less interest in her baby. He's in the care of a wet nurse, which has allowed his mother to play games with the ladies who keep her company.

My emotions are stirred as if on a turbulent sea. I'm nearly wrenched apart by my longing for my daughters, my husband, and my grandparents. I worry nonstop about Meiling. What if she dies by her own hand or through my inadequacies? Assuming she lives, will she blame me for the loss of her baby? If all this weren't enough, I doubt myself. How could I have missed that Meiling's problems were so serious? It makes me question my worth as a doctor of women, as a doctor of anyone.

Life Without a Friend . . .

My labor begins seven weeks after the birth of the future emperor. Meiling is still too unwell to help me, but I'm in the lodge and have Midwife Quon to assist the delivery. This is my fourth child, and my labor is swift. That is not to say I am without pain, but it's bearable. We follow all but two rules. First, I insist that Miss Zhao and Poppy remain in the room with me. Second, when the baby comes out and is snipped from my body, Miss Zhao quickly announces, "It is a boy."

My tears of happiness begin. I've accomplished my main duty as a woman: to provide a son who will care for the Yang family ancestors through offerings and prayers. Poppy puts him in my arms, washed and swaddled. He has a fine head of black hair. His mouth is pink and perfectly formed. I pull away the blanket so I can count his fingers and toes. Ten and ten. I count his three precious things. All there.

"It is not my place to give him his official name," I say, looking up at Miss Zhao and Poppy. "For now, we will call him Lian."

And suddenly, I am less a refined woman than I am a peasant who gives birth and then goes back to the fields the next day, because even though Empress Zhang has completed doing the month, she still insists I come to the Great Within.

"Congratulations on the birth of a son," Empress Zhang says when she sees me.

Widow Bao and Lady Liu echo these sentiments and present me with gifts large and small, some for the baby and some for me.

"I'm touched. Thank you," I say, but I ache, and I can feel blood seeping into the cloth folded between my legs.

"You have been a good companion," the empress says, "and the next emperor's birth was indeed slippery. As slippery as could be expected anyway." She laughs lightly, and the ladies of the court join in. "While I would enjoy keeping you here, you have my permission to return to Wuxi."

"Of course, no one would call it a gift to consign a woman to do the month on the Grand Canal." This comes from Widow Bao, who alone has the age and rank to say something of this nature in front of the empress.

It is neither right nor proper for women to do the month outside the inner chambers, let alone on the Grand Canal, but if I can see to the empress the day after giving birth, then surely I can take care of myself on a boat. I can get home sooner and tell my husband in person of the joyous arrival of our son even faster than if I send a courier. I sit up. Blood oozes, and I feel momentarily light-headed.

"The empress looks well today," I venture. "May I take your pulse? Will you drink the tea I've prepared?"

The next few days are challenging as plans are put into place for our journey home. Poppy begins to pack, while I perform my duties to the empress. Lin Ta assigns a wet nurse to feed my son during the day, but at night when I return to my room, I bring him to my breast. Lian's suckling causes the child palace to cramp and squeeze back into its original shape. I find this even more painful than the contractions of labor and certainly worse than what I felt after my daughters were born. My breasts ache with milk that doesn't have enough opportunities to be released, but I won't give up. As hard as I'm trying to tie myself to my son, my heart is never far from my friend.

"I would like to see your baby," Meiling announces. She's conscious enough to see my child no longer resides inside me. "Did you have a son?"

"I did. You can see him another time," I respond.

"I won't harm him, if you're worried about that."

"Of course you wouldn't, but let's make it another day." I worry that holding Lian will cause her both physical and emotional pain.

"I understand." After a moment, she continues. "I thought when you joined me in Beijing you would finally see me as someone worthy, but I realize now that could never happen." She pauses. "You were a pearl in your family's palm. I'm merely a pebble that has been tumbled and smoothed to give a pleasing appearance, while inside I am but packed mud."

"Meiling—"

"No, listen. You've lived a life of purity and been rewarded for it with children. I've put my hands on the dead. I'm so polluted and fouled, how could a baby ever find nourishment in my child palace or sanctuary in my arms? Or maybe my sad fate is punishment for sins I committed in a previous life. Either way, how could you—a good mother—allow me to touch your son? You couldn't."

"You are neither polluted nor fouled. What happened is my fault. I missed something—"

She interrupts with a question. "Do you ever regret that your grandmother and my mother brought us together?"

I take her hand, the same one that has grabbed mine when she's begged me to let her die. "Never. Now try to go back to sleep. You must grow as strong as you can. In three days' time, we will leave this place. We're going home."

She begins to cry and shake. "What if Kailoo won't take me back?"

I smooth the hair from her forehead and then rest my palm there. She's still hot with a fever I have yet to break. "Don't doubt for a moment that he'll be happy to have you home."

"I—"

"You and Kailoo have a marriage I can only envy. He loves you with his heart and not out of duty."

She takes small panting breaths—like a child who's cried too long—but for now she's empty of tears.

On our last night in Beijing, Midwife Quon comes to check

on Meiling and says she can switch from packing to the regular padding we use for monthly moon water. I spoon-feed Meiling a soup of pickled bamboo shoots, chicken skin, and jujubes, knowing these foods will provide both warmth and healing properties. Poppy quietly packs the last of our things. She seems despondent. I would have thought she'd be eager to return to the Garden of Fragrant Delights.

In the morning, Lin Ta accompanies our palanquins and donkey-pulled carts to the dock, where our boat and people have waited for us all these months. Poppy carries my son, while our bodyguards help Miss Zhao and Meiling board the boat. The tiller woman escorts the traveling party to the cabin we'll once again share. Seeing the familiar faces fills me with quiet joy. We're going home.

I'm required to stand with the eunuch to watch as my imperial gifts of gratitude are loaded onto the boat, giving me a preview of the rewards that I alone have received as a result of this journey: ten pecks of rice and many catties of coal; several kinds of edible delicacies—tea from the farthest reaches of the empire, lingzhi mushrooms for prolonging life, and fiery mao-tai for the men to drink in their celebrations; bolts of cloth (originally from our province); furniture, lanterns, bamboo screens, and bronze braziers and other ceremonial vessels; ceramics for every purpose; jade and ivory eating utensils; brushes, ink, rice paper, and books; rain hats and oil-paper umbrellas; and strings of cash, and gold and silver in the form of ingots and jewelry. Information about a royal allocation of land to the Yang family has, apparently, been sent ahead by sealed decree.

Lin Ta gives me a wry smile. "You're returning home with sumptuous gifts, while Young Midwife is lucky to still be breathing."

"It's neither right nor fair."

Lin Ta glances around to make sure no one is listening, and whispers, "If it were me, I might use some of the time on the boat to inspect my gifts. They might be better redistributed into more manageable jars, chests, and other containers."

"You've taken my desire and phrased it in a manner both

polite and discreet," I say, for I was already hoping to reorganize some of my spoils so they might be siphoned off to Meiling upon our arrival in Wuxi.

Lin Ta raises his voice back to a normal level. "The boat is well stocked with live poultry, wheat noodles, tofu, and walnuts. Your meals will be easily made from these ingredients, which will mean fewer stops on your way home."

"I thank you for your kindness," I say. "Maybe one day I can repay your hospitality and generosity."

He's clearly touched, but he waves away the idea. "No need. No need."

I stay on the deck until the dock disappears behind a curve in the canal. I don't feel ready to go to Meiling and the others. I make small talk with the tiller woman, who holds up her hands and wiggles her fingers.

"I'm fully recovered!" she exclaims.

"Indeed, you are."

"I now have so much energy it's put the boatmen on edge," she confides. I had not anticipated this problem. She doesn't seem to care, though. "Let them cower from a woman with a renewed spirit. Let them call me feisty. I'm still the boss who pays them." She pours a cup of tea from an earthenware jug, hands it to me, and says, "Here. Sit awhile."

We drift into silence as the outskirts of the capital slide past. I hear a cry from my son and feel my milk let down. I'm about to go to him when another boat glides north past us. A eunuch in full court regalia stands on that deck. Armed with a bow and arrow, he takes aim and shoots at a man carrying a basket piled high with cabbages strapped to his back as he walks on the towpath toward the city. The peddler falls to the ground. From across the water, I hear the eunuch's high-pitched laughter. The man onshore stands. He pats his body to make sure he isn't injured and then begins to pick up his scattered cabbages. The eunuch draws his bow again and aims for another passerby. This time the arrow flies past the intended victim and disappears into a scraggly field. The eunuch reaches into his quiver for a third arrow. The Hongzhi emperor may be hoping to bring righteousness back to the realm, but he'll never succeed if members of the court would shoot at common men for amusement.

———

We have the wind at our backs, but some days it feels as though we're being propelled by a river of Meiling's tears. We spend most days inside, curtains drawn, with the only light coming from a single flickering lamp wick. Meiling usually wears one of the simple gowns she brought with her from Wuxi, and her hair is knotted into an unadorned bun. Both accentuate her thinness. I keep thinking about when I first saw Meiling upon reaching the capital. How happy she was . . . But happiness is transient. Yin and yang always struggle for balance, with the darkness of yin sometimes winning and the brightness of yang striving to bring things back into balance.

"I blame myself for Meiling's miscarriage," I confide to Miss Zhao one night as we sit together on the deck after I've nursed Lian. "I should have seen something was wrong."

"I doubt she blames you," Miss Zhao says.

"But I think she does."

"Then you should talk to her."

"It doesn't seem like she wants that."

"Are you sure? Have you tried?"

I haven't, but I've taken Meiling's silence for reproval. "How can she forgive me when I can't forgive myself?" I ask Miss Zhao as I adjust Lian in my arms. "Whatever she's feeling toward me is made worse now that I have a son. Every sound he makes must feel like another stab from a sword." I hesitate, afraid to reveal my deepest fear. "I don't know if a path can be found back to the trust and the deep-heart love Meiling and I first discovered as girls."

"Every minute of silence you allow to continue will push the two of you farther apart. *It takes a lifetime to make a friend, but you can lose one in an hour,*" she recites. "*Life without a friend is life without sun. Life without a friend is death.*"

I nod in acceptance of her wisdom. "Can you take the baby for a while?"

Lian doesn't even open his eyes as I transfer him to Miss Zhao. I return to our room and Meiling's seemingly unbreakable reserve. I tell Poppy to go to the deck. After she leaves, I sit on the edge of Meiling's cot. She rolls away from me. I put a hand on her ankle, hoping to send the message that I'm not going anywhere.

"I keep thinking about what I could have done differently," I begin, although it feels like I'm talking to the air. "I've reexamined everything I gave you and reviewed all the times I performed the Four Examinations on you. I should find a mistake—a fault in one of my formulas perhaps—but it eludes me. I wonder if what happened might be the working out of some destiny that is not clear to us. Perhaps something afflicted the baby—imbecility or a deformity. Can a miscarriage ever be looked at as a fortunate misfortune?"

"A fortunate misfortune?" Her voice comes to me as though from the bottom of a well.

"That wouldn't mean I'm not at fault," I add quickly. "I am, and I will surely pay for my errors in the Afterworld." She doesn't move a muscle. I take a breath and attempt to go on. "Your loss—"

"Stop!"

"I'm trying to apologize—"

She lurches to a sitting position so suddenly that I'm taken aback. Her eyes are filled with the same anguish I've seen in them since she first told me she was in labor. "This wasn't your fault. It was mine."

"You mustn't blame yourself—"

She shakes her head vehemently. "You have it all wrong," she blurts. "I was taking a formula made by Doctor Wong. What I took was meant for *you*. My selfishness protected *you*."

My body draws up, confused. "What do you mean? Doctor Wong prescribed nothing for me."

"But he did."

I wait, feeling that if I press her, she'll retreat back into silence. But once she begins to speak again, I wish beyond all wishing that I couldn't hear the words.

"Lady Kuo asked Doctor Wong to make his best formula to protect you and your baby in the final stage of pregnancy," she stammers.

"She gave me no such thing."

"Because she probably knew you wouldn't take it." Another long silence. Then, "She gave the herbs to Poppy."

"Poppy?"

"She was to make the formula and give it to you when you entered your seventh month. I stole the ingredients and made them into a brew for me instead." Meiling drops her head so I can't see her eyes. "So many sayings cover my greed and envy. *The sight of treasure provides the motive . . . A plan is born when a man is desperate . . .* But none is more apt than *Carelessness in putting things away teaches others to steal.* I knew where the ingredients were, and I took them. I wanted a baby so badly, but I lost the one thing I wanted as punishment for stealing what was meant for you."

Her confession doesn't make the waters any clearer. "Why would you take something meant for me, Meiling? Why?"

"I thought if it was good enough for you, then why shouldn't I take it?" She begins to weep. "Remember when my mother said that a Metal Snake can have an envious streak? I paid a price for my envy. My baby died."

I shake my head. "Something's wrong here. Doctor Wong and I may have different ideas about Blood-warming and Blood-cooling during pregnancy—and his prescription could have counteracted what I gave you—but that wouldn't have resulted in a miscarriage. Do you still have any of the ingredients? I want to see what he used."

With effort, Meiling rises from the bed, goes to one of her bags, digs through the contents, and returns with a silk pouch tied with woven cord. I open it and pour the contents on the quilt. As my fingers go from item to item, my heart feels as though it's dropping to the pit of my stomach.

"Well?" Meiling asks.

"Ox knee is often used to expel old monthly moon water or clear the child palace of lingering blood after birth," I answer, my throat tightening around my words. "But it can also be used on wives thought too sickly to carry a baby to term. Expelling the embryo gives the woman a chance to live."

Meiling draws a hand across her mouth as she takes this in.

I can hardly get the next words out. "And here are peach kernels."

"Yes. So?"

"They're in every abortifacient recipe." I avert my gaze as she absorbs this fact. "This is Tibetan crocus," I press on, "which is a Blood-moving medicine. Some women use it to regulate their monthly moon water, but it can also cause an abortion or miscarriage. If not taken properly, a woman can easily bleed to death, which you almost did. These tragedies would have happened to me too if I'd taken this formula."

The implications of what I'm saying cause Meiling to cry out, "But why?"

I don't know the answer, but there's someone on board who might. I leave Meiling sobbing on the bed. I return to the deck and ask Poppy to come with me. Miss Zhao follows, with my son in her arms.

When we get to the room, I look at Poppy. "Tell us about the herbs you were to give me."

My maid's face falls. It's as if she's been waiting for this moment and been dreading it. "I'm so sorry, Lady Tan, but I must have misplaced them."

Meiling, weak and broken, admits that she took the ingredients.

Poppy's eyes widen, her relief clear. I question her, and she answers.

"You were going far away, and Lady Kuo wanted you to deliver a grandson safely. She wanted you to live long enough to bring him home. I was to follow Doctor Wong's orders for preparing the tea and make sure you took it. He gave them to me."

Live long enough to bring him home? That's irksome, but I have to believe Lady Kuo thought she was doing what was best for me. That doesn't explain Doctor Wong's prescription, however.

"Why would Doctor Wong have given Poppy these ingredients unless he meant to do me harm?" I ask my traveling companions. "Or is he *that* inept?"

"We'll find no answers until we return home," says Miss Zhao, always a champion of logic and calm.

"As soon as we reach Wuxi . . ." I'll do what exactly? Confront my mother-in-law? Demand an answer from Doctor Wong? I force myself to regain my composure. "Wuxi is still weeks away," I say to the room at large. "Now that I know what Meiling took, I can use the time to figure out how better to treat her." I turn to my friend. "I'll start with herbs to end your bleeding and continue administering the Decoction of Four Substances and the Decoction of Two Aged Ingredients. I'll supplement the latter with cardamom to regulate your qi, calm your stomach, and increase your appetite, nut grass rhizome to settle and regulate your blood flow, and the immature fruit of bitter orange to promote wound healing. Does that sound all right to you?"

———

As we move south, the days get warmer. We're coming to the close of the fifth lunar month, and each hour brings increased heat and humidity. To find relief, our little party sits outside under a canopy and watches clouds scud across the sky. The slightly cooler air—and the changes in the landscape—are healing for my friend, though she still struggles with fatigue and listlessness. Often, after dinner, we return to the deck, where the boatmen silently pole or row us through the water. But on some nights, after my traveling companions fall asleep, I employ the tiller woman to help me go through my imperial gifts. I reallocate many of the items—textiles, home furnishings, and basic foodstuffs—into several large trunks and arrange with the tiller woman to have them sent to Meiling's home upon our arrival. I'm not sure how my friend will feel about this, but I hope these things will serve as tangible—and very visible—proof to her neighbors and would-be patients of the success she achieved in the capital. No one needs to know the truth of what happened, and, fortunately, they'll have no way to find out. Nor will they understand that the gifts she received are paltry compared to what, in my opinion, was due her for delivering the next emperor.

We know we've entered our province when we begin to spot orchards of oranges, pomelos, longans, and lychees. Other riches reveal themselves: ducks, geese, and pigs; stands of pines and bamboo; fields of rice, rapeseed, and other crops; mulberry leaves being plucked to feed silkworms; the smells of fish being dried in the open air and pots of rice steaming. When we're two days from Wuxi, our boat stops so a messenger can run ahead to let our families know we'll reach home shortly.

On the morning of our arrival, I rise early and step outside. The heavens appear as a low, glowing blanket of humidity. The hours ahead will be hot and miserable. I feed my son, eat a simple breakfast, bathe, and dress for my husband, not knowing if he'll be in residence in the Garden of Fragrant Delights, in Nanjing, or traveling. From one of the trunks filled with my gifts of gratitude, I put on a rose-pink dress over a pleated white skirt that does much to hide that I recently had a baby. Over this, I wear a black satin sleeveless jacket. My ensemble may not send the message of longing for the bedchamber, but it will tell my husband and his family I was successful in their ambitions for connections and rewards.

Men tie the boat to Wuxi's main dock. I had hoped to see my husband waiting for me. That he is not here to greet me and meet our son is a disappointment. Beside me, Meiling stretches her neck like a roosting goose looking for her gander. Not finding her husband, she appears hurt and confused. Three palanquins and several wagons, however, have been sent for our transportation. While the mood on the dock is more subdued and the activity far from being as bustling as I remember, plenty of men hop on and off the boat, yelling orders, hefting trunks. All of this makes our farewells feel hurried. Miss Zhao gets into her palanquin, the bearers hoist it, and in seconds she's on her way to my grandparents' home. I hold Meiling close.

"You're so lovely that you shame the flowers," I say. I mean it. Somehow the hardships she's endured have left her as beautiful and ethereal as a fairy in a dream. "Your husband will be happy to see you. Do you think your house is finished?"

"I'll go wherever the bearers take me. Whether it is to the tea shop or to our new home remains a surprise." She sounds wistful and uncertain when she asks, "Will you come see me?"

"As soon as I can. I promise."

Then she too is gone. *All the sorrows of the world arise from parting, whether in life or by death.*

I stay on the dock until the last of the cargo is unloaded and put on the wagons to be taken to their respective destinations. "When you reach the Garden of Fragrant Delights, take the trunks with my wardrobe and medicines to my bedchamber," I instruct the men as sweat trickles down the backs of my legs. "The rest is to be overseen by Lady Kuo."

I say thank you and goodbye to the tiller woman and then get into the palanquin with my baby. Poppy runs alongside us, as usual. I'm anxious to introduce Lian to my husband, and I'm ready for whatever form my confrontation with Doctor Wong will take, but another part of me senses something is wrong. I hear no merchants boasting about the attributes of their wares, no men shouting at each other to get out of the way, and no women calling above the street noises for their children to come home. Only the soft padding of the bearers' footfalls comes to me through the palanquin's walls. Indeed, arriving at the Garden of Fragrant Delights is not at all what I expect.

A Sapling in a Typhoon

No guards stand at the gate to greet me. I carry my son over the threshold and into eerie quiet. Not even the sounds of the women who sing at their looms reach us. I swiftly glide from the first to the second courtyard and keep moving. In the Courtyard of Whispering Willows, I find two men at the entrance to the garden for which the house is named. They draw back as I approach.

"Come no closer," one of them says.

"Her face is clear," the other man observes. Then to me, he orders, "Show us your arms."

With those words, my heart sinks. "Is it heavenly flowers disease?" I ask.

Silence gives me the answer. *Ailan . . . My baby . . .* Neither has been visited by the smallpox-planting master.

"Are the ill in the garden?" I ask.

"They've been put in the Hermitage," the first man answers. "We're here to keep anyone from leaving the garden."

"How many are inside?" I ask, gesturing with my head to the barred gate behind them. My breath is so ragged that each word comes out frayed and uneven. "Are there children? Any girls?"

The two men exchange glances. I'm not sure what this means. Maybe no one's been counting . . . Maybe there are too many to count . . .

My next question is the most important because the answer will tell me what has already happened and what is still to come. "How long has the pestilence been in residence?"

"The first cases appeared two weeks ago," one of the men answers, which means the worst effects of the disease have arrived.

I try to slow my racing heart. "Is my husband here?"

"Young Master Yang is in Nanjing."

Relief. He's safe, but then I'm drawn back into the frightening reality. I'm not brave enough . . . I'm not knowledgeable enough . . . I put three fingers over my lips. *Tap, tap, tap.* The motion is calming, while at the same time the pattern echoes the calculations I'm making—like moving the pieces on an abacus to arrive at a solution. I must protect my son . . . I must find my daughters . . . *Tap, tap, tap.*

I turn to Poppy. She is white with fear. I try to reassure her. "You have nothing to worry about. You already survived smallpox, as did I." She slowly nods, but I'm not sure she believes me. "Follow me."

I hurry to my chambers. Once inside, I give the baby to Poppy, who mutely stares at me.

"Keep him here," I tell her. "Do not leave for any reason, and do not let anyone in."

I exit the room, pull the door closed, and wait until I hear Poppy clamp the lock into place. I stay alert, placing each foot carefully in front of the last, not wanting to fall in my haste. When I reach my daughters' room, I try the handle. The door is locked, which I take to be a good sign. I knock and call to my eldest daughter in a low voice, "Yuelan."

I hear movement inside. Then close, so close, just on the other side of the door, Yuelan says, "Mama."

"Are you well?"

"Chunlan and I are fine, but Ailan . . ." Yuelan starts to cry. "We put her outside when the fever came. Someone took her to the garden."

With that, as filled with doubts as I am, I know what I must do. First, though, I try to bolster my daughters' spirits for whatever might come next.

"You did everything correctly," I say. "I'm proud to have you as my children. Don't ever forget that."

The wrenching sounds of my two oldest girls weeping follows

me down the corridor back to my bedchamber. Poppy unbolts the door and lets me in. I hurriedly scan my shelves, putting whatever herbs I think will be useful into satchels. When I tell her what I'm going to do, she starts to cry big, gulping sobs. I'm working hard to tamp down my own fear and have neither the time nor the will to comfort her. Poppy puts my satchels in the corridor, I take Lian in my arms, and together we go to my mother-in-law's room. I'm afraid that if I slow for even one second my insecurities will put up a blockade across which I won't be able to pass.

My mother-in-law's door is locked, but I hear her familiar *keeck, keeck*. She's alive.

"Lady Kuo," I call. "Lady Kuo."

Just as it was with my daughters, I hear movement inside.

"Yunxian?"

"Yes, it's me. I'm here."

She doesn't open the door.

"Many are sick." The way these three words roll from Lady Kuo's mouth tells me she's been drinking. "At first, we thought the children were simply suffering from childhood Fright."

This is a common mistake in the diagnosis of smallpox. The symptoms of Fright can range from fretfulness to crying, from refusing to nurse to turning away from or not keeping down food, from fever to convulsions, all of which can make their presence known long before the heavenly flowers pustules of smallpox erupt.

"Is Doctor Wong in the garden?" I ask.

For the first time, my mother-in-law says something critical of him. "He showed himself to be too much of a coward to enter." Then, "Yunxian, can you help?"

No cure exists for smallpox—either people live or they don't—but I promise to do what I can. I ask a few more questions, while trying not to reveal my trepidation. I have some requests, the first of which is that Lady Kuo must find a wet nurse who either received variolation as a child or survived smallpox to feed my son.

"A grandson!" she exclaims. The door opens. Even in these most calamitous of circumstances, she can rejoice at the good news. She's somewhat unsteady, but not so much that I can't leave my son with her. I have to trust she'll do everything possible to keep him fed, safe, and well.

"It is my husband's right to name our son," I say, "but please let Maoren know I call the baby Lian."

I put my lips to his forehead. If I see him before this scourge is over, then I'll probably lose him forever. Fetal poison is still fresh in him, making him too young to survive should the malevolent miasma of the disease reach him.

Lady Kuo carefully takes Lian from my arms. Here at last is the grandson she's been waiting for. She puts a hand on my sleeve and says, "Manzi is in the garden. Please save him."

I understand she loves Manzi as her second son. She's doted on him his entire life and has without doubt spent more time with him these past fourteen years than with her own birth son, my husband. Her affection for the boy has been reflected in the bride-price gifts that have been sent to the salt merchant's family for their daughter and in the plans that are already under way for a marriage celebration two years from now that will rival my own.

"I'll do all I can," I promise her.

Could there be anything harder in the cosmos than turning my back on my mother-in-law, son, and servant? My heart pounds in my chest and my breasts ache, but I retrace my steps, pick up the satchels, and go to the entrance to the Garden of Fragrant Delights. The two guards let me pass, and in moments I'm surrounded by the beauty and tranquility of plants and rockeries. I make my way along the pebble paths to the Hermitage, where I see bundles on the terrace. Only as I cross the zigzag bridge do I realize these lumps are people, which means that the interior of the Hermitage must already be full.

Stepping onto the terrace, I get my first glimpse of the scourge. In my mind I thought it might look like any other rash—in patches, red, maybe flaking or oozing—but I was wrong. We call smallpox *tian hua*—heavenly flowers—but it's also considered a *dou*—bean—rash, because the eruptions look and feel like hard beans under the surface of the skin. *Very* hard beans.

I must find my daughter.

As I walk past each person, I let my eyes travel over exposed skin. Some of the ill have only a few beans, but others have beans on beans, covering every inch of flesh. I cross the threshold into the Hermitage. My hand covers my mouth and nose. The stench is dreadful. Like anything in nature, the bean must grow, sprout, and open, only instead of blossoming into a flower or producing ripe fruit, this bean ultimately bursts to release the poison inside. Those before me have entered this stage of the disease. Now they will either die like my brothers did or survive as I did. If they survive, some will be scarred beyond recognition. They might have marriage contracts canceled. If they are servants, they might be dismissed. The lucky will end up like me, with only a few pockmarks to show the world of their inner fortitude.

"Mama."

I spin in a circle, looking for the source of the voice. In a corner, two women sit with their backs against the wall. One of them lifts a hand and motions to me. I step over people lying on mats haphazardly spread across the floor. Nearing the two women, I see that one holds a baby. Her face is so covered with beans that I don't recognize her. Her clothes are decorative and lovely enough that I conclude she must be a concubine. The other woman is similarly dressed. She sits with what appear to be bundled children on either side of her.

As I approach, the second woman says, "It is I, Miss Chen." I'm startled by how much weight she's lost since I last saw her. It's as if her body has been transported back in time to when she first attracted Master Yang's eye, which only emphasizes the few beans that dot her face. Miss Chen places her hands on the mounds nestled against her. "My son, Manzi, and his first sister." It's been years since the boy left the inner chambers and I've seen him up close, yet I'm struck by how little he looks like his father or his half brother. His cheeks are angular, while their faces are as exquisitely round as the full moon. Even under the coverlet, I can see the broadness in Manzi's shoulders, while my father-in-law and husband both have the carriage and build of men whose work is more of the mind than of the body.

Miss Chen clears her throat to get my attention. She tips her head in the direction of the other woman. "Snowpink and her son."

So my husband now has two sons. I can't help but wonder which one is the older and what fights over the order of succession lie ahead of us. I dismiss this from my mind, for it can't matter right now.

"My daughter? Have you seen her?"

Miss Chen reaches over the child on her left to touch the next mound. "Ailan is here with me."

I step around and over more of the sick until I reach Miss Chen's side and the mound she's pointed out. Two eyes peer up at me.

"Mama . . ."

I drop to my knees, lift strands of hair from Ailan's face with a fingertip, and tuck them behind her ear. The beans on her face are too many to count. Later I'll examine her body, but for now, I say, "Don't be afraid. I am here, and I will take care of you."

The smallest of smiles lifts the corners of Ailan's lips, while voices plead from every direction in response to my words.

———

Snowpink's son—only ten days old—returns to nothingness on my first night in the Hermitage. My husband's concubine dies three days later. During that same period, four children, whose mothers didn't invite the smallpox-planting master to do variolation or for whom the process didn't give them enough protection, lapse into delirium and drift away in the night. One is a girl; three are boys. Of the boys, two had already left their mothers' sides in the inner chambers and were studying with tutors in the family school. I learn from Miss Chen of others who died before I came home, including her two youngest daughters, one of whom was seven and the other who had recently turned four and was getting ready to have her feet bound. Her second daughter has yet to be touched by the disease.

Miss Chen keeps her body as still as a statue and her voice even when she tells me all this. "There will be time to mourn those I lost," she says. "But now I must do everything possible to save Manzi and Fourth Daughter."

Her son, Manzi, I know. But Fourth Daughter? I raise my eyebrows in question.

"Lady Kuó has three daughters with Master Yang," Miss

Chen explains. "I have four daughters with him. This one is my first, making her Master Yang's fourth daughter." The clouds in her eyes tell me she's used this tactic to help secure her daughters' positions. She turns away, embarrassed perhaps.

There are so many children, each one in a different stage of the disease. Initial fever and vomiting. Sores in the mouth and nose. When those pustules break, the disease flowers down the neck and arms and onto the torso. A few children have reached the point of scabbing, but they'll remain infectious until scars form. In some cases, I do not have the time or a chance to learn a child's name. Late at night, after I've made a round of the Hermitage to visit each patient, I stretch out a mat on the terrace and try to lose myself in the stars. Sometimes the keening and wailing of brokenhearted mothers reaches over the wall of the garden to overwhelm us all with added misery and dread. In these moments, I wish I could hold my son.

I fight my feelings of powerlessness by staying busy. I prepare Live Pulse Infusion. The ingredients boost the qi, especially in those who have lost vitality through fever sweats. I create ointments and salves using soap bean, one of the fifty most important ingredients in Chinese medicine, which I remember Grandmother using to treat carbuncles and other skin problems. I attend to ruptured and suppurating pustules as I might try to heal scrofula nodes or tumors hardened by cancer by burning mugwort cones on the skin. I recall the case of a woman with a fiery rash that I wrote about in my notebook. I treated her—successfully—with Decoction of Four Ingredients and Decoction of Two Aged Ingredients. I try it on a few patients, and it seems to slow the eruption of new pustules and reduce suffering. But everywhere I look I see Fright in children's eyes and hear it in the whimpering calls to their mothers. The light of life quickly dims in adults, who, petrified and panicked, often give up too quickly. The babies, of course, don't understand what's happening to them, which is a mercy. With each passing hour and day—and with every dead body that must be shrouded in cloth and moved to the back gate—I have to accept that, ultimately, I'm failing. Still, I try.

I have many people to look after, but my heart never leaves my daughter. One minute, she boils with fever, overcome by Heat.

The next minute, she shivers as Cold skulks in like a terrible frost. I keep watch on her hands and feet, because once Cold settles in those extremities and begins creeping toward the torso, little can be done to reverse its course and keep it from reaching the heart when death is imminent.

One day when I unwrap Ailan's bindings, I'm horrified to discover that beans have flared up on the soles of her feet. While I was away, Ailan completed her footbinding, but her feet are still in a fragile stage. Now they need to stay exposed to the air so that when the pustules burst, they'll drain freely and not molder into infection under binding cloth. I do not know what this will mean for the future of her feet—if refinement will be needed or if we'll need to start the process from the beginning. I survived smallpox and I'm a doctor, so I tell myself not to be afraid. But I'm terrified of what the disease might mean for her future.

Miss Chen, who has a relatively mild case of heavenly flowers, is as devoted to the care of her son and daughter as I am to Ailan. When she offers to help me, I accept. We may have been competitors when it came to the seniority of her son and whether or not I would ever give birth to a son who would supersede Manzi in stature and position, but this did not stop her from caring for Ailan until I arrived, for which my gratitude will last an eternity. Miss Chen says not one fearful word about what will happen when Master Yang lays eyes on her, assuming she recovers. Instead, she's diligent and selfless as she applies pain-relieving salve on a boy of seven, dabs at suppurating pustules on the cheeks of a girl of fifteen, and wets the lips of a toddler too weak to lift his head. She helps me measure ingredients and sometimes stirs the pot as herbs are brewed. Not surprisingly, given that she's a Thin Horse, she has knowledge I haven't been exposed to, which gives her insights into our situation.

"How can we as women not blame this scourge on men?" she asks with a hint of bitterness one night as we sip tea next to our sleeping children. "When men travel, they stay in crowded inns. They eat food and drink tea prepared by strangers. They converse with other sojourners. They're exposed to typhoid and cholera . . ." She takes a breath before rattling off the rest of her list. "Diphtheria, typhus, and smallpox. When they come home, they bring these malignant elements to those of us—wives, children, servants, and concubines like me—who reside in the inner chambers. Tell me. Are men not the cause of every woe the world must endure?"

I glance around at the sick on their mats. "I blame mothers."

"Mothers?"

I can't disguise the disdain in my voice when I say, "Any mother who has the opportunity to hire a smallpox-planting master and does not do it has failed in her duty not only to her children but to the future generations of her husband's family."

A long silence follows this. Miss Chen sets down her cup and rests her fingers against her son's forehead. I sense her trying to suck his fever into her body. Manzi seems to be rallying. His cheeks are filling out again, although they'll never reach the roundness that Master Yang and my husband were born with, but his sister is deteriorating, having reached the stage when all she does is sleep. I've given her doses of ginseng, burnt licorice, astragalus root, and cinnamon heart in a final attempt to reverse the course of her fate, but my hopes are ebbing. Still, when I watch Miss Chen's devotion, I'm reminded how lucky her children are to have a mother who can nurse them at any hour of the day or night when so many others are in here alone.

Miss Chen turns and meets my eyes. "I don't remember my mother, and I don't remember seeing a smallpox-planting master after the Tooth Lady bought me, but obviously I never received variolation. And now you reproach me for not doing my duty as a mother to my children?" She pauses to let her accusation sink in. "Not everyone is a believer in variolation. How sick will a child get? Will he or she die or be scarred from the process? Things can go wrong—"

"I know, but—"

"I've also had to consider my daughters' futures. I don't know what their father has planned or what Lady Kuo might arrange for them. I could not risk that they might end up with even a few scars on their faces caused by variolation. Unlike you," she adds pointedly, "Fourth Daughter doesn't have extra attributes—an education or generations of imperial scholars in her lineage—that would guarantee a bright future even if her cheeks are slightly marred."

Fourth Daughter shifts on her mat and opens her eyes. The younger children don't understand what's happening to them, but I suspect she knows what's coming.

"Your mother must have done something to preserve your face," Miss Chen says to me. "Is there anything you can do for my daughter's coming scars?"

Scars are the least of Fourth Daughter's problems, but I'm guessing Miss Chen is focusing on this concern to allay her daughter's fears about the path before her. I try to sound optimistic.

"This is not a case of trying to restore virginity with a decoction made of pomegranate skin and alum," I say. "But ointments can be applied that will help in the healing process."

Only a few hours later, I find not a trace of pulse in either of Fourth Daughter's wrists. When an infant dies, it's painful for the mother to endure, but their connection has been fleeting. This is not so with an older child, even if it is only a daughter. Miss Chen weeps as I wrap the girl in cloth. Then the concubine and I drag the shroud to the back gate of the compound, where we've left other bodies to be fetched and buried. Miss Chen sways unsteadily as we turn to walk away. When I take the concubine's elbow to buoy her, she speaks in a low voice—to herself, to me, to the universe, I can't tell which. "At least my daughter won't have my life."

The doubts I had after Meiling's miscarriage threaten to overwhelm me now. Can I honestly say I'm helping anyone? Has one smallpox patient fully recovered under my care? Maybe Doctor Wong had the right idea: stay away, let nature follow its course, and protect his reputation by avoiding a long tabulation of death marks next to his name. I can almost hear his sneering words. *You are not a proper doctor. You are only a woman.* I wish I were a giant gingko tree hundreds of years old, with the deep roots it takes to stand strong against mighty winds. Instead, I feel like a sapling in a typhoon, desperately trying to hang on.

Neither Miss Chen nor I gets any sleep that night as we sit vigil over Manzi and Ailan. Both children have taken a turn and now seem to be following Fourth Daughter's path. I can't let this happen, but I've done all I know to do. Only one person can help me. To ask for this sacrifice is almost more than I can bear, but I must do whatever is necessary to keep my daughter on this earth. When daybreak comes, the air feels as heavy as a goose-down quilt. I go to the gate that leads to the main part of the compound. Three more people have taken sick overnight. I let them in and point the way to the Hermitage. Then I wait on my side of the gate for one of the guards to fetch Lady Kuo. Soon enough, I hear her *keeck, keeck* as she approaches.

I report on the situation and end by asking, "Can you send a palanquin to bring my grandmother?"

My request shocks her, for it tells my mother-in-law just how dire things are inside the garden that I would be so unfilial as to invite my grandmother into such a dangerous situation.

The new patients are settled when Grandmother Ru arrives, bringing Miss Zhao with her. Instead of wearing fine silk gowns and decorations in their hair, they're attired in cotton tunics and skirts dyed in indigo with matching scarves tied around their heads. Grandmother wastes no time on niceties. "Take me from patient to patient," she says. "I want to see each case. We will decide now who will live and who will die. We will not spend time on those we cannot save."

Over the next several days, I'm humbled to watch Grandmother. Both her wisdom and her emotional strength help me through the frightening hours. No one in the Hermitage is more important to me than my daughter. And no one is more important to Miss Chen than her son. Having two new sets of hands to treat the sick allows the concubine and me to spend more time with Manzi and Ailan, especially during those hours before sunrise when evil spirits come to prey on the weak and mothers need to attach themselves to their children to keep them from being dragged to the Afterworld.

———

Two weeks pass. A night comes when all seems quiet and peaceful. Ailan is recovering, and she sleeps soundly, with breath flowing gently in and out through her slightly open mouth. Miss Chen dozes next to Manzi. Their inhales are low and jagged, caused by exhaustion for her and frailty for him. As Miss Chen and I did earlier in the epidemic, I now sit and sip tea with Grandmother and Miss Zhao. My father's concubine looks tired. Grandmother is another matter entirely. Her vitality has always impressed me. Now she appears drained. This ordeal is hard on all of us, but she's seventy-seven years old.

"Tell me about Meiling's miscarriage and what happened in the capital," Grandmother says seemingly out of nowhere.

These past weeks I've put that out of my mind to focus on the ill and dying. Now it's a reminder of all I still need to understand.

"I'm waiting," Grandmother says, and sends me an encouraging smile.

Haltingly, I tell her about the herbs meant for me that Meiling took, the loss of her baby, and the beating she survived. Grandmother's face grows darker with each word I speak. I end by saying, "I'm still inexperienced compared to Doctor Wong, so maybe his prescription was something I don't understand—"

"*Ha!*" Grandmother snorts. "That man is like a fly following a horse's tail, while you have benefited from learning passed down from generation to generation in my natal family." She pauses, fuming. "What can we say about Doctor Wong? He has a greater desire for fame than he does for producing a good remedy. Many doctors like that exist, you know. They use exotic ingredients—the fuzz from deer antlers in spring or the shavings of rhinoceros horn—to make their benefactors feel special. At least Doctor Wong doesn't pretend that an immortal revealed to him the secret for a unique tonic that only he possesses."

"Are you saying you think he made a mistake—"

"A mistake? No doctor should make a mistake when it comes to abortifacients. I know I don't." When I look at her questioningly, she asks, "Do you remember Red Jade?"

"Of course. She was one of Grandfather's three Jade concubines."

"When you were a girl, I diagnosed her as having a ghost pregnancy."

As she speaks, it starts to come back to me. Ghost pregnancies occur in widows long after their husbands have passed away, in unmarried servant girls, and in wives and concubines whose husbands and masters work far from home. When Grandmother treated Red Jade, Grandfather had been in Nanjing for several months attending to duties at the Board of Punishments.

"Grandfather wasn't the father," I say in understanding.

"*An old horse knows the way*," Grandmother recites. "It was better to guarantee Red Jade's loyalty to me by helping her than it would have been to replace her. I gave her those items that would purge the embryo from her body, save our family from embarrassment, and provide me with a set of eyes and ears that I'd be able to trust going forward."

"That doesn't explain what Doctor Wong did," I point out. "I'm not a concubine or a servant, and Doctor Wong knew my husband had planted a baby in me before I left for the capital. Is it possible that he could have created this particular remedy in an effort to help me with my pregnancy?"

Grandmother doesn't have an answer apart from "I don't see how." She holds out her cup for me to refill. "We'll rest awhile longer," she says, "and then we'll make a final visit to our patients before we try to sleep."

As I always have, I obey Grandmother Ru's orders, knowing I am not done with trying to figure out Doctor Wong's actions. I visit each patient. Everyone is recovering except for Miss Chen's son. I've done everything I can think of and so has Grandmother, but the boy continues to drift away from us. In Miss Chen's concern for her son, she's let go of all vanity. She's lost more weight, her complexion is gray, her hair hangs in strings, and her eyes have a vacant look. I put a hand on her shoulder, then quietly move on.

When I get back to Grandmother, she's slipped into night-clothes and lies beneath a light quilt next to Miss Zhao. I'm too tired to change, but I rinse my mouth with tea, spit it into the pond below the terrace, and stretch out on my mat. I stare up at the sky as I've done every night since I came home from the capital, trying to let the anxieties of the day float to the heavens. But my earlier conversation with Grandmother and Manzi's worsening condition gnaw at me.

"Grandmother." I glance her way. "Smallpox is the great sadness of the world, but why does this scourge continue when it's preventable?" I pause before blurting the question that has tortured me these past weeks. "Why didn't Respectful Lady hire a smallpox-planting master for my brothers and me?"

"Those are two very different questions." Grandmother sits up, and Miss Zhao rises next to her. They stare at me with concern in their eyes. "I can only guess at the answer to your first question. Maybe those mothers were afraid of variolation. Maybe they were ignorant—"

"But what about *my* mother? Why didn't she—"

"When the smallpox-planting master returned to Laizhou after your brothers died and I had been brought in," Miss Zhao interrupts in her quiet voice, "I made sure your brother, Yifeng, received the treatment. The old man used the method of wrapping a scab in cotton and sealing it in his nose."

"And he's alive and without a single scar!"

Miss Zhao looks at me in sympathy, while Grandmother regards me with equanimity.

"Your mother came from an elite family," Grandmother says. "She should have known better. Your father too."

"Then why didn't she—"

"There are people in the world who believe nothing bad can happen to them. Your mother was like that. She had not suffered a day in her life, but . . ."

"But?"

"How much do you remember about her?" Grandmother asks.

"Respectful Lady was beautiful." My mind fills with images: her pleasing countenance, the grace with which she moved, and the expression on her face when she was teaching me the rules to become a proper wife and mother.

"Yunxian," Grandmother says, cutting into my memories, "try to think of her not as her daughter but as a doctor. Use the diagnostic tools I taught you."

I cast myself back in time, but as a physician and not a little girl. I summon a vision of Respectful Lady in her room, sitting on the edge of her marriage bed. "She was always pale," I remember. "Even before my brothers died, melancholy hung on her. She bound my feet. She taught me how to read and write. She listened to me recite rules for girls. But now that I'm a mother myself, I see how removed she was from her actions. Her heart wasn't in the room with me."

"The first time this happened was when your oldest brother was born," Grandmother says.

"It happened again after your second brother entered the world and again when you arrived," Miss Zhao adds.

"After your brothers died, your father wrote to your grandfather and me because he was worried," Grandmother goes on in a gentle voice. "You were all far away in Laizhou, so your grandfather and I could only send recommendations by courier." She tightens her jaw as she recollects that time. "When I look for patterns in the human body—the relationship between the Five Depot Organs, the Five Influences, and the copiousness with which women feel the Seven Emotions—I focus on that most common of feelings, which is—"

"Anger," I finish for her. "Often when I get to the root of a woman's ailments, anger is the spark, the fuel, and the creator of ash."

"All true," Grandmother agrees. "But I consider sadness to be the most powerful and destructive of the Seven Emotions. Even when your mother first married into our family and lived in the Mansion of Golden Light with your grandfather and me, she was pensive and inward looking. Now think about how she must have felt after your brothers died. How could she have not blamed herself?"

Miss Zhao reaches out and touches my hand. "Many times after your father fell asleep in my bed, I'd go to the courtyard and find your mother weeping. As you might imagine, she did not want my comfort, especially after I became pregnant. When I gave birth to Yifeng, she now had a new son."

"But he was a ritual son and a daily reminder of everything she had lost," I say in sudden understanding. It's all I can do not to cry, because didn't she see that she still had me? But as I know all too well, a daughter is not a son.

"Respectful Lady knew what would happen if she didn't take care of her feet," Miss Zhao resumes. "To this day I wonder if she neglected them so she might be reunited with your brothers or if she did it to punish herself for believing she was above tragedy."

A dismal silence encircles us. Finally, Grandmother speaks. "I see so much of your mother in you."

With a pang, I perceive all the worry I've given her over the years, but then Miss Zhao says something that changes how I interpret what Grandmother said. "You are even more beautiful than she was."

"You are both being kind," I say. "But I'm not a typical Snake with flawless skin."

I touch a finger to one of my smallpox scars. Grandmother and Miss Zhao exchange glances, then return their faces to me, both of them smiling.

"Don't you know that those heavenly flowers marks are what make you so beautiful?" asks Miss Zhao, who I've always considered to be even more exquisite than Respectful Lady. "Total perfection is not so desirable."

———

We sustain a few more deaths, but we begin to have many successes, with family members and other residents returning to the main part of the compound. On the morning Ailan is to be released, I wrap her feet in clean bindings. Her soles are badly scarred but once she reaches adulthood they will not be seen by anyone except her and perhaps a servant. Her future husband will be able to hold her embroidered shoes in his hands and never know the ugliness that lies beneath the bindings.

I support Ailan as we walk together over the zigzag bridge and along the paths to the gate to the Courtyard of Whispering Willows. Yesterday I informed the guards that she would be going home. Throughout the invasion of the disease, I've stayed on my side of the gate to prevent infection from spreading into the household. This time I position myself in the threshold in the hope that I'll find Yuelan and Chunlan waiting for their sister. They've come. My husband too. He looks well and strong in his black scholar's robes. Poppy is nearby. She lifts up Lian so I can see him. Maoren tells me that he's officially accepted the name I gave our son, for which I'm grateful, and I can see Lian's grown a lot while I've been in here. I hope he'll remember me once I can take him back in my arms.

"Only a few more days," I say.

"I await your return to me with my full heart," my husband responds.

The guards shut and bolt the gate, leaving me to wonder if Maoren knows about Snowpink and the death of their newborn son and what he might mean by "my full heart."

I'm nearing the Hermitage when a high-pitched scream pierces the silence, echoing off the surrounding walls. I hurry to the terrace to find Miss Chen covering Manzi's body with her own. She suffered when her daughter died, but this? Utter devastation . . . When I reach her, she looks up to the sky. I hear her whisper something to herself, words that barely reach my ears but immediately agitate my mind. "I always assured him our son would become master of the Garden of Fragrant Delights. Now Manzi never will." She begins to weep as only a mother who has lost a son can. I know I should comfort her, but I am too distracted by what she has said. Her words have turned a key in my mind and opened a door.

Manzi never looked like Master Yang. If my unborn son died, Manzi would have eventually become the new master, according power to Manzi *and* his natal family. Spinster Aunt had something to tell me after Manzi's birth but her death came before she could tell me . . . It has taken me many years to stitch these pieces together. Now I realize Manzi's father could be only one person. And that person schemed and plotted from the day his son was born, which also means . . . Spinster Aunt's death was not an accident.

The Washing Away of Wrongs

After the heavenly flowers disease disappears completely from the Garden of Fragrant Delights, the last survivors return to their families or, in the case of concubines and servants, to their masters, and I'm free to go back to my rooms. I'm determined to visit Meiling, since the suspicions that arose from Miss Chen's utterance directly concern my friend and the herbs that were meant for me, but I need to get settled with my family before I do anything else. I also have much that I'm eager to discuss with my husband, but my first night home he doesn't come to my bedchamber. A disappointment. I fall asleep feeling exhausted and dispirited. The next morning, when Poppy pours my tea, she brings the gossip that Master Yang is going to remove Miss Chen and her sole surviving child, Fifth Daughter, from the Garden of Fragrant Delights. I dress and then rush to find my husband. He's in his library.

"Is it true your father is casting off his concubine and her daughter?" I ask. Perhaps this is not the correct approach as Maoren and I have not been alone together since I left for Beijing seven months ago. So much has happened, including the birth of our son, but I haven't given my husband a chance to express his joy or thank me for doing what I could during the smallpox outbreak.

"Since when have the hens begun to crow?" he asks, squinting his disapproval.

I take a breath and remind myself that I'm a wife before anything else. "I'm sorry," I say, bowing my head. "I spoke sharply."

Maoren stands up and walks toward me. He reaches out and brushes a loose strand of hair from my cheek. "You look tired."

"I'm tired to my marrow." I raise my eyes to meet his. "Maoren, why is your father expelling Miss Chen?"

"She is no longer a beauty," he states.

It's true, but I can't let this go. "Don't let your father turn her out. She helped me during the sickness. She was courageous when—"

"The concubine has already been dismissed," he says, swiveling away from me. "She will take her daughter with her—"

"Her only surviving child," I emphasize. "And Fifth Daughter is your half sister."

I can see him tasting this idea on his tongue and finding it bitter.

"Without a son and without her beauty, Miss Chen has no value to my father."

"Fifth Daughter is only ten years old," I press.

"There is nothing I can do. It is my father's decision."

I nod and leave Maoren to his books. I realize there's little time. I go straight to the front gate, where I find Miss Chen and her daughter.

"I don't know what's to become of us," the concubine whispers.

I have no words to reassure her. Few options exist for a woman like her. Watching her leave with only the clothes on her back, the scars on her face, and her child is sad beyond measure.

A few days later, my husband abruptly departs for Nanjing. Although he offered kind words when Ailan was released—*I await your return to me with my full heart*—he did not visit me before he left. I tell myself he must be happy about Lian, but is he upset that I didn't receive more rewards from the palace or that I didn't do enough to keep Snowpink and their son from dying? Maybe Maoren and I have simply spent too much time apart . . .

Life in the Garden of Fragrant Delights is different now as we all adjust to the changes resulting from the heavenly flowers disease. I sit for hours with mothers who lost children. No remedy exists to relieve their anguish, but I can cry with them. I visit former patients, making sure they're eating well and providing formulas to rebuild their strength. And, of course, I cherish every moment I have with my daughters and son, who has reached three months.

Two weeks later, with my husband gone and feeling reconnected to my children, I decide it's time to visit Meiling. I step over the main threshold of the compound and get into my palanquin. Eight weeks have passed since we arrived back in Wuxi, and I'm unsure of what I'll discover when I reach her new home. Meiling and her mother received variolation, but I don't know about her husband or his customers. I hope they haven't been affected.

When I arrive, a servant opens the gate, and I enter a small courtyard that reminds me of the first house where I lived. Meiling appears in a doorway and calls to me, breathless and nervous. "Yunxian!"

We hold each other in a tight embrace. I don't want to let go, and she doesn't release me. "We're all fine. I'm so glad you're alive," she murmurs. "I was terrified for you and your children. Tell me. Is Lian well?" All I can do is nod into her neck. She takes my shoulders and pushes me away to study my face. Wordlessly, she reads the grief that has etched my features. Staring back at her, I see not a woman who recently came close to death but my friend who is as beautiful as the day we first met.

She releases me and asks the polite questions. "Have you eaten? Would you like some tea?"

We sit together at a table by an open window overlooking the courtyard. The sounds of the city rise up around us, a reminder that life goes on. We exchange pleasantries. I compliment her on her pretty home. I gently inquire about her injuries, all of which she says have healed. After a proper amount of time has passed, I say, "I'm not here just to visit." I tell her what Miss Chen said when her son died. *I always assured him our son would become master of the Garden of Fragrant Delights. Now Manzi never will.*

When Meiling stares at me blankly, I realize I've jumped too quickly into the subject. "Let me start over. We know Doctor Wong gave Poppy herbs intended to harm my baby, but we couldn't figure out why."

Meiling blinks a couple of times, still adjusting to the turn in the conversation. For a moment, I think that maybe she doesn't want to revisit what happened.

"Yes, I remember," she says at last, "but what does that have to do with what Miss Chen said about her son?"

I lean forward. "Who do you think she was talking about when she said, 'I *always* assured *him*'?"

"Master Yang, the child's father," Meiling answers.

"But that doesn't make sense. She would never need to say such a thing to Master Yang, let alone multiple times, because he would never have a question about who would become master when he died. First it would be Maoren. Then, if something happened to Maoren or if Maoren and I never had a son, Manzi would become the master."

"Manzi," she repeats.

"My father-in-law would know that down to his bones." I watch as she considers what I've said. "So I asked myself, with whom would she discuss this?" I pause. Meiling waits. "It made me wonder if Manzi wasn't Master Yang's son."

Meiling tucks her chin. "Do you have any proof of what you're suggesting?"

"Manzi didn't look like a Yang man. Not his father, my husband, or Second Uncle—"

"That is hardly proof. It could be argued Manzi resembled Miss Chen's father or her brothers. There would be no way to prove otherwise."

"Maybe it's better to think about who would have a motive to make sure I didn't have a son. If I didn't give birth to a boy, then Manzi's succession would have been guaranteed. The ingredients of the formula you took are evidence that someone intended to kill my baby, securing Manzi's place."

"The formula came from Doctor Wong." Meiling's eyes widen. "You think Doctor Wong and Miss Chen—"

"Miss Chen and I had our pregnancies diagnosed together by him. I realize that was a long time ago and I was mainly concerned with my own condition, but I remember how familiar their conversation was. Miss Chen said to the doctor, 'You know me. Have you helped me become full with child?'"

"That could mean anything. Maybe he gave *her* a formula—"

"Maybe, but there's something else, and I suspect it's related." I hesitate, nervous to voice what I've come to believe. I take a breath and let the words rush out. "The night Miss Chen had her baby, Spinster Aunt came to see me. I could tell she was upset, but she wouldn't say what was wrong."

"So?"

"Even back then, I thought she saw or heard something when Miss Chen was in labor. Maybe Spinster Aunt was killed to keep her from telling me, from telling anyone."

Meiling gives me a doubtful look. "Her death was an accident."

"But what if it wasn't?" Before she can ask, I volunteer, "No, I don't have proof she was murdered. But something happened in the labor room that disturbed Spinster Aunt enough that she wouldn't confide in me. I think it also caused her to enter the courtyard at night alone, which is not something she would have ordinarily done. Perhaps she went to meet someone." I pause. Again, I worry I'm going too fast. "There's a witness to what happened during Manzi's birth."

Meiling nods slowly as understanding comes to her. "My mother was in the room to catch Miss Chen's baby." She stands. "Wait here. I'll get her."

A few minutes later, Meiling and her mother return. I don't know what Meiling told her, but the midwife regards me warily. I take her measure too. After all these years, Midwife Shi finally looks like a granny. She's rounder, and gray threads through her hair.

It takes much prodding and cajoling, but eventually Midwife Shi confesses what she knows. When she's done, we sit in silence for several minutes.

Finally, Meiling takes a breath. "If all this is true—"

"It is," her mother says.

"Then why didn't Doctor Wong try to end Yunxian's second and third pregnancies?"

"Daughter, you're a midwife. You know the answer. Many children don't live to seven years. What need of a plan for the future could there be until Manzi reached that age? Better yet, until he was eight years old?"

"By that time," I cut in, "I had three daughters. They offered no threat. And who knows? What may have started out as an unlikely seed of an idea took years to grow. Maybe Doctor Wong thought fate would intervene and bring me a son the fourth time I was full with child. In the end, you were the victim."

Several emotions wash over Meiling's features as she considers all this. At last, she asks, her voice tremulous, "What should we do?"

"If we act," I answer, "there could be repercussions for my husband's family. And for the two of you."

"I'm afraid," my friend admits, "but can we in good conscience do nothing?"

Midwife Shi and I remain silent as Meiling rises. She crosses the room, rummages through her shelves, returns with paper, inkstone, and an earthenware jar filled with calligraphy brushes, and sets them before me. "You need to write to your father."

I hesitate. Maoren and I have been married for fifteen years. In writing this letter, I feel like I'll be betraying him. "What if I'm wrong? Shouldn't I ask Maoren about all this first?"

"But what if you're right about everything?" Meiling asks. "Would he let you send the letter? Would he want the truth to come out?"

I'm helpless as Meiling reads my face, seeking the answers in my expression. Then she reaches into the brush holder, selects a brush with a fine tip, and holds it out to me. I take the brush, dip it in ink, and begin a letter to my father, outlining my suspicions about Meiling's miscarriage and Spinster Aunt's death and asking him to come to Wuxi. Then Midwife Shi, Meiling, and I spend hours compiling a list of possible witnesses and the questions that could be asked if my father decides to answer my appeal.

———

Three weeks later, the sounds of drums and gongs let us know that the procession bearing my father is nearing and for those in its path to clear the way. My husband, father-in-law, and Second Uncle wait with their hands folded inside the sleeves of their robes. Lady Kuo and I stand behind our husbands. I'm nervous.

The last time I saw my father was twenty-two years ago, when I was eight years old and he came to my grandparents' home with his new bride.

The procession comes into view led by a twin column of bannermen, criers, and musicians. My father rides on a horse whose black hair and mane have been brushed to shiny luminescence. Braiding and tassels swing from the saddle and bridle. My father's erect posture and his official cap give him height and authority. Behind him follow an assortment of men—also on horseback.I take them to be clerks and secretaries, who will assist my father in the hours to come. It would be an honor for any family to have a guest of such high standing, but the purpose of my father's visit is a cause of great concern and embarrassment: a re-inquest about Spinster Aunt's death and an investigation into the physician of the household and how his actions may have affected the Yang family.

My father dismounts, and one of our grooms takes the reins. Maoren, my father-in-law, and Second Uncle bow in supplication as they should before a Prefectural Judge on the Board of Punishments. I'm ready to perform a full obeisance when my father steps forward and takes hold of my elbows.

"Daughter, I would recognize you anywhere. You look so like your mother."

My hand covers my heart to hold the sentiment inside me forever. My father turns to the men in the family.

"Master Yang, I will do my best to complete the proceedings with as little fanfare as possible. Maoren, it is good to see you—"

"I'm afraid, Prefectural Judge Tan, that you'll find your trip was unnecessary," Master Yang interrupts. "I've known Doctor Wong for many years. He has served our family well. To see him accused—"

"Is no doubt a difficult situation," my father finishes sympathetically. "No family wants to have a re-inquest either. Please be assured I will perform my duties according to the highest ideals of the Great Ming Code."

Master Yang is not placated, but as he opens his mouth to continue to object, Second Uncle quickly places a hand on his older brother's shoulder, conveying the message that this battle cannot be won.

Around us, servants offer cups of tea to the lesser members of the traveling party and grooms lead away the horses, giving Master Yang a moment to get his emotions further under control. "Under the circumstances," he says at last, "I'm honored to have an official of such integrity here to preside over the proceedings. All the parties are present."

"Then we will begin at once," my father says.

Hearing this, Lady Kuo quickly steps forward. "Let me first show you to a room where you can refresh yourself from your journey," she offers, to which my father nods his agreement.

Although he had seemed in a hurry to get started, nearly an hour passes before Lady Kuo escorts my father to the same colonnade where the first inquest about Spinster Aunt took place. My mother-in-law's bow is deep and respectful. He's a dignitary and an honored guest, but I've never before seen her act so humbly. I'm further surprised when he touches her sleeve, leans toward her, and whispers a few words. She tightens her jaw, nods, and then backs away.

My father takes his place at a table, where he's flanked by his secretaries, each of whom has paper, brushes, and an inkstone before him. Spinster Aunt's exhumed body lies on a table, covered with muslin. A diagram showing the front and back outlines of a body stands on an easel. Next to this is a small table with the tools required for an inquest on one end and brush and ink on the other end.

Doctor Wong sits on one of two chairs placed between my father and his secretaries and Spinster Aunt's body, facing the audience. He looks as he always has to me: handsome, with an air of superiority about him. While custom and law say that the entire family of the dead may attend, only thirty chairs have been set up. My father-in-law, Second Uncle, and Maoren are in the front row in the same positions they took at the first inquest. Most of the other chairs are filled by Yang men, but a few women, including Lady Kuo, are also seated. Miss Chen has been summoned. She's in an alcove, with a gauze veil covering her face to hide her few scars. Next to her are other nonfamily women: Meiling, her mother, and Poppy. Meiling and I give each other a subtle nod.

My father begins with some preliminaries, noting the day, month, and year of the Hongzhi emperor's reign. His secretaries keep their heads down as they write every word spoken to create the official record. My father then announces that he'll follow the rules and directions laid down in *The Washing Away of Wrongs* as he considers the forensic evidence, quoting: "*If even one tiny mistake is made, the repercussions can stretch ten thousand* li." He pauses to let us consider these words, which were spoken to us years ago by Magistrate Fu.

"This is an unusual situation, since we have two accusations of crimes before us," my father goes on. "The first dates back fourteen years to the death of Yang Fengshi—a woman known by her family as Spinster Aunt. The second allegation regards the deliberate use of abortifacients—with the resulting death of a fetus and near death of its mother. The intended target of this second crime was, apparently, my own daughter. I will hold myself to the highest tenets of integrity and objectivity as I perform my duties as investigator and judge, but to further assure impartiality and your confidence I have asked Coroner Sun, who is not from these parts or familiar with the victims, witnesses, or the accused, to review the evidence. If someone objects to any of this, now is the time to speak."

My father's eyes slowly pass over the assembly. If this had been Magistrate Fu, then perhaps there might have been arguments from different quarters, but my father's position as a Prefectural Judge allows nothing of the sort.

"We will look at the facts chronologically," he continues, "beginning with the re-inquest, moving on to the second accusation, and then consider how these two crimes—if indeed we find what occurred to be unlawful in nature and not a matter of misfortune, accident, or incompetence—are connected and the intention behind them. The accused is the physician of the household, Doctor Wong."

While news that Doctor Wong would be the target of this investigation has caused much gossip throughout the Garden of

Fragrant Delights, hearing the accusations spoken aloud in an official manner has produced what feels like a wall of disbelief from those seated around me. For his part, Doctor Wong lifts his chin, forms his lips into a small smile, and gently shakes his head as if to reassure everyone that this occasion is of no concern to him nor should it be to anyone else.

My father gestures to the coroner. "You may begin."

"I will start with a procedure called To Disperse Vileness," Coroner Sun explains. "My assistant will hand out gum made from liquidambar or, if you prefer, he can give you a piece of candied ginger to suck. These will help to wash away the taste of death. He also has a bottle of hemp seed oil. You may wish to smear some of it under your nose. The odor of decay won't disappear entirely, but it will be lessened." He turns to my father. "When the grave-diggers opened Yang Fengshi's coffin, we discovered the worst foul liquids had evaporated, but in the interests of the family, I've dabbed the body with wine and vinegar."

With that, he pulls off the sheet of muslin to reveal what's left of Spinster Aunt. A chorus of gasps comes from members of the household who are seeing someone they knew now badly decomposed. Spinster Aunt's flesh appears withered and leathery. Her lips have retreated, exposing protruding teeth. Her nose and eyes are gone, leaving three gaping holes. The skin that once covered her shins has completely disappeared, leaving bare white bone.

Memories of the original inquest return as the coroner relates findings not unlike those Midwife Shi outlined fourteen years ago, while his assistant dips a brush in red ink and marks what is relayed onto the diagram of Spinster Aunt's body. The water originally found in Spinster Aunt's belly, which pointed to drowning as the cause of death, is still evident in the way this area has been slower to decompose. The coroner also reviews prior documented evidence, some but not all of which has been erased by time.

"Here we see dried mud," Coroner Sun says, using a thin bamboo stick to point to Spinster Aunt's yawning mouth. He moves the stick to one of her hands. "The nails have continued to grow in the grave, and they extend like talons. But you can clearly discern dried mud not only under the nails but also in what remains of her palms." Moving on, the tip of the stick touches a spot just above Spinster Aunt's upper teeth. "Dried mud cakes the cavity where her nose once was."

My father clears his throat and reads from a paper: "In the first inquest, it was determined that Yang Fengshi had an accidental fall, hit her head, and drowned in the pond. The physical evidence, however, does not fully support this theory. Yes, water was found in her belly. And yes, the pond is shallow enough for most people, even a child, to escape. But if she lost consciousness, then she would not have had the ability to fight for her life, yet she has the remnants of mud in her hands and under her fingernails. Even if she had rested for days—and not hours—on the surface of the pond, mud would not have become so embedded in her nose and mouth cavities."

I glance at my husband, who has his head tilted in low conversation with his father. Lady Kuo and some of the other ladies of the inner chambers wipe their eyes. Doctor Wong stares at his hands, which lie open, palms up, on his thighs. It's impossible to guess at his emotions.

"There is something else to consider," Coroner Sun says. "I would respectfully ask Prefectural Judge Tan to join me here."

My father rises and steps purposefully to the table.

"I need help," the coroner says, handing his assistant two pieces of cloth to drape over his hands. "We need to turn over the body."

Once Spinster Aunt is facedown, the assistant returns to the easel.

"At the first inquest, Midwife Shi reported that Miss Yang hit the left side of her head." The coroner once again uses his stick to point to Spinster Aunt's corpse. "If that were so, then why is the indentation on the *back* of her skull?"

My father scratches his beard, pondering the problem, and asks, "If she fell and hit the back of her head, then why was she found facedown in the pond? And, from an administrative perspective, how did the discrepancy about the location of the injury to the victim's head come to be in the official record?" His questions are greeted by muttering. He raises a hand for silence. "The answer to the second question will need to come from the original coroner and magistrate. I would also ask if they are acquainted with the accused, and if they benefited financially or otherwise from him. As you all know, lying in an official investigation is cause for severe punishment, but issues about the coroner and magistrate will need to wait for another time. As to the first concern, I want to remind everyone that the reason we gather at the site where a death occurred is to gather evidence. I now ask Master Yang and his son to follow me. The rest of you will remain seated."

My father-in-law, husband, and father now disappear down the path lined by azaleas, which have grown taller these past years. I keep my eyes down and my ears attuned, hoping to catch the conversation coming from the pond. I hear nothing apart from some splashing. We all wait. Finally, the three men come back up the path. They carry rocks of varying sizes, some of which are wet. My husband's boots and the bottom of his robe are also wet. The men set the rocks on the table and return to their seats.

My father states a truism. "*One or two decades will not change a rock.*" He gestures to the coroner. "Please try to fit these specimens to the dent in Yang Fengshi's skull."

A few women shield their eyes. A young man whom I treated as a boy for his frail disposition and who is now deep into studying for the imperial exams faints and is carried away. My husband and his father have gone as white as death garments.

After a few minutes, Coroner Sun holds up a rock still shiny with water. "This cracked Miss Yang's skull. It is an exact fit to the indentation. When she did not die at once, she was held facedown in the pond. She must have struggled very hard as we can see from the water and mud evidence."

I look at Doctor Wong to see how he reacts to this information, but he remains still, as though he hasn't heard a word of what's been said. His stare remains steady, focused just over our heads to, I suddenly realize, the alcove where Miss Chen, Poppy, Meiling, and her mother wait to be called as witnesses.

My father shifts in his seat so he can address the doctor. "Please stand and face the table with the body." Doctor Wong obeys, as he must. "It is said that when a suspect is questioned before a corpse and its relatives, he—or she—will be more inclined to confess. Would you care to do that now?"

Doctor Wong sniffs contemptuously. "Absolutely not. I have done nothing wrong."

Unmoved, my father calmly places a hand flat on the table and turns his attention back to the gathering. "We have heard about evidence found on Miss Yang's body that suggests she was killed. I will come back to the motive or motives for her death later, but now let's turn to the second accusation as, I believe, we will discover that the reason for both crimes stems from a single source. Doctor Wong, stay where you are. Shi Meiling, will you please approach?"

Meiling leaves the alcove, walks up the center aisle, and sits in the second chair positioned to face the audience. My father asks her just five questions.

"What was the cause of your miscarriage in Beijing?"

"I took a remedy that I thought would help me have a safe pregnancy."

"Do you have any of it with you?"

She shows what's left of the herbs and other ingredients that made up the formula she took.

"Can you describe the medicinal properties of each?" he asks.

"I am not a doctor," she answers. "However, I have learned the effect each ingredient will have on a pregnant woman."

My father gives her permission to list them, which she does, and then inquires, "How did you come to have the herbs?"

"I took them from a maid."

"For whom were they originally intended?"

"Tan Yunxian, Master Yang's daughter-in-law."

This fact is met with profound silence.

My father next calls for Poppy to sit in the chair Meiling just vacated.

"Who gave you the herbs that ultimately caused the young midwife to miscarry?" he asks.

My longtime maid cries so hard she can barely speak. "Doctor Wong."

Amid gasps of surprise, Doctor Wong's face remains a mask of indifference.

"I only did what I was told to do by the doctor of the household," Poppy sobs. "I would never hurt Little Miss."

My father dismisses Poppy, and she returns to the alcove, covering her face with her hands.

"Doctor Wong, is there anything you would like to say to refute what the midwife and the maid just said?"

"I am disappointed to see that a man of your standing can be so swayed by the mutterings of women, especially from a member of the Six Grannies who desecrates the rules of proper behavior set down by Confucius," he answers.

Perhaps Doctor Wong believes that by acting disdainful he'll convince everyone of his innocence, but the family's sentiment has turned against him, and my father does not appear to be swayed either.

"So for now you will not be confessing," he says. "No matter. Please remain where you are, so we can see your reaction to the next witness. Midwife Shi, come forward." Once she's in position, my father questions her about how she learned her trade and how long she's practiced. Then he begins to probe more deeply based on what Midwife Shi confessed to Meiling and me. "When was the last time you came to the Garden of Fragrant Delights?"

"It was for the birth of Miss Chen's son," she answers.

"Am I right that it's not always necessary for a doctor to be present at these events?"

"You are correct. Childbirth is bloody. Doctors usually stay away unless there are complications."

"Were there complications in this instance?"

"None at all," Midwife Shi answers.

"But a physician was in attendance."

"Yes, Doctor Wong was there."

"Please tell us what happened."

"Many women cry out during labor. Often they complain about their husbands or their masters. Never again will I allow him into my bed, and that sort of thing." The midwife gives a half smile. "Of course, we would not have a society if every woman followed this course."

No one laughs.

"What did the concubine say?" my father asks.

"She yelled at the doctor that if a son exited her body, then she would never again open her legs for him."

"No!" The scream slices through the stunned crowd. I turn to look at the source of the sound and see into the alcove, where Miss Chen rises so quickly that the veil covering her face lifts and then gently falls as though blown by a breeze. I swivel back to catch Doctor Wong flinch and then quickly compose himself.

"Sit down, Miss Chen," my father orders, "and remain quiet." He returns to Midwife Shi. "Are you suggesting that Master Yang was not the father of his concubine's son?"

"That is correct."

"Who else knows this?"

Midwife Shi sets her jaw and straightens her back. Her voice is strong when she says, "The woman I knew as Spinster Aunt was present to assist me during Miss Chen's labor. She heard everything. Later, the two of us talked about what we should do. This baby, the one named Manzi, had entered the world as next in line to become the headman of the Garden of Fragrant Delights should the young master die or die without a son."

The lines on my father's forehead deepen as he considers this information. I wonder if the Yang family is looking at Doctor Wong and seeing what I see: the carved cheekbones, the broad shoulders, and the set of the jaw that he and Manzi shared.

My father asks his next question in such a low tone I barely hear it. "And you kept this secret all these years?"

"What choice did I have?" Midwife Shi asks in response. "Not long after Miss Chen gave birth, I attended to three other laboring women, each of whom had an unfortunate outcome." She sighs. "This happens, but thanks to a few well-placed words from Doctor Wong, elite families no longer invited me into their homes. Anything I would have said in my defense would have been seen as—"

"But that was not your only motivation," my father interrupts before Midwife Shi can finish.

I grip my hands together so hard that my fingernails bite into my skin, afraid Meiling's mother will lose her courage.

"Every mother does what she can to put her child forward—especially a fatherless girl child," the midwife says at last. "Doctor Wong promised me that if I spoke not a single word about the secret he and Miss Chen shared, he would protect my daughter. 'I can ruin her as I have already done to you,' he said. 'Or I can help her.' I agreed to his terms. Our arrangement began immediately."

After my father dismisses Midwife Shi, he leafs through his papers as if to make sure he's not forgetting anything. If he follows the suggestions I wrote to him, then three witnesses remain: Miss Chen, Lady Kuo, and me. Each of us has important information to share—willingly or unwillingly—but he doesn't call on any of us, leaving me confused and disheartened. Instead, over the next hour, my father tries to get Doctor Wong to admit to his crimes. He gives the doctor opportunities to offer explanations, some of which could be colored as careless mistakes. When asked why he didn't try to kill Maoren instead of my unborn son, the doctor laughs. "I've told you I'm not a murderer."

My father waves away this answer as though it were a bad smell. Then he says, "The easy way is the sloppy way, but I will ask you nevertheless. After you killed Miss Yang with the rock, why didn't you remove it from the Garden of Fragrant Delights?"

"I didn't kill the spinster," the doctor answers.

My father runs out of patience. "Can you offer *any* evidence that you did not kill Yang Fengshi?"

"I cannot," he answers.

"Can you refute the claims that the child Manzi was your son and that you were trying to secure his place as future head of the Yang family?"

"I cannot."

"Let us be clear. Are you admitting you are guilty of these things?"

Doctor Wong refuses to respond.

"I will give you one last opportunity to explain yourself," my father says.

Master Yang rises and shouts in indignation. "We deserve that at the very least!" Around him, a chorus of male voices led by Second Uncle support this demand.

Doctor Wong lifts his hands, casually, disinterested. What he says proves that Grandmother was right about him all along. "I confess to wanting to be a famous doctor remembered long after my death. I wanted to be like the man who created the methods for the washing away of wrongs." He permits himself a small smile. "The very methods you've employed today—"

My father brusquely cuts him off. "Your actions were not those of a man desiring fame. Rather, you sought the benefits and power found in siring what you hoped would be the heir of this family's holdings."

Doctor Wong lets out a breath in resignation. "What difference does any of it make now? Manzi is dead."

This produces such consternation from the Yang men—and even some of the women—that for a moment I'm worried they'll take matters into their own hands. My father pounds his fist on the table, silencing the assembly.

"A woman died. Another woman lost her child and nearly died. And we don't yet know what else you did." My father looks down at his papers. "There are other roads of inquiry I can still take," he says. "I would be happy to continue the investigation and employ the usual interrogation techniques—beatings and the like—if that would suit you. But understand that for each new lie uncovered, especially after the time and effort men will have spent extracting the truth, your physical punishment will increase." He pauses, and then adds, "I am giving you the opportunity to take the coward's way—confess, avoid torture, and begin your sentence."

Doctor Wong sighs and his shoulders slump as his boldness melts away. I'm reminded of the story Spinster Aunt told long ago about the so-called brave man, who ended up hiding under the bed like a frightened kitten to escape his wife. At last, Doctor Wong speaks. "I respectfully ask for the coward's way. Torture will not be necessary. I will accept your verdict based on what you've heard and the sentence you believe I deserve. Now, without the addition of pain or blood."

"The coward's way then." My father sweeps his eyes across the audience to convey his opinion of the doctor's complete lack of honor or courage. "Let me begin by saying that I was raised in a household devoted equally to scholarly endeavors and to medicine. From my mother, in particular, I learned that in medicine we must look at the entire cosmos—both within and without the body. Are they in harmony?" He gestures to me. "What pride I have in this moment to see that my daughter has learned to see these patterns not only in those who ail but in the world around her, which is how she was able to bring this matter to me. Just as my daughter or my parents might have felt the pulses, asked questions, and so on, I now follow a similar course to find what in the evidence is out of harmony with the cosmos and what traces have been left behind that reveal past movements."

My father pauses so his secretaries can take down all his words. Once their brushes stop moving, he picks up again. "Fame is a dream some men chase. Sometimes they catch it and manage to hold on to it as if hanging on to the tail of a kite in a tempest. Sometimes they are blinded by desire for recognition or influence, as if they have drunk a flask of fairy wine. We are talking about the basic elements of yin and yang, are we not? The constant push and pull between good and evil, love and hate, honor and disgrace, all of which follow each other in an unending cycle. In this case, Doctor Wong, you were not alone in your misdeeds. I now ask Midwife Shi and Miss Chen to stand next to you."

Once the two women are in place, my father says, "All punishments are dictated by the Great Ming Code: beheading, banishment, penal servitude, and flogging."

Hearing these words, Midwife Shi seems resigned. Miss Chen stays silent beneath her veil. Doctor Wong goes pale, perhaps reconsidering his choice of the coward's way.

"I will begin with Midwife Shi," my father goes on. "The punishment for lying at an inquest is severe—one hundred blows with a heavy rod."

"No!" Meiling cries out. This is far worse than what she received at the palace.

My father ignores the outburst. "While the Great Ming Code says I can't suspend a sentence, it can be reduced, which I believe is warranted in this case. After all, Midwife Shi—as a woman and as one of the Six Grannies—could not disobey Doctor Wong's orders. At the same time, we must admire her Confucian fealty. She sacrificed her reputation to secure her daughter's future. That daughter—another member of the Six Grannies—has also exhibited the precepts of Confucius. In helping to expose Doctor Wong, Young Midwife has helped clear her mother's name. Midwife Shi will receive one hundred blows from the lightest bamboo rod available in the district."

Hearing the sentence, Meiling's mother remains as still as stone. Miss Chen's veil—light and diaphanous—trembles.

"As for Miss Chen," my father says, "she is property. I leave her punishment to Master Yang. But if it were me, I'd have the concubine banished from the household immediately."

He couldn't know that Miss Chen has already been thrown into the street.

He dismisses the two women and turns to Doctor Wong. "The dead will not rest, and the living will not be at ease without retribution. Punishment for those who kill an unborn child whose mouth, eyes, ears, hands, and feet have not fully formed is nearly nonexistent. In this case, however, Young Midwife's fetus—a girl—had developed these physical characteristics." He pauses as Doctor Wong begins to sob. Then, "I want to give you a punishment that will discourage others from attempting something similar while in pursuit of power and financial gain. You will receive one hundred blows from a heavy rod and wear a cangue around your neck for a year so the populace may see your humiliation. If you're still alive after twelve months, I sentence you to be decapitated in Wuxi's public square."

As two guards approach, Doctor Wong struggles to rein in his emotions. By the time he stands to be led away, he's once again himself—arrogant, and fully in control.

———

Tonight the men of the Yang family are to host a banquet in honor of my father. I will not be permitted to attend. With what remains of the day, I go in search of my husband and find him alone in his library. He doesn't look pleased to see me.

"The matchmaker said you were smart," he says wearily, "but

your cleverness has brought embarrassment to our home and our name."

"Writing to my father was the right thing to do—"

"For whom? For Spinster Aunt? She cared for me when I was a boy. I have fond memories of her. Then to see her like that . . . As for Young Midwife—"

"Remember *I* was the target."

"But nothing happened to you, did it?" Our eyes meet. "Yunxian, what bothers me is that you didn't talk to me first. How is there love or even duty in your choice?"

I put a hand on his sleeve and feel the warmth of his arm through the silk. "I'm sorry if I hurt you."

He pulls away from me and wordlessly returns to his desk.

I feel unsettled as I walk through the colonnade. I've righted wrongs but at what cost? When I get back to my room, I find a note from my father informing me that he's arranged for us to meet before he departs. The next morning at the appointed time, I go to the Hermitage terrace. All traces of the sorrows and pain that transpired here are gone in another example of the washing away of wrongs. I pour tea for my father. The koi swim close to the terrace, looking for handouts. This is the most time I've spent alone with my father in my life, or at least that I can remember.

"Let us not waste these precious moments," he begins, breaking the silence. "If Respectful Lady were here, she'd be as proud of what you've accomplished as a doctor as I am."

"Thank you, Father," I say, bowing my head.

He regards me. "We do not know each other. For this I blame myself."

I'm unsure how to respond.

"After your mother died, I was brokenhearted." He slowly nods as if to acknowledge the truth of this assessment to himself. "I turned inward and away from my children. I thought only of myself and my career. I had studied so hard to take the imperial exams—"

"And look what happened," I interrupt, throwing aside decorum. "You were awarded by the emperor. You rose high on the Board of—"

"I achieved much success, but I abandoned you and your brother when you needed me."

"We had Miss Zhao."

"A concubine."

"She has always been loyal to you and to Yifeng and me."

He twists his beard between his fingers. For a moment I wonder if this meeting was a good idea. Then I decide to make one last plea. "Many years ago, Grandfather and I sat on this same spot. He told me that he became a doctor to balance the cruelties he'd delivered as a Grand Master for Governance on the Board of Punishments."

"I understand," my father says. Then he recites, "*Store up good deeds and you will meet with good. Store up evil actions and you will meet with evil.*"

"When I was at the Forbidden City, Empress Zhang, the ladies of the court, and I interceded on Meiling's behalf to reduce her sentence."

"Were you successful?"

"Meiling is alive."

My father concedes this fact with a tip of his head.

"Now I want to help Miss Chen." I go on to explain her circumstances.

My father listens, but he doesn't respond in the way I wish. "As I said earlier, I'm proud of what you've accomplished as a doctor, but perhaps you've interfered enough in household affairs."

"Or maybe I haven't done enough!"

He frowns in disapproval.

"Miss Chen showed great courage during the invasion of smallpox into the Garden of Fragrant Delights," I continue.

"It's not your place to—"

"Miss Chen didn't get pregnant by herself," I press on. "Was she a schemer or a victim? You didn't ask! You didn't even call on her!"

"This line of questioning would have humiliated your father-in-law and had the potential to upset the balance of power in the family. Leave it to him to decide whether or not to confront anyone else who might have been involved."

"But some consideration should be given to Miss Chen, don't you think? Why punish her for a man's conniving?"

My father's eyes narrow. "Your grandparents tell me you are good at the Four Examinations. I suggest you use that practice to consider what happened here. You asked if Miss Chen was a schemer or a victim. She schemed. No question. If she was also a victim, then who put her in that position, and why? I am less concerned with the Yang family's reputation *outside* the gates than I am with the impact these disruptions to power and decorum will have *inside* the gates. Think on this, Yunxian, and I believe you will come to the same conclusion I did. I was trying to protect you from further intrigues." He rises. "It was good to see you, Daughter. I hope not so many years pass until the next time."

I could weep, if my mind wasn't already running down the pathways he's opened for me with his questions about Miss Chen: *If she was also a victim, then who put her in that position, and why?* I can think of only one person.

At the Border of the Sky

My father has planted ideas in my head, and I want to pursue them, but the stresses of the past year now catch up to me: The time in the capital, plus the rigors of travel to and from Beijing. Being pregnant and giving birth. Taking care of Meiling. The heavenly flowers outbreak. The re-inquest. My head pounds, and my body aches. I go to bed, and Poppy pulls the draperies. I sleep. I feel like I could stay here for a month, but on the third day Poppy comes with a note. Miss Zhao has sent word that Grandmother is seriously ill. I dress and hurry to my husband. "I must go to her," I tell him.

He doesn't offer objections. I may have my husband's approval, but I need Lady Kuo to agree as well. When I walk to her room, I carry Lian in my arms. He grew a lot when I was treating the sick. His thighs are chubby, and his cheeks full. He's an agreeable baby, and I don't want to leave him again.

Lady Kuo greets me at the door to her room with her customary *keeck, keeck*. There are things I want to say and things I want to know, but they'll have to wait. Like my husband, she is amenable to my leaving.

"Our family wishes to extend its continued gratitude to your grandmother for her help during the weeks of the heavenly flowers invasion." She claps her hands, and Sparrow comes running. "Go to the front gate. Order the bearers to get a palanquin ready."

As soon as Sparrow departs, I say, "Once again I must leave my son—"

She brushes aside my concern. "I'll make sure the wet nurse fills his belly."

I put Lian in his grandmother's arms and turn away, promising myself that I'll make up for my absences from him as a baby when it's time for him to learn to read, write, and recite.

When I arrive at the Mansion of Golden Light, Inky whisks me through the courtyards to Grandmother's bedchamber. Grandfather slumps in a chair. Miss Zhao hovers over him in the gloom. I approach the bed but am brought up short by the sight of Grandmother. Her skin is the color and texture of clay, and her gray hair is splayed out as though floating on the surface of a pond. I ball my hands into fists to fortify myself. Then I step forward, with a smile on my face, my heart fully open, and my mind thrumming with ideas of what I can do to help her.

"Do you think I'm unaware of you trying to do the Four Examinations on me?" Grandmother asks.

Before I can respond, Miss Zhao says, "Maybe Yunxian can do something."

Grandmother's eyes drift to the lantern as she considers this. Then, "I'm beyond help."

Grandfather tries unsuccessfully to hide a groan. Miss Zhao shifts her gaze so Grandmother won't see her expression.

"No one is beyond help," I say, trying to convey confidence.

Grandmother's lips form into a delicate smile. "*Birds fly home to die, and foxes retreat to their burrows. Some things are inevitable.*" She takes my hand and presses it to her left breast. Through the padding of her clothes, I feel a lump as hard as a rock. My brain skitters, trying to find a solution.

"There are formulas you can take—"

"Do you think I haven't taken them already?" Grandmother asks. "For years? Until now I've kept the death demons in the shadows." After a long pause, she adds, "If I could cut it out, I would. Hopefully, I have many months left."

Grandfather buries his face in his hands. I'm trying to absorb this news but failing miserably. Grandmother was already long sick when she came to help me at the Hermitage. Knowing her time was limited, she came. Maybe that's *why* she came. I try to get Grandmother to tell me more about her illness—what herbs she's been taking, what suggestions for treatment Grandfather has had—but she deflects me, stating, "The time for all that is past." Which, of course, is the opposite of saying she might have many months left.

I go deep within myself to find the strength and ability to help her. I'm driven by one thought. When I was a little girl, I couldn't save my mother. I can't cure Grandmother, but I can ease her journey to the Afterworld. Grandfather and I work together, looking through books and ledgers, trying to find ingredients that will dull her pain and settle her qi. Miss Zhao and I take turns spoon-feeding the medicinal teas we brew.

On the third evening, Grandmother motions for me to come to her after Miss Zhao escorts Grandfather from the room so he can get some sleep.

"*Qi is finite, like a lamp's supply of oil,*" she recites in a weak voice. "*Death is a sickness no one can cure.*"

Her words lay bare the truth of the situation.

"You're sad," she continues. "I understand. But . . ." She closes her eyes, seeking strength. Then she once again recites. "*It is impossible to change the fate time has allotted, for even the best banquet must end and the guests depart.*"

"Grandmother . . ."

She struggles to gather herself. "I want you to have my books and medical supplies. Take special care of my copy of *Profound Formulas.*" She smacks the bed with her hand—a gesture made all the more important because of the effort it takes. "As you know, it is the last copy in existence. Study my notebooks, which are filled with my best treatments—"

"Grandmother, please. Let us have more days together."

She shakes her head. "I wish I could give you that, but death is coming."

My eyes tell me she's right even as my heart struggles to accept it. I offer to get Grandfather.

"No," she says, grabbing my hand and holding it with surprising vigor. "Just women . . ."

Before I can protest, she goes on. "If you memorize my

formulas—as I taught you to do when you were a girl—I will die content." She tells me of one notebook in particular in which she's recorded her best successes. "Keep that one extra safe."

I bow my head and promise to do her bidding. A few minutes later, Miss Zhao returns. She pulls a chair next to mine, and we sit together in silence. My father was gone for Respectful Lady's final hours, just as Grandfather is away from us now, which makes me wonder if a death vigil is something we women are compelled to do. I would not want Maoren to watch my final attempts at breath or see the messy things that happen as my soul departs my body.

I have witnessed many people die, but in Grandmother's last hours, her terrible mask of pain disappears, and a golden hue infuses her cheeks as though she's lit from within. Her breathing slows, but it isn't labored. She doesn't seem frightened. She presses my hand over her heart, and even in the final minutes I can feel her strength. And then she's gone. Miss Zhao goes outside to inform Inky. Immediately, the sounds of lamentations rise throughout the compound. Miss Zhao brings Grandfather. Tears trickle down his aged face as he stands next to the bed gazing at his wife.

I remove myself so I can change into mourning clothes made of the coarsest raw linen. Miss Zhao and Inky help me wash Grandmother's body and dress her in her burial garments. The next day, Grandfather meets with the geomancer, who chooses a date and place for Grandmother's burial. My brother is in the capital for his final studies to take the imperial exams, but my father comes to Wuxi to attend his mother's funeral rites. He brings with him Respectful Lady, who performs her duties well with Miss Zhao's assistance. As for my father, I had not thought I would see him again, let alone so soon after the re-inquest. He holds me when I weep tears of loss.

On the day of Grandmother's interment, a delegation that includes Master Yang, Lady Kuo, my husband, his uncles, and my two oldest daughters arrives from the Garden of Fragrant Delights. What seems like hundreds of others whom Grandmother treated over the years also come to venerate her and make offerings. I see Midwife Shi, Meiling and her husband. Every mourner wears a shade of white—like the autumn moon, snow, chalk, or mother's milk—all within the spectrum associated with death and bereavement. I prostrate myself on the ground and wail when Grandmother is laid in her inner coffin, which is then set inside a larger coffin made of the finest wood. Mourners burn paper money for her to use to pay off demon dogs and spirits that might hinder her journey to the Afterworld and burn even more for her to use to buy necessities when she reaches her new home. For the next forty-nine days, I make offerings of food and pour libations of rice wine before Grandmother's spirit tablet, so she won't go hungry or thirsty. But I eat and drink little. My head hurts, and I'm so tired.

And then it's time for me to return to my husband's home. I take with me Grandmother's books and notebooks, as well as the equipment she used for brewing tonics and teas and mixing poultices and ointments. Workmen build extra shelves in my room, and my mother-in-law sends rosewood cabinets for me to place against the walls—all to store my inheritance. I hide Grandmother's special notebook behind the panel in my marriage bed. Beyond these tasks, which are many, I'm useless.

I should open each and every book Grandmother gave me. I should examine the contents of every vial and jar. I should begin memorizing Grandmother's formulas. But I'm paralyzed by grief and exhaustion. My headache is blinding. I develop a sore throat, which turns into a deep, wet cough. I burn with fever. I prepare different formulas, but they don't help. The weakness that has plagued me off and on since I was a child has found residence in my body. I retire to my bed and the images of marital bliss that surrounded my mother when she lay dying.

Meiling comes daily. She reports on Doctor Wong, who, for the weeks I've been in mourning at the Mansion of Golden Light, had been roaming Wuxi's main square with a cangue around his neck to show the world his disgrace. She says the cangue's weight has produced sores on his shoulders that suppurate with blood and pus. People look at him and see a man so gaunt that it's as if he's half man, half ghost. I find not one drop of compassion for him. My father gave Doctor Wong the punishment he deserved.

His suffering would have ended too quickly if he'd lost his head in one quick chop of the executioner's sword.

I am not myself . . .

As the hours and days pass, I lose will and the last of my energy. I stop eating. I have no desire to drink. I sleep but never wake refreshed. The longer I stay in bed, the weaker I become. I have fever followed by chills. I feel as though part of my soul leaves me until one day I'm so frail that my body seems barely strong enough to bear the weight of my garments. The passing of a single day feels like three winters.

Meiling does for me a great intimate kindness. Every four days she unwraps my bindings, washes my feet, applies alum between the toes, and wraps my feet again. I continue to decline, drifting closer and closer to my grandmother. My temperature soars. Each breath takes effort. What I cough up is as dark in color as cheap jade. My chest feels as though someone has placed an anchor on it. A doctor is brought in. He sits behind a screen and asks questions, but I haven't the strength to answer them. One night, Maoren and my mother-in-law come to see me. They think I'm unaware of them, but I hear them discuss my health in serious terms. "You had better send a messenger to her father," my mother-in-law advises. First, though, my husband brings my daughters to my bedside. They are good girls, and I apologize for not seeing them into their marriages. "Take care of Ailan," I tell Yuelan and Chunlan. "Make sure her bindings stay tight, and that she practices her embroidery." Parting from my son is hardest of all. I waited so long to have him, yet I have not spent the time with him that a good mother should.

Later that night, the lamps are dimmed. Meiling perches on a stool so she can watch over me, but she falls asleep, holding my hand, her head on my quilt. All is quiet except for my ragged breathing. I'm unafraid. I've accepted what's coming, knowing I'll soon be reunited with my grandmother and mother. Then, at the border of the sky and earth's most distant corner, Grandmother Ru comes to me. Is this a dream? Am I having a fever vision? Is she a ghost? I cannot say, but she is before me as clearly and as solidly as the first time I met her. And she is *very* upset.

"As a Snake, you've always been vulnerable to those emotions and illnesses that attack from the inside, but now you must be strong," she booms as only a resident of the Afterworld can.

"I can do nothing to change course," I try to explain. "I fell ill when I married out. I fell ill after my first child was born. Now that you've left me, how can this sickness be a surprise? Sad emotions have always overtaken my body. Now is no different."

"It *is* different! This is the last time!"

"*You* are not real." I close my eyes, trying to drive away the apparition, but Grandmother doesn't—*won't*—leave.

"I *am* real." Her voice finally begins to lower as she returns to the matter-of-fact approach I know so well. "Like Guanyin, the Goddess of Mercy who sees into the hearts of all women, I've always felt that I could see through to your heart. Forever I've worried about your melancholic turn of mind and how it physically affected your body. This is your weakness, and it has been the pattern in your life. Why do you think I paired you with the daughter of a midwife? Her qi is exuberant, and I knew she would always take care of you. But now you must change. Do you think being feeble and pitiable presents a good example to your children?" When I don't answer, she goes on. "You may think this illness is fatal, but it isn't. I'm going to help you one last time. You have my special book of cases. Go to page fifty-eight. Follow the directions. In a few days, you will begin to feel better."

I consider this possibility.

"You have done your duty to your husband and his family," Grandmother goes on. "Now you must turn your attentions elsewhere. You were born to be a doctor of women, and a special destiny awaits you. You'll use the arts you learned from me to save the sick, and you will have a good, useful, and extraordinarily long life—living until you reach seventy-three years."

Could her prophecy possibly be real?

"But know this," she continues. "The sickly constitution you have endured will help you going forward. A doctor who understands her own nature—and the sufferings of her own body—can better treat another woman, for their natures and bodies are in sympathy." She starts to back away. I watch to see if she'll open the door, melt through a wall, or simply vanish. "You still have an important task ahead of you. I couldn't help Meiling, but you can. Give her the gift she desires. And remember, follow my medicine."

I jolt upright. Meiling still sits on the stool, asleep, with her head on my quilt. Poppy is curled on the floor in the first antechamber. I pry loose the hidden panel in my bed and pull out Grandmother's notebook. I gently touch Meiling's cheek. Her eyes widen to see me sitting up.

"Can you help me?" I ask.

She nods uncertainly. I rise and steady myself by grasping the carvings that grace that half-moon entrance to my bed. Meiling supports me as I wobble forward. The only reason I can walk at all is that she took care of my feet. We pass through the dressing room, step over Poppy, out of the marriage bed, and into my room. I sway as I turn over in my mind everything Grandmother told me.

"Take me to my desk," I request.

When we reach it, Meiling raises the wicks on two lamps, and I open Grandmother's notebook to the page she specified. As I read aloud, Meiling begins to pull ingredients from my shelves and drawers.

———

Grandmother was right. My fever comes down and my lungs slowly empty of phlegm, although it will take months to fully recover and rebuild my strength. My convalescence gives me time to contemplate. I've been lucky to have been cared for and loved since childhood by a circle of women. Now it's time for me to create a wider circle, so I can do for my daughters and other women in the household what Grandmother, Miss Zhao, Meiling, and even Poppy have done for me.

Spring begins to make an appearance, although the blossoms on the plum and crabapple trees remain vulnerable to frost. This is when we're supposed to say goodbye to the past and hello to new beginnings, and I do. I think about the contributions I can make with what remains of my life. In visiting death, I've found the inner strength Grandmother said I have. Just as she once told me to speak if I wanted to be heard, I finally understand that I must act in ways I haven't had the courage to do in the past and resolve some of the issues and problems that have existed in my life.

Now that I'm strong enough, I decide it's time to visit my mother-in-law. When my father and I had our time together on the Hermitage terrace after the re-inquest, he warned me against pursuing further intrigues within our gates. Maybe he was right, but I can't move forward with my life until I can pack away what happened to Spinster Aunt and Meiling once and for all. My father chose not to call Lady Kuo as a witness, but I still have questions for her I'd like answered.

Keeck, keeck. The familiar sound greets me when I enter Lady Kuo's room for the first time since I left for the capital so many months ago. Sparrow opens the windows to let the dawn light filter in and the suffocating smell of liquor breath disperse. My mother-in-law sees me and beckons me to her bed. I stand with my hands tucked up my sleeves, signaling that I'm not here to make obeisance or serve tea. She must see the change in me, or she intuits my purpose for being here, because she says, "I have good news for you. I've decided you may practice your medicine openly. You have proved yourself to be a *ming yi*—a famous doctor."

After all these years and everything that's transpired, I say, "I will not be so easily bought or silenced."

Lady Kuo sucks her lips into her mouth as though to swallow what she wishes to say. I don't doubt this will be a difficult conversation, with me pulling truth from her tongue painful word by painful word.

"Did you invite Doctor Wong to Miss Chen's bed?" I ask. "Or did something else happen—rape or an agreement between the two of them—that you decided should be kept a secret?"

I expect resistance, if not outright denials. I'm prepared either way. What I didn't anticipate is that she would look at me squarely, pat a spot next to her on the bed, and say, "Sit." Naturally, I do as I'm told.

"I love Maoren," she begins. "He is my son. But he was my *only* son. I tried to make another with my husband and got three daughters instead. Although we were still young, there came a point when he couldn't or wouldn't complete the task. I thought he was no longer interested in me."

"Which is why you purchased Miss Chen."

"When she didn't become full with child during her first months here, I thought she might be having the same problems with my husband that I'd experienced. Remember, years had passed since I'd last gotten pregnant. Desperate, I sought Doctor Wong's advice." She falls silent for a few moments. "If something happened to Maoren, especially once he started traveling back and forth to Nanjing, everything would transfer to Second Uncle. Power. Money. Land. Decisions. I had to do whatever I could to secure the Garden of Fragrant Delights and all the Yang holdings for our direct descendants, even if it meant going behind my husband's back—to spare him the humiliation—and sending a doctor to a concubine's bed." She takes my hand and stares into my eyes. "In Manzi, my husband and I had a ritual son in case something happened to Maoren. But of course, all I wished for was that you would give us the grandson we needed, which you did—"

"Eventually." We stare at each other. Finally, I say, "I keep thinking back to the day Miss Chen and I told you we were both pregnant. I thought you were angry."

"I wasn't angry. I was surprised. If I'd known you were full with child, everything might have turned out differently."

"I still only had a daughter. Your problem remained."

"That's true." Her eyes get a faraway look. She wouldn't be my mother-in-law if she didn't surprise me completely. "One day when you're the head woman of the Garden of Fragrant Delights, you might do as I did."

"I would never—"

"Wouldn't you? It's been my responsibility to make sure the family endures and that we have a son to make offerings to the ancestors. You'll eventually carry this burden. It's what I've been training you to do all these years. It's been my supreme duty as your mother-in-law."

I consider this. Have I misinterpreted her actions and her treatment of me? Perhaps. But that's not what's at issue here.

"In any case," my mother-in-law continues, "Doctor Wong gave the Yang family the son it needed. What I didn't realize at the time was that his desires would stretch far beyond mine."

"You could have stopped him."

"How? Think about it, Yunxian. What could I have done that would not have caused unending disruption, and disgrace to my husband, son, you, and everyone else in our line? And I include Miss Chen's daughters in that."

I hadn't thought about them. "Are they Doctor Wong's too?"

Lady Kuo shakes her head. "Fate. My husband eventually gave her four daughters—one more than he gave me."

"What about Spinster Aunt?"

"Until the re-inquest, I thought her death was a sad accident." She goes on to ask what would have been my next question. "The herbs Doctor Wong sent to give you in Beijing? I swear I did not know they would be harmful." She squeezes my hand. "These things I confessed to your father when he first arrived for the re-inquest. There were choices to be made to protect the descendants of our two families, and together we made them. He told me that for my punishment I will suffer in the Afterworld for all eternity. I told him I was content with that."

"So now, to keep me quiet, you'll allow me to treat patients?"

"I would hope you'd keep silent for the family. As for your medicine, you proved yourself to me long ago when you cured Yining."

The concubine's daughter I treated when I first married in . . .

"You've always turned a blind eye to my activities," I say, finally understanding.

She lifts a shoulder. Silence hangs between us. Then, "I hope that you'll continue to remain as discreet as you've always been."

I wait, feeling there's more.

After a moment, Lady Kuo continues. "So here we are. I have not been a particularly good teacher for you, but this is not uncommon. After all, having a daughter-in-law and mother-in-law in the same room is like tying a weasel and a rat together in a sock. The weasel and rat are enemies by nature. The weasel may be larger and have sharper teeth, but the rat is smarter and faster. I hope that going forward we can work together, and you will allow me to teach you to be the head woman of the household. And, as I said earlier, you may continue to treat women and girls. But please, *please*, remain inside the compound. Always consider how your activities affect the reputations of *all* the women and girls in our home, including your own daughters, who will be married out to other families one day."

"What about visiting Grandfather and Meiling?"

"You may continue to visit your family home and that of Young Midwife. But that is it. No treating patients *outside* our compound." She pauses, considering. "I will give you one additional gift, and that is to right the wrong against Midwife Shi. I will send a message to Wuxi's other elite families by allowing both Young Midwife and her mother to bring babies into the world here at the Garden of Fragrant Delights."

I weigh all this and decide to accept her conditions. Still, I will remain cautious. *Things always change to the opposite. The road up is the same as the road down.* If Lady Kuo's mind goes in a new direction tomorrow, then what? If all this weren't enough for me to take in, she adds one more request.

"I've longed for years to ask a kindness of you." She rests her wrist palm up on my thigh. "Can you find what is wrong with me?"

My mind is jumbled with thoughts and emotions, but I have the wherewithal to say, "I don't need to read to your pulses. I have long known what ails you."

There will be days and months—maybe even years—to sort out and understand all that's transpired, but for now I send Sparrow to my room to gather what I'll need. When she returns, I put Sichuan pepper flower in a pot of water and set it on the brazier. While I wait for the mixture to brew, I blend ingredients for an emetic to induce vomiting. Once both infusions are ready, I pull a small table to the bedside and set out two pairs of chopsticks and a bowl filled with the liquor my mother-in-law likes to drink.

"Sparrow, bring a lamp to the bed and hold it still," I order. Then I ask my mother-in-law to gargle the fiery pepper flower liquid until her mouth and throat are numb. Next, I give her the emetic to drink. The results are immediate. She vomits into the bowl until the watery traces of last night's meal are expelled. Sparrow cries out and backs away when she sees movement in the bowl. This prompts Lady Kuo to peer into it as well. When she sees baby worms swimming, she retches several more times, but nothing more comes out. She falls back to the bed, exhausted and pale. I put a hand on her shoulder to soften my warning.

"This next part will be uncomfortable."

"I'm ready," she says, bracing herself against the bed's back wall.

"Open your mouth as wide as you can." I use a flat piece of jade to hold down her tongue. "Relax," I instruct. "I'm going to massage your throat." To Sparrow, I say, "Hold the lamp a little closer."

Lady Kuo's tongue quivers as I use my left hand to massage from the hollow of her neck upward along the pipe leading to her mouth. After a couple of minutes, something white appears at the back of her throat. My right hand grabs a pair of the chopsticks.

"Close your eyes," I tell my mother-in-law. As soon as they're shut, I use the chopsticks to reach to the very back of her throat, grab hold of what I believe to be the head of the mother worm, and begin to pull. As it rises past Lady Kuo's lips, my flesh crawls. Sparrow whimpers next to me, but she keeps the lamp steady. I pull out the piece of jade, drop it on the floor, and move the chopsticks to my left hand. I pick up the other pair of chopsticks, reach down to pluck what I hope is the middle of the worm, and keep pulling. It looks like the type of long noodle we serve on special occasions to bring to mind long life, but noodles don't wiggle and squirm. And this is no mere garden worm. Its body ripples like that of a snake. *I was born in the Year of the Snake,* I tell myself. *I am not afraid.*

Using the chopsticks in my left hand, I put the upper part of the worm in the bowl of liquor where the babies continue to swim, and then reach back into Lady Kuo's mouth to latch on to the next segment. Finally, the tail snaps out of her throat. I drop the rest of the worm in the bowl. It must be a meter in length.

It wasn't my mother-in-law who had a thirst for liquor. It was the worm and her babies.

———

I next devote myself to completing the task Grandmother set for me: to help Meiling get pregnant. I stay up late to read by lantern light Grandmother's books and notebooks. I study the medical classics about pregnancy and birth. I pull my notebook from its hiding place in my marriage bed to review my own cases. I go over in my mind the herbs Meiling told me Grandmother and Doctor Wong gave her and why they were ineffective. I consider the words of the great physician Chen Ziming from two hundred years ago: *Men think of the bedroom when their Essence is exuberant; women crave pregnancy when their Blood is exuberant.*

A path becomes clear to me. I decide to use cooling and tranquilizing herbs for Meiling's husband in a formula composed of lotus buds and snake-bramble seed to boost his potency, and deer horn and a particular species of rose hips, which inspires the male body to gather and consolidate fluids, especially Essence. For Meiling, I make Beginning of Joy pill, which has sixteen ingredients, including ginseng, licorice, angelica, and atractylodis, to strengthen her qi and Blood and, crucially, prevent miscarriage. I also burn moxibustion on her belly to build welcoming warmth in her child palace.

When Meiling's monthly moon water doesn't arrive, she dismisses the symptom, saying, "It has been an infrequent visitor since we left Beijing." The week after that, she looks tired and pale. She rejects these signs too. "The fish I ate last night did not agree with me." With those words, as innocuous as they are, it finally comes to me why Grandmother and Midwife Shi thought *I* would be a good match for Meiling. If I had physical and emotional flaws, which Meiling's caring heart could rescue me from time and again, then she had the weakness of feeling she was not worthy of the blessings of the world, which I could help through my unconscious acceptance of the gifts and privileges I was born into. In our friendship—with all its twists and moments of tumult—was the yin and yang of life.

The next week, although I'm confident of my diagnosis, I decide to test if Kailoo has successfully planted a baby. Meiling places her wrist in my hand so I can feel her pulse. I let my heart and breath slow until I am one with my friend, and there it is. I find striking yin and salient yang. I smile and tell her the good news, but she remains skeptical, afraid to be disappointed.

"I anticipated this, and I'm prepared," I tell her. "I knew you wouldn't be satisfied with the usual tea made from lovage root and mugwort, though you know that it stimulates the fetus to jump and twirl so that a mother can feel it at just a few months. So, I've added honey locust fruit as a male doctor would." I hand her the cup. "We say, *Joy at its height births sorrow*, but couldn't we look at it the other way around and say that extreme adversity can be the beginning of good fortune?"

She regards me, a hopeful look on her face.

"Trust me," I say. "Drink."

Meiling swallows the tea and—happiness of happiness— promptly throws up.

Her morning sickness turns out to be relentless. I include perilla stalk in a tonic to strengthen her stomach. To ward against miscarriage, I create a formula using purple thyme and skullcap to cool maternal Fire.

"Be calm," I tell her. "Follow my instructions, and all will be well."

———

There is soft happiness in sadness and deep sadness in happiness. This aphorism can be applied to many situations, but perhaps none is more poignant than preparing a daughter to go to her husband's home. What joy it is to pin up Yuelan's hair, signaling to the women and girls in the inner chambers that she is ready for marriage. What sadness it is to see her clothes packed into trunks and the most precious of her dowry gifts of jewelry, scrolls, and strings of cash wrapped in red silk and placed in lacquer boxes inlaid with gold. What satisfaction I feel to give Second Aunt, as the woman in our household with proven fecundity at giving birth to sons, the honor of sending her to Yuelan's future home to "make up the room" in preparation for her arrival. What surprising pleasure I get from imparting words of advice alongside my mother-in-law. "Always respect your mother-in-law," I say. "Always obey." Lady Kuo hears this, folds her hands together, and adds in a sweet—mocking?—tone, "Listen to your mother-in-law, but follow your mother's example: *Obey, obey, obey, then do what you want.*" I never could have imagined that my mother-in-law and I would one day find a way to laugh together, and yet we have.

I think back to my own wedding day, the first time I saw Maoren, and our first night of bedroom affairs. No one expects passion to last forever, but ours dissipated too soon. I've told myself that perhaps he lost interest in me during the time I was away on the Grand Canal and at the palace, caring for the ill in the Hermitage, observing weeks of ritual mourning for Grandmother, and being bedridden with my recent illness. Or maybe what I did to get to the truth of what happened here in the Garden of Fragrant Delights tainted me in his eyes. In the end, the cause doesn't matter, because we've accomplished our obligation to secure the Yang family line. (And in truth, it's been years since we enjoyed night sports by day.) I could harbor disappointment in my husband, but I prefer to look at it this way: I'm a wife with responsibilities, and he's earned the right to have the company of a woman whose only purpose is to entertain . . . and provide treats in the bedchamber. He seems pleased when I offer to buy him a concubine.

"I trust she will be pleasant," he says.

"I will find someone as pleasant of disposition as she is of face," I promise.

And I do. I think of my grandfather's three Jades when I name the girl I buy for my husband Snowgoose. (In time, I might find Maoren another Snowpink, but now is too soon for him to be reminded of her and their son.) Already I imagine all the other Snows who might enter the compound one day—Snowlight, Snowcrystal, Snowdawn. For now, though, Snowgoose evokes purity, lightness, and the ability to carry someone away from earthly concerns. Her face is unmarked by smallpox scars or lines of worry. Her eyebrows curve like willow leaves, and her lips are so pink that she need not apply color unless she so chooses. She has a slender form, with a swaying walk. When she's brought to the household, I personally help her dress in an aqua silk gown with a pattern of butterflies and flowers in raised silver thread. I supervise as her hair is styled into a bun and enclosed in a circlet of gold filigree. I tuck into her hair long pins on which shimmering blue butterflies made from kingfisher feathers decorate the ends, giving the effect of a garden at the height of spring. I walk my husband to the concubine's door, open it, and give him a gentle push.

As I head back to my own rooms, I consider something I learned from my grandmother. Every woman must treat her husband's concubines well. Our behavior in this regard raises the quality of our benevolence in our husbands' eyes. But I believe we have even more to gain than a husband's admiration, and that is compassion. We may not care for concubines, but it's important to remember that each one came from the womb of a woman. Every girl—no matter how small-minded or unfortunate—had a mother who nursed and cared for her. Each one—no matter how jealous we might be when our husband visits her—is still a human being.

These thoughts lead me to Miss Chen. Even though my father warned me against interfering in other people's lives, I still want to help her. I discreetly ask the concubines in the household about her whereabouts. They direct me to a rooming house, where I find Miss Chen, protected by walls and shrouded in veils so no one will see her ruined face. She has always been skilled at embroidery. A few words placed here and a few placed there, and soon elite women in Wuxi are buying embroidered sleeve guards, the tops of bound-foot shoes, and nightclothes from a mysterious unnamed woman. For Miss Chen's part, she has perfected the art of imperfection by deliberately leaving out a single stitch that might complete a peony, goldfish, or cloud. The message is clear—and one that makes a good gift to daughters who are marrying out: be humble but also recognize that no one is perfect. Meiling and Kailoo hire Fifth Daughter, Miss Chen's surviving child. She works in the tea shop, assists Meiling in her midwife duties, and cleans their home. These are not the chores typically given to a bound-footed girl, but at least she will earn a living. By the time Meiling's baby announces it's ready to breathe the air of this world, Fifth Daughter is able to help Midwife Shi deliver her grandson.

When I step out from behind the screen that has shielded me from the sight of blood and mess of childbirth, the baby has already been placed in Meiling's arms. She gazes up at me and says, "My heart will forever be attached to my son's." When I look down into his face, I'm reminded of the aphorism that says, *No mud, no lotus.*

As the Hongzhi emperor completes the fifth year of his reign, my oldest daughter is pregnant with her first child. Chunlan and Ailan are both betrothed. Lian is nineteen months old, and Poppy spends her days chasing after him. My brother has successfully passed the highest level of the imperial exams and been presented to the emperor. As for myself, I have just turned thirty-one. I've had many challenges over the last thirty-two months, and I still have many years of rice-and-salt days ahead of me, but I see my future in a way I never have before. I will use all that my grandparents, especially my grandmother, taught me to heal women. Without fear. Without hesitation.

PART IV

SITTING QUIETLY

The Fifth Through Sixth Years
of the Zhengde Emperor's Reign
(1510–1511)

White-Haired, Growing Old Together

How is a life located in time? By the movement of the sun and the moon, by the changing of seasons, or by the marking of the New Year's Festival? By how we note the stages of a woman's life in milk days, hair-pinning days, rice-and-salt days, or sitting quietly? A famous couplet tells us *Heaven adds time and people get older; spring fills the world and blessing fills the door.* The young get married and have babies; those of middle age grow old and die. We make offerings to our ancestors in the Afterworld in the anticipation that they will reward us in this world. We try to make good decisions—by choosing wives for our sons, creating good alliances through the marriages of our daughters, planting crops, buying land and businesses, and hiring the best tutors for our sons—in hopes that we will secure goodness and prosperity for future generations. But nothing is guaranteed. An unblemished face will grow wrinkles in time and the white petals of the azalea will turn brown and fall. It is a never-ending cycle that will continue through eternity.

Nineteen years have passed since the smallpox invasion, and I have officially entered the time of sitting quietly. This is the period in a woman's life when, by definition, she waits for death to remove her from the struggles of life, but no one would know it from observing me. When my father-in-law died five years ago, my husband became headman of the Garden of Fragrant Delights. Maoren retired from the Board of Punishments and currently oversees all matters pertaining to the Yang family with help from

Second Uncle, who has proved himself to be wise, loyal, and hard-working, as well as an excellent model of behavior to his great-nephew and my son, Lian, who will one day lead the Garden of Fragrant Delights. I now preside over a four-generation household and hope to live long enough to see the next generation. *An extended family line is like a tree with a sturdy trunk, deep roots, and many branches.* To that end, I'm responsible for the health not only of all the children and women in the Garden of Fragrant Delights but also for the working women who come to the back gate to seek my help.

As Lady Tan, I also bear all the burdens and obligations of running the household—managing the budget, receiving rents paid by those who work our lands, overseeing construction projects and repairs, purchasing staples like coal, rice, and salt, as well as all other foodstuffs, selecting and hiring servants and tutors, and arranging for weddings and funerals. I like to think I'm straight-forward in my approach to my duties and to our servants. Not once—at least not yet—have I drawn on the strategies that were so much a part of Lady Kuo's way of presiding. All of which is to say I do not have time to sit and watch the flowers grow in their leisure or enjoy the moon's travel across the night sky. Rather, I am the gatekeeper of the family resources. As such, my days begin early, and they are very long.

I'm already awake and dressed when my daughter-in-law taps on the door to my bedchamber, enters, and serves me tea. She recently turned seventeen. She is the mother of my first grandson and will soon give birth to another child, hopefully another son. My concern, the same one that preoccupied Lady Kuo, is that the Yang wives are not producing enough sons, despite my best efforts to make the women in the household fertile. What's worrisome is that if we keep on this path, the family will continue to grow smaller and money will become scarcer, as we won't have enough men to run our businesses or sons to do well in the imperial exams.

"When Midwife Shi comes for her weekly visit," I say to my daughter-in-law, "I expect you to visit the Hermitage so we can both examine you." (I still have a hard time thinking of Meiling as Midwife Shi, but she took on the title after her mother died.)

"I will be there, Lady Tan," she answers, her head politely bowed.

I count on this girl to be an extra pair of eyes and ears for me, so I ask, "Are there others in the household I should see today?"

"Fourth Aunt is having trouble with her granddaughter's footbinding—"

"Fourth Aunt should have told me!"

"She blames herself that she hasn't been more vigilant, and she didn't want to disappoint you."

"Tell her not to worry about my opinion. What matters is that infection doesn't settle in her granddaughter's feet. I will visit the child after Midwife Shi leaves."

"Yes, Lady Tan."

I smile at the girl. "How are Lian's studies progressing?"

"He was in his library, working all night."

My smile broadens. "He has always been a good student."

"As you have told me."

"Then you shall hear it again, so you might be a good mother to your sons when they are old enough." I move to my dressing table to apply rouge and lip color. "I started teaching Lian when he was three. I thought to myself if a child can memorize a nursery rhyme, then why not something more important? I opened the *Book of Odes*. I remember well the first lesson Lian learned by heart. *He who depends on himself will have the greatest happiness.* And look! It has turned out to be so."

My daughter-in-law begins to brush my hair. I like the girl. She's obedient, with a kindly disposition. And she's particularly adept at styling high buns and attaching ornamental pins and other decorations.

"Lian is already a *juren*," I go on, as if she didn't know this already. "He passed this level of the imperial exams at an age earlier than my father, my grandfather, or Lian's father. Oh, such a bright future lies ahead." As if in agreement, my daughter-in-law steps to my side so I can see her pregnant belly. I nod to acknowledge her silent message. Then, "Please go ahead to the inner chambers. I shall be along shortly."

My first stops this morning are to the kitchen, the granary,

325

and the weaving room. Next, since the Dragon Boat Festival is nearly upon us, I check to make sure preparations are under way to protect the house and its inhabitants from the Five Poisonous Creatures that wake up at this time of year. Servants have burned ruby sulfur throughout the compound to ward them off and hung bouquets of mugwort over the gates to keep evil spirits at bay.

By the time I reach the inner chambers, everyone is already deep into their morning activities. As the model who sets the example for womanhood, it's my duty to pass proper values on to the daughters in our family so they might marry out into good families, while my actions—if in alignment with the cosmos—maintain tranquility and decorum among the wives and concubines who live within the protective walls of our compound. I pay obeisance to Lady Kuo, who sits with the spinsters and other widows. I check to make sure Poppy is nearby. For the last two years, she has loyally served as personal maid to my mother-in-law, who needs help with everything. My youngest daughter, Ailan, is also part of this group. Her betrothal was canceled after the matchmaker saw the extent of her heavenly flowers scars. My poor girl is the new Spinster Aunt, although she's only twenty-four.

I give special attention to the young mothers to remind them to take those formulas that promote fertility, encourage them to continue teaching their sons and daughters, and supervise those who are binding a daughter's feet. "*A plain face is given by Heaven,*" I recite, "*but poorly bound feet are a sign of laziness.*" My instructions and warnings are met with a chorus of "Yes, Lady Tan," and "Thank you, Lady Tan." Last, I nod to the concubines. These women, who rely on their beauty for power and prestige, are as catty and petty as they are in every home. I prefer peace be kept, but I try to maintain control from a distance. *Sit on the mountaintop and watch the tigers fight.* Best not to get scratched.

Once I've made my rounds, I stand in the center of the room and clap my hands to get everyone's attention. It's taken me a few years as the head woman of the household to reach this decision, and I'm not sure how everyone will receive it. "We have just entered the fifth month," I begin. "The custom in the Garden of Fragrant Delights has always been for the concubines to accompany

their masters to Lake Tai to celebrate the Dragon Boat Festival."
In their circle, the concubines gracefully nod to each other in acknowledgment of this special privilege. "This year all concubines
will stay home. Whoever else would like to attend the Dragon
Boat Festival may do so—from babies to grandmothers."

My announcement is greeted with surprised gasps from the
wives and sullen looks from the concubines, but no one can fight
me on this. I am, after all, Lady Tan. Later, when I seek out my
mother-in-law, she comments, "You've always been a different
kind of thinker." I suppose that's true. She adds, "I hope this
doesn't cause trouble with the men." I hope it doesn't either. Then
she gives me a steely stare and says, "I will be coming. I have always wanted to attend the festival." A hidden desire of the heart
can now be achieved.

Two days later, on the fifth day of the fifth month, every female from a six-week-old infant to an ancient auntie—apart from
the concubines—arrives in the inner quarters dressed in her best
finery. I wear a silk gauze dress with a train that snakes out behind
me like a pearly tail. Jade earrings in the shape of feathers dangle
from my ears. As we make our way to the front gate, the rustling
of silks and satins and the tinkling of hair ornaments nearly drown
out the birdsong, while our rose-cloud capes float in our wakes. I
hope I'm right about this decision. My grandmother disapproved
of attending the Dragon Boat Festival, because she wanted to
maintain her integrity as a doctor. Lady Kuo believed that when
she sent the concubines with their masters, those men would come
home ready to sire sons with their wives. My wish: let the wives
tantalize their husbands and make the husbands woo their wives.

I've arranged for palanquins, sedan chairs, and a carriage to
take us to Lake Tai, where we'll meet our sons and husbands. At
the drop-off area, we carefully step to the ground and join hundreds, maybe thousands, of residents of Wuxi from every level of
society—from the poorest of the poor to high-ranking officials
and their families—as they walk to the shore. At one of many
docks, we board a leisure vessel to take us across the lake. In the
distance, we see the boats that will be competing today. On each
one, the upturned bow has been shaped into a dragon's head, with

an open mouth and painted eyes. Just glimpsing them builds excitement in us. To be able to behold the races . . .

We reach the far bank and disembark. Half the women of my household ooh and aah at every new sight, while the other half have been awed into contemplative silence.

"Please be mindful," I warn them. "Older girls, hold your younger sisters' hands. Mothers, aunts, and grandmothers, I caution you as well. I've been told the pathways are not as manicured as what we have at home. Be careful not to fall."

Murmurs of agreement reach my ears. Not one woman or girl will rebel, because each one knows I give the care of her feet prime importance. Over my years as a doctor, I've seen too many cases where gangrene has set in. Many girls die—drifting off like leaves falling in autumn winds, like lamp wicks burned to ash. As worthless branches on the family tree, as girls who are being raised by their natal families only until they are married into their husbands' families, they are not memorialized. No records of their deaths, no memorial tablets, and no great mourning. As for the adult women who are haphazard in the care of their feet, each one reminds me of my mother.

"Poppy?" I call out sharply.

"I'm here."

I spot her in the crowd. She has a firm grip on my mother-in-law's elbow.

"Then let us begin. Everyone stay together. And please remain vigilant." I offer one last caution: "This is our first time here. Let's not allow a tragedy to make it our last."

We climb a short hill, heading to a private pavilion where the men of our family have gathered to watch the races. Cypress, gnarled pines, and osmanthus trees, as well as towering stands of bamboo, paint the shoreline and surrounding peaks a thousand shades of green. The lake stretches out fifty *li*, maybe more. The embankment is built of stone. Bridges—one with four hundred arches—bisect the lake at different spots. Shrines dot the hillsides. A pagoda rises like a ladder fourteen stories into the heavens. A crane swoops and cries out. Up ahead, I see Maoren, who greets me with a beckoning wave. When I reach him, he takes my hands in his.

"I'm happy to have you here," he says.

Servants have set up a picnic of freshwater crabs, for which Lake Tai is known, soup, rice dumplings wrapped in leaves and tied with string, pickles, and jars of rice wine. Couples sit together—sometimes by themselves, sometimes in little groups. Second Uncle and Second Aunt have their own circle, with their sons, their wives, and grandchildren. He has rightfully earned the respect befitting an elder in the Yang family, and, after all these years, Second Aunt is content, if not actually happy. Elsewhere, some of the usual divisions have been forgotten as boys and girls play together. Below us, the lake shimmers, reflecting the hills and clouds. In addition to the dragon boats, pleasure vessels—decorated with brocade curtains and fluttering banners—sweep back and forth across the water, each with its own party onboard.

The time arrives for the races to begin. The first two boats line up side by side in the middle of the lake. From this vantage point, I can see more clearly the ways in which each boat's dragon carries its own unique personality—from the curl of its whiskers to the intricacy of its scales. A gong is hit. The lead man on each vessel rhythmically bangs a drum, summoning the dragon heart of his boat to inspire the rowers. Oars fly, disturbing the glistening reflections and sending rippling waves across the lake. Maoren and some of the other men loudly urge their favorite boats to win. During the second race, some of the ladies of the household completely forget themselves and call out too. By the third race, the men and women of the Yang family are shouting together and raising cups of rice wine when their preferred boat crosses the finish line first.

Next, the winners of the first heats compete against each other. More favorites are eliminated. In the early afternoon, the two finalists pull into position. I'm happy to see that Maoren's top pick has made it this far. It would be unseemly for me as Lady Tan to express my emotions by cheering as the gong is hit. Unseemly or not, sounds burst forth from me with such exuberance that I'm forced to clasp my hands over my mouth. For many years my husband has followed the adage that instructs *Ascend the bed, act like a husband; descend the bed, act like a gentleman.* But in this moment, decorum is forgotten. He wraps his arm around my waist and pulls me close.

More wine is poured. Couples, families, and groups of unmarried boys leave our pavilion to ramble the shade-protected pathways. Other festival guests are doing the same. I'm pretty sure I glimpse Oriole, the brickmaker, with her head bent toward a man who must be her husband. Not only has she remained healed, but over the years she's recommended me to women like herself who have suffered from taxation from toil. I'd love to approach her to say hello, but Maoren says, "As Master Yang and Lady Tan, we must stay here and let others pay their respects."

It is said that marriage and fortune are predestined, but Maoren and I also worked closely with the matchmaker to make sure that our two oldest daughters married well and, as it's turned out, happily. Yuelan and Chunlan live close enough that I can visit them regularly. It has been a gift in my life to help them through their pregnancies and births. Still, to see them here—with their young children in tow, all dressed as though they're on their way to the imperial palace—gives me great joy. How kind my daughters are to their younger sister, who's come on this excursion covered by a veil that reaches longer than her fingertips.

While I wait for Meiling and her husband to arrive, others come to say hello. My brother, Yifeng, steps into the pavilion wearing the gown, hat, and embroidered insignia that announce to all his status as a magistrate. His son, my nephew, is now studying for the exams. I believe he will follow his father into the ranks of civil service. Yifeng and I visit often—at New Year's and on those dates when together we make offerings to those we've lost. Grandfather died three years after Grandmother's passing. Not long after, my father retired. He returned to Wuxi with his wife to live in the Mansion of Golden Light, where he could use his connections to benefit young men hoping to rise in official-dom. He died two years ago. His second Respectful Lady died within a year. Yifeng performed and continues to perform all the rites.

"Where is Miss Zhao?" I ask, looking over my brother's shoulder.

"Now that she's attained the status of Honorable Mother," he answers, "she felt it was not proper for her to come."

"Honorable Mother," I echo. It pleases me that Yifeng remains thoroughly devoted to Miss Zhao. But if for some reason his wife should grow to dislike Miss Zhao, then I will welcome her into the Garden of Fragrant Delights. It took me many years to realize she's not much older than I am, so maybe we will be old ladies together, embroidering and telling stories in a special corner of the inner chambers.

Meiling arrives at last. She is now well-to-do in her own right, wearing fine gowns purchased with her own money. Her husband, also prosperous, walks proudly next to her. Between them, Dairu, their son of eighteen years. Following a few steps behind is Miss Chen's surviving child, Fifth Daughter, who some in Wuxi now call Young Midwife.

Dairu hurries ahead of his parents, bows to my husband and me, and then asks if Lian is here. The boy is polite, educated, as I promised Meiling, in our home school. "Let me take you to him," Maoren says. My husband rises and leaves with Dairu.

Kailoo turns to Meiling. "Wife, I want to walk to the pagoda. Will it be all right if I leave you here for a bit?"

Once our husbands are gone from sight, Meiling sits next to me. So often we hear of companionate marriages, but I have found deep-heart love with Meiling.

"Do you remember when Grandmother discussed with your mother the possibility of a match between the two of us?" I ask.

Meiling nods. "*Friendship is a contract between two hearts. With hearts united, women can laugh and cry, live and die together.*"

"Did you imagine then how true that would be for us?"

"I didn't, but I also couldn't have imagined seeing you here at the festival," she answers with a delicate chuckle.

I gaze out across the lake. "Your word pictures brought this to me for many years. It is exactly as I thought it would be."

"And in exchange, you taught me how to read and write actual words."

I pour two cups of wine, and we watch the children play for a while.

"Have you chosen which cases to include in your book?" Meiling asks.

I sigh and hold my palms open skyward. "I don't know why you persist in nagging me about this."

"Because I think you should write it. You know the saying. *Old men have much knowledge and experience just as old trees have many roots.*"

"Are you calling me an old man?" I ask in a teasing tone.

"I'm pointing out that you're a doctor who has treated women and girls for decades. You should share your knowledge."

"I'd like to reach more wives and mothers," I confess, embarrassed to voice this desire even to my friend. "But if—and I mean *if*—I wrote what you suggest, wouldn't people think I'm seeking fame?"

"You are not Doctor Wong," she replies sternly. "You'd be writing this to help women."

I mull over the idea as I do every time Meiling brings it up. "If I could write descriptions of symptoms followed by recipes for formulas with exact measurements and times required for brewing, then wives and mothers wouldn't have to risk their modesty or that of their daughters to find paths to wellness—"

"That's what I've been telling you."

"Women would need to be able to read," I point out.

"Not every woman has this skill," my friend admits. "But who knows? Maybe a woman could ask a neighbor to read it to her."

We fall into silence, both of us in thought.

Meiling touches my wrist to get my attention. "If you choose simple ingredients—"

"Inexpensive, you mean!"

We laugh, but she's right.

"No one would ever say my remedies are showy," I say at last. "I always think about the tie between emotions and the body. *Fierce joy attacks yang; fierce anger damages yin.* If I were to write a book, I'd want to include Liver-related conditions that are affected by the different types of anger we women must hide from our husbands, mothers-in-law, and concubines. And then there are the ailments connected to Lung emotions—sadness and worry."

"Do you remember the brickmaker?" Meiling asks.

"I think I saw Oriole here today—"

"Could you also say that women not only struggle with their emotions but also are burdened by too much labor, while some women, like Oriole, are harmed by excessive labor?"

I nod, taking in her words. "I don't know of a single male physician who has recorded cases related to working—common—women."

Kailoo strolls toward us, which means Meiling's and my time together is coming to a close. My friend squeezes my wrist. "Say you'll do this. No, promise me you'll do it."

"But I don't know where to start."

She gives me a look that could not be clearer in its message. *Stop acting like your mind is empty of thoughts and ideas.* Then she goes ahead and creates a path for me. "Your notebooks. You've recorded every case."

But instead of convincing me, her suggestion makes the idea of this project all the more daunting. "If—and again I say *if*—I do this, I'll need your help."

She tips her head coyly. "All you had to do was ask."

A few hours later, my family begins the journey home. No matter the age, everyone looks tired but happy. It pleases me greatly to see husbands sitting with their wives as we glide across the water. I hope that a year from now we will see many infant sons.

That night Maoren comes to my bedchamber. He sits cross-legged at one end of my marriage bed. I sit across from him, my legs tucked to the side, my gown flowing about me, my feet peeping out just so. While he has his trio of Snows to keep him entertained, he still likes to come to my bedchamber now and then. I may have given birth to four children. I may not be as slender and lithe as I once was. I may even have a few lines at the corners of my eyes, but my feet are as perfect as the day my mother finished shaping them. Maoren takes them in his hands. Men may be heaven and the sun, but nothing can change the essential weakness of Essence. Despite all we women are taught, I suspect that in time every wife on earth comes to understand this fundamental truth.

———

The next day, I stay in the inner chambers through lunch and then absent myself to go to the Hermitage. The gingko trees have grown and the stands of bamboo thickened, but the sound of wind through branches and water trickling over rocks has remained the same. I cross the zigzag bridge to the Hermitage terrace. The building may have originally been intended as a place for men to meet, but it's fully mine now. The interior looks much like my grandparents' pharmacy did in the Mansion of Golden Light. Eight teak chairs are lined up with their backs to a wall. Grandmother Ru's books and jars of herbs fill shelves on the opposite wall. After Grandfather's passing, I moved his library of medical books and the larger furniture, including my grandparents' three pearwood medicine cabinets with all the little drawers to hold ingredients, into the Hermitage as well.

Never force an illness to fit an existing formula. What matters is to find balance between the body, emotions, and the world. Almost everything I use to make medicines I keep here in the Hermitage. My herbs of choice are peony, angelica root, and lotus leaf—all of which strengthen a woman's yin. In addition to the standard herbs suitable for women and girls, I also stock the usual ingredients that a wife can give her husband to promote his liveliness in the bedchamber or extend his longevity.

The first woman who comes today is from the outside. She's as thin as a reed. Her pulses lack vitality, and her flesh has a yellowish tint to it. "I've given birth to ten children," she mumbles as though she doesn't have the strength to push the words from her mouth.

"You have done your wifely duties well," I praise her.

"But I don't want to have another baby. I *can't* have another one. I'm so tired."

Of course she's tired. Too many women suffer from at least one of the Five Fatigues, three of which are brought on by grief, worry, and enervation. None, however, is as difficult to avoid or overcome as the fatigue that comes from giving birth and raising children—especially for the poor, who are without help. The symptoms are easy to recognize: loss of weight due to malnutrition, pallor brought on by exhaustion, feet and hands that go from cold to hot and back again, and dreams that interrupt the restorative nature of sleep. I have yet to meet a man who would be able to sustain a balanced qi when faced with such difficulties and challenges.

"You want control over your body," I say, "but you're afraid of what will happen if you tell your husband you will not perform bedchamber activities."

"Very afraid," she admits.

"I can give you herbs to regulate your monthly moon water, guaranteeing that it will arrive on time," I promise her. "You must take the remedy without fail. If you don't and you forget yourself one night, you may become pregnant."

The wife of one of my husband's cousins arrives next for a follow-up visit.

"I can't wash away my anger," she tells me as she weeps into a handkerchief.

"Cases like yours are difficult to treat," I say.

"I'm grateful that your father helped my husband get appointed to a post on the Board of Punishments, but—"

"I'm sorry for my father's part in your suffering." I try to sound placating, but inside I think about how levying punishments—beatings, banishment, and death—is so contrary to the purpose of women, which is to bring life into the world. But this is not the only issue. To celebrate a recent promotion, my patient's husband has acquired a concubine just fifteen years old. What woman wouldn't become ill from anger?

I hold her wrist to feel her pulse. "I've been thinking about your case, and this morning I made adjustments to your formula. You will taste the difference."

She nods to let me know she understands.

"You and I can do nothing about your husband and his concubine," I go on, "and I don't know that I can extinguish completely the fire that burns in your heart, but let us try to smother the flames until they're smoldering embers."

My third case is one I know only too well and have suffered from myself: the inability of a wife to give her husband a son. The patient is thirty years old and married to another of my husband's cousins. I perform three of the Four Examinations and then consider how they've changed in the months I've been treating her. Then I begin to ask . . .

"Tell me about your monthly moon water. Has it become regular yet?"

The woman shakes her head, keeping her eyes focused on her hands.

"Would you call it heavy or light when it arrives?" I inquire.

She whispers her reply. "So heavy I feel dizzy when it comes."

And on it goes.

Later, after the last patient leaves, I make a pot of tea and sit on the terrace. My mind is filled with ideas about the kinds of cases I could include in a book. I want to write about those problems that stem solely from *being* a woman. Oh, our feet may take different shapes and mark us by class, but we share breasts and the travails of the child palace. We are connected through blood and Blood. We also share the same emotions. When suffering, how can a woman not feel despair, frustration, or anger—whether rich or poor, educated or illiterate, childless or a mother? In other words, we are all trapped to some extent by our physical and emotional selves, but each woman is trapped in a different way. The empress—the most important woman in the world—is confined to the Great Within. Women like those who live in the Garden of Fragrant Delights and the Mansion of Golden Light may be among the most elite in China, but we're also the most constrained, having lived our entire lives in the inner chambers in first our parents' homes, then our husbands'. Concubines and servants get glimpses of the outside world, but they are bought and sold. Common women— those married to farmers, butchers, and shopkeepers, those who labor in silk factories or sort tea leaves, and those who fall under the category of the Three Aunties and Six Grannies—may work in the outside world of men, but they can't avoid the hardships that come as a result. Just look at Meiling. She can go where she wants when she wants, but a midwife like her must suffer the disdain of husbands and fathers. Isn't that just another version of being trapped?

When Meiling arrives the next morning, I sit at a respectful distance as she examines the women in our household who've entered the month or are doing the month. After each woman, Meiling looks my way and says, "All is well." I never doubt her assessments.

When her examinations are complete, I invite her to my bed-chamber. Poppy brings in a light meal. As my friend and I eat, I relay the ideas I've been pondering about medicine for women.

"This is exactly why I think you should write a book," she says, her enthusiasm bright.

"Then we shall begin after lunch."

Later, she follows me through the antechamber and the dressing room of my marriage bed and onto the sleeping platform. We sit side by side with our backs against the cushions as we have since we were little girls. I wiggle loose the panel where I've secreted the notebooks with my most important cases.

"Here," I say. "You take one, and I'll take one. We can decide together which are the best cases."

It's not long before Meiling looks up and says, "You should include the story of Yining."

"She was my first patient in the Garden of Fragrant Delights—"

"A little one who suffered from food damage."

"I like the idea, because any child can suffer from excessive love in the form of overindulgence."

This sets us on a path to find cases of common ailments—coughing, vomiting, sore throats, jaundice, worms, lychee nose, and Wind rash—that afflict men and women, boys and girls alike. I believe a woman will be able to use my treatments to help the boys and men in her household if a male doctor isn't available or if her family can't afford one. Meiling and I are so engrossed that before we know it, the candles have burned down.

Over the coming weeks, Meiling and I continue to pore through my notebooks. Once we've identified the cases that illustrate everyday problems and the ways to treat them, we turn to what will make this project unique among all medical books ever written. Meiling is indispensable—encouraging me, questioning me, and sometimes rejecting my ideas. With her counsel, I narrow the list down to thirty-one cases, many of which are related to monthly moon water, pregnancy, the effects on the body from childbirth, nursing, and menopause. Once the cases are selected, Meiling retreats, saying, "Only you can write the introduction."

With that, she leaves me to my thoughts, brush, ink, and paper. I understand I must act servile and self-effacing before men—other doctors, especially—so I adopt a humble yet confident tone. I begin with the history of my family. *I, Tan Yunxian, am descended from generations of respected and acclaimed imperial scholars.* I go on to note the high ranks achieved by my great-grandfather, grandfather, uncle, and father. Then I recall my childhood: *Grandfather Tan noted my precociousness and suggested that I learn "his" medicine, but my greatest teacher was Grandmother Ru, a hereditary doctor of great skill and wisdom. At fifteen, my hair was pinned up and I married out. I suffered from maladies of qi and Blood. When doctors treated me, I considered their prescriptions, deciding for myself what would and wouldn't work.*

———

The following spring, Meiling and I sit on the terrace of the Hermitage. I wear a silk tunic dyed in mulberry juice, a sleeveless jacket of cerise brocade embroidered with gold and silver threads, and a pleated skirt in midnight blue. Meiling's dress is colorful and bright—the gaudy pink of crabapple blossoms, the extravagant green of plantain leaves, and the joyful red of New Year—to befit her status as a midwife. A copy of *Miscellaneous Records of a Female Doctor* sits on a table between us, having just been published, on the sixteenth day of the third lunar month in the fifth year of the Zhengde emperor's reign. Around us, newly sprouted leaves shiver on their boughs and blooming peonies scent the air. The girls of the household pursue different activities based on their ages. They play guessing games, do puzzles, embroider, sew, pluck at instruments, practice their calligraphy, and recite from the classics. Farther away in the garden, two little boys fly a kite. Another group of boys races along the garden's pathways, ignoring warnings from their mothers and servants to be careful, until I raise my voice and order them to stop this instant. To reward them for their obedience, I give them each a date. Soon enough, the other boys and girls have gathered around me, so I can dole out the treats I keep for them in my pockets.

As soon as the children leave the terrace, I regard Meiling's and my paired images in the mirror of the pond's reflection. A couplet about married couples comes to mind: *White-haired, growing old together.* The same could be said for Meiling and me. With each passing harvest, Kidney qi weakens. Men start to lose their hair— women too, sometimes. Our teeth seem to grow longer. Our bones become brittle. What were once lines of smiles and laughter turn into marks of regret and grief. Or, sometimes, into grooves of anger or arrogance. But looking at our reflections, I see no loss of qi, though we both recently turned fifty.

I hear the sound of voices. Miss Zhao, Lady Kuo, and Poppy come into view and begin to cross the zigzag bridge to reach Meiling and me. For much of my life I felt alone, but over the years a circle of women came to love me, and I came to love each of those women in return. As Miss Zhao raises a hand to wave, I consider the path my life has taken. I remember my mother on her deathbed, saying, "Human life is like a sunbeam passing through a crack." I remember when my grandmother visited me in a dream and her prophecy that I would live to reach seventy-three years. If this is to be, then I have lived two-thirds of my life. But who knows, really, how many days might be left for a woman such as myself, and what yet I might do when surrounded by so much beauty and love?

POSTSCRIPT TO THE REPRINT OF
MISCELLANEOUS RECORDS
OF A FEMALE DOCTOR

My grandfather's sister was a woman doctor named Lady Tan Yunxian, a wife, mother, and daughter-in-law of high standing. I remember when I was a boy and still losing my milk teeth, seeing my great-aunt treat patients in the Mansion of Golden Light, where I lived and still reside, and in her marital home, the Garden of Fragrant Delights. She was beyond reproach, and she achieved fame in her lifetime for her medical skills, which she applied to rich and poor as a humanitarian art. She lived to be ninety-six, outliving long-believed predictions for an earlier death. She died in the thirty-fifth year of the Jianjing emperor's reign [1556], having survived the reigns of five emperors and proving she must have been a very good doctor.

It is said that the descendants of a person who saves lives will prosper and thrive, but such did not transpire in this instance. Lady Tan's son, Yang Lian, died at a young age. Many years later, Lady Tan's only grandson, Yang Qiao, was beheaded for crimes of a political nature. All his descendants were killed in this purge as well, leaving her without any male heirs to make offerings to her in the Afterworld. Without them, there was no one to see to the preservation of her work either, and her book slowly disappeared from book purveyors. I searched until I met a man who had a copy in his personal library. He lent it to me so I might transcribe her words and have new woodblocks made, allowing the book to be printed and distributed again.

Mysteries remain for this great-nephew. The cures Lady Tan formulated in her old age were said to have been even more inspired than the ones found in her book. Many believe she achieved the wondrous abilities of the greatest practitioners of the past, who could simply look at a person—could see *through* a person—to discern what was wrong. But if Lady Tan had reached these heights, why did she not record those cases? Did she write them down but choose not to share them? If so, where are those writings now? I worry that a servant or lesser wife in the Garden of Fragrant Delights may have found her notebooks, thought them worthless, and used the pages to cover pickle and sauce jars.

Now, at the time of this new publication, I hope that Lady Tan's original cases will provide help not just to one village or city but to the multitudes spread throughout the land.

I offer this postscript in the thirteenth year of the Wanli emperor [1585] with one hundred obeisances.

Respectfully,
Tan Xiu

ACKNOWLEDGMENTS

During the early days of the Covid-19 pandemic, I was, like many people, in lockdown and feeling at loose ends. One day as I was walking past one of the bookcases where I shelve my research books—something I do at least ten times a day—the spine of one of the volumes jumped out at me. I don't know why, because it was gray with very subtle lettering in a muted tone. I pulled it from the shelf: *Reproducing Women: Medicine, Metaphor, and Childbirth in Late Imperial China* by Yi-li Wu. I looked at the front material and saw that I'd had the book on my shelf for a decade and had never opened it. I thought, *Well, here I am in the middle of a global pandemic. Maybe now's the time to read this.* I sat down right then and began to read. On page 19, I came across a mention of Tan Yunxian, a woman doctor in the Ming dynasty, who, when she turned fifty in 1511, published a book of her medical cases. Curious, I put down the book, went to the computer, looked up Tan, and discovered that her book was still available not only in Chinese but in English as well. I had a copy of *Miscellaneous Records of a Female Doctor,* translated by Lorraine Wilcox with Yue Lu, the following day. So, within the space of about twenty-six hours, I knew what my next book would be.

The spine of the book leaping out at me and its immediate availability were happy moments of serendipity, but my good fortune didn't end there. I tracked down Lorraine Wilcox—thank you, Internet—and discovered that she lived about fifteen minutes from me! Vaccines were still unavailable, and it was many months before we would meet in person, but Lorraine and I spoke often on Zoom. She recommended online lectures for me to watch, put me in contact with many scholars, and sent me all kinds of material, including a xeroxed copy of the second edition of *Miscellaneous Records of a Female Doctor*, reprinted by Tan's great-nephew in 1585. Lorraine gave freely of her time and resources, and I am deeply indebted to her gifts of knowledge and insight.

Tan Yunxian was a remarkable woman by any measure. According to the scholar Charlotte Furth, in a standard catalog of the twelve thousand known Chinese medical works to be found in Chinese libraries, only three were written by women, with Tan Yunxian's text being the earliest. (Charlotte Furth passed away as I was working on the final edits on the novel. Not only did she bring Tan Yunxian back from the brink of oblivion, but her influence on women scholars focusing on women's lives in China cannot be overstated. Some would argue the field would not exist if not for her.) Many of the formulas Tan listed in her book are still used today in traditional Chinese medicine and are based on traditions more than two thousand years old. Still, little is known about her life beyond the few pages she wrote in the introduction to her book and from the prefaces and afterwords written by her male relatives. She did record words spoken by Respectful Lady on her deathbed and recounted her grandmother's ghostly visit, including the prophecy about the length of Tan's life, which turned out to be wrong.

The greatest keys to her life are found in her cases. She opens each one with a description of her patient, usually a woman or girl described as living in an elite household. Scholars believe that most likely these women, girls, and servants lived in Tan's husband's household. Their real-life cases are reflected in the fictional stories in the novel: Yining, the girl who suffers from food damage caused by excessive love (Case 11); Widow Bao's problems with menopause (Case 24); her daughter's ailments caused by excessive weeping and which Tan treated from afar (Case 18); the young wife suffering from postpartum Wind itching (Case 15); and Meiling's problems (Cases 4, 23, 27, and 31). Then there are the cases that involve women who reside in the outside world: the brickmaker (Case 3) and the tiller woman (Case 2). I asked myself how Tan might have met those women. I also thought about what may have happened to Tan after her son and grandson died and why she never recorded additional cases, despite the fact that her remedies were reported to have improved in her later years and were considered by many to be miraculous. Did being a doctor change for her as she aged? Did practicing medicine become a necessity—a way of earning money, of personal survival?

I'd like to acknowledge some of the women scholars who have inspired me and so many others with their work on women's lives in imperial China: Victoria Cass's *Warriors, Grannies, and Geishas of the Ming* and "Female Healers in the Ming and the Lodge of Ritual and Ceremony"; Patricia Buckley Ebrey's *The Inner Quarters*; Dorothy Ko's *Teachers of the Inner Chambers, Cinderella's Sisters,* and *Every Step a Lotus*; Susan Mann's *The Talented Women of the Zhang Family*; Wang Ping's *Aching for Beauty*; and Yi-li Wu's "Ghost Fetuses, False Pregnancies, and the Parameters of Medical Uncertainty in Classical Chinese Gynecology" and "Between the Living and the Dead: Trauma Medicine and Forensic Medicine in the Mid-Qing," as well as her Zoom lecture "Myth-Busting the History of Chinese Medicine: Going Beyond the 'Function, Not Structure' Stereotype." My gratitude extends to Tobie Meyer-Fong, who answered questions by email and gave of her time in a telephone interview on topics that ranged from details about women's lives to how large family compounds functioned day to day.

With this novel, perhaps more than any other, I got to research clothing, cosmetics, jewelry, and other personal adornments. So much fun! When I wanted inspiration for a particular outfit, I looked at images in *Chinese Dress* by Valery Garrett, *Chinese Clothing* by Hua Mei, and *Traditional Chinese Clothing* by Shaorong Yang, as well as at Ming dynasty paintings. For information about the lives of children during the time that the novel takes place, I turned to *A Tender Voyage: Children and Childhood in Late Imperial China* by Ping-chen Hsiung and *Chinese Views of Childhood* edited by Anne Behnke Kinney.

The following journal articles and books helped me to understand different aspects of traditional Chinese medicine, with an emphasis on women: "Dispersing the Foetal Toxin of the Body: Conceptions of Smallpox Aetiology in Pre-modern China" and "Variolation" by Chia-feng Chang; *A Flourishing Yin: Gender in China's Medical History, 960–1665* by Charlotte Furth; *Thinking with Cases* edited by Charlotte Furth, Judith T. Zeitlin, and Ping-chen Hsiung; *The Web That Has No Weaver* by Ted J. Kaptchuk; *The Expressiveness of Body and the Divergence of Greek and Chinese Medicine* by Shigehisa Kuriyama; "Women Practicing Medicine in Premodern China" by Angela Ki Che Leung, who also served as editor of *Medicine for Women in Imperial China;* *Oriental Materia Medica* by Hong-yen Hsu et al.; "Between Passion and Repression: Medical Views of Demon Dreams, Demonic Fetuses, and Female Sexual Madness in Late Imperial China" by Hsiu-fen Chen; "The Leisure Life of Women in the Ming Dynasty" by Zhao Cuili; and "Female Medical Workers in Ancient China" by Jin-sheng Zheng.

Concerns about female reproductive health are probably as old as humankind, and I had many interesting conversations with people listed in these pages on this topic, but perhaps none were more important or more poignant than the ones I had with Marina Bokelman, folklorist, healer, family friend, and second mother to me. In our last conversation before she decided to leave this life, she spoke at length about Hildegard von Bingen, a Catholic nun born in 1098, who became an abbess, composer, writer, and medical practitioner. In her medical texts, *Physica* and *Causae et Curae,* she described herbs and provided recipes that would regulate menses, offer contraception, end unwanted pregnancies, and see a woman through pregnancy and birth.

A few comments on medical terms and issues I addressed in the novel: The term *child palace* dates to the first or second century C.E. and is still used in contemporary Chinese for the uterus. Today we can recognize *infant-cord rigidity* as tetanus presumed to have been contracted while squatting on straw to give birth or sitting on wet ground during or after labor. (Tetanus is still one of the main causes of death for postpartum women in the third world.) In her book, Tan wrote of her treatment of scrofula lumps and sores in Cases 5, 7, and 16. Today medical professionals would understand these symptoms as mycobacterial cervical lymphadenitis related to tuberculosis. She treated these patients with moxibustion, which was recognized in China as a successful remedy for the condition since ancient times, as well as herbal remedies. Last, I'd like to recommend a fascinating article, "On the Origins of the Midwife" by Sarah Bunney in *New Scientist,* in which she explains why childbirth is more dangerous for humans than for any other primate.

I was also inspired during the creation of this story by Brian E. McKnight's translation of *The Washing Away of Wrongs* by Sung Tz'u (Song Ci in pinyin). This is known to be the first book of forensics in the world and is datable to 1247. It precedes similar works in the European Renaissance by nearly four hundred years. (That said, state-ordered forensic records in China date back to the second century C.E.) *The Washing Away of Wrongs* continued to be used by forensic scientists in China well into the twentieth century. Maybe that's not all that remarkable. The indicators of death by drowning, hanging, stabbing, or poison have not changed through time. I have followed Sung Tz'u's practices for inquests, including revealing a naked body for all to see, the accused standing to face the corpse, examining the spot where a victim drowned, and the concept that the family and the accused must have the opportunity to face each other.

I've always taken great pride in going to every place I write about. I couldn't do that for this book. (As I write this, China continues to have lockdowns in major cities, and the quarantine period for visitors is three weeks.) However, when I researched *Peony in Love,* I went to several water towns in the Yangzi delta. I was confident about writing about a water town, but I still felt sad that I wasn't seeing Wuxi with my own eyes. Serendipity came to the rescue once again. One day when I was looking at Twitter, I saw a post about a Ming dynasty building in Wuxi. I sent a direct message to @TheSilkRoad inquiring what else they might know about Ming dynasty sites that still exist in Wuxi. Within a day, Zhang Li sent me links to forty-three Ming dynasty buildings, gardens, and waterways that have survived in Wuxi, along with photos, history, and, in many cases, videos. Soon enough, I was on a boat floating on Wuxi's canals—during the day, at night, and in a black-and-white documentary made in the 1950s. You can find many of these links on my website in the section called "Step Inside the World of Lady Tan" at www.LisaSee.com.

The garden for which the fictional Garden of Fragrant Delights is named is modeled on two gardens, both of which I've visited many times: the Humble Administrator's Garden in Suzhou and the Garden of Flowing Fragrance at the Huntington Library, Art Museum, and Botanical Gardens in San Marino, California. The Garden of Fragrant Delights compound is very much inspired by the Qiao family compound near the ancient city of Pingyao, which I visited many years ago. The home boasts 313 rooms, six large courtyards, and nineteen smaller courtyards. You might recognize it as the setting for the film *Raise the Red Lantern*. The marriage bed has been in my family since long before I was born. Generations of See children have played in it. When I was a little girl, the drawers were filled with clothes and shoes so I could play dress-up. My children and their cousins used to watch television in the first antechamber, where a servant once would have slept on the floor. Today, all these years later, I marvel at the beauty of the window paintings, the carved vignettes, and the three separate rooms—all held together without a single nail. You will find photos of the two gardens, the Qiao estate, and the marriage bed on my website. My author photo was taken at the entrance to the marriage bed, so you can see a bit of it there too.

As we all know, works of fiction can create mind pictures and give us emotional experiences. During the first year of the pandemic, I decided to reread the David Hawkes translation of Cao Xueqin's *The Story of the Stone* (also known as *The Dream of the Red Chamber*), which is considered to be one of the greatest, if not the greatest, Chinese novels. While the story is set in the Qing dynasty, it does give a stunning portrait of what life was like in a grand household with many courtyards and gardens and inhabited by a large family, countless concubines, and retainers of every sort. My reading was further enhanced this time around by listening for *hours* to a podcast called, aptly enough, *Rereading the Stone*. The weekly conversation between the hosts, Kevin Wilson and William Jones, led to my further understanding of Chinese culture, history, literature, and philosophy.

For information about the Ming dynasty, I read *A Ming Society* by John W. Dardess, pertinent sections in *Chinese Civilization and Society* edited by Patricia Buckley Ebrey, *The Censorial System of Ming China* by Charles O. Hucker, and a collection of short stories, *Stories from a Ming Collection* compiled by Feng Menglong and translated by Cyril Birch. But sometimes trying to find a detail for a story can be like looking for the proverbial needle in a haystack. I'm here to tell you those needles can be found . . . with lots of help. I must begin by giving my heartfelt thanks to Jeffrey Wasserstrom, Chancellor's Professor of History at the University of California, Irvine. Over the years, I've asked him numerous times for help and advice, and he's always gone above and beyond. While I was writing this novel, he acted as a go-between, connecting me to people who helped me with details I couldn't track down myself. (Remember, the big research libraries were closed.) He first introduced me to Emily Baum, a professor of modern Chinese history at UCI with a subspecialty in traditional Chinese medicine, who discussed with me the differences between western and Chinese medical traditions. (Western medicine is focused on material structures. You can hold a heart in your hand and see bacteria through a microscope. Traditional Chinese medicine is more focused on processes and interactions in the body.)

Professor Wasserstrom also connected me to Christopher Rea, Professor of Chinese Literature at the University of British Columbia, who answered many questions I had about the Ming dynasty: If there was a mail system in China five-hundred-plus years ago, how did it function? How long would it have taken to travel from Wuxi to Beijing on the Grand Canal in 1490? He sent me Chelsea Zi Wang's in-depth essay "More Haste, Less Speed: Sources of Friction in the Ming Postal System," and pointed me to a diary kept by Ch'oe Pu, a newly appointed Korean Commissioner of Registers on Jeju—the island I wrote about in *The Island of Sea Women*—who was shipwrecked off the coast of China in 1487 and was taken to Beijing on the Grand Canal. I then found

John Meskill's translation of *Ch'oe Pu's Diary: A Record of Drifting Across the Sea*. The diary is filled with wonderful details about clothes, food, customs, and, of course, how long it took to get from here to there each day exactly three years before Tan Yunxian, Miss Zhao, and Poppy make their journey.

Last, when I was struggling with the differences I found in various texts—what were the responsibilities of a Prefectural Judge, Magistrate, and Chief Investigating Censor, and who would preside at an inquest or a re-inquest?—Professor Wasserstrom made a wonderful email introduction to Michael Szonyi, Professor of Chinese History at Harvard University and the former director of the Fairbank Center for Chinese Studies. Professor Szonyi shared with me his article "The Case in the Vase: Legal Process, Legal Culture, and Justice in *The Plum in the Golden Vase*." We also had a fascinating correspondence, a tiny bit of which I'd like to share with you. When I wrote to him because I was confused that some sources used Ministry of Punishments (or Justice) while others called it the Board of Punishments (or Justice), he replied with the following:

> On the Board of Punishments, I can't speak to the motivations of other translators, but I think the real issue is just the degree to which we are confident about inserting our own assumptions into the terms we use. The standard reference work for official titles, Hucker's *Dictionary of Official Titles in Imperial China,* uses Ministry of Justice. But that came out in the 1980s, based on earlier work. From my perspective, it's not reasonable to infer that some notion comparable to our idea of "justice" is embodied in the original Chinese term. But the notion of punishment certainly is. Board vs Ministry is easier to explain—in the British system, a Ministry is headed by an elected official who also serves on the Cabinet. The Chinese office we're talking about here is a high-level office headed by a senior bureaucrat. So it can't be translated as a Ministry. If more early Sinologists had been American, we might use the term Department of Punishments to indicate a very

high-level administrative body headed by a senior bureau-crat. But somehow we've settled on Board.

Complicated and nuanced, but fascinating.

For all matters concerning tea, I turned to Linda Louie, the owner of the Bana Tea Company. She has created a tea package for book clubs, featuring some of the teas mentioned in the novel, which you can find on her website at www.BanaTeaCompany .com. I also want to thank Linda for acting as the liaison between her sister, Meiyin Lee, and me. Meiyin sent along interesting material on traveling in the Ming, Thin Horses, and Tooth Ladies.

This is a novel, and I took some liberties. While the method of writing a message on a baby's foot during labor to send it back to the child palace is real, it did not happen to Tan Yunxian. There is also nothing in the historical record to indicate that Tan Yun-xian ever left Wuxi, let alone traveled to the Forbidden City. But I wanted her to make the trip for three reasons. First, to give a pos-sible answer to how and where Tan encountered the tiller woman. Second, I was fascinated and intrigued by the details of the true story of a "matron of medicine" named Peng, who gave birth in 1553 to a son right before Empress Xiaoke, the fourth consort of the Jiajing emperor. When he heard that his beloved's eyes had been sullied by seeing such a sight, he ordered the midwife to be executed. The consort and other ladies of the court fought for a lighter sentence and won. The emperor sentenced Peng to thirty strokes and expelled her from the Forbidden City. Third, and most important, including the interlude at the Forbidden City al-lowed me to write about women in every level of society—from a servant up to the empress. And, as a side note, the story of the eunuch shooting arrows at passersby on the Grand Canal is true.

I'm lucky to have many extraordinary people who support me as a writer and a woman. My agent, Sandra Dijkstra, and her staff of wonderful women—Andrea Cavallero and Elise Capron, in particular—stay attuned to the business side of things. This is my third novel with Scribner, and what a wonderful journey it's been. Thank you to Nan Graham, Kathy Belden, Katie Monaghan, Mia O'Neill, and Ashley Gilliam for your unwavering support and abounding energy, and to everyone in marketing and sales who astound me almost daily by thinking outside the box.

My sister, Clara Sturak, knows and understands my writing better than anyone else on earth. Not only do I trust her editorial eye, but I also trust her to help me get to the story I'm trying to tell. I'm fortunate to have two sons, two daughters-in-law, and a grandson to remind me what's important in life. I love them all so much. Last, I want to thank my husband, Richard Kendall. They say absence makes the heart grow fonder, but I beg to differ. During these strange and wondrous pandemic years—as the two of us have spent twenty-four hours a day under the same roof, working in different rooms, finding simple joys in music, streaming ever more esoteric television shows, and lounging in the garden—my love and respect for him have grown more than I could have imagined on the blind date set up by his father and my mother so long ago.

LADY TAN'S CIRCLE OF WOMEN

—

LISA SEE

This reading group guide for Lady Tan's Circle of Women *includes discussion questions and ideas for enhancing your book club. The suggested questions are intended to help your reading group find new and interesting angles and topics for your discussion. We hope that these ideas will enrich your conversation and increase your enjoyment of the book.*

Topics and Questions for Discussion

1. The opening of this novel begins with a preface which includes the line "My cousin has excelled at treating women because she has shared in the losses and joys of what it means to be a female on this earth." How does this set up the novel and what is to come for Yunxian? After reading the novel, what does it mean to be a "female on this earth?"

2. How does the death of Respectful Lady shape Yunxian? What lessons from Respectful Lady does Yunxian carry with her? When Respectful Lady is near her end, she mutters: "To live is to suffer." How is this a warning for Yunxian early in the novel?

3. Grandfather Tan and Grandmother Ru have very different ideas about childbirth. Whom do you agree with, and why? Although five hundred years have passed since the time the novel takes place, do you think these contradictory ideas still hold true today—not just for childbirth but for women's medical care in general?

4. Lisa often writes about friendship: Snow Flower and Lily in *Snow Flower and the Secret Fan*, Youngsook and Mija in *The Island of Sea Women*, and now Yunxian and Meiling in *Lady Tan's Circle of Women*. These two girls shouldn't have contact with each other, let alone have a relationship formalized and sanctioned by Grandmother Ru and Midwife Shi. How do Yunxian and Meiling each benefit from the relationship? Are there downsides for each of them? Talk about what friendship means to you. And, since you're all in a book club—typically a circle of women—share what it means to you.

5. Each character—and Yunxian's relationship to that person—changes and evolves over time. How does Yunxian come to

see and understand the characters of Miss Zhao, Miss Chen, Lady Kuo, Doctor Wong, and her husband and father?

6. The importance of having a son was critical in ancient China. It still is in many countries and cultures around the world. What are the main plotlines in the novel related to this issue? Consider the perspectives of Spinster Aunt, Miss Chen, Doctor Wong, Midwife Shi, Lady Kuo, and Meiling and Yunxian. Were these characters out for his or her own self-interest?

7. Lisa often uses aphorisms to help illuminate a character or a plot point. One of the most significant in this novel is *No mud, no lotus*. Discuss how this aphorism is important to the story. On page 256, Miss Chen recites a series of aphorisms to Yunxian: "*It takes a lifetime to make a friend, but you can lose one in an hour.*" "*Life without a friend is life without sun. Life without a friend is death.*" What message is Miss Chen trying to convey to Yunxian? Lisa considers these aphorisms to be true across time and cultures. Do you agree? How have they played out in your life, if at all?

8. A case could be made that Yunxian was a modern woman. What are some of the ways she balances work and family? Do you see yourself in her?

9. The Dragon Boat Festival looms large in Yunxian's imagination. What does it mean for her—and the other women who reside in the Garden of Fragrant Delights—to finally get to attend?

10. Lisa was inspired to write this novel during the height of the Covid-19 pandemic, walking past her bookshelf to find a text she had but hadn't read in the decade that she owned it. How does time and memory inspire us to examine neglected objects? Have you experienced newfound inspiration or ideas by the objects around your home?

Enhance Your Book Club

1. Host a tea tasting for your book club. Bana Tea Company has put together a package featuring the special tea dried in the mandarin orange that Yunxian serves Lady Kuo on page 166 and the jasmine tea that Meiling and Yunxian share on page 177. Access the custom tasting kits here: www.banatea company.com/pages/Lisa-See-Tasting-Kit-2023.html

2. Share with your book club the year in the Chinese zodiac in which you were born. What are the characteristics of your birth sign? Do they ring true to you? What other signs are you compatible with, and why? What signs should you avoid?

3. Design your own Ming dynasty outfit. Use this link (https://lisasee.com/books/lady-tans-circle-of-women/#guide) to find an outline of an outfit along with some symbols and their meanings. You can do this as a group activity with the host providing crayons, colored pencils, felt-tip pens, or even watercolors. Or you can create your outfit at home and bring it to your book club to share. What symbols did you use, and why?

4. "Step Inside the World of Lady Tan" on Lisa's website www .LisaSee.com to see photos, videos, and more about the people, places, customs, and traditions that inspired the book.

A Message from Lisa See

Dear Readers,
Thank you for reading Lady Tan's Circle of Women. *It has been a great honor to bring Tan Yunxian's remarkable life to all of you. She was as inspiring five hundred years ago as she is today.*

The most frequently asked questions about the novel involve footbinding Well, entire books have been written to explore this practice, but I'll share, in brief, some of what I've learned. Bound feet were primarily a sign of economic status. A man could say, "I am so wealthy that my wife has bound feet," meaning his wife didn't have to work. Or he could say, "I am so wealthy that not only does my wife have bound feet, but even our servants have bound feet." That was a seriously wealthy man!

There was a whole sexual aspect to bound feet. Whatever you can imagine that they might have done with those feet, they did that and more. Tied into this was the sense men had about the sacrifice and pain women had gone through to give them this particular pleasure and beauty. Prosaic reasons existed for footbinding as well. A woman would always have to lean on a man. A woman wouldn't be able to run away. A girl who had gone through footbinding was also sending a message to potential in-laws: Here is a girl who is so obedient that she successfully completed footbinding. Here is a girl, who, having borne the suffering required to achieve a pair of bound feet, will be able to endure any difficulties she might encounter in married life.

But these reasons—as logical and legitimate as they may have been at the time—still don't explain how mothers could do this to their daughters, generation after generation for a thousand years. Can you imagine inflicting the same kind of pain on your daughter that you yourself experienced as a child? Alas, at this point in time, footbinding was one of the few things a mother could do for her daughter to give her a better chance at life. If she could give her daughter a pair of perfectly bound feet, then her daughter might be able to marry into a more prosperous family and have a different life.

Few other options existed for most girls in those days. A girl could grow up to work in the fields—a life of physical labor in extremely harsh conditions. I haven't been able to find the life expectancy for a peasant living in the Ming dynasty, but in 1850, the life expectancy for a Chinese peasant was just thirty-two years, and in 1949 it wasn't much better, ranging from thirty-five to forty years. A girl could also be sold by her family to become a courtesan, concubine, or prostitute. She wasn't given a choice. If she was unhappy, too bad. Even if she was happy, her life was unstable as she lived at the whim of her owner. Girls could be sold at around five years of age to become a "little daughter-in-law," who, as children, would do simple chores around the house, but as they grew up their main purpose was to become a sexual plaything for the males in the household.

Understanding the social context for most girls and women during the time described in the novel makes it easier to be sympathetic about a family's decision to bind their daughters' feet. While the custom of footbinding is behind us that doesn't mean women aren't still held to what can be a punishing standard of beauty today. Take a walk down Rodeo Drive, and you'll see what I mean: fillers, augmentation, lifts, and tucks. How different are these contemporary practices?

At least today, we can decide for ourselves.

Lisa